secret of the rose

secret of the rose

Escape *to* Freedom

MICHAEL PHILLIPS

Tyndale House Publishers, Inc., Carol Stream, Illinois

Visit Tyndale's exciting Web site at www.tyndale.com

TYNDALE and Tyndale's quill logo are registered trademarks of Tyndale House Publishers, Inc.

Escape to Freedom

Library of Congress Cataloging-in-Publication Data

Phillips, Michael R., date
  Escape to freedom / Michael Phillips.
    p. cm. — (The Secret of the rose ; 3)
  ISBN-13: 978-0-8423-5942-9
  ISBN-10: 0-8423-5942-7
  I. Title. II. Series: Phillips, Michael R., 1946-   Secret of the rose ; 3.
PS3566.H492E83   1994
813'.54—dc20   94-23235

ISBN-13: 978-1-4143-0789-3
ISBN-10: 1-4143-0789-6

Printed in the United States of America

13   12   11   10   09   08   07
 7   6   5   4   3   2   1

Acknowledgments

Acknowledgment is made for use
of the following book:
The Berlin Wall, by Deane and David Heller,
Walker & Co., New York, 1962.

Thanks also to . . .

The original of the baron's poem
in Chapter 104,
"Escape to the West," is entitled "Tell Me."
(*Knowing the Heart of God,*
by George MacDonald,
Bethany House Publishers,
Minneapolis, Minn., p. 224.)

CONTENTS

Part V: *Dieder Palacki—August 1962*

Part VI: *E. Brecht—September 1962*

Part VII: *Escape to Freedom—*
September–December 1962

Prologue

When the Creator paused to take stock of the heavens and the earth he had made, he declared: "It is good!"

When he later stood back to survey his completion of the creation of man—a man who occupied the center of the vast array of plants, animals, stars, suns, moons, and galaxies—his divine proclamation resounded through the universe: "It is very good!"

In man did the Creator, the Almighty I AM, raise the holy creative act to its very pinnacle, calling into life a being apart from himself that yet reflected his divine nature. Here was a being, says his Word, created *in the image* of God himself, who yet was also given that ascendant capacity, distinct from all the rest of creation, called free will—the power to *choose* whether to walk in that image so intrinsic to his making.

Ah, God our Father, does such intimacy truly exist between us and thee, that we may lay claim to such hallowed origins? Have we truly—incredible thought!—been created in thy very image! Expand our minds, open our hearts to absorb the lofty and life-changing truth, that in thee we can discover all that a perfectly loving Fatherhood was meant to be!

Through the creation of the first man and woman did God embark upon the lengthy process of fashioning a family—*his family. This family stood as the centerpiece of creation itself. It was likewise intended as the focus, the hub, the causing, pulsating, foundational nucleus of all history that would follow.*

The ways of God concerning *his people*, therefore, ever after took preeminence over all else. Notwithstanding that the working out of his divine plan through the human drama soon became marred with sin, suffering, and death, he—known to his created beings as *YHWH*, or *Elohim*—never for an instant nor for an eon lost sight of the heavenly purpose for which he brought his creatures into being and breathed his own life into them.

God will accomplish his purpose for the sons and daughters of his creation. Some of them are aware of those holy objectives even as he carries them out. It is they who yield themselves to the influence of his hand, bow before their creator, and give thanks.

Some are unaware of the overarching potency of his sovereign design, thinking even that he is against them or that he has forgotten them altogether. Still others set themselves in opposition to him, unknowingly countering his every attempt to impregnate their lives with his love.

But his timing is perfect where his creatures are concerned. His purposes are never rushed. A day . . . a thousand years—it matters not to him. Whether it takes ten weeks or a thousand generations of mankind upon the earth, the creating Lord God of the universe will do what is necessary to fulfill his ultimate design.

Nothing in his economy passes away. Nothing of his intent *can* pass out of the heavenly ken. He loses sight of nothing, from objects of his creation to the deepest motives within the heart of man.

The unseen guiding hand of his rule remains ever present. He, the Hound of Heaven, relentlessly pursues his quarry, sending his voice to call unto wakefulness, his light to open the windows of men's souls heavenward. Ever do the reminding influences of his presence go forth upon the earth, from the tiny primroses peeking through the wintry ground to the lubricating oil of the conscience.

If it exists within God's mind to do, it *will* be consummated.

Over the passage of years, and centuries, and millennia, man may—in the selfish, short-sighted, and foolishly independent exercise of the will he was given—cease to look up into the face of the Father-Creator who made him and who has a divine *Will* for him. But his Father will never cease looking down upon him with a heart so full of love that no price is too high for him to pay to bring that man back into the garden-fellowship intended from the beginning.

The Father yearns to give man again a land wherein to dwell in familyness with him—Creator and created walking together in the heat of the morning, and in the cool of the evening . . . perfectly as one.

In the beginning, Yahweh stooped down to the earth he had made, drew from it the dust from which he created man, and breathed his own life into his nostrils. God then said to him: *Be my son. Be fruitful, multiply, occupy the land I have given you. . . . Take dominion over the whole earth . . . and be my people.*

God will not rest until mankind is ready, capable, and eager to obey that most foundational of the Genesis commands. When the time is nigh, then will he fulfill what he purposed on that day.

All history points toward that single end.

PART I

Roots of Evil, Threads of Promise
From the Beginning–1962

∾ 1 ∾
A Land and Its Mysteries
2000 B.C. – A.D. 69

It had always been called the Land of Promise, that prehistoric patrimony on each side of the Jordan pledged to Abraham.

He, known to men of old as almighty God, Yahweh, the LORD, had said to faithful Abram of Ur, *Leave your country, your people, and your father's household and go to the land I will show you. I will make you into a great nation, and I will bless you. I will make your descendants more numerous than the stars in the heavens. I am the Lord, who brought you out of Ur to give you this land and to take possession of it.*

Six hundred years later, on the mount of Sinai, God made the promise to Moses: *I will deliver my people from the hand of the Egyptians and bring them up out of that land into a good and spacious land, a land flowing with milk and honey.*

It must have seemed to Abraham's numerous offspring that the Lord's optimism had failed to take into account the singularly persistent efforts on the part of the Egyptians, the Assyrians, the Babylonians, the Persians, and the Romans to prevent them from occupying that land between the eastern desert of Arabia and the Great Sea. If he intended to give them such an inheritance, the less faithful among them must have wondered why did he not raise his divine hand a little more aggressively against those so bent on wresting it from them.

In Eden had the Creator established the perfect garden for men to dwell. But with their expulsion had begun six millennia of wandering, ever seeking but never permanently coming to rest in that new Eden, that land of milk and honey that had been covenanted to Abraham's offspring as a homeland forever.

He had cast them from the first garden with the words "Cursed is the land because of you." It must have seemed that the covenant with Abraham for the second garden was infused with the same curse as well. Occupying that divine endowment for brief interludes between defeats at the hands of conquering giants appeared their only lot.

The gloomy words of the Almighty to Abraham following the promise—*Know that your descendants will be strangers in a country not their own, and they will be enslaved and mistreated*—of a certainty spoke not merely of the relatively brief sojourn in Egypt, but set the course for Israel's entire future on earth.

The land itself, however, had never been as important to the ancient Hebrew God as those offspring of his loving covenant themselves. That the Hebrew children were of the Creator's family was a truth that rose preeminent in the heavenly equation above their nationhood. That they were a *people* was a deeper truth than the possession of secure borders. That they had been chosen to carry news of the Almighty into all the world came before having a place of their own to lay their heads.

He they called Yahweh was in the process of building a different kind of nation than could be contained by boundaries crisscrossing the earth's surface. Even the perimeters of that ancient land laid claim to by Joshua's invasion, held by the might of that great warrior-king David ben Jesse, lamented over by Isaiah and Jeremiah, were borders merely lining the earth, without necessary correlation in the regions *above* the earth where higher Principalities ruled.

At length, when the time was fulfilled and the season for his kingdom was at hand, God sent his Son, the awaited Messiah, to his people. The Messiah told them that the temple he would build and the race he would fashion were not to be built by hands, fortified with weapons, nor held by armies. Rather it would be a temple made by the living stones of men and women, and a nation built by the knitting together of men's hearts.

Alas, the children of Abraham received neither Jesus the Anointed One nor his message, and thus their pilgrimage to rediscover the meaning of the ancient covenant had only begun.

∽ 2 ∾
A Holy Theft
A.D. 70

A black-clad, bearded priest of the ancient order of the Levites stole quietly under the darkened covered cloister through the South Gate into that most sacred edifice in all the Jewish world, the temple of Herod.

What he was about to do, if discovered by his peers, especially by the High Priest or by Herod Agrippa himself, would cost him his priestly vestments . . . and probably his life as well.

He made his way through the Court of the Gentiles, through the Beautiful Gate, across the Women's Court, into the Court of Israel, past the altar, and finally into the Holy Place itself. Slowing his step now, he stole nearer his destination, that innermost sanctum where God himself was said to dwell.

Would he be struck dead for tampering with the holy articles of their faith? If such was the case, so be it. He prayed Yahweh would be merciful to his soul in the next life.

A premonition of evil had been growing upon him for days.

There had been reports for some time that the emperor Vespasian was sending his son Titus to Judea. But Roman legions and governors and centurions had come and gone through this region for a century. None of his fellows in the Sanhedrin seemed to think anything of it.

But never had there been an ambitious emperor's son leading the legions of soldiers. And Jehoiachin ben Azor, faithful priest and rabbi of the stock of Aaron, knew that this time was destined to be different. Frightfully and woefully different.

Among the temple priests Jehoiachin was considered atypical at best, downright astonishing, some would have said. Some of his views were clearly too broad, especially his tolerance of the Christian sect. In his favor, his friends maintained, at least he kept his unorthodox notions of brotherhood mostly to himself.

He had such a peculiar predilection as well for divining the future. In another age and another time, he might have been considered a prophet. In this, his own age, however, he was merely looked upon with mingled annoyance and scorn, while his words—both warnings about things to come and strange teachings about Yahweh's desire to become familiar and close to his people—went largely unheeded, which perhaps was the strongest indication of all that the prophetic spirit did indeed live within him.

Jehoiachin had been poring over the Scriptures for days, ever since the terrifying vision that had awakened him six days ago.

Daniel had spoken of evil things that would befall the temple of God—*this* very temple, Jehoiachin was now convinced. With threefold emphasis, the prophet had warned of the abomination that causes desolation that would one day be set up in the very temple itself. His warnings had been written, the Scriptures said, so that the wise would understand.

"O God," he had cried out, "*help me to understand the mystery sealed away in the book, and show me what you would have me to do.*"

Again he had sought the words of the prophet.

The king of the North will return to his own country with great wealth, but his heart will be set against the holy covenant.

He stopped. Most of his colleagues and rabbinical scholars took Daniel's words to refer to that tyrant Antiochus of Syria. But Jehoiachin had never agreed with such an interpretation. *Rome* was farther north than Syria. But Jehoiachin was alone in viewing the dreadful prophecy as yet awaiting fulfillment, and as coming from that great power of the northern Mediterranean.

At the appointed time he will invade the South again. He will vent his wrath against the holy covenant. His army will rise up to desecrate the temple fortress and will abolish the daily sacrifice. Then they will set up the abomination that causes desolation. . . . He will invade many countries and sweep through them like a flood. He will invade the Beautiful Land.

What else, thought Jehoiachin, *could the prophet refer to than the might of Rome?* He was more convinced than ever, especially since his vision, that just such an invasion was imminent. The results, he was sure, were unmistakable—the temple, the very holy place itself, would be destroyed.

The king of the North, that emperor who sat on the imperial throne of Rome, would plunder all its wealth for himself. For did not Daniel say, *He will honor a god unknown to his fathers with gold and silver, with precious stones and costly treasures.*

He had even consulted the words of the crucified Jesus. Jehoiachin was student enough of the new sect to remember that he too had quoted Daniel's words concerning the abomination of desolation. A new collection of his teachings by a tax collector called Matthew had been circulating for a year or two. He had himself sought out this Matthew secretly, by night, and interviewed him at length. Jehoiachin was a Jew, not a Christian. But Jesus had been a Jew, and a faithful one he personally believed. Most of his followers were Jews too, and Jehoiachin was broad enough in his outlook to desire the truth from whatever quarter it came. Their claim that Jesus was the Messiah was difficult to comprehend, he had to admit. Yet if it were true—as the Christians maintained but his fellow priests denied—that he had actually appeared alive following his crucifixion, it certainly lent an authenticity to their claim.

In any case, he would worry about who the Christ was later. His mission right now concerned his vision, Rome, and what he might do to save at least a few items from falling into its conquering clutches.

Now as he made his way, he thought back to his conversation with the fellow Matthew. He was one who had heard the startling words with his own ears. He had then written them down in what he referred to as his Gospel. Jehoiachin was therefore confident that Jesus' words were just as Matthew had recited to him that night:

When you see the abomination that causes desolation standing in the holy place, spoken of by the prophet Daniel, then let those who are in Judea flee to the mountains. Let no one on the roof of his house go down to take anything out of the house. Let no one in the field go back to get his cloak. For there will be great distress.

Whether Jesus was a prophet or not was another thing he couldn't resolve right now. But his words were clear—*"Don't wait . . . flee to the mountains."* They confirmed Daniel's warnings, and his own vision. Jehoiachin, therefore, intended to follow his advice.

He would have warned his fellow priests, warned the whole city of Jerusalem, if he thought it would have done any good.

But he knew what they did in this city to prophets of all kinds, especially ones deemed false. He had not been in Jerusalem at the time of the crucifixion of the Nazarene, but he was scholar enough to know that he was not the only Jewish rabbi or holy man to be put to death by his own countrymen. This was no friendly place to prophetic types.

No, it would do no good to issue warnings. They would only kill or discredit him, and then he would be prevented from doing what he felt he had been shown he must do. Grieve him as it might, this was one task he must undertake, and one journey he must embark upon . . . alone.

With stealthy step, Jehoiachin crept through the Holy Place, and now at last stood before the curtain into the Holy of Holies itself.

A lump rose in his throat. He could feel the sweat breaking out over his back and chest. A lifetime's teaching and training rose up to argue one last time against the foolhardy thing he had come here to do.

Only the High Priest could enter the Holy of Holies. Jehoiachin was about to commit sacrilege against the essence of the Jewish faith, against the very character and holiness of Yahweh. Yet he felt compelled to do so, as if Yahweh himself were urging him on.

One final time he paused to pray.

Stay my hand, Lord God of Israel, if what I am about to do is grievous in your eyes. Do not let me sin against your Law nor your temple nor the dwelling place of your Glory.

He waited a moment.

The only impulse he felt was that which had been with him so persistently since his vision—the impulse to continue forward.

Taking in a deep breath, he parted the curtain and entered the Holy of Holies.

His heart beat wildly, and he half expected any moment to hear a roar of thunder and have a bolt of lightning explode from the sky to strike him down where he stood.

With effort he sought to quiet himself. He took quick stock of the sacred surroundings he had never before laid eyes upon.

There it was—the pouch worn on the High Priest's chest that

contained the stones from Aaron's breastplate that possessed divine power.

Slowly he reached forward and laid hold of the pouch.

His hand trembled as he opened it, reached inside, removed the two large diamonds known as the Urim—which signified the answer of *no* when the High Priest removed it to render some thorny decision—and the Thummim, which, if selected, signified *yes*.

He paused only briefly to glance at the exquisite gems, then placed them carefully in a piece of cloth, which he deposited in a pocket in his robe. From another pocket he took two small common stones he had brought for just this purpose, and put them in the pouch. He would not have the Urim and Thummim discovered missing any sooner than was necessary.

Jehoiachin set the pouch back in its resting place exactly as he had found it, then hastily left the place, still breathing hard, heart beating rapidly. He strode back across the white stones of the temple courtyards as noiselessly yet as quickly as he could, and in a few minutes was again safely alone in the streets of Jerusalem.

He was only one man. He could not save the temple. But perhaps he could save a few of those priceless treasures of their heritage for another time when yet again God would raise a temple of worship upon this place, atop the rubble which he was sure Rome was about to create.

He paused to look back one last time at the magnificent temple of Herod.

A tear rose in his eye. He knew that he would never lay eyes on it again.

His gaze swept back around the city through which he made his way. Neither would he set foot inside its walls again, he was sure, for as long as he lived.

"O Jerusalem . . . Jerusalem—sacred city of old," he sighed. "I will miss you. . . ."

A pause came to his inner spirit. The next thoughts to cross his lips were whispered words of prayer.

"Raise this city again, O Lord, even out of the rubble the legions of Rome are about to cause. Bring back your people to this holy mount. Go with them to wherever in the world they are scattered. Protect your

*people . . . and protect these stones, that they too may find their way
again to this temple of your presence, at the time when you appoint for
their return."*

A multitude of feelings and prayers he was unable to utter
swept through him.

Finally he turned again and continued swiftly on his way.
There were yet preparations to be made. And he must be on
his way, through the Essene Gate and out of the city, before
dawn.

∽ 3 ∽
Wanderers without a Home
A.D. 70–1382

God offered to make of Abraham's children a holy nation
indeed by bringing them into the divine family through the
sacrifice of his firstborn Son. His people chose instead to continue placing their hopes on a passing earthly kingdom—a
dream brought to a sudden and cruel end, thirty-seven years
after that Son's death, at the hand of the Roman emperor's son
Titus.

With Jerusalem in flames, the heights of Masada finally
scaled, and the first-century nation of Israel in ruins, thus began
the greatest Diaspora of all. Indeed were the children of Abraham now cast to the winds and spread abroad to the four corners of the earth. Truly did they become peregrinators and
pilgrims, roaming not merely the deserts of Sinai, Shur, Paran,
and Zin, but the continents and byways of the whole earth.
With vaster scope were the words of God to Abraham now fulfilled, not for a mere four hundred years, but for nearly five
times that many: *Your descendants will be strangers in a country not
their own, and they will be enslaved and mistreated.*

In every country did they encamp, but nowhere did they find
a home. Nowhere did the family of man open its arms or its
heart to Abraham's seed, to this historic people with no soil in
which to send down the roots of its venerable and ancestral cul-
ture. Hence they wandered without a homeland—mistreated,

slandered, vilified, in some eras even slaughtered, yet miraculously remaining a *nation* in the purest sense, bound together by threads of common heritage and belief—for no mere Mosaic two, but for ninety-five score of years. Persecute it as the world might, the divinely imbued Hebrew blood could never be eradicated from the face of the earth, nor could the remarkable tenacity and verve it gave its people be diluted.

Truly did Yahweh honor the ancient prayers of his faithful servant: *Go with them wherever in the world they are scattered. Protect your people.*

They wandered—taking with them whatever treasures, relics, and memories of their historic and ancestral heritage they had managed to preserve—making a temporary home of every community where men gathered, learning the tongues and the ways of the Gentiles around them, until at length the Lord seemed to say, as he had on Sinai: *I have seen the misery of my people. I know their afflictions and sorrows. I have come to deliver them, and to bring them to that ancient land I promised their forebears, a land flowing with milk and honey.*

From Abraham through the ages, from father to son to son to son in an unbroken link through time, the treasures of Jewry passed in generational succession, giving vivid and substantial reality to the truth that all those who came after actually *touched* the ancient patriarch by being numbered among his seed.

Numbered among the most prized of all Jewish artifacts, which had somehow been preserved through the years, were these two—the ancient Urim and Thummim of Aaron's breastplate, the former a great clear diamond of fifteen carats, the latter also a diamond, but of an exquisite pale blue and smaller, of some twelve carats.

By any standard, both were of inestimable value, added to immensely by their historic connection to the period of the Exodus. Whether the two surviving diamonds were in fact the mysterious Urim and Thummim could not be known with certainty. But the legends and traditions surrounding the precious stones gave them tremendous historical and religious significance for all of Jewry. What hands had kept them safe all those years was a secret that would never be known.

Some said, though they knew not how, that they had been smuggled safely out of Jerusalem before its destruction in A.D.70, beginning a period of extensive travels through Egypt, Ethiopia, the Orient, and finally to Russia.

❧ 4 ❧
A Mysterious Pilgrim
A.D. 1382

He bore the look of mystery the moment the monks of Troitsa saw him approaching their chapel in haste, with an expression of dread in his eyes.

The mystery only deepened when, two days later, he lay dead, leaving no legacy behind him but the priceless treasures he had brought them for safekeeping.

The abbot of the monastery knew what they were, according to the bearded rabbi who had identified himself only as ben Israel, *a son of Israel*. Whether anyone would believe the remarkable tale he had heard in private at the dying rabbi's bedside, if Sergius told it, was another matter.

The Jews of the first-century dispersion spread widely through the continents of the world. Their travels took many families northward, beyond the seat of conquering might of that now-fallen king of the north called Rome, and into the expansive regions of a heterogeneous European continent.

The peoples moving between Europe and Asia in those northern climes were no people particularly friendly to the wandering children of God. The collapse of Rome had caused a free-flowing migration of a multitude of tribes, many of them mere barbarians. In the very disunity of the times, however, were God's people able to put down roots alongside other sects and clans and races. No single nationalistic fervor was present to rise up against them.

They began, therefore, with many other bloodlines, to people eastern Europe, and within the next few centuries had made their way throughout the huge land of *Rus* and were, by the fourth century, joined there by their cousin Christians.

Six hundred years later, Vladimir, fifth grand duke of Kiev, was visited during his reign at the end of the first millennium by representatives of Islam, Judaism, Roman Christianity, and Byzantine Greek Orthodox Christianity, all hoping to expand their influence in these northern regions.

It was the Greeks who made the strongest and most lasting impression. Vladimir sent a deputation of his own to Constantinople. They reported back to him, regaling him with tales of the splendor of the cathedral in that great city between the Black and the Mediterranean seas. He therefore chose to cast his lot with the Christians of the East and set about the widespread conversion of his people.

Vladimir brought priests to Kiev, ordered mass baptisms, built many churches that modeled their onion-domed, ornate style after the architecture of Byzantium, founded monasteries, and sent out missionaries to spread what had begun in Kiev into the rest of his domain. Thus was Russia made a "Christian" land by imperial decree.

Even though Judaism lost in the opportunity to become the official religion of Russia, many of Hebrew descent continued, through the centuries, to migrate into those northern Slavic and Russian regions between the valleys of the Rhine of central Europe and the Urals separating that continent from Asia to the east. As different as it was from their native Israel, which now was in the pagan hands of Arabs and Muslims, it seemed to suit them here. Northeastern Europe gradually became one of the great strongholds where the children of Abraham's seed—except for periodic inquisitions against them—were able to live in relative peace, while their numbers continued to grow.

It was no peaceable land, however. Warlike barbarians fought for control, and the peasants of the land paid for the savage greed with their own blood.

A constant stream of invaders attempted to conquer the land from every direction as well. The most savage—and successful—of these came from the East.

Mongol hordes led by descendants of Genghis Khan invaded from China and Mongolia in the middle of the thirteenth century with a cruel and overwhelming might that could not be resisted. Within but a few short decades, all of Russia had come under their control.

The Golden Horde, as the Mongol overlords were known, left the religious institutions of Russia virtually untouched, however. During these times when terrible financial tolls and cruelties were exacted upon Russia's peasantry, Jewish rabbis and Christian monks found themselves conscious of their links of faith to a more than usual degree. If they were not exactly brothers, certainly they were cousins who could occasionally help one another amid the difficult—and sometimes desperate—circumstances of their people.

Thus it was that the bearded ben Israel, who was too old and not strong enough for such a hasty journey, had left Moscow late one night on the ride that would prove to cost him his life.

He was well familiar with the Holy Trinity Christian monastery known as Troitsa. Though the Trinity was a Christian doctrine no Jew could believe in, how could he not admire the monastery's founder, Sergius, who as a young man had left home to live in the forest, where he dedicated himself to prayer, self-denial, and holiness. The small chapel he built in the woods gradually attracted others. A neighboring abbot made him a monk. Eventually the monastery called *Troitsa* grew from the original chapel, some forty miles outside Moscow, and gradually the quiet man's reputation spread.

The Jewish rabbi from Moscow found common chords resonating within himself at the Christian monk's teaching. His own people had known oppression, not for mere centuries, but for three millennia. When he heard of Sergius's teaching that compared the Mongols with the Egyptians who had oppressed his own Hebrew ancestors, he knew that this must be a man in whom he had discovered a kindred spirit. It became his desire to journey one day to Troitsa and meet Sergius face-to-face and to express the bonds of commonality between their sister faiths.

Unfortunately, the day for such a meeting did not come soon.

In 1382, word of an approaching Mongol army reached Moscow. A terrible premonition swept through the heart of the rabbi of Israel. Fearing not only for his people, but also for the legacy of their heritage that had been placed in his hands, he decided to take it to the monastery. There, should anything happen to him, he was certain the protection of God would surround it, for was it not already evident that the God of his fathers walked closely with the Christian monk of Troitsa?

His daring ride, mostly in the black of night, had taken him over unfamiliar terrain and had taxed him far beyond what his frame could endure. It was not, however, a mission he could entrust to anyone else.

His exhausted steed, jumping a small earthen dike some eight miles from Troitsa, had stumbled, throwing the poor rabbi to the ground. Groaning in pain, he glanced around to where the dying horse lay in a heap, its great sides heaving but without even the energy to lift its head and make an attempt to rise.

He would have to continue alone on foot. He crawled to the poor animal, patted his long head and nose, whispered a few words of apologetic comfort, prayed for God to take him quickly and gently, then rose and set about the remainder of his journey.

It was midmorning when he collapsed on the steps at the Troitsa monastery, to the amazement of the monks at the door who had observed his approach. They immediately sent for Sergius.

Offering a feeble hand and a thin smile as the abbot superior knelt down to greet him, the prostrate rabbi identified himself, then requested a private audience with the monk whom he had wanted to meet for so many years.

The monks proceeded to make him as comfortable as they could under the circumstances in one of their available rooms. They brought him water and some warm broth, and within the hour their guest was fast asleep. Sergius visited him, alone, later in the afternoon when he had, if not recovered his strength, at least revived sufficiently to converse with the abbot. He explained his mission, the need for secrecy, and some of the history of the two diamonds, wrapped in the folds of a thick protective leather pouch, which he pulled from inside his coat and handed to the astonished abbot.

"There is no one else to whom I can entrust them at present," he murmured when he had completed his remarkable tale. "But they must find their way back to my people . . . when it is safe."

"As they shall, my friend and brother," assured Sergius of Radonezh. "As Joseph's bones were preserved during the sojourn of our fathers—your people and mine—in Egypt, to be returned to the Land of Promise when the season of their exile was past, so too shall these precious stones be preserved for that time when *this* exile of Abraham's offspring has come to its end. We will pray for their protection, and that our Father's hand will guide what hands of men they pass among, until that appointed time when they shall again rest upon Mount Zion in the holy city of Jerusalem."

"Thank you—may I call you my brother?" breathed ben Israel.

"You may," replied the monk. "It rejoices my heart to hear you utter the word. Now you must sleep, and eat what you can when my monks attend to you. We must have you recover your strength to continue about God's business."

The aged, weary Jew smiled weakly and nodded.

In his soul he knew that his work was done. This was not how he had envisioned his meeting with the Christian leader he had long admired. There was much he had wanted to ask him, so many common threads of their respective faiths he had wanted to explore.

Yet he was content, and would die a happy man.

Two days later, ben Israel had gone to join his fathers Abraham, Isaac, and Jacob, and the multitude that had followed them.

Sergius placed the valuable relics into the monastery's repository, where but a handful of other earthly treasures lay, for safekeeping. The very day of the rabbi's death, he commissioned two of his monks to fashion a small clay box, fitted and studded with metal braces, inlaid with lesser jewels, to be painted with symbols significant to Russian Jewry and folklore, in which the two diamonds would be kept, awaiting the day when they could be returned into the hands of those ben Israel had called his people. He took care as well to write of the event in his journal, making sure instructions were clear as to the disposition of the Jewish heirlooms in the event his own passing should precede their return to the people in whose care they most rightfully belonged.

A week after the rabbi's death, the Mongols invaded Moscow with redoubled force. The city was sacked, burned to the ground, and twenty-four thousand of its inhabitants massacred.

❧ 5 ❧

Preservation of the Legacy
c. A.D. 1500

The legacy continued, but was hidden again in invisibility.

Yet the eyes of God never sleep. They now turned themselves toward an obscure youth called Wizanski, and placed within his heart the hunger by which the Almighty would continue to heed the ancient prayer of Jehoiachin.

A century after Sergius, with the Mongols gone and the huge land mass consolidating into modern nations, differing forms of Christian monastic life in eastern Europe and what was now Russia began to come into sharp conflict. A trend among many monks was to live alone, without property, to disavow all connections with earthly life, and to give themselves completely to meditation and prayer.

Another faction within the Russian Orthodox Church took the view that, while perhaps individual monks should possess no wealth of their own, it was right and even desirable for monasteries to collectively accumulate what goods they could, even to the acquiring of sizable holdings. The chief proponent of this latter trend was one Joseph of Volokolamsk, a Russian nobleman turned monk.

Josephites were orthodox in their doctrine, strict in their discipline, opposed to heresy in any form, and insistent that all rites of the church be diligently observed. But they were far from mystics, and spent little time in meditation and prayer. They considered theirs a "practical" faith. Their utilitarian view of property resulted in the construction of great buildings at their monastery, where the furnishings, vestments, sacred vessels, altars, windows, chairs, tables, and rooms for the conducting of their affairs were always beautiful, and occasionally lavish.

Over the years, it began to be rumored that somewhere on the premises a vast hoard of gold and silver items had been laid aside and was now hidden, in preparation for a time of famine that had been predicted by one of the monks.

A certain young nobleman who sought the monastery early in the sixteenth century came from Pinsk in the neighboring Lithuanian region of Poland. A Jew by blood, his religion was a strange but effective mixture of Judaism and Christianity. His reception, in the midst of the unbending orthodoxy of Josephite tradition, was cool at first. But he entered into the form of their ways and bent himself to an intense study of their doctrine. Calling himself a "complete" Jew, young Wizanski remained at the monastery fifteen years, during which time he matured greatly in the synthesis of his system of belief, absorbing the mystical heritage of Orthodoxy with greater devotion than he had the Roman Catholic tradition of his native Poland, though never being fully accepted into the priestly order. A great student of the past, he made a diligent study of whatever documents he could lay his hands on that might point to indications of post–first-century unity between Jewish and Christian leaders. At the end of his sojourn in Russia, he returned westward to Poland to reacquaint his hungry heart once again with the Judaism of his past.

The predicted famine never came exactly as prophesied, nor was the rumor of hidden wealth ever substantiated, though it persisted.

It was known, however, that the monastery at Volokolamsk had inherited many possessions from other monasteries through the years. These included, other rumors maintained, the personal trunk that had belonged to Sergius of Troitsa, which was said to include his devotional books, a journal, his robe, a few earthly possessions of reputed value, and the bones of his earthly tabernacle.

No doubt around all these rumors clung some vapors of truth, corrupted and enlarged and given added interest by the dust of falsehood. Along with the known and visible accoutrements of the monastic life in clear evidence at Volokolamsk, these rumors led to widely exaggerated reports of the wealth of the Josephites and to the disdain the more contemplative monastic orders had for what they judged their inordinate involvement with the affairs of the flesh.

When, still another century later, a Josephite monk took it upon himself to open the ancient trunk from Troitsa, he declared the old rumors to have been false, for he could discover nothing whatever that would indicate earthly wealth.

The journal of Sergius also, he said, was missing.

ᕯ 6 ᕯ

A New Homeland
1948

Out of holocaust—victory!

The Nazi Pharaoh was dead, his chariot wheels of death stilled at last.

The new exodus had begun!

Arise, children of God, from out of the whole earth. Yahweh has heard your cries and will take you to the Land of Promise again!

In 1948 at last did the tribes of Jacob's sons possess a homeland once more to call their own—*Israel!*—the same land given to Abraham, journeyed to by Moses, tramped across and fought for by David, and sung about by their ancient kings and prophets.

And if the delivery and provisional aspect of the prophecy was of more expansive duration than the sons of Abraham would first have thought, so too was the extent to which the latter portion of it was fulfilled as well: *But I will punish the nation they serve as slaves, and afterward you will come out with great possessions.*

Indeed had their persecutors been punished. The mighty Egypt of the Pharaohs boasted only silent stone sentinels out in the Nile desert of Thebes to remind the world of its former greatness. Babylonia and Persia were so lost to the passage of time no monuments even stood to remember them by. Rome's mighty empire had collapsed from within, and even its language that had once ruled the world was now dead.

Still the Hebrews they had all disdained lived on.

Now the latest of their persecutors, the tyrannical German *Reich*, lay also in ruins.

The new Jewish homeland was peopled, however, with but a scant trickle from out of all the nations of the earth. The second exodus, made up of men and women crossing each of the seven seas in their twentieth-century Palestinian pilgrimage, made not nearly so cohesive a conglomeration as that which Moses led across the Red Sea almost exactly four thousand years earlier.

Notwithstanding the massive Nazi carnage, assuredly had Abraham's descendants become as numerous as the stars in the heavens. The vast majority of those remaining, however, did not discover emigration to Israel from those lands in which they found themselves such an easy task. For some the constraints were financial. Most, after so long, considered themselves citizens of their adopted homelands and sought no change.

There were others, in certain parts of the world, who could not, as easily as they might hope, get out from the borders that enclosed them. The defeat of fascism caused new walls to be raised against the offspring of God. *Communism* now set itself up to purify the world's genealogy of both Abraham's bloodline and that stalk that had been grafted onto it by the miracle of Ephesians chapter two, the followers of Christ known as *Christians*.

Persecution continued, therefore, against *all* those who made the ancient Hebrew God, Yahweh, *I AM*, the object of their worship. In the postwar era, however, the continued massacre of Jews was one of the most skillfully concealed of the world's lies. The Holocaust had nowise ended in 1945, only shifted its focus eastward and taken its atrocities out of the public eye.

Some sought to endure, some sought to hide their lineage, others sought means to escape to either the West or their new homeland; still others made it their business to help their kinsmen and alert the global community that its Jewish problems were far from solved.

The children of Abraham had come out of World War II with their numbers decimated by annihilation, yet with character, national pride, and a vibrancy of spirit that earned the respect of a world that had for so many centuries despised and ignored them. They emerged from the Nazi holocaust with that great possession which more than fifty generations of them had so passionately yearned to call their own—the land of their fathers.

They were, however, still a people incognizant of their Messiah, and therefore, to that extent, unfulfilled as a race of God's children. They again occupied their patriarchal homeland, but they had yet not taken possession of Yahweh's heart—that most prized possession of all that he had been waiting to give them now for six thousand years.

Still he waited.

Many things had been accomplished . . . but this highest calling of their destiny yet waited to be fulfilled.

❧ 7 ❧

Dark Secrets

1953

As the faint images slowly came into view, the man hunched over the developing tank, squinted, and bent forward for a closer look.

He sloshed the picture about gently in the developer as if he would hurry the process, though the film continued just as slowly to reveal itself.

The ordinarily routine work of processing the Kremlin's film usually turned up nothing more interesting than photographs of factories, fields, farms, and military installations. Occasionally something of minor interest might be requested for *Pravda* or Tass.

But never had Stoyidovich seen anything like this!

Clutching the corner of the print with his sponge-tipped

tongs, he held it up to the thin red light bulb above the tank. Even as he squinted again, his eyes immediately opened wide in shock.

What he had suspected at first glance was true. He recoiled in disgust at the grisly sight, threw the photograph back down in the developer, and turned away.

His wits as a photographer, however, remained with him sufficiently that he knew the images would darken beyond recognizability if he left the print in the developer too long.

He turned back, checked it again, then lifted it out of the solution once more with the tongs and tossed it, face down, in the pan of acetic acid stop bath to his right. Then he sat back on his stool and exhaled a long breath, as if developing the single eight-by-ten had exacted an enormous physical toll from his bodily strength.

As indeed it had.

He had been taught reconnaissance photography during the war. He had learned his trade well and had parlayed it since into as good a position as a man like himself could hope to have in the Communist order. Working for the revolutionary government was not safe. Nothing in Russia was safe. Stalin had not only slaughtered millions of peasants, he had ordered the murder of eleven hundred delegates to one Party Congress—all of them Stalin supporters! Of the 139 Central Committee members, 98 were shot.

No, nothing was "safe" here. But working for the government meant slightly increased benefits from time to time. At least it kept him from poverty.

He was one of millions who had changed his name. But nothing could change his blood. Nothing could take away the ache of persecution, even if he happened to have been lucky enough to be born with features that looked especially Russian so as to avoid the grief that came to so many.

His young assistant had *not* been so lucky. *His* features could not be hidden, nor the intensity of his political leanings. He had tried to hide both, and his alias certainly gave nothing away. But Stoyidovich was not so naive as he let his superiors at the Kremlin believe.

He knew.

It was why he had brought in the young fellow as his assistant, even though he realized the possibility existed that it might endanger him as well. Actually, it had been a foolhardy move. And after the young man had been arrested, he *had* been interrogated . . . more than once. But the KGB seemed satisfied in the end, and he hadn't seen anything of them in a year.

He made sure his present new apprentice was Russian through and through, and loyal to the Communist cause besides.

Still, he thought, he missed the sense that he was somehow involved, however thin the association, with someone brave enough to do something . . . with someone brave enough to even face prison if it came to that, for the sake of his people.

Stoyidovich thought another moment or two. Then, in a sudden moment of resolve, he rose from his stool, turned, and walked several paces across the darkroom. The negative was still in the enlarger. They would be careful to retrieve it when they returned.

He would make an *extra* print—a small one . . . small enough to hide easily.

He would make extras of anything else on the roll, too, that might be useful.

Quickly, beginning to perspire with fear now for what he was about to do, he readjusted the enlarger for the smaller size paper, made a quick calculation to account for the closer intensity of the light, then flipped the switch to expose it for a second and a half. With hastily fumbling fingers he took out the negative and peered at the reversed image, then the next, and the next.

Yes, he would make prints of those too.

He reinserted the negative, corrected the focus slightly, then flipped the switch once again, then off, then repeated the process yet a third time.

The deed was done!

Stoyidovich lifted the enlarger's heavy arm back up to eight-by-ten size so that his work would not be discovered.

He took out the small squares of exposed photographic paper, then glanced around hurriedly for a place to hide them.

He would not develop them . . . not now.

No one would know of the existence of these photos. Even if

they were found, they would appear harmless—just a few pieces of unused photographic paper.

When the time came—if he needed them for whatever purpose those of his bloodline might require—he could develop them then. It would do the people in the gruesome scene he had just seen no good.

But his efforts just might save their children.

Until then, however, no one but he himself would know these photographs existed.

∽ 8 ∽
A People and Their Heritage
1948–1961

A certain Heziah Wissen, faithful husband, father, rabbi, and Jewish man of God, now found himself chosen the unwitting, though no less diligent and resourceful, protector of the ancient spoil from the Most Holy Place of Jerusalem. He could not know how many venerable hands his touched as a result of his honored position . . . nor what hands now sought him for their own evil purposes.

Various networks of underground activities sprang up in the postwar era of which the rabbi was a part, especially in Eastern Europe. These established a flow for both people and information to get out of the Soviet Union, either to the newly created democratic nation of West Germany, the BRD—though few wanted to remain on that tearstained soil for long—to the United States, or to Israel itself.

They went by various names, denoting their purposes. Some were political, some humanitarian, others Zionist in their orientation. One was called the Fighting Group against Inhumanity . . . another went simply by the name of *The Rose*.

Information and people were by no means the only commodities of exchange on the secretly linked tracks of these invisible railroads of life stretching north and south, east and west, across Europe.

The industrious people of Jacob's descent had applied

themselves through the centuries, though their wealth was not now measured in flocks of goats and sheep, by head of cattle, or by the number of a man's wives, slaves, or oxen as in the days of Moses. The gold and silver they took from the Egyptians in times of old was, in this latter-day exodus, the hard-earned wealth of their own hands. But no less did modern Pharaohs and their henchmen attempt to lay their hands on such wealth for themselves.

The nation of Israel had grown particularly affluent through the centuries in artifacts of its religion. Objects of gold and silver were numerous, as well as certain relics of enormous antiquity that had been, miraculously their more zealous would say, preserved through history for this time so that they might again find their way to that land where originated all things. At the midpoint between the great river Euphrates and the Nile sat the holy city Jerusalem, where, one day in the not-too-distant future it was hoped, would again rise against the desert sun a great new temple wherein Yahweh's people might renew their worship of Solomon's God. It was there, in that new dwelling place of the Spirit of God, that the relics and wealth of the Jewish past most rightfully belonged.

Getting them there from the four corners of the earth, however, was not always an easy task. Israel had been badly plundered of both its human wealth and its earthly treasures by the Teutonic despot. There were those in the regime of the new Russian tyrants as well who still sought what Hitler had not been able to lay his hands upon.

But *Einsatzstab-Rosenberg* had been unsuccessful in tracking down all such valuable Jewish resources. Early in the 1700s, the legendary Urim and Thummim had arrived, by whatever means, in Warsaw, where eventually, two centuries later, they came into the hands of the faithful Polish rabbi, who made it his business to protect them from the greedy and nefarious hands of the Nazis.

How his possession of them came to the attention of a ruthless Gestapo mercenary during the war only added to the mystery, for the poor Jewish peasant, killed by the agent trying to obtain the information, took whatever he might have known to his grave.

Rabbi Wissen, however, knowing thereafter that he was being hotly pursued, managed to get the small, ornately painted box containing the two stones, two ancient dreidels, as well as several minas of precious metals, safely from Warsaw and out of the sight of the Gestapo. With help from a sympathizing German nobleman by the name of Dortmann, whose wife shared the rabbi's Jewish blood, a temporary hiding place was found for both rabbi and stones, though it lay deep inside the Third *Reich* itself.

After the war, with Dortmann imprisoned in East Germany, the rabbi sojourned in the new state of Israel before returning to Russia to help his people who remained in captivity there. Nothing of the stones and the relics accompanying them had been heard of again.

After some years, Rabbi Wissen gradually became aware that his life was once more in danger. That any connection could exist between this and his wartime pursuer after such a passage of years the rabbi seriously doubted. It was clear, however, that the time had come for him to leave Russia, with wife and daughter, and make a new home in Palestine for good.

Unknown to him, however, information was about to come into the hands of the network, whose commitment he shared with Dortmann's daughter, which would graphically and unmistakably inform the whole world of the plight of their people. Once he saw it, he realized he must get that information safely to the West first. Then he would see to his own emigration. He was Jew enough to realize that the cause of his people mattered more than his own life.

If only he could also have known that the messenger about to bring the vital new documents into the hands of the *Network of the Rose* was the same young man he had been searching for during his whole time in Russia since the war.

But identities were closely guarded. Many names giving away Hebrew ancestry had been changed. And though the paths of an aging Jewish rabbi and a faithful young Zionist came close, they did not meet.

There was a time for all things . . . but the appointment between these two was not yet.

⮜ 9 ⮞
A Son of Jacob
May 1961

Fog lay thick over all Moscow.

The night was silent and still, and what distant noises there were in the sleeping Russian capital were muffled yet further by the deep cloud that had descended upon it.

A figure shrouded in a long black overcoat glanced furtively right and left, then quickened his pace, crossed a wide intersection, and began the long walk out across the black, slow-flowing Moskva River on the Kamenny Bridge.

Two or three times more he glanced behind him, then paused some third of the distance out. If he was found at this late hour he was sure to be searched. That was why they had chosen the bridge. Disposing of the incriminating packet would be easy enough from here, the river providing a permanent grave for its contents if the KGB or any similar danger presented itself.

The son of Jacob, an alien in a land unfriendly to those of Hebrew blood, was grateful that he had learned his trade well enough to be rehired by the aging Russian Jew who had shown interest in him after the war. He still could scarcely believe what had fallen into his hands and what a risk the old man had taken to preserve these for such an opportunity. This new power that had arisen in the north threatened those remaining under its evil dominion as much as had any of the conquering empires of old. Too many had already been murdered. What he held in his coat would prove it to the world.

A low whistle came through the night fog. It was the signal from his contact that the other side of the Kamenny was also clear. He waited precisely ten seconds, then returned the sound. Both knew they were alone on the bridge and that the exchange should be a safe one.

He began walking again, slowly, as if the fog itself lent a subdued effect to the very movement of his legs. Those he counted among his friends called him foolhardy for continuing such clandestine and perilous work. He had spent too many years in prison already, they said. Others could continue. It was time for him to leave Russia. No doubt in Israel he could locate the family of his betrothed—if they even remembered him after all these years, he added silently.

It was true, he thought. Times had changed, and even his passion for the work had faded. But he had not become involved in the underground during the war to desert it now when an occasional opportunity to help arose. Perhaps he should have gone with them to Switzerland, he mused, questioning for the thousandth time his decision to remain behind with the Polish underground. That decision had led him after the war to Russia, where, apprenticed to a governmental tradesman by day but involved with a Zionist faction by night, he had been arrested and imprisoned in 1951, the beginning of eight lonely years in exile.

But he was free again at thirty-six, as free as any of his blood would ever be in this Communist prison called the Soviet Republic. He was free, and yet a listlessness was encroaching that, try as he might, he could not seem to fight off.

Was he destined to remain in Russia forever? Was he going to become like everyone else here—uncaring and unfeeling?

He had heard of a sister underground network that went by the name of *The Rose*. Though not Zionist in its orientation, it had links into West Germany and was considered one of the more successful of such organizations at getting information out of the Communist sphere. That was why he was delivering this particular parcel to a contact who had links with their people, whoever they were. It was more important that this information reach Western governments even than that it reach Jerusalem.

Could they of *The Rose* get people out too? He would think about it later. The information he held inside his coat could not wait.

With his reflections to occupy him, he proceeded to the center of the river, where the arch over it reached its midpoint.

Hear, O Israel . . . he said, speaking low in modern Hebrew as a figure approached through the fog. The language had been outlawed some time earlier. The dialect itself was better than any password. No one would return it unless he was a friend.

The Lord our God, the Lord . . . he heard softly back through the night in the criminal tongue.

. . . is one, he concluded.

"Do you have the parcel?" the other voice asked, now in Russian.

"Yes."

He pulled it from his coat, then handed it to his contact.

"It must get out of Russia immediately."

"One of our number will take it across the border."

"Whoever touches it will be in danger."

"Why, were you followed?"

"No."

"Why, then?"

"They will soon discover it. I don't know how. But they always do. They will track it somehow. You will have but a few days. The KGB is never far behind."

"The man into whose hands this will be placed will, it is said, himself be leaving Russia soon. Where he is bound even the KGB will not be able to follow."

"Our homeland?"

"Perhaps," came the answer vaguely.

"Do not be too sure that he will be safe even there, my friend. The reach of the enemy's arm is a long one."

"He walks close to God, they say. He will be protected."

"What is his name? I seek one who—"

"You know I cannot tell you that," interrupted the other, "even if I knew his real name, which I do not. I am not even myself personally acquainted with him. Whatever it is you have given me will see many hands other than mine before it reaches him. It is the only way safety is assured."

He placed the packet under the folds of his coat, hoping he would not have to drop it in the river on his way to meet the next contact among the many he spoke of, then turned.

"Shalom."

"And to you," said the deliverer of the parcel, disappointed that he was unable to penetrate the veil of secrecy that surrounded the very network in which he was placing such important hopes.

The two men parted, returning in the directions from which they had come.

If only I could find them! he thought as he made his return back across the bridge. Whether or not the rabbi was presently in Israel, he was sure he had been in Russia within the last year or two. There were reports that had unmistakable hints of his identity. Since his release from that dreadful prison in Leningrad two years ago he had done whatever he could to follow the leads.

But the man on the bridge was right. Secrecy surrounded every movement of the underground, and no one used their real names.

Had she waited for him? Would she still want him after all this time?

The flames of love had nowise dimmed in his soul, though many years had passed.

Joseph ben Eleazar was a man who honored his commitments. And to Rabbi Wissen's eldest daughter he had given his heart.

❧ 10 ❧

A Daughter of Israel
October 1961

A daughter of ancient Hebrew heritage walked slowly along Friedhofstrasse, glancing now and then at the ugly cement-and-barbed-wire wall on the opposite side of the street—and the green lawn of the burial site on the other side of it—that divided the once-great German capital. Berlin had been her home now for enough years that she no longer felt a stranger here, though she wondered if people of Jewish blood would ever be at home anywhere, especially in Germany.

She knew many who had made the migration to Israel. She herself had helped hundreds get there, including her own family just recently. Her mother and father and sister were all there now. She had received a letter from Gisela just yesterday.

But even Israel was not yet "home" to them. They were Polish—she here, her family there, Joseph, her betrothed, wherever he was by this time.

The Holy Book's Rachel had waited seven years to be united with her betrothed, by the cruel hand of her father, Laban.

She smiled sadly as she walked. She had waited seventeen. Should she even still think of herself as betrothed? Most Jewish women in her position would consider themselves widowed by this time, at the cruel hand, not of a father, but of what the Germans called their fatherland.

Her family had been Poles for generations. How many new generations would it take before they could claim to be Israelis . . . and *only* Israelis?

Her mother and sister had begged her to accompany them. Only her father seemed to understand. He too was a man of mission. He understood her commitment to the cause she shared with her whose father had hid them during the war . . . the cause of *The Rose*.

She would follow them in time, Ursula had assured them, but not until she knew Sabina and her father were safe and could carry on without her, whatever their future might hold.

They might still need help, she added. The ugly wall across from which she now walked had changed everything. She would not leave West Berlin until she had done all she could for them.

How ironic, Ursula thought, that the wall had cut right across the cemetery, now mostly in the eastern sector, and cut it off from the very street here in West Berlin named for it. No more ironic, she supposed, than that it had cut blocks in half, cut businesses off from their customers, cut families cruelly off one member from another . . . and taken life itself from so many.

Through a portion of wire fence where the concrete blocks had not yet been raised to full height, her glance fell on the contingent of East German *Vopos* patrolling the border on the other side along the edges of the cemetery itself. They were a familiar sight now, though no easier to accustom herself to than calling Hitler's Berlin her home. Beyond them, less than a hundred meters away from where she walked but as removed from her as if they had been on the far side of the world, a few scattered mourners could be seen in the Fischer Street cemetery placing flowers upon graves, while others cleaned and tidied family burial plots. She wondered if they were mourning any of the brave individuals who had been killed attempting to cross this very wall between her and them since it had been laid down across Berlin two months ago.

How long would this wall be here? Ursula wondered.

How long would this division, and the death it had already caused, remain? How fittingly symbolic for it to snake its silent and evil way alongside the final resting place of those attempting to cross it to freedom.

How oppressive it must be over there, thought Ursula as she walked, glancing beyond the cemetery to the buildings in the heart of East Berlin, *if even the elderly, with but a few more years to look forward to anyway, were willing to risk death and leave everything behind, simply to live out their remaining days in freedom.*

How could a vital young woman like Sabina, she thought, *have endured it so long?* And yet, after so many years when it was possible simply to walk across the border to freedom, now the wall had risen between her life here . . . and Sabina's over there.

Her friend was trapped in the Communist tomb, from which escape was becoming more dangerous and more difficult every day.

❧ 11 ❧

Der Mauer

Ursula's thoughts drifted back to many of the frightful escapes that had already been attempted in the two short months since the partition had gone up.

Daring flights over, under, and through *der Mauer* had begun the very day the barrier had been erected in August. Ursula had even been part of a few of them, for in the early days after the building of the wall, before security measures had been tightened, almost anyone could help escapees if they dared.

The Wall of Tears, as it soon came to be called, though difficult, was not impossible to get across during those first several weeks. Hundreds of escapes proved successful. Even as it was being fabricated—crudely at first—many small groups were able to slip over to the West, scrambling over the low wall or crawling under the wire. Cars and trucks were even driven at full speed through the incomplete and poorly built barricades. And before the evacuation of Bernauerstrasse and Harzerstrasse, where buildings and apartment houses literally fronted the wall itself, many simply jumped or climbed down the walls of their homes to freedom.

But as the days went by, the wall went higher, the cement was poured thicker, the patrols of guards were increased, and East Berlin became more and more like the prison it was destined to become. Escape, for those who dared attempt it, required by necessity steadily more ingenuity.

A nineteen-year-old East German girl was smuggled across the border to safety in a large hand suitcase.

East German schoolteacher Fritz Berger transformed himself into an American Army officer by scrounging from friends whatever used bits of military attire he could lay his hands on. When ready, he walked through Checkpoint Charlie on the Friedrichstrasse one evening and was given the customary military courtesy—a heel-clicking salute—from the East German border patrol, motioning him through. Had the guard been more alert, he would have noticed the "American officer" was wearing parts of a Czechoslovakian army uniform, a World War II German shirt, Russian shoulder straps, and buttons from an old U.S. Army uniform, given him by a girl who had once been in love with an American soldier.

A husband and wife, with their little child, made a desperate leap to the freedom of the West from the window of the fifth floor of an apartment building on Bernauerstrasse into a firemen's net while the crowd of men holding it choked and gasped from the tear gas bombs being thrown by the East German police. Still they clutched the net for dear life, lest the small family crash on the pavement.

The very day after the first barricades of barbed wire were strung, a young East German soldier, in full uniform and carrying his Russian-issue submachine gun, sprinted toward the barrier on Bernauerstrasse and leapt high over the wire. His daring jump to freedom was captured on film and made front-page news all over the world. Immediately after reaching the other side, he threw down his gun, shouting, "I'm free! I'm free!"

Many tunnels were also dug, though the underground method was one of the most dangerous escape routes of all. The loose, sandy soil of the region around Berlin was not nearly compact enough to create dependable tunnels and gave way far too easily. Many collapsed.

Considering the extreme hazards, however, and that buildings near the border were watched with extreme vigilance, a great number of people managed to tunnel their way to safety, sometimes with nothing but spoons and small shovels, taking great care to hide every spoonful of dirt. A taxi driver from Frohnau dug for two sleepless weeks and finally led twenty-five people underground to freedom, including a child of eight and a woman of eighty. Three hours after the escape, the tunnel was discovered by the *Vopos* and sealed up, never to be used again.

For a time, one of the easiest and most dependable routes of passage from East to West Berlin was to wade and swim and crawl along Berlin's underground drainage canals from one part of Berlin to the other. The most popular in the first month after August 13 was the Ragenwasser-Kanal, a clear rainwater canal that flowed under Esplanadestrasse, directly between the two halves of the city. Huge numbers of refugees sought freedom along this wet highway, but after only fifteen days it was detected, and bolted manhole covers replaced the open gratings that had allowed such easy access.

The closed passage was quickly replaced by another at Glockengasse, where some 150 passed to freedom in three weeks. However, this canal route was also discovered and access to it likewise closed.

In just two months, most such easy escape routes—underground, over ground, and directly through gaps in the wall itself—had been plugged.

Not all the stories were pleasant ones. With every account of heroism and escape, there was an equal tale of heartbreak and tragedy.

Countless families had seen their lives suddenly torn apart by the cruel hand of the cold war's random geography.

One West Berlin couple had decided upon the open street

beside the wall as the site for their wedding so the bride's mother, trapped in East Berlin, might hope to catch glimpses of the ceremony from a block away with binoculars.

Proud West Berlin parents regularly took newborn infants to crossing points in the wall, where, holding the infants high above their heads, they hoped grandparents on the other side might be fortunate enough to see them.

Many were the plights mirrored by that of one elderly man who had long lived in East Berlin but worked as a watchman on the night shift in West Berlin. At work on the night of August 13, he had not been allowed to return home and was separated from his family thereafter. Every day he came to the wall, climbed high atop a ladder, and attempted to wave to his family on the other side. They could not come to him, and he was unable to get back to his own home to them.

Separation was only part of the anguish. Many tragic deaths had occurred, Germans killing brother Germans, spilling the blood of their countrymen upon the stones and sidewalks and streets of the divided city.

Dieter Wohlfahrt, a young Austrian studying at the Technical University in West Berlin, trapped like so many others in the eastern sector of the city on August 13, crept to the barbed-wire fence in the suburb of Staaken and began cutting his way through. Before he was successful, however, he was spotted and fired upon, and fell. While helpless West German border guards watched in agony, the young student bled to death and was then silently dragged away to his final resting place in East Berlin by the *Vopos* who had killed him.

Several were shot trying to swim across the Spree. The *Vopos* and all East German authorities less and less considered West Berliners their fellow countrymen.

It was not only the young who braved death in heroic and solitary flights to freedom.

Ursula herself had been in the crowd watching the drama unfold when a seventy-seven-year-old, white-haired East German climbed out the window of her second-story apartment on the border to attempt the climb down to the ground. Reaching her to prevent her escape, three *Vopo* policemen grabbed her by the shoulders and tried to pull her back. A

young West German man, witnessing the scene, leapt up to a
window ledge, clasped the woman's legs, and after a tussle that
lasted several minutes, managed to wrestle her from the hands
of the East Germans and down to the ground and to freedom.
The only possession she was able to save was a cat, which she
frantically clutched throughout the entire ordeal.

Unfortunate Ida Siekmann had not been so lucky.

When the Communists began bricking up the doors and
windows of the lower floors of her apartment building on Bernauerstrasse and followed those moves with the forced evacuation of the families living in the upper stories, the fifty-nine-
year-old woman made a rash decision to attempt a most desperate means of escape. Heaping together her featherbed and
all the blankets and pillows and other soft materials she possessed, she opened her window and dropped them to the
ground below. Then, hoping that the bedding would break the
impact of her fall, she leapt from her window. She missed her
pile, however, and seconds later lay moaning and dying on the
cobblestones of the street below.

Now the only reminder of this one of many lives lost in the
attempt to escape the shadow of Communism was an occasional wreath of flowers left on the sidewalk in front of Nr. 48
Bernauerstrasse so that no one would forget Frau Siekmann's
fateful fall.

Ursula shivered at the memory.

Notwithstanding the accounts of successful escapes, the
Vopos seemed more numerous daily, and with each attempt
they redoubled their efforts to plug every possible leak over,
under, or through the hideous grey barrier bisecting the
city. Already, in just two short months, the difficulty of getting from the East to the West had been increased a hundredfold.

The penalty for helping escapees mounted daily too. Prison
awaited those caught in the East. She would continue to do
what was possible to help on this side, thought Ursula.

But she could not keep from wondering what the escalating
danger would ultimately mean to her comrades in the *Network
of the Rose*, whose very lives were suddenly much more in danger than before.

∽ 12 ∽
Anxious Thoughts
November 1961

Andrassy Galanov, twenty-one-year-old KGB apprentice, strode with more confidence than his years could account for through the deserted Kremlin corridor.

The limp from his injuries three months ago was only barely recognizable. He had been summoned home as soon as he could make the trip, but was then made to wait nearly two weeks before any meeting of consequence took place, a result of one of many idiosyncrasies about his uncle that annoyed him. But the delay had allowed him to heal further, and for that he was thankful. He would not appear weak and would hide what remained of his limp as best he could.

The manly bearing he sought to exude as he walked along, however, belied the fact that deep down he was more than a little anxious concerning the interview toward which he was bound.

He would not reveal it, of course.

Russian men learned not to show their fears from an early age if they intended to rise out of the obscurity of the masses to any position of prominence in the revolutionary regime. That creed bore all the more importance if the KGB was one's chosen route of advance. It was the ruthless, unfeeling, and coldly efficient who made their mark. Such had distinguished his uncle, and such, the young man was determined, would in time set him apart from his youthful peers as well.

Galanov had wanted to be an agent since before he could remember.

Born in Germany of Russian parents during the war, he remembered practically nothing of that time. His first definable memories were of fear—first of their fellow Russians, then that they would not be able to get out of Germany at all, then later, back in Russia, hearing his parents talking about the American threat, and about the need to protect the motherland from invasion and attack.

As he had grown into his teen years, talk at home and at school and in the newspapers was of the imperialist aggression of the United States in attempts to gain military dominance over their homeland through those countries bordering the Soviet Union. Crisis after crisis had required the sending of brave Russian soldiers to such places to secure their safety, and even—where the American threats were most severe—sending troops to help the innocent nations by occupation. Only so could they be saved from destruction by the cruel American bombs and vicious, plundering GIs.

He remembered being told of U.S. and British attempts to rape and ransack Eastern Europe and how Stalin had saved those countries. He remembered personally the crisis in Egypt and the American-led revolts in Poland and Hungary in 1956, as well as growing anxieties in Asia and Latin America. There was no place, it seemed, that the Americans were not trying to take over.

Many young Russians like him were eager to go to war against the imperialists. But he had always loved the world of intrigue and mystery. He set his course early to help the motherland by being part of the KGB, like his uncle. But by now, at the ripe young age of twenty-one, he was already experienced enough to have made the transition from wanting to help his country to merely wanting to help himself.

His recent assignment in Germany had been of short duration, only a little over a year, yet he had learned a great deal. He had observed the mechanics of Soviet influence in the plum of its satellite states—the East German *Deutsche Demokratische Republik*, known simply as the DDR. He had had opportunity to work closely with that nation's secret police, and his association with *Stasi* Section Chief Schmundt had afforded him rare personal glimpses into the German psyche. How typical Schmundt was he had no way of knowing. But the exposure was one he considered invaluable, even if it did mean putting up with the German's middle-aged lusts after a phantom beauty he had once known but hadn't laid eyes on in years.

Galanov smiled to himself at the thought.

Schmundt was a fool, albeit a powerful one.

His countenance darkened at further memories. So powerful the idiot had nearly had them both killed! He would be more careful of Schmundt's passions next time . . . if there was a next time.

That, of course, depended on what his uncle had in mind concerning his future.

He wasn't exactly *afraid* of Korskayev.

Andrassy Galanov possessed that commodity of constitution—rare among the general population but absolutely essential for those who sought to distinguish themselves in the spy game—known as nerves of steel. Fear was not something that entered into his calculations, and though he remembered it as a youngster, the personal feelings associated with it had never touched him closely. Besides, childhood was already a distant memory, and he had long forgotten anything resembling fear by this time in his life.

He was, however, *wary* of his uncle.

He well knew what power the man wielded and what came to those who took such men lightly. He would be respectful, even grovel a little if necessary. And above all make every effort to produce satisfactory results. His uncle wasn't a young man anymore, and the day would inevitably come when he would be replaced. Why shouldn't it be with him? Therefore, it behooved him to load his own dossier full of successes.

Galanov cut a striking figure as he made his way along, almost imperceptible limp notwithstanding. His time in Germany had influenced him more than he realized, from the erect posture of his spine to the crisp footfall of his steps. He strode with a purpose that contrasted noticeably with the bureaucratic lethargy so characteristic of these hallowed halls of Communist power.

It was already 7:15 in the morning. In Bonn or Berlin the corridors and rooms would be fairly abuzz with activity by this time. But the offices of the Kremlin still slept . . . all except for his uncle's.

Galanov wondered if Korskayev ever slept.

Under more favorable circumstances he might have enjoyed this return from Berlin to Moscow. He had not been home in more than a year, and if the snows stayed away, late autumn could be a most pleasant time in the Soviet capital.

Unfortunately, his uncle's insistence to learn about the incident of the prison escape in more detail would probably not make this a trip primarily to be enjoyed.

His uncle was not one you refused. Ties of blood counted for little in his estimation, only obedience.

When he had first been assigned to Berlin, Andrassy had thought it fate's way of getting rid of him. But fate had smiled on him after all. No sooner had he landed than Berlin had become the hottest of the world's hot spots—a veritable greenhouse for the rapid elevation of an aspiring KGB agent, even if he did have to take a backseat to the German clown of a *Stasi* section chief.

Now, returning to Moscow, he had the sense of being removed from the source of action. His uncle had assured him it was only to discuss these recent developments in a more personal way, but Galanov knew that displeasing him could mean he would never see Berlin, or continue his climb up the KGB ladder, ever again.

Most of his uneasiness stemmed from the awareness that he had not really achieved much in the way of the purpose for which he had been sent to Berlin in the first place.

Every lead of Schmundt's had dried up, and he hadn't been able to turn up anything on his own. Just when they had been about to break the case wide open, the imbecile had started tossing grenades, and everything had blown up in both their faces.

He was not unaware that his uncle's annoyance was heightened by the fact that he had almost laid his hands on the old Jew he had been seeking, only to have the man vanish before his very eyes. He now had some people down in the Mediterranean region following a scent that looked promising.

He knew his uncle was angry and frustrated and that, given sufficient time, some of that frustration was bound to come his way.

Galanov didn't like to even think about what could be the result.

✍ 13 ✍
Frustrated Greed

In the office toward which young Galanov was bound, the man about whom he had been thinking stood silently brooding over the early morning meeting he had scheduled with the son of his younger sister.

The eyes, peering absently outside through the smoke that drifted around his head, were dark, deep-set, and full of visions that should occupy the brain of no mortal.

It had been sixteen years since he fled that land from which he had recently summoned his nephew.

Those years had been reasonably good to him. They had seen a vast shift in the matrix of world power, a shift he had successfully ridden to the top of his chosen profession, if "profession" the field of his nefarious endeavors could legitimately be called. He had power and position in a regime where neither could be taken for granted, and money enough to live more comfortably than 90 percent of his Communist comrades. And he was feared, a factor which, for a character such as his, was perhaps most satisfying of all.

Still a gnawing dissatisfaction ate at him, a constant reminder that there remained one episode in his life in which he had been bettered by another and, as he considered it, a lesser mortal. The vexation such knowledge caused in the innermost regions somewhere near his soul—that singular dominion of vengeance within the human constitution from which a man capable of such hate drew its viperous strength—was a fire that could not be quenched, a worm, eating at the twisted pride of his manhood, that refused to die.

He took one last drag, then turned, strode to his desk, and crushed out the fire on the remaining butt of cigarette with a grinding force from his fingers as if he were crushing the life out of the enemy who had come unbidden to his mind.

He stood there a moment, contemplating the heap of ashes in his ashtray, then wandered toward the window again.

He had himself cheated, deceived, lied to, swindled, killed, and thus by his estimation got the world's "best" of a thousand others during that time. But they could not erase the one most painful black mark from the memory of his past.

Hatred was at the root of this man's essential being. The soil for its growth had been provided in ample supply—as it is for all men and women in all ages and in whatever conditions they find themselves—by the circumstances of his early life. With a lifetime's choices motivated by that most subtle, powerful, and lethal demon of all the enemy's ranks called Self had he sent the roots of his character deep into that soil. There they drew strength and nurtured that cousin evil spirit, Ill-Use, such that all attempts toward growth of the inborn roots of *true* character were suffocated and choked off at an early age.

The soil of circumstance is fertile and full of nutrients, capable of nourishing all range of human character development. Pride, greed, bitterness, and revenge thrive in its black depths, as do selflessness, forgiveness, compassion, and kindness. The embryo human soul sends down tender roots of all kinds, there for the will, which sits on the throne of character development, to determine *which* will be nurtured, encouraged, and fed—thus growing mighty and sending out new and similar shoots in all directions—and *which* will be clipped off before they have a chance to make themselves permanent in the subsoil below.

He had learned to hate from an early age, in both this land and that of Germanic exile. The fortunes of his childhood had not been pleasant, and he had allowed evil roots to flourish. He learned to hate Germans. He learned to hate aristocrats. He learned to hate Jews. He learned to hate Christians even more.

It was doubtful whether he had ever felt that thing people called love. It was a root he pruned from his character almost immediately. His memories about his parents were too contorted for him to even think about, and he hadn't in decades.

The only slit in the self-protective armor of his hatred opened toward his younger sister, whose release from Germany he had arranged after the war. A certain shallow bond of shared fate caused him to remain at least moderately well-disposed toward one who had suffered with him. He had made arrangements for his sister's husband, who had climbed alongside him in the new regime, and now their son aspired toward a future in the

KGB as well—an aspiration he had himself made use of by taking the boy under his wing, so to speak, and sending him to Germany as his personal and secretive liaison into the office of a certain section chief of the German secret police, *Staatssicherheitsdienst.*

Thoughts of the young man brought his mind back to his present vexation and the reason for the meeting with him that was about to take place.

He had himself been getting so close. He had been about to break the Jewish ring in and around Moscow. There had been signs of increased Jewish and Christian activity in Germany that his German contact and his nephew had been pursuing in hopes of dropping a net on the prisoner's people.

Suddenly it appeared he had been bettered again—and by none other, he was now convinced, than both that old fool of a German and the cursed rabbi himself.

He should never have consented to keep the baron alive all this time. That idiot Schmundt and his boyish fascination with the daughter! He had thought that eventually one of them would lead him to the rabbi and his holy box. But now they were *all* gone—they had let the rabbi flee Russia and the baron escape prison, both within two months.

He had let the fools win yet another round in this lengthy and deadly game of chess!

He turned away from the window and slowly paced about the moderately sized office.

It was not by any consideration plush. Nothing in Moscow, even the premier's private chambers, would be considered luxurious by Western norms. But according to the austere standards by which the Revolution measured the hierarchy of its most loyal servants, Vaslav Korskayev was most fortunate indeed. The mere fact that his office had a window at all was enough to reveal at least something of his status.

No one was calling it the Fourth *Reich* these days. The terminology of the idiot Nazis had died with its leaders in the bunkers of Berlin even as he was making good his opportune absquatulation back to the motherland. But over the years the stretch of its domination had greatly outreached that of ancient Rome, and now here he was with an office in the mighty

Kremlin itself, in the heart of Moscow, the city to which the entire world looked . . . and trembled.

Yet he had not been able to bring the power and might of the Soviet colossus to the aid of the one thing that had eluded him all these years.

He walked absently again to the coveted pane separating him from the outside air of the city, pulled another cigarette out of his pocket, put it between his lips, lit it, and stared vacantly out into the increasing grey morning's light.

The thin face the light fell on was not a pleasant one. Its sunken, narrow-set eyes seemed like they should have belonged to a smaller man. The cheeks below them were sallow and sagging, giving an altogether unbecoming, unhealthy impression. A coat of black leather was still draped around his shoulders since he had arrived an hour earlier, and it complemented perfectly the black oily hair bent around the side of his head, combed as if attempting to make up for its diminishing supply. The grey of the skin would seem to indicate like coloration of hair, but in fact hardly a trace of grey was to be found despite his fifty-five years. In truth, there wasn't much hair at all. A high forehead had receded steadily through the years and had by now all but entirely consumed the top portions of the skull, across whose apex the skin seemed to have been stretched almost too tightly. In any event, the balding scalp was far smoother than the whiskered cheeks and neck, which gave evidence of having been pockmarked early in life.

The tip of his cigarette showed red as he drew in a deep inhalation of smoke, then let it slowly drift out his nose, rising to encircle his head.

His eyes squinted slightly from the smoke, as if they were attempting to bring something across the square outside into focus. But his thoughts were only on the upcoming interview he had scheduled and how best to approach it.

It would not do to admit defeat, nor to betray any sign of weakness to a subordinate. In the Kremlin, even the slightest hint of weakness was the blood whose scent brought out the jackals of opportunism. Once the wolves were on the trail, the end could not be far away. He had seen it too many times and was determined such an evil fate would not come to him.

He would couch his words carefully in bringing his nephew in on the search, now from this end.

Almost the same moment the words came into his mind, a knock sounded on the door behind him, interrupting his reverie. He started momentarily, then spun around, instantly bringing his faculties back under his tight control, and commanded entry.

∽ 14 ∾
KGB Schemes

Galanov opened the door at the command of the occupant of the office behind it and walked in.

"So, young Andrassy," greeted the elder of the two as they shook hands formally, "how goes your convalescence?"

Galanov inwardly winced at the pointed use of the word *young.* But like the aspiring agent he was, gave no hint of it.

"Well, Uncle Korskayev," replied the younger.

Not a word of familial warmth passed between them. Except for the appellation given by the younger, no observer would have known that an atom of kinship existed between them.

"I scarcely notice your limp."

Galanov nodded, as one receiving a fact appreciatively. In truth he was chagrined that anything had been noticed at all. He had tried with great effort to conceal it. It would appear his uncle had won the opening salvo in the subtle exchange for the high ground of the interview.

"I will be back to full strength in no time," Galanov said with attempted enthusiasm.

"That pleases me," rejoined Korskayev, "for we have a great deal to do. Sit down, sit down!"

Galanov did so. Korskayev took his own chair behind the large metal desk.

"Now," he continued, "fill me in on everything that happened during the August incident and where the investigation stands at present."

Galanov did so. Korskayev listened intently, asking many

questions along the way. After forty or fifty minutes a silence fell between them. Galanov waited. His uncle appeared deep in reflection.

"There are no clues, then," he said after several long moments, "about what might have become of them after the escape—that is, if the German and his daughter are still alive, as you are convinced they are?"

"*I* am convinced of it, though I am not sure the truth has dawned on the good Herr von Schmundt as yet. He will no doubt discover it in time, perhaps already has."

"What makes you sure?"

"Schmundt has a secretary—altogether an unremarkable woman except for the fact that she is in love with him. While Schmundt has been in the hospital, she has been busy. Busier than she realizes I am aware of. Yes, they are alive—though, to answer your question, there are at present no clues to their whereabouts."

"Do you think they can be located?"

"Given time."

"You were unable to locate the girl earlier."

Korskayev's voice carried none too obscure a barb regarding his nephew's lack of success. It did not go unnoticed, but again, Galanov did not flinch.

"The events of the escape left a trail. I am convinced it can be located and followed. Other people had to have been involved. And now that the old baron is out of prison, the logistics of the situation are more complex. They will give themselves away at some point."

"Is there any evidence whatever that the old Jew might have contacted them?"

"Not the slightest thread."

"Is it not possible that his disappearance from Russia, coinciding as it did with the prison escape, was no accident?"

"Anything, I suppose, is possible, but no evidence regarding the rabbi came into the *Stasi's* hands. It was my understanding that *you* were about to close the net on *him?*" he added, with a pretendedly innocent tone.

The young man's query contained implications his uncle did not like. He should have known by now that he had trained his nephew well in the subtleties of this game of verbal repartee and that there was no reason to expect gratitude, only cunning, in repayment.

Galanov, however, was playing a dangerous game with a powerful man. If the day was eventually to come when he might replace his uncle, that day was nowhere near yet at hand. For the present, pleasing Korskayev was his only possible route of advancement.

"Perhaps I shall send you back to do what you can on that end," mused Korskayev dryly after a moment, "though I must say your previous year's efforts did not produce anything as substantial as would justify the confidence with which you speak."

"I was—" Galanov cleared his throat, betraying for the first time his nervousness—"uh, hindered by the Schmundt fellow. It took a great deal of time simply, ah . . . winning his confidence so that he would trust me."

"I see," intoned Korskayev with significant undertones.

"If I had a free hand—"

"If you had a free hand, then what?" interrupted Korskayev with sudden and unexpected sharpness. "What would you do, with no office, no manpower, no files, no dossiers . . . in a foreign country where no one trusts you, where you are not at home. Yes, my young friend, just what *would* you do?"

"I only meant—"

"I know exactly what you meant! You were trying to blame your own incompetence on Schmundt. I know all too well that he is a fool. But even fools have their uses, and in his own way he has become a powerful man in the DDR. Learn this lesson well, young Galanov—success can rarely be gotten alone. In this business we are in, you need to know how to use people. You failed because you were so confident you did not think you needed the German. Well, I tell you, if Berlin is where we are, then we need the Germans. If we are in Warsaw, we need the Poles. Do you hear me?"

"I hear you, Uncle Korskayev," answered Galanov as contritely as it was within his nature to sound.

"If I do decide to send you back, if I even decide to keep you on this case at all after so little to show for it thus far, then I advise you to learn to *use* Schmundt, not disdain him."

Galanov did not reply, but sat waiting for what would come next. He had made the one mistake he had sworn beforehand he could not make—he had aroused his uncle's anger. Not that he wasn't himself fuming inside at the things his uncle had said to him. But he would keep his feelings, and his thoughts, to himself.

"Before that time, however," Korskayev went on, giving a show of moderating his emotion, "we must regain the rabbi's trail here. I have had some men on it, with certain success, I might add. Two are in Israel at this very moment, closing in upon him at last.

I have reason to hope. But I am concerned about what he has left behind. We have pieced together clues and traces of what is surely a Jewish network of some kind. I want it penetrated, exposed, and put out of business."

"And the photographs?" asked Galanov.

Now it was his uncle's turn to inwardly wince, though he likewise did not show it.

"They are most surely with the rabbi in Israel. When we lay our hands on him, they will be back in our possession. But just in case—which brings me to another aspect of what I have in mind for you—I have been looking into the rabbi's family. I have reason to believe they are not all with him. If we can lay our hands on any of them, that will no doubt provide us with a full supply of bargaining power with which to secure the rabbi's cooperation in returning the photographs."

"I am still uncertain how the photographs came to your attention in the first place," said Galanov. "Last year when you contacted me I thought I understood them to have been stolen."

"You understood wrong. When word of them first surfaced, that was assumed."

"How did word surface?"

"An informant—not one of ours—approached an official with connections in the Politburo. He had gotten wind of something, he said, that they might be interested in. He was paid handsomely, of course, and described the photographed scenes in remarkable detail, although he swore never to have actually seen them. The thing was looked into, but the photos were found safely in the same file where they were originally put eight years earlier. The informant knew nothing more, where they had come from, where they were presently—he had only heard vague reports. The bunglers paid him and let him go. My office was not brought in until later."

"What did you do?"

"I immediately put all the resources of the KGB on the case. I knew there had to have been duplicates made. But by that time, the Politburo informant was gone without a trace and everything we could turn up indicated that we were too late, that they had left the country. All we were certain of is that Zionists were involved. They were the only ones who could possibly benefit from the photographs. I called you in Berlin, and later alerted your superior."

"What is it you want me to do?"

"I want you to infiltrate this Jewish network I speak of. I want you to learn all you can of Rabbi Wissen and his family. I will, of course, open all my files on the matter to you and will expect you to become personally familiar with all aspects of the case. But you they will not know, as they do me and all my more experienced agents. Even if the photos are gone, we must trace them back to their source. There are others involved besides the rabbi who I am sure are still in Russia. This will, therefore, be an opportunity for you to prove yourself once again."

"I understand."

"It may be that in time your investigation will require a return to Germany, for in all likelihood there remain connections between the rabbi and the German prisoner Dortmann, perhaps between their families. But I would know more before making such a decision."

"I will not disappoint you, Uncle Korskayev."

"I am certain you will not. In any event, I am convinced that whichever trail we follow will lead us in the end to the rabbi's box and to the photographs. Put one of them in my hands and you will find yourself promoted to chief of operations in the sector of your choice."

"You are more than generous, Uncle Korskayev."

"Place them both in my hands, son of my sister, and I will ensure that this very office, with its window, and all the power that goes with it, shall one day be yours."

∽ 15 ∾
Acrid Memories

As the door closed, the KGB chief was again left alone with his thoughts. The interview had stirred unpleasant waters within him.

Once more he sought the window, as if staring outside might distract his pricked pride and personal annoyance.

He knew what his nephew wanted and had, through the years, become a shrewd manipulator of the motivations of young rising KGB aspirants for the purposes of achieving his own ends.

It was one of the most powerful tools inherent in his position. He had just used it skillfully and would continue to do so in order to achieve the one thing in his personal file that still remained undone.

As he stood, his thoughts drifted back to that morning during the war, on the deserted country road, when he had last laid eyes on the two men who on this day occupied his thoughts.

He had outwitted their escape attempt and was about to capture the whole lot of them. But the moment he had spoken to Baron von Dortmann, a sudden haze had come over his eyes. The black-clad man behind him, whom he now knew to be the rabbi he sought, faded from sight. So did all the others. His own voice shouted for them to stop, but it seemed to die in the air. None of those fleeing, not even his own men, heeded it. Never had he felt so powerless in all his life.

When a few moments later—he never knew how much time went by—the eerie trance passed and he came to himself, no one but the baron was visible. He still stood where he had been, unmoved, staring intently forward. He had not been able to hold the German's gaze and knew, though he would never admit it to another, that his enemy was a stronger man than he.

Then the German had done the unthinkable.

Not only had he made no effort to escape, he had begun

walking forward, straight toward the pistol he held aimed at him, still staring into his eyes, straight *toward* his enemy.

How he remembered his words! They had burned a hole in his memory ever since—words of command, spoken as if the fool thought *he* was in authority over the might of the Gestapo: "You may not prevent them," he had said. "They are under my orders to go."

And then—though even after all these years he could hardly believe that his memory of the incident served him correctly—the idiot had actually surrendered.

"It is me you want," he had said.

He had turned and ordered Schmundt to open fire. Turning back around toward the prisoner, again he met the penetrating gaze he could neither avoid nor resist.

"In the name of the most high God, I command you to hold your tongue. You may arrest me, but you will seek these people no more."

Who did the fool of a German nobleman think he was, issuing orders *to him!*

Those were the words he had tried hardest of all to forget. "I command you . . . I command you to hold your tongue. . . ."

Fury rose in his heart again at the very thought of another *commanding* him with such quiet authority.

Well the others may have escaped, but the baron had paid for his idiocy with sixteen years of prison. The thought of it, however, did nothing to assuage his wrath. Now he had escaped, and his secrets with him. Where had the fool come by such courage and power?

But he would find him!

He would find them both . . . or his name—!

He had vowed never to let his German name escape his lips since the day he had gone out to meet the advancing Russian army and pass himself off as one of them. But he would break his own vow now in order to make an even greater oath to himself, and utter those words he hadn't been called in all these sixteen years.

He would find them . . . he would find them both, and make them pay with their own lives for making him appear the fool!

He would find them . . . or he wasn't Emil Korsch.

～ 16 ～
Three-Way Search
November 1961 – March 1962

What he had originally anticipated would be a brief interlude in his homeland turned out to be a hiatus two months in duration.

Andrassy Galanov was busily engaged during that time in his new assignment. With his uncle in the background, the agent managed to infiltrate, as Korskayev had hoped, what they were confident were the fringes of the Jewish network responsible for the duplication of the compromising photographs.

Despite his efforts, however, he was able to learn little more than what Korskayev already was sure of—that the photographs had gotten into Jewish hands (where they had been made and how they had passed from hand to hand remained unknown) and had indeed been smuggled out of the country, and that Rabbi Wissen had apparently fled the Soviet Union with his family almost immediately afterward.

Though the results of Galanov's efforts were not sufficient to produce direct links to either the photos or the legendary sacred artifacts, he did establish covert ties with two Jewish underground organizations, putting in place a low-level lackey who, if anything turned up, would be able to get the information into KGB hands.

Shortly after the first of the year, therefore, Korskayev sent his nephew back to Germany, with instructions to remain incognito for a time, observing the moves of his German superior, before assuming once again his former role with the *Stasi*. He was certain, Korskayev said, that there had to have been contact between the rabbi and the German baron who was of such interest to Schmundt. If so, he would have them learn what they could on their own, without having to rely on Schmundt to forward any vital information to them.

They would use him, but not be forced to depend on him.

It was not Korskayev's way to depend upon any man, though he would take advantage of any man he could for his own ends.

The rabbi had gone to the baron once before. Why might he

not again? Korskayev reasoned. It was entirely possible, he said, that through the Jewish network he had known of the baron's escape before the fact and had fled for the very purpose of contacting the baron. The networks involving both men were no doubt connected. Perhaps both events were even connected.

If his people in Israel did not turn them up, it was not inconceivable that the photographs could be, even now, in the German's hands or those of his daughter.

"Whatever may be Schmundt's reasons for wanting the girl, Galanov," Korskayev had said, "I care about nothing but the box and those photos. The Kremlin has been extremely concerned ever since it was discovered that a duplicate set existed— and I mean at the highest possible levels, Andrassy. Recovering them would be sure to mean advancement for us both. Find the rabbi, the escaped baron, or the girl—I don't care which. One of them is bound to lead you to the photographs."

In his new role, Galanov learned of Section Chief Schmundt's latest search to locate the woman of his absurd fancies, and he set himself to follow him to see what might turn up.

Before the month of January was out, he was certain Schmundt was on the trail of the two Germans, though all those he questioned insisted the *Stasi* chief had only been inquiring about an American.

No matter, thought Galanov. If it was the same American, the fellow by the name of McCallum whom Schmundt had had him investigate before, the trail could not help but likewise lead him where he wanted to go. He wasn't sure what the American's role in all this was. But if Schmundt was after him, it had to have something to do with the girl and would thus prove useful in helping him locate either the Jew or the German baron for his uncle.

∽◞◟∾

Thus the quests of the three Communists—Schmundt's passion for Sabina von Dortmann, Galanov's search for the photographs that symbolized his rise in the KGB elite, and Korskayev's private lust after Rabbi Wissen's holy box containing relics of inestimable worth—all converged on the trail of the two Dortmanns and their would-be American rescuer, Matthew McCallum, none of whom knew how fervidly they were being pursued or how close indeed was the danger.

∾ 17 ∾
Multiple Trails

Galanov followed the trail of his former German superior into many corners of East Germany and Poland, where he lost it for a time, picking it back up again in Warsaw, then south into Czechoslovakia, and northward again through Prague.

By mid-March he found himself in Leipzig, where, to his annoyance, he had foolishly allowed himself to get too close to the American.

The man had turned around quickly and had laid eyes on him at nearly point-blank range. He had spun around and walked off hurriedly, compounding his error, chagrined at having blown the most elemental creed of a Soviet agent. Had his uncle seen the incident he would have yanked him off the case, recalled him to Moscow, and stuck him behind a desk for the rest of his inglorious career with the KGB!

Luckily his uncle had *not* seen it, nor had Schmundt—he hadn't seen the German for three days now.

Neither man would ever know of it. *No one* would know he had botched the surveillance but the American, and if he minded his business in the future, it was the last time their eyeballs would conduct business together.

He had drawn back immediately, not wanting to exacerbate his blunder, and had given the American a looser line. He only succeeded, however, in accomplishing exactly what he had been trying so hard to avoid. Within forty-eight hours he realized he had lost him altogether. Nor could he regain Schmundt's trail.

Perhaps, he mused morbidly as he sat in his hotel room, he was not as ready to carry the KGB mantle as he had thought. But even if that depressing conclusion was true, he would never admit it to his uncle. He would *make* himself ready. He *would* crack this case.

The whole Leipzig incident was a black mark across his memory that he determined to forget . . . and never to repeat.

He spent the next day trying to piece together everything that had happened so as to make the most educated guess possible as to the next moves of *Stasi* Section Chief Schmundt and the American he was following.

They had been moving north.

There was nothing due north but farming villages. What could they possibly find there? Dessau or Wittenberg, perhaps . . . Magdeburg farther to the west—no, he doubted that, although it was in the direction of the border.

No, he thought to himself—there could be only one likely destination.

He would return to Berlin.

That must be where they were bound eventually. If he happened to arrive there first, then he would be ready and waiting for them.

Besides, there was one in Berlin who had seemed kindly disposed toward him of late. She was certain to know where her boss was.

It was time to renew his acquaintance with Lola Reinhardt.

✎ 18 ✎
Happy Reunion
March 1962

Meanwhile, in a small and humbly appointed house located on the inconspicuous street called Graulinger in the East German city of Magdeburg, a great reunion was underway between the very persons who had been the object of such an intense but unsuccessful search by both *Stasi* and KGB.

As the three newly rejoined friends completed their long and talkative breakfast, former U.S. State Department attaché and presidential adviser Matthew McCallum rose from the table and gave a great stretch.

"That was a marvelous breakfast!" he exclaimed as he and his hosts—she whom he had first met as a teenager before the outbreak of the war, Sabina von Dortmann, and the beautiful lady's father, who had been imprisoned by the Gestapo and had only recently been freed by the two, Baron Heinrich von Dortmann—walked toward the adjacent living room.

"I hope it will cling to those sparse ribs of yours," commented Sabina with a laugh.

"Like I told you, my provisions these past months haven't been the most plentiful."

"And you really think someone was tracking you?" asked Baron von Dortmann.

"Positive of it. I caught a good look at the one fellow in Leipzig about a week ago. A very young man. I have no idea who he was, but I'm certain he was watching me."

"Has he bothered you again?" asked Sabina.

"No, I've seen nothing of him since that day, though I'm fairly certain I saw your old friend Schmundt about three days ago."

Sabina and her father glanced at one another with an expression of anxiety.

"But we're not going to worry about either of them right now," said Matthew. "We're all together again. They don't know where we are. So for the moment, we're in the driver's seat."

Matthew patted his thin stomach with satisfaction as they took seats.

"I haven't had such a satisfying meal since I walked through Checkpoint Charlie!" he added. "Now it's time to give some thought to the next phase of this operation."

"What do you mean by the next phase?" said the baron.

"And what operation?" asked Sabina.

"The operation to get the two of you out of here!" answered Matthew.

"What . . . out of where, Magdeburg?"

"I didn't give John Kennedy my resignation, break across the Berlin Wall and into East Germany, and search through half the Communist world in every disguise I could think of just to *find* you. I came to rescue you from this place and to take you back to the West with me."

Sabina and her father looked at one another with astonished expressions.

"As long as your father remains in the DDR, Sabina, he will be a fugitive from the East German police. You will both be in danger. We *must* get to where we can live together in freedom."

"But what can be done?" asked Baron von Dortmann. "This country is walled up. How—"

"I'm talking about breaking across the border—the three of us."

"Breaking out—I am an old man, Matthew!"

"Not so old as when I saw you last, Baron. You look fit and well. We will find a way. Escape is always possible."

"And dangerous."

"True . . . but possible."

"People have been killed. When that horrible wall went up last year, everything changed."

"We will manage it . . . somehow."

"But . . . but you are trapped behind what your people call the Iron Curtain . . . *just like us,*" said Sabina.

Matthew nodded with a wan smile.

"I'm on my own, without as much as a single ostmark to my name," he said, "driving a broken-down Trabi with half a tank of fuel remaining. It's parked a ways back up the street. Other than that, and a couple forged passports, I've got nothing."

"You're not being encouraging, Matthew," said Sabina.

"What can I say? If we're going to get out of here, we're on our own . . . except, of course, for your *Network of the Rose.*" Matthew's expression turned pensive for a moment. "Actually," he added, "that's not really true at all, as I'm certain you both know even better than I do."

The other two waited patiently, realizing that what was trying to find expression came from deep inside him. When he finally spoke once more, his tone reflected the deep reservoirs of faith that had slowly been expanding within his being.

"These past two months have taught me something," he said. "Something far beyond what I think I would ever have been able to learn by any other means."

"What?" asked Sabina with sincere interest.

Again Matthew was thoughtful for a while.

"That God's protection and guidance . . . are very, very practical and real."

"Amen!" rejoined both Dortmanns with soft and heartfelt acknowledgment. Their very lives were breathing testimonies to the veracity of Matthew's words, and they knew it.

Again it was quiet several moments.

"There are so many principles you learn," Matthew began once more. "Principles of faith . . . *good* principles . . . *true* principles. I'm not even saying you learn them in a superficial way . . . they might be very meaningful to you . . ."

He paused, index finger pressed thoughtfully against his lips. After a moment he began punctuating the air in front of his face with it, as if to underscore the words that were coming even before uttering them.

". . . *Until*," he went on, "until a moment comes when you have to take some principle down to a totally new level of awareness . . . when it is severely tested, when your back is to the wall and everything seems to depend upon that one thing you have said you believed all this time. Then—when that moment comes—you find out how much you *really* believe it. Do you believe in that truth enough to entrust your life and your whole future to it?"

He sat, nodding his head back and forth in obvious memory of things that had recently taken place.

"I have discovered, in a more personal and present and down-to-earth way than ever before, that we really can depend upon God's protection. I prayed for protection every night, and two dozen times every day—both for myself and for the two of you. I knew our very lives depended on it.

"I prayed also that he would guide my steps, that he would make straight my path before me. I've known of Proverbs 3:5-6 for years. They were two of the first verses I memorized after giving my heart to the Lord. But suddenly I found myself in situation after situation where I literally did not know where to turn next, where to go, what to think, what to do.

"The moment of truth—the moment when your whole belief system is tested by the fire of circumstance—had come. Did I *really* believe that Proverbs 3:5-6 was true—all the way down to the bottommost places when I literally had nowhere to turn, not the remotest idea where to take my next step?

"The stories I could tell you!" Matthew sighed, "how God did in fact 'guide my steps' after I gave my way to him. I ran up against so many dead ends! And yet . . . God does direct our paths! He really, really does—if and when we are complying with the responsibility given us in the first portion of that wonderful promise—when we trust him with all our heart, when we don't rely on our own understanding, and when we acknowledge him in all our ways—not such easy conditions!"

The baron smiled knowingly.

"Ah, Matthew, my boy," he said, "you have indeed put your finger upon the very essence of walking in close communion with our Father. No easy task indeed—to lay aside our own understanding, to lay aside all the other things that we by nature try to trust in rather than him. I have been living for more than half a century with that as my desire, and yet there are times I feel I fail so miserably."

"Is that why he sends trials upon his people," mused Sabina, "so that we will be forced not to depend upon ourselves, but to rely upon his protection and his guidance?"

"I don't know that I'm comfortable with the notion that God sends trials upon his people," remarked the baron. "Perhaps he occasionally does so, but I question whether that is his intent. But I do think it is the reason he tells us to rejoice in our trials and be thankful, because they provide an environment to enable us to learn truth on a deeper level than we can learn in the normal routine of an untroubled and carefree life. What do you think, my boy?" he asked, turning to Matthew.

"I tend to agree, Baron," replied Matthew. "Clearly God uses life's difficulties, but I'm not so sure they originate with him."

"As with my years in prison, and your recent months."

"His using them is why we are to thank him for them. The soil of circumstance, as I like to think of it, is capable of producing much more fruit when it contains manure than when it contains nothing but lifeless sand."

"Well put."

"In any case, getting back to our predicament—I can now say that what we do and where we go from here depend upon the

Lord's guidance, not our own cleverness . . . and not even, in the final analysis, on the *Network of the Rose* either. He will protect us, he will show us what to do, he will guide our steps. I'm more confident in that than I could ever have been six months ago."

"I'm so happy to hear you say so, Matthew," said Sabina.

"I'm nervous, even afraid—who wouldn't be? But I know we may trust him."

∽ 19 ∽
Revisited Proposal

More talk followed, during which Matthew retrieved from his car the baron's old journals he had rescued from the ancient Dortmann estate, known as *Lebenshaus*, now in the hands of the Communist government of the DDR.

As the baron glanced through the books of his youth and early manhood, tears filled his eyes. He had never expected to see these writings of his heart and innermost thoughts again. They could not help reminding him of his dear wife, Marion, Sabina's Jewish mother, who had died in Switzerland during the final year of the war.

A quiet time of talk, gratitude, and prayer followed.

Suddenly the baron's countenance brightened. He set down the volumes and glanced up with an expression full of exuberance and life.

"That reminds me, my boy," he said, "Sabina told me the two of you talked of being married! That is, before you dreamed up your madcap plan to break me out of prison."

A sheepish expression came over Matthew's face.

"We spoke of it, yes, sir," he said. "Such was my hope . . . except for one thing."

"What could that possibly be?"

"I felt it was only proper . . . that is, I wanted to speak with you first, tell you of my intent, and ask for your consent to make your daughter my wife. Unfortunately, things got a little mixed up before I got a chance to talk to you."

"There's no time like the present," rejoined the baron, throwing Sabina a quick wink.

Taken by surprise at the suddenness of it, Matthew glanced over at Sabina, then back toward the baron, who had risen forward in his chair and now sat as one waiting expectantly.

"Then here goes," said Matthew after a moment. "But I've never done anything like this before, so you'll just have to let me stumble along."

"Stumble ahead!"

"All right," said Matthew, pausing to swallow, then going on. "You have called me your son. Now I would like to request that you allow me to inherit that title by right of marriage. Would you, Baron Heinrich von Dortmann, consent to allow me the honor of proposing to your lovely daughter, Sabina?"

"Request granted!" boomed the baron with delight, rising to his feet and striding forward to shake Matthew's hand vigorously.

"Thank you, sir."

"Well, what are you waiting for, Son . . . there she is, right over there, tears running down her face. Don't keep her in suspense any longer!"

Matthew grinned, then turned and walked the few paces to where Sabina stood, face wet, smiling from ear to ear. He took her two hands in his.

"Sabina," he said seriously. "I love you so much! So I'm asking you now, again, with your father's approval, if you would marry me . . . and be my wife."

"Request granted," whispered Sabina softly and still smiling through her tears.

Matthew took her into his arms, and they stood together several long moments.

"Well then," said the baron boisterously, enjoying the role of elder gadfly to the romantic moment, "what I want to know is when this wedding is going to take place. I've never given away a daughter, or had a son of my own for that matter, and I'm getting older every day!"

Matthew and Sabina laughed.

"We can't proceed without *my* father," answered Matthew, "and he's in Bavaria."

"I presume what you're suggesting is not that we bring him here?"

"No, sir. For more reasons than a wedding, I believe, as I said before, that it is imperative the reunion take place . . . in the West. The three of us have to somehow manage to get there."

∾ 20 ∾
Unpleasant Broodings

The gates to a man's soul are guarded by the most invisible legions of all the world's armies. Whether they are friend or foe to that soul is for every man himself to determine.

A more serious campaign than had hitherto been launched had begun in and around the hearts of those connected with a certain office of the East German secret police force. How different, however, were the ultimate responses to that unseen yet forcefully invading army.

It had not been a happy two days for *Staatssicherheitsdienst* Section Chief Gustav von Schmundt.

He tossed the folder he had been carrying onto the plain dresser, removed his gun and its silencer from his coat pocket, then eased himself down onto the squeaky hotel mattress without taking the least stock of the sleazy room surrounding him, exhaled a weary sigh from an expressionless face, and sat staring straight ahead.

He had not planned to come back to the hotel until he was through the list. He had business, important business, to finish. Somehow, though, he needed a break. An inexplicable feeling of fatigue had come over him throughout the day. He needed to rest and gather his thoughts. He would lie down for a few minutes. Then he would go out and follow up on the remaining leads he had recently acquired.

After a moment or two he lifted his pistol from its resting place on his lap, fiddled momentarily with the silencer, then unconsciously lifted the barrel to his nose and sniffed at the remains of powder that could still be detected from its firing the previous evening.

The action was neither habitual nor planned, a mere reflex of the animal instinct that was slowly coming to dominate the nature of this man who yearly was becoming less and less worthy of the name. It contained no more meaning than a dog sniffing at the feces of some fellow creature. It was not the instinct of the heavens, toward which man was meant to reach, that impelled the crude gesture . . . but rather the earth.

Without knowing it, he had been drawn by the smell of death.

The faint aroma brought neither sense of victory nor pang of remorse to his heart, but only a slightly heightened vividness to the reminder of what had taken place twenty-four hours before.

The killing of seven months earlier had stirred up wrath and fury within him. This killing, however, brought quietness to his soul. Some long-closed doors within him, as a result, had been attempting all day to budge on their rust-hardened hinges.

Still he sat, still without expression, replaying the incident through his seared brain.

"I know that you spoke with a man late today in the *Postamt!*" he had said to the frightened postal employee after bursting in upon him at his home. "What did he want?—"

"He asked about some rare issue floral stamps, *mein Herr.*"

"What did you tell him!"

"I said that the *Postamt* did not deal in stamps for collectors. I referred him to a specialist in rare stamps."

"Why did he come to you?"

"I do not know, *mein Herr.* Perhaps he had heard that I too was a philatelist."

"Bah! You are lying!" yelled Gustav. "He came for information . . . not stamps!"

He had searched the main room of the man's apartment, then stalked into the adjoining bedroom.

"Please, *mein Herr!*" the man had implored, receiving the butt of Gustav's gun against his head in reply.

Quickly Gustav had spotted his small bureau with attached secretary and proceeded to rummage through the drawers and compartments. Within moments he laid his hands upon a book of stamps, and hurriedly flipped through it.

"What are these names at the back of the album?" he had demanded.

The man said nothing.

"The names, you fool! Do you care so little for life?" A sharp booted kick in the side of the man's ribs followed.

"They . . . they are my dealers . . ."

"What dealers!"

"Of stamps," groaned the poor man in obvious agony.

Gustav scanned the list quickly.

"There are no shops listed here. Some of these are nothing but little farming villages! What kind of fool do you take me for!"

"Private . . . private collectors . . . ," murmured the man. "Please . . . there is no need to bother any of them. . . ."

Gustav had smiled at the time, although the memory brought no smile to his lips now.

"So . . . there is no need for me to bother any of these people, eh?" he had said mockingly. "We shall see about that. I have the distinct feeling that one of the people on this list will be able to tell me all about our American friend who paid a visit on you. Now, if you want to live through the night, tell me which of these *dealers* you sent him to!"

Nothing but silence came in reply.

Gustav's taste for the recollection turned to gall in his mind's mouth. He rose from the bed and walked slowly to the single window of the small room, as if mere bodily motion might help him forget.

Only blackness met his absent gaze.

He did not care to replay the rest of the interview. What was the point of remembering the man's helpless look, the pressure of the trigger against his finger, the color of the blood. . . .

Yes, it had been easier at the moment to kill this man than that fool called Schlaukopf who had tried to swindle him. But it still wasn't a pleasant business under any circumstances. And now he found it sticking with him in a most provoking fashion. Easier at the time, perhaps . . . but with deeper personal complications.

The compunction that now spoke to him from out of the depths of the frayed edges remaining around what had once been his conscience came in such slight whispers as to be barely audible. But he had to admit that the man's face was difficult to erase from his memory—a man who two days ago had been warm and breathing and alive, but who was now a cold and life-less corpse . . . because of him.

Gustav was not quite so dead yet as to be able to recognize that fact without it causing a momentary catch in his psycho-logical breathing apparatus. Nothing could altogether take the manhood out of him—not even he himself, though he had himself spent the better part of a lifetime trying to do just that.

His thoughts turned to Sabina and unconsciously drifted back through the years.

"Sabina . . . Sabina—where are you?" a young boy's voice cried.

He was running through Baron von Dortmann's immense garden, made all the more enormous for a seven-year-old who did not yet know his way from one end of it to the other with-out getting lost. On this occasion, his young five-year-old neighbor had run ahead out of sight and was now hiding from him.

"Sabina!" his voice had pled, the rising fear he felt beginning to betray itself. It was getting dark, and he didn't know which of the many paths to take.

Suddenly she had jumped out and into plain view no more than a meter in front of him, laughing with glee.

"Why must you always tease me?" he said, displaying the first hints of the frustration that would more and more through the years characterize his half of the relationship.

"I wasn't teasing, Gustav. I was just playing hide-and-seek. I wanted you to come find me."

He could still see her smiling, happy, innocent face. No, she hadn't meant any harm by it. She was just a gay, fun-loving little girl.

That's all she ever had been—even as they had grown older. She never understood how seriously he took things, never un-derstood that he had wanted more to exist between them than mere childhood memories of chases through the garden.

She *still* didn't understand.

She was still hiding from him. Still he pursued her along

circuitous pathways that had thus far led him nowhere. Nothing had changed in all those years.

But everything *had* changed. He was a formidable man, and this was now no game of hide-and-seek . . . but of life and death.

The brief melancholy memories of the past caused a question he had never before considered to bubble up from the depths of his being. When it burst into his consciousness, he found it so alien to the shape his character had taken that he could scarcely hold it in his mind in such a way as to accurately consider it.

The question was no more nor less than this: *What would Sabina think of me if she saw me now?*

For years he had fantasized meeting her again, marrying her, living the rest of his life with her, deluding himself that he held it within his power to make her happy.

Suddenly the unthinkable dawned upon him: that perhaps she would turn with revulsion at the very sight of him. This thought, along with the residue remaining from the memory of postal employee Fritsch lying dead on his apartment floor with blood oozing out of his head, caused a momentary gag to seize Gustav.

He turned quickly from the window and tried to find somewhere to go, but only the bed and dresser met his path of retreat. There was no escape. He paced two or three lengths before returning again to the black, silent pane of glass.

The thoughts were not only unfamiliar, they were so alien as to be capable of finding no place to lodge within him. They entered his brain as an unfriendly invasion force that must be fought off . . . and quickly!

Sabina *didn't* understand, he said to himself again.

He had, of course, realized long before now—not without some pain that he did his best to ignore—that she did not love him, never had loved him, and was doing everything she could to avoid ever laying eyes upon him again. But he managed to convince himself that she was deceived, that she would change her mind when she saw all he would be able to do for her.

Gustav was engaged in that ancient and masterful art of self-deception at the point of his own being. The vague sense was growing upon him that Sabina might not appreciate what kind of man he was, but he was unable to connect what he had become with any kind of value to do with ethics or honor. He could not see that perhaps Sabina was morally a better individual than he, and that that was the reason for her antipathy toward him. Rather, he had deluded himself into thinking that Sabina was simply different from him as a person, but neither better nor worse.

She might not like what he was, but he was unable to bring his conscience to bear upon the issue in a personal way. She simply didn't grasp, he told himself, what a real man had to be in a real world.

Suddenly, at a deeper level of mingled consciousness and conscience than he had ever explored before, the possibility slowly occurred to him that perhaps *he* had been the one who had deceived himself all this time.

Then came the more profound question of conscience: *What kind of person have I become? Am I the sort of man that a woman like Sabina would ever—could ever—love?*

The answer was too noisome to consider.

The invasion was underway. Would the guardians of his gates be friend or foe?

The inner hinges were trying to break free of their casings. Oil from on high had been sent to lubricate them. A few scant drops had already penetrated into the inner workings and would have their result, but they were not yet enough to break apart those hinges and swing the doors wide.

Again he turned away from the window, this time in disgust.

No! He would not consider it!

He stalked about the small room in agitation, though there was scarcely enough space to do so. He appeared as a caged animal, suddenly uncomfortable with the box into which he had been placed.

He was who he was, he tried to tell himself. He was a product of difficult times. He had done what he had to do in order to survive. Who cared what kind of man he was? He had become a man of standing and power and influence—what else these days mattered?

Besides, he tried to console himself further, it was too late to do anything about it. He was forty-two years old. He was part of an opportunity-less regime, where change was not merely frowned upon, but in some cases was forbidden altogether.

Change was not an avenue open to one such as him. Why should he change? Who did Sabina think she was! She was no more righteous than he!

Gradually he cooled. Once more the self-deluding reason that had always stood him in good stead with himself began to gain again the upper hand.

If he wanted her to love him, he thought—after he *had* her— he would simply have to put on a veneer of goodness like he would put on an overcoat. His way of coming out where he wanted to be in the end required that he convince her that he was different from perhaps what he really was.

Of course he would have to get his hands on her first, and that might require some unpleasantness here and there. But once it was over and done with, he had no doubt he could be successful with the ruse. There were no moral rights and wrongs here, he went on with his inner argument. Everybody wore overcoats by which they tried to deceive those around them. He just had to select his with care and make sure it was the kind of coat whose style would suit Sabina.

His unsettled walk back and forth landed him eventually in front of the dresser. There was the stamp album the man had been so protective of as to be willing to die without divulging its secrets.

Casually he flipped through it again.

His mother had tried to interest him in stamps when he was a boy. But he had been more interested in guns, and eventually she had given up.

There was nothing remarkable here, Gustav thought. If the man considered himself a philatelist, this was certainly a sorry collection. He scanned the names at the back of the book for at least the tenth time that day.

These were his contacts all right—stamp dealers . . . or members of the underground network.

He had located six of the addresses by now, each of which showed a line from his hand through it. He had dismissed all but four. One of them, he was positive, would know something of Sabina and her father. Fritsch would not have remained silent unless one of these individuals was important enough to die for.

Stuffing his gun and silencer back in his pocket, still holding the stamp album, Gustav opened the door and left the small room. He would lie down and rest later. He had to interrogate every person on that list. Though his private broodings had taken some of the fervor out of the search, the job yet had to be completed.

He sighed wearily as he descended to the lobby with heavy step.

Whether Sabina would like him if she saw him was really beside the point. Whether he was even successful in fabricating an overcoat of goodness by her standards was equally beside the point.

Her father was an escaped prisoner. She had broken the law. They were both traitors and fugitives. His job demanded that he find them and bring them to justice, notwithstanding his personal stake in the affair.

If he didn't, he could wind up behind bars in the baron's place. It was how this system worked.

It had to be done.

He had to find them.

His course was set . . . and nothing could stop it. He'd have to settle it about the overcoat in his mind later.

∾ 21 ∾
A Quiet Talk of Love

The remainder of their day of reunion, Matthew, Sabina, and Baron von Dortmann visited, laughed, prayed, and talked over plans together, though most of the time was spent reminiscing and catching up on the months since they had so calamitously parted. In the case of the baron and Matthew, a whole new basis for relationship was rapidly being formed, for they had not spent more than a few moments together in twenty years.

That evening, after supper, Matthew took two chairs out onto the small porch, then asked Sabina to join him. The night was chilly though not unbearably cold, and the nip of the March air felt refreshing against their faces.

They sat down and allowed the stillness of approaching night to settle over their spirits. It had been a day neither would ever forget.

"I have something for you," said Matthew at length.

"Nothing could surpass the gift you gave me this morning," said Sabina in a contented voice.

"Nothing?" repeated Matthew.

"It is the first red rose I've been given in my life. I should say, it's the first I've *accepted*."

They both laughed lightly.

"I will keep the rose you gave me this morning forever. I will find some special place of honor to preserve it. Do you still have the box we bought in Berlin?" she asked.

"It is safe and sound with my father," answered Matthew. "But," he added pointedly, "I have another gift for you. Are you absolutely certain nothing could surpass this morning's red rose?"

"Positive."

"Not even something from *Lebenshaus* itself?"

"I don't know what you mean."

"Not even . . . this?"

As he said the words, Matthew pulled out from where he had kept it concealed in his clothing the rose-painted china box.

Sabina gasped when she realized what it was.

"I didn't only visit the dungeon when I was there," he said. "I had this one other errand to attend to as well."

She took it tenderly from his hand, holding it for several moments.

"We promised we would not peek inside until we could open it together, remember?" said Matthew coyly.

"I . . . I remember," said Sabina, reddening slightly and trying to keep from smiling.

"We said we would enjoy the roses we put inside . . . *together*," Matthew added, emphasizing the last word with deliberately feigned innocence.

There was a moment of silence.

"I don't know how to tell you this, Sabina," Matthew went on, his tone now sounding contrite and apologetic, "but . . . well, when I was there, down in that dark room with only my flashlight . . . and not knowing if I would ever see you again . . . I'm sorry, Sabina, but I'm afraid I could not help myself."

She glanced over at him.

"You . . ."

"Yes . . . I opened the box. I hope you'll forgive me."

At first Sabina's expression was blank, not quite grasping the full implications of his humble and repentant tone.

"But . . . then, you *know?*" she said, more in statement than inquiry.

"Know what, Sabina?" replied Matthew, eyes wide in pretended ignorance. Gradually a smile played at the edges of his mouth, and she finally realized the game he had been making of her.

"Oh, Matthew, I couldn't help it!" she said with apologetic exclamation. "I didn't know either if I'd ever see you again, or *Lebenshaus* either for that matter! You can't imagine how badly I wanted to take it with me that night. When Papa went down to seal up the dungeon and the whole bottom part of the house, I went to look one last time at our box. I decided to leave it, hoping that somehow it would be safe. But I *had* to look—I had to know! I said to myself, 'Oh, I hope Matthew will forgive me this once!'"

Matthew laughed.

"All is forgiven! On both sides?" he added.

Sabina nodded.

"It would appear we both broke the promise," he said.

"Only out of love."

"Perhaps, then, we are excused."

Again silence fell.

Without another word, Matthew reached over and placed his hand on top of Sabina's. Together they removed the white lid and peered inside, sharing now together the sight they had both already seen alone—Matthew's small note and the rosebuds.

"Two white roses," said Matthew after a moment.

Sabina sighed. "Two white roses," she repeated.

After a moment Matthew leaned close so that he could see deeply into Sabina's eyes even in the scant light from inside the house.

"Friends . . . *forever*," he said.

"Forever," she repeated, holding his gaze.

Their lips met, each holding the other's for several long seconds.

They eased away, both sighing with pleasure, and sat back beside one another, Sabina still holding the china box on her lap, and now slipping the fingers of her right hand through those of Matthew's left.

Contented enough to spend two years sitting as they were, neither moved nor spoke for some twenty minutes. Both their hearts were too full to give expression to words.

"I won't soon forget what you have done, Matthew, coming here to find my father and me," said Sabina in scarcely more than a whisper, after a long time had passed and the night seemed deepening around them.

"What else could I do? The lady I loved was in prison behind the walls of the Communist dragon! I had to rescue her!"

He stopped and became serious, though still with humor in his tone.

"Now all I've got to do is figure out how to get us *out* of the dragon's lair!" he added.

After two or three minutes, Sabina glanced up at Matthew.

"Do you mind if I ask you a question?" she said.

"Of course not—what about?"

"Roses."

"I can't think of anything better to be asked about."

"How long did it take you . . . ," Sabina began, "I mean, when did you finally discover what the secret of the rose really is?"

"I don't know," replied Matthew. "Maybe sometime last June and July when I was bringing a rose to you every day. . . ."

He pondered quietly for a moment.

"It might not have even been until this morning, as I was walking along holding the rose I'd found, thinking of what I would say when I saw you."

"Papa used to say that the secret was only given to those who came to understand the depths of the red rose. How blessed we are to have been able to discover the secret together," said Sabina, "first as friends, and then now . . ."

She hesitated.

"You know what I mean," she went on, "being able now to discover the secret of the rose together after all these years. God has been good to us!"

She took Matthew's hand and pressed it between her own two.

"I do love you, Matthew!"

"And I you, Sabina. I'm so happy that God allowed me to be the one to discover the secret of the rose . . . with you."

∽ 22 ∾
Somber News

A quiet and gradually more somber mood fell between them, and they were silent for several long minutes. When Matthew broke their silence, it was to bring them back to the realities of their situation.

"We're going to have to make more definite plans tomorrow," he said. "Gustav, or whoever has been following me, could show up at any moment. Now that I've secured your father's permission and your formal acceptance of my proposal, I don't want to risk anything getting in the way of our future again."

Before Sabina could reply, the telephone rang.

She got up and walked back inside. Matthew could hear nothing of the brief call. But the moment she returned he could tell from the look of shock on her face that the news was not good.

"What is it?" asked Matthew.

"One of our friends," she replied in a dazed voice. "Spreading word of possible danger."

"Bad news, I take it?"

"Another of our number was killed last night, shot in the head . . . right in his own apartment."

"Why? What happened?"

"No one knows. His place had been ransacked, and his stamp collection stolen."

"His stamp collection?" repeated Matthew, suddenly more alert.

"He disguised his network connections as stamp dealers."

"Are you and your father listed?"

"No, we've only been here a short time. But a few of them would know our whereabouts. There has been a rash of inquiries last night and throughout the day today. There is much fear among them."

"Did the man by chance work at the *Postamt?*" asked Matthew.

"Why yes!"

"And his name was Fritsch?"

"Yes . . . but how did you know?"

With the sickening realization that he had almost certainly led the man's killer into the city, Matthew explained his interview at the post office.

"I don't see that we have any alternative," he concluded. "The danger is too close behind."

Sabina sighed and nodded.

"We'd better go in and talk to your father," Matthew added, rising and walking back inside with Sabina. "We're going to have to leave here immediately. . . . I'm afraid that means tonight."

∽ 23 ∾
A Raid at Number 42

The street called Graulinger was even more deserted at this hour than when Matthew had walked along it some eighteen hours before, when dawn was about to break both over the cobblestones and into his own life.

Now, at one in the morning, the city was silent and black.

No little urchins, not even a stray roaming cat met the stealthy pedestrian who had parked a block away and was now making his way along the sidewalk beneath the tall brick apartment building. This was no walker cognizant of the flower box high in the darkened window across the street.

It was something other than roses he had on his mind.

He had finally unearthed the information he was certain would lead him to his prey.

He had not had to kill to obtain it this time. But in spite of that fact, *Stasi* Section Chief Gustav von Schmundt—who had earlier in the evening been experiencing some uncharacteristic and highly discomforting pangs from regions within himself he was unacquainted with—had had to swallow hard more than once at the memory of his last interview just an hour ago.

Now he walked briskly though silently along, heart pounding at the thought of seeing Sabina's face once again. Despite his soberingly reflective personal evaluation of five or six hours previous, he could not deny that his heart still longed to hold her, to kiss her lips, to feel her long blonde hair between his fingers. . . .

Unconsciously his pace quickened as he tried to shake the fantasies from his brain.

There would be plenty of time for all that later.

First he had to entrap them and make sure he had both of them safely in tow. The baron, of course, for now would have to be returned to prison. He would let Sabina beg, then he would see what his influence could accomplish in securing the old man's release. It wouldn't do for an important *Stasi* official's father-in-law to be sitting in prison as a traitor to the Republic.

If the McCallum fellow was with them, however, he would throw him in prison until he rotted! Or maybe toss him as a bone to the KGB, to let them do what they wanted with him.

Gradually his reflections turned toward the likely results of the multiple arrests he was about to make. He would probably be a hero, Gustav thought.

McCallum was an important U.S. diplomat. His capture within the DDR and his implication in a prison break and an underground spy network would cause front-page news all over the Western world. It would be highly embarrassing to the United States president, whether McCallum's business was personal or not.

And he, Gustav von Schmundt, would share the front page with him!

He would be known as the agent who had single-handedly cracked the case and taken the American spy into custody. It would certainly mean a promotion. It might even mean an honorary trip to Moscow for a medal from Premier Khrushchev.

Let Korsch, let Sabina . . . let any of them look down on him then! She would crawl to him, begging to marry such an important man.

The implications of the information he had discovered, and what future awaited him in the house just ahead, caused Gustav's previously morose spirit to brighten considerably.

What had been wrong with him? How could he have allowed himself to get caught in the web of such gloomy broodings? Everything he had done would be worth it soon enough. What a fool he had been to worry about what kind of man he had become!

He was soon to be one of the most important and famous men in the entire DDR—that's what kind of man he had become!

He paused.

He had come to the intersection. He glanced at the building on his right, barely able to read the number 40 on the wall.

There was the address he sought, on the other side of the street . . . Number 42.

A dim light shone inside.

Certainly they could not still be awake.

He crept into the street, then made his way across it, eyes riveted on the windows of the small house.

By heaven!—there was a figure with its back turned . . . on the couch . . . next to the lamp that was on.

What was . . . did he see . . . could he be sure?

Was it not the back of a head of long, flowing blonde hair?

His heart began pounding wildly in a paroxysm of frenetic and uncontrollable emotion.

With gargantuan effort of will he forced himself to remain calm, proceeding noiselessly across the street, through the open gate, and toward the porch.

His perspiring hand sought the inside of his pocket, where its fingers closed around the cold steel grip of his pistol. He hoped there would be no occasion to use this now, but he had to be ready for anything.

Should he knock or burst in without warning?

Both methods had advantages . . . both contained risks.

Bursting in might cause screaming and panic and arouse an unwanted ruckus in the neighborhood. If the baron, and perhaps even McCallum, were asleep in other rooms of the house, crashing through the door might awaken them too quickly and give them a few precious seconds to get away through a window.

No, he decided, he would let Sabina come to the door quietly.

She would open it. He would slip his foot in instantly. If she tried to bar his way, then he would take appropriate measures. If she started to scream, he would grab her and clamp his hand over her mouth. In either case it would be best to take care of Sabina first, then get the drop on the two men while they still slept.

With cautious tiptoeing, he crept up the three wooden steps to the small veranda, glancing at the two empty chairs sitting there.

He could not see through to the figure in the living room from here, but his ears had detected no movement coming from within. She had to still be there.

He paused, drew in a deep breath, then lifted his fist to the door.

He rapped upon it lightly three or four times. He would not alarm Sabina's nighttime reverie with the heavy-handed pounding of the KGB.

He waited a second or two. No sound came from within.

He knocked again, with slightly more force.

No response.

A quiet panic began to seize Gustav's throat. He retreated down the steps and ran to the street, glancing back toward the lit window.

Sabina still sat on the couch, back turned. Relief surged through him.

She is sound asleep, he thought.

Hastening back to the door, he knocked louder and deliberately this time.

But yet a third time no answering reply from within met his imperative query.

He tried the latch. It was locked.

Again he knocked, this time with the fleshy bottom of his clenched fist, the pounding sound betraying the beginnings of heart-sinking and angry anxiety.

He waited this time no more than a second before raising his booted foot, smashing it against the latch and lock, then bursting through into the small house and running with mounting desperation into the dimly lit sitting room.

The sounds of the shattering door and his heavy step echoed through the night.

Gustav stopped. His face went pale as a ghost.

There on the settee were propped several large pillows held together with a sheet, around which had been draped a woman's blouse. On top, resting against the couch's edge, a woman's blonde wig had been carefully arranged around a smaller pillow, to look from the outside as if a woman were sitting, reading, or dozing beside the lamp.

From his present vantage point, the absurd thing looked like a faceless snowman!

Rage and incensed humiliation rose up like a suddenly roused flame within him. Before he knew what he was doing, he had emptied four screaming rounds from his pistol into the lifeless thing that had made such a mockery of his passions just minutes earlier.

With smoking pistol clutched in a vice-grip of madness, eyes frantically searching back and forth for any sign of life, Gustav spun about the room and ran recklessly into the single bedroom, then out of it seconds later and toward the kitchen of the small house.

He knew the truth without having to search the place: They were gone.

But search he did—like a madman.

It took several minutes for his tornado of vehemence to begin to cool, during which time he was heedless of the lights and sounds awakening in the buildings nearby at the commotion coming from inside Number 42.

Coming to himself where he stood in the center of the living room—the entire place ransacked, drawers strewn about in every room, the two beds upturned, closets thrown inside-out, kitchen utensils still rattling to their resting places all over the floor—breathing heavily, face still pale but body hot and sweating, Gustav collapsed into a nearby chair and tried to force his mind to think.

The room was still warm. He could feel Sabina's presence, just like that night so long ago when they had raided *Lebenshaus*.

They could not have been gone more than an hour . . . two at the most.

They must have expected him; otherwise, why the ruse of the pillowed snowman set up to look like Sabina was home? If they had gone to all that trouble to conceal their movements, they could not have left by the front door, where they might have been seen. They must have been trying to keep their movements from their neighbors as well.

Gustav rose again and walked through the kitchen and to the back of the house. He opened the back door and peered out.

Not a trace of light was to be seen.

He stepped out into the blackness, nearly tripping over the bottom step, cursing, then landing with both his feet on the thin grass of a tiny backyard. Inching out across it, feeling his way with outstretched hand, he came after only six or eight meters to a back fence, a gate of which still stood open into an alleyway behind.

This had to have been their route of escape. He turned and walked back into the house.

The moment he entered, a faint sensation came to him.

Could it be that she still wore the same perfume after all these years! In the bedroom he could have sworn—

He would not torture himself with such fantasies!

He had succumbed to that mistake too many times in the past. He had been a fool ever to think she might love him!

The spirit of revenge rose up within his heart. This was it— this was the last and final straw!

There would be no more delusions about marrying the wench, no more kindly thoughts toward her treasonous father, no more quarter given her spy of a lover! He would imprison them all—Sabina with them!—and never think twice about it!

Momentarily he calmed again to think. Might they come back?

No. The house had been vacated of all personal belongings. Only furniture remained. Hardly a piece of clothing had been left behind.

It was clear they had left abruptly . . . with no intention of returning.

He would have the house staked out just to be sure, but he placed little hope in such an exercise.

This cat-and-mouse game would have to start over once again. Only from now on he would not be so naive.

They had outwitted Gustav von Schmundt once too often.

But this time would be the last.

He continued on through the house, then stalked with determination over the shards of the front door his boot had demolished.

It was time to pay return visits to a few of the late Herr Fritsch's personal so-called stamp dealers!

PART II

Lola Reinhardt
March–May 1962

∽ 24 ∽
Lonely Decision

It had been a winter of sad disquietude for Lola Reinhardt, assistant and secretary to *Stasi* Section Chief Gustav von Schmundt.

The army laying siege to her boss had turned several of its flanks in her direction at the same time. Similar promptings had come whispering at each of their inner doors, begging invitation to enter. The Voice speaking to each was the same, though the ears through which the whispers attempted to pass caused the words to ring with a much different timbre indeed.

The construction of the Berlin wall, less than a kilometer from the office where she now sat, had exercised a completely unexpected impact upon her.

She turned from the file cabinet where she had been standing in front of an open drawer and listlessly moved toward the window, then gazed down toward that section of the wall that was visible to her eyes. It was certainly ugly, and why she looked at it several times a day she could not have said. There was something about it that compelled one to stare at it . . . to stare and to wonder what it all meant.

A sound disturbed her.

Lola glanced away from the window and turned around to see an unexpected figure approaching through the door.

"Herr Galanov!" she exclaimed in genuine surprise.

The young Russian KGB agent smiled warmly and extended his hand.

"*Guten Tag*, Fräulein Reinhardt," he said.

"How nice to see you again," she rejoined.

"And you, Lola," he returned, taking the only other chair in the room. "How are you?"

The question was such a simple one, a rote comment of everyday conversation. Yet these days, even the most routine things went deeper than they ever had before and caused Lola to think more than she ever had in her life.

She had never particularly been an idealist, nor had her life been an especially happy one.

Neither was she a philosopher concerning her lot. She expected no more than a certain predictable dreariness to the ongoing routine of life, in spite of the private dreams she had allowed herself to harbor in connection with her superior. She coped with the tedium of existence in East Germany, in many ways, as well as if not better than most of her comrades.

Yet when the wall that she had been looking at a moment ago had gone up, she began to feel inextricably trapped. It was an unusual response for one such as she, for whom that illusive thing called freedom was a commodity she neither sought nor even thought much about.

The freedom that beckoned to her, however, was not political or societal, but of another kind altogether.

The feeling had not come upon her immediately. It was delayed, in fact, by several months.

The frightful incident of the helicopter crash involving her boss and his young assistant had been such an emotional drain that first news of the blockade between sectors of the city had gone by her almost unnoticed.

Then through the months of September, October, and November she had been busily engaged in her own private and daring quest to get to the bottom of the people—and especially the girl—involved in the underground network Herr von Schmundt had so long and so fervently sought. That activity had preoccupied her with a greater sense of purpose than she had ever felt in her life.

She reflected again on the calls she had made during that time and the investigations she had set in motion as she had acted in the authority of the section chief during his convalescence. She had surprised even herself with the command she was able to bring to her bearing and by the obedient cooperation she received.

She had personally visited Potsdam. She had gone to Teltow. She had familiarized herself with all the principal players in her boss's private drama, from the baron and his daughter to the American he had been trailing throughout the winter since that time. She had gone over every millimeter of every file connected with the case.

And how greatly her probings and confidential inquiries had paid off!

Lola halfway suspected what the contents of the packet revealed before it had been delivered to her, but once she read through it, the papers confirmed her every hunch, including the changeable loyalties of the lackey at the morgue. All the pieces finally fit. She had held the solution to her boss's *Hauptleidenschaft* in her very hand.

To present him with it, she had known, would earn his temporary gratitude . . . but it would never win his devotion.

The decision she had subsequently made was forever irrevocable and had begun to change her life immediately.

No one else would ever know what Lola had discovered, she thought as she watched the packet she had worked so diligently to obtain settle into its permanent grave in the oozing mud under the slow-flowing waters of the Spree.

∞ 25 ∞
The Deep Call of Life

"Lola . . . ?" sounded Galanov's voice again, interrupting the persistent flow of her reflections.

"Uh . . . oh, I'm sorry. I was distracted for a moment," said Lola, fumbling to bring herself back to the present. "I . . . I am well, thank you, Andrassy."

"I am delighted to hear it."

"But I am surprised. . . . I did not know you had returned to Berlin."

"I arrived only yesterday."

"You are looking very well. Your injuries appear to have healed completely."

"I am feeling fit as ever."

"You are here to resume your former duties with our office?"

"Eventually . . . yes," replied Galanov vaguely. "There are one or two other matters I must attend to first. Tell me, is the section chief in?"

"No, he is not here."

"He is not . . . still in the hospital?" asked Galanov, though he knew the answer well enough, for he had been following Schmundt loosely for two months.

"Oh, no."

"He is well recovered then?"

"Yes."

"When do you expect him back?"

The subject of her boss lay at the very heart and center of Lola's changing mental and emotional horizon.

The moment she had decided not to provide him with what he so desperately sought concerning the young woman and her father, the very instant she had turned from the middle of the bridge to begin walking back toward her dreary flat, the metamorphosis had begun for Lola Reinhart.

To engage the human will in any determined direction forward unlocks the sluggish wheels of growth and sets the becoming of personhood in motion.

What Lola had done was unremarkable in itself. That she had decided to do it, had made a decision affecting her future, and had carried through her resolve—the consequences of such internally willed motion could not be denied.

She had climbed out of the backseat of the carriage called cause-and-effect in which she had ridden along for so many years—unquestioning of her lot, taking whatever came her way—and set herself down instead in the causing front seat, where direction and momentum are determined.

From that very day forward, life began to look different to the eyes of Lola Reinhardt.

Not that it began to appear instantly brighter. The dreariness of her days continued, especially with the purpose gone for which she had expended such energy of late.

Yet henceforth the vague seed-thought that had sprouted to life within her continued to grow—the idea that she herself could take an active, causing, initiating, *will*ing share in her own being . . . that she could become someone perhaps a little different from what she was before . . . and that she could exercise a determinative hand in that process.

Two seemingly contrary feelings began to develop within her, one toward death, the other toward life. It was during this time that she first became personally aware of *der Mauer* and considered its implications . . . to her.

She began to feel a certain vague choking sensation in some deep region of her psyche. It must be the wall, she thought at first, and the sense of entrapment that had settled upon the free-spirited German people of the DDR like a dull fog. But in her case it was far more than that, though she did not realize it yet.

Lola herself could not know that what she was feeling, even below the region of specific cogitation, was the first tentative and distant hint that her consciousness of being was at last beginning to come awake. The discontent she was experiencing was not from finding herself in the DDR, nor from the realization that Herr von Schmundt did not love her. It was rather a discontent of soul, which was slowly reviving to its hunger for a kind of life that mattered.

Alongside this disharmony within her, as the winter of 1962 had drawn to a close, Lola found herself noticing things her eyes had not beheld in years—daffodils and tulips and crocuses appearing from out of the cold, wet, wintry ground . . . birds making their songs heard once again. The blue of the sky began to appear bluer, the occasional orange of a sunset or reddish glow of a sunrise more orange, more red, more full of a strange kind of delight . . . even mystery.

None of these sights yet brought a smile to Lola's sad countenance. But they spoke to her heart, watering and bringing light to the thin green sprout of life within it . . . and the time for smiles would one day come.

Her thoughts began to revolve around a cousin and an aunt, her only living relatives, whose home was in Hamburg. They had never been close. She had scarcely found herself reminded of them in years and hadn't lain eyes on them since the war.

But as life calls to life, and as ties of family and bonds of kinship are at the very foundation of life's created matrix, suddenly an acute longing rose up within Lola's bosom to see them again.

Alas, but it was too late!

Why had she not thought of it a year ago? Now a visit was impossible.

With the realization again came the vague feeling of spiritual strangulation—the awareness that in her present environment she would never know the life, the freedom, the laughter, the joy that her heart longed for . . . but that she knew not how to lay hold of.

❧ 26 ❧
Acquaintance of Convenience

I . . . I must confess I don't know where Herr von Schmundt is at present," replied Lola, again after a lengthy reflective silence. "I have seen him but rarely since the first of the year. He moves in and out of the office."

"He is . . . very busy?" queried Galanov.

"He is in the field . . . on surveillance. I have seen nothing of him now in two weeks."

"Surveillance?" repeated the Russian. "Anything, uh . . . new?"

"He is tracking the escaped prisoner from last August."

"Ah, . . . I see."

Andrassy Galanov had been well trained by his uncle, and of course by the KGB training manual. He was always alert to anything—a look, a flinch, a dart of the eye, a hesitation of the voice, a shift in tone—that might convey more by subtlety than intended by the words being spoken. He was ever alert for anything that could be capitalized on and turned to his advantage.

On this day, though he had not seen her for several months, he immediately noticed a change in the *Stasi* chief's secretary. It took him some time to identify it, and he found himself pondering it even as they spoke.

Then it came to him.

There was—despite the long pauses and expressions that looked as if she were far away—a new spark of life present in Lola's countenance. He wondered what it was. Was she in love? In Schmundt's absence had she finally gotten over her fetish for him—despite his youth, Galanov was a shrewd judge of human character and had seen it immediately—and met someone else?

Whatever its cause, he was ready to exploit it as soon as an opportunity presented itself.

Lola, on the other hand, had been, of late, so hungry for human contact of any kind that the mere sight of young Galanov brought a spark to her eye.

"Will I be resuming that case as well?" Galanov added after a slight pause.

"I am not certain," replied Lola. "Perhaps . . . if he has not found the prisoner by now."

"When do you expect the section chief back?"

"I am sorry," answered Lola, with a slight smile, "I do not know that either. It seems I am not much help to you. I do, however, think it will be soon. It has been his custom to check in personally with the office every week or two and calls still more frequently. He will no doubt be happy you have returned."

"No doubt," Galanov said with a smile, keeping his thoughts of the irony of her comment to himself. He doubted Schmundt had much use for him, except when it suited his own purposes.

"Would you like some tea or coffee, Herr Galanov?" asked Lola, warming up to the presence of another human to talk to.

"Why, yes, thank you, Lola. . . . Tea, I believe," replied Galanov.

As Lola prepared a pot, she and the young Russian continued to chat amiably. They took chairs and continued to visit as they enjoyed tea together. Within thirty minutes, Lola had become more than relaxed.

"Was your visit home an enjoyable one, Andrassy?" she asked.

Galanov nodded. "Mostly business, however. My . . . uh, my superior there kept me rather busy on a surveillance case of my own. Has there been any contact that you know of, Lola," he asked in a nonchalant tone, "between the prisoner Herr von Schmundt is seeking and a Jewish rabbi?"

"A rabbi . . . hmm, nothing that I am aware of."

Galanov eyed her carefully. She appeared to be telling the truth.

"He is being sought by my government," said Galanov. "It is possible there may be a connection between the two men."

"Have you returned to seek him specifically?" asked Lola.

"If I am able to learn anything, it would certainly be highly appreciated, although my assignment is merely to carry on as before, as Section Chief Schmundt's assistant."

"What is this rabbi's crime?"

"He has stolen some documents that my superiors consider a major breach of security."

"He is now in the DDR?"

"His exact whereabouts are unknown. It may be that he will attempt, or already has handed them over to the German Herr von Schmundt seeks."

Now it was Lola's turn to keep her own counsel. Her brain hurriedly scanned back through the months of her own investigation to determine if anything she had run across suggested such a connection.

Again Galanov noted the pensive pause and wondered as to its cause. He would definitely, he said to himself, continue the cultivation of this relationship with the suddenly intriguing Fräulein Reinhardt.

∾ 27 ∾
House of Refuge

The house where Sabina and her father had been staying for the better part of a week was, though not one Sabina had known before, yet in familiar surroundings. It was just outside the village of Grossbeeren, south of Berlin, and she had been here many times.

They had left Magdeburg suddenly at Matthew's insistence, in the middle of the night, and had known from the dreadful news about Fritsch that Gustav could not be far behind them. To attempt to contact any of their acquaintances and associates there would only be to risk further compromising the entire network in that region.

They would have to leave the city without a trace, for their own protection and everyone else's.

They had, therefore, hastily stuffed Matthew's broken-down

Trabi as full with their few needful possessions as possible, carefully arranged the house to appear still lived-in with a life-sized doll of Sabina sitting on the couch, crept out the back door and to the alley where the vehicle of escape was now situated, and then stuffed themselves in around the blankets and boxes and suitcases and headed as noiselessly as the dilapidated automobile would allow out of the city toward the north.

Where they would go, praying for guidance as the city disappeared in blackness behind them, they didn't know. The Trabi did not have fuel to drive all night, nor did they have a destination that would have required it. Nor further could they risk being stopped by an inquisitive *Vopo* or *Stasi* patrol. One look inside the car would have aroused such profound suspicion that they would likely have been detained, if not outright arrested, on the spot.

Getting well out of the city, therefore, Matthew drove for something less than an hour, taking numerous turns, side roads, and detours so that by the end of it he scarcely knew himself where they were, and then pulled off onto a wooded side road, extinguished the lights, and stopped the engine.

There they had spent the remainder of the night, talking, praying, and curling up with the blankets they had with them and dozing as much as possible.

They awoke in the grey light of dawn, cramped and tired but in good spirits, thinking how wonderful right then would be the smell of freshly brewing coffee—and the taste to go with it!—but wishing even more for a place where they could get out of sight and be safe for a while, until they could decide what was to be done.

They realized their most faithful network contacts, and some of Sabina's longest and most trusted allies in her work over the years, lived in and around Grossbeeren. There had been no association with any of the people there in months, so there should be no immediate danger. They would make for the village, contact either Willy or Erich Brumfeldt, and see if there might not be a place they could hide the car . . . and themselves.

Both father and son rejoiced to see the wandering outcasts of Abraham's lineage, and both begged them to do them the great honor of taking refuge in their humble home.

Sabina, however, refused, in consideration of Clara. During the months of her fugitive hiding out with her father, Sabina had returned to Grossbeeren twice more and had learned every detail of the events of that fateful day the previous August. She well knew of the beating Clara had received and the other injuries and death that had been the price her colleagues had paid for the baron's freedom, and never would Sabina knowingly bring such upon anyone again unbidden.

"Is there anyone else who would have us?" she asked. "I will not put your wife in that position a second time."

"But, Karin—," insisted Erich, still calling Sabina by her former alias.

"I'm sorry, Erich," interrupted Sabina. "That is final. I know, perhaps better than you yourself, that you would be in danger too. We are still being pursued. Your name is, I fear, already known. I would have us seek refuge, if possible, with one who is new to our number and yet who is aware of the potential consequences. A man without a family, perhaps."

In the end, they had been put up with a hulking, good-natured mechanic of farm implements by the name of Josef Dahlmann, a widower with a large house and no children. He still occupied the family home where he had been raised with his brothers and sisters, all of whom, except for his youngest sister, Erich explained, had since left. Josef and his sister had lived in the home together for years, since the death of their parents, though in constant fear of its confiscation by the Communist regime. His sister had been married the previous August, but since that time had been forced to remain with her brother. Dahlmann had made Brumfeldt's acquaintance and had become involved in some of the group's clandestine activities.

"We appreciate your taking us in like this, Herr Dahlmann," said Baron von Dortmann as the three shook hands with their new host after they were all inside and Erich had completed the introductions.

"Anything I can do to help God's people I will do," replied the large man. "My wife was half Jew. She survived the war, but was so weakened from the camp where she spent two years that she only lived another five years."

"I am sorry," said the baron sincerely. Of all men, he could understand the depth of the loss.

"I am concerned about the car," said Matthew. "I am reasonably certain it is known."

"We will hide it out of sight in my barn among the equipment."

"But if it should be found, it will bring danger upon you."

"I do not fear for myself, my friend. But if it will alleviate your concern, we will change the license."

"Change . . . ?"

"I have several plates that should do nicely without arousing the least suspicion."

"Did I not tell you he was a resourceful man!" laughed Erich. "You will be in good hands here."

"Then while my sister fixes you some tea or coffee," their host now said to Sabina and her father, "we shall empty the car and get it quickly into the barn."

Now they first noticed a young woman approaching from the kitchen.

"May I present my sister Angela," Dahlmann said.

A new round of greetings followed.

Matthew, Erich, and Josef turned and left the house to begin emptying and concealing the Trabi, while Angela led Sabina and the baron into the kitchen, where they took seats as she checked the coffee that was brewing and then took the pot off the stove, where water was boiling. She then proceeded to make preparations for tea.

"I understood Erich to say that your brother lived alone here," said Sabina to their hostess. "Are you . . . visiting?"

"No," she answered, "I have lived here all my life."

"Is it your sister, then, who was married last year? Perhaps I mis—"

"No, it was me," said Angela, a sad smile now appearing on her countenance. "My wedding took place on August 3."

"Then . . . but why—?"

The bewilderment in Sabina's voice was evident, though she suddenly felt awkward about all the questions she was asking.

"I'm sorry," she said. "I have no right to pry. You are very kind to open your home to us in this way."

"I do not mind your questions. I will tell you what happened as we enjoy our refreshment. What would you like?"

"You cannot imagine how wonderful that coffee smells!" said the baron.

"I'll have tea, thank you," answered Sabina.

A few moments later, Angela sat down beside them, setting a plate of small cakes on the table between their three steaming cups.

"My husband is an engineer," she said after a long and thoughtful pause. "He must travel a lot. When we were married, we had a week's honeymoon before he was scheduled to leave on a brief business trip. That was the eleventh."

She paused and glanced away, obviously filled with emotion.

"Where . . . did he go?" asked Sabina.

"Hamburg," replied Angela. "He was only to be gone four days, but—"

"He did not come back?"

Angela shook her head.

"The wall went up . . . and . . . I have not seen him since—" Her voice broke off, and she looked away as her eyes filled with tears.

Sabina stretched a comforting hand across the table and rested it upon that of the young woman, who was probably ten years younger.

"I am very sorry," she said. "I had no idea."

Angela wept softly for a moment. Sabina kept her hand where it was, and she and her father waited patiently.

"He did not come back for you?" Sabina asked at length.

Angela shook her head sadly.

"I'm so sorry," said Sabina again, her tone indicating that she had misunderstood.

"Oh no . . . please," said Angela, anxious to make herself clear. "It is not that he does not care. He *could* come back."

Again Sabina's face registered confusion.

"We had spoken of going to the West. That is one of the reasons he went to Hamburg, to look for a job there so that we could move to the BRD. We have friends, another couple who had been married only a month before. We were all going to

West Germany together. But now the two men are there, and we are left stranded behind the wall."

"But . . . I don't understand why your husband does not return."

"If he came back now, we would *never* be free in the West."

"Would that not be better than to be separated?"

"Perhaps," sighed Angela, "but we still want to be free. That is why he has remained in the West, in hopes that I can somehow get to him."

"Have you tried?"

"Oh yes—I have applied for an emigration permit many times."

"And?"

"They are all denied."

"Have you heard from your husband?"

"Only messages delivered by people coming into the DDR."

"What does he say?"

"He says to be patient . . . and that he will get me into West Berlin somehow."

"Is he still in Hamburg?"

"He and his friend are in West Berlin now. Oh, you cannot imagine how difficult it is to know that he is so close!"

Now it was Sabina's turn to smile a melancholy smile of remembrance. She knew Angela's sadness. Many Germans shared it. Separation was an anguish that went deep.

"But you don't know how he intends to accomplish it?"

"I have no idea. But ever since the wall, my brother Josef has been so angry—angry at our government for allowing itself to be a pawn of the Communists, as he says. He does not show his anger. He is good-natured. But he wants to help everyone escape that he can."

"I hope he will be able to help you see your husband again soon."

"It is so difficult not to lose heart."

"Have faith . . . love makes many things possible," said Sabina. Perhaps, she thought, she would have the opportunity to tell Angela what the love of her man had driven him to do. If Matthew could do what he had done already, why might not they hope that one day they would all be free on the other side?

Before she could carry her thoughts further, the object of those thoughts, along with their host and Erich, returned into the kitchen from outside, through the back door.

"The car is safely hidden, and all your things are inside," announced Josef to Sabina and the baron. Then turning to Matthew he added, "Now it is your turn to enjoy some refreshment with us."

∿ 28 ∿
Discussion of Options

As they drank their coffee and tea, the conversation quickly turned to practical matters.

"What are your plans?" Dahlmann asked, glancing first at Matthew, then at the other two of his fugitive guests.

"We don't have any," laughed Matthew. "Other than getting to West Germany, that is!"

"It is becoming more and more difficult every day, my friends," put in Erich seriously. "The escapes of the first months have slowed to a near trickle, while killings at the border are rising in converse proportion."

"How could it have come to this!" said Angela with a shudder.

"We allowed it two decades ago—that's when it happened," rejoined the baron softly and with deeply significant tone, offering one of his extremely rare comments on the temporal world situation.

"Are any of our former contacts still active, Erich?" asked Sabina, turning to her longtime comrade of The Rose. "We ourselves—Papa and I—have been moving so much in the past months that I do not know nearly so well as before what is happening with our people."

"We have lost touch with many," he replied. "People are afraid, Karin—forgive me, I forgot! It will take some time for me to accustom myself to Sabina, although it is a beautiful name."

"Thank you." She smiled in return.

"To continue," he went on, "it has changed greatly. The wall, the killings, the climate of fear—many who helped previously have retreated. Our numbers are not what they once were."

"You have no direct contacts with the other side . . . no leads?"

He shook his head.

"It has all changed. I was involved with a couple escapes in the first two months, and then only indirectly, but nothing since."

"How are people escaping?" asked Matthew, looking toward both men with raised eyebrows.

"There are no patterns," replied Erich. "It is every man for himself these days. It has all become personal. Underground networks such as ours are not responsible for most of the attempts. Whoever comes up with the most ingenious idea to slip over or under unnoticed, he is successful."

They all fell silent. The afternoon was by now well advanced, and unconsciously Sabina yawned.

"Oh," she exclaimed, catching herself. "I didn't realize how tired I was."

"It was a long night!" said Matthew.

"You will be able to sleep as long as you like tonight," said Josef. "You are welcome as long as you need a place. As you can see, we have an abundance of space."

"But we mustn't put you out longer than necessary," said Sabina.

"Think nothing of the duration. You are among friends."

"I think perhaps I ought to drive into Berlin tomorrow," said Matthew.

"Alone?" said Sabina, waking up and with concern registering in her voice.

"That is the best way. I have my German identity. If I can obtain some money from the rest of you," he added laughing, "I will find a cheap hotel and poke around and see what I might be able to learn. I don't know if he's still around, but I'll try to find my old CIA contact Paddy Red and see if he's got anything up his sleeve that might be helpful."

"You shall take my car," said Josef.

"I will be fine in the Trabi."

"Not if it is known. Besides—" now he laughed—"you will *still* be driving a Trabi. Is there any other automobile in the DDR? But you will drive *my* Trabi."

"Have you been in touch with Hermann?" Sabina now asked Erich.

"I see my cousin from time to time. But we have had to take great care since before the prison break. There is the possibility we are known."

"I heard just a few days ago," now said Angela, "from my friend—who I was telling you about," she added, turning to Sabina—"whose husband is with mine on the other side." Then facing the others again, she continued, "She told me that a man named Hermann—I'm certain it's the same fellow you've spoken of, Josef, in connection with Erich—she said that he was involved in many attempts and that perhaps she and I ought to see him. She thought he might be able to help us."

"Hermann is, I must admit, more daring than I," chuckled Erich. "I too have heard these rumors about him, but out of respect for my wife have maintained a comfortable distance.

"I'm going to Berlin with you," said Sabina to Matthew. "I'll get in touch with Hermann. He'll help us if anyone can."

"It's too risky," said Matthew, shaking his head. "If Gustav is behind us, I want you and your father out of sight."

"But, Matthew, I—"

"I'll go in alone," Matthew interrupted with finality. "You can tell me how to contact Hermann just as well as if you were there yourself."

"He's a gruff and suspicious man. Would you not agree, Erich?"

"I think you have my cousin diagnosed to perfection," responded Erich with a laugh.

"Then you'll have to help me be convincing," said Matthew, not to be deterred. "If it doesn't work, I'll come back and get you and we'll try again. But first, I'm going in to Berlin alone . . . after a good night's sleep!"

∽ 29 ∽
A Daring Plan

Matthew was gone six days.

Sabina was well past the edgy stage and progressing far down the road toward full-fledged anxiety when, on the afternoon of the sixth day, suddenly there was Josef Dahlmann's Trabi pulling up behind the house.

She leapt from the chair where she was sitting, ran outside, and smothered him in an excited embrace before he had the chance to get both feet well planted on the ground.

"Let's go inside," he said, laughing. "We have some things we need to talk over—and soon."

So saying, and with Sabina beaming on his arm, they walked inside the house.

"I was beginning to get worried," she said.

"I told you I'd be fine."

"I couldn't help it. The separations before . . . you know."

"You haven't forgotten the promise of the pink rose already, have you, my dear?"

"Oh, Matthew, don't tease. I'd only had you back for two days when you were gone again. Surely you can't blame me for that."

"Of course not. I missed you too."

"I just don't want to lose you again!"

"And you shan't. I promise you—again."

"Did you see Hermann?"

"Yes."

"And?"

"All in good time. Let's gather the others. Baron!" Matthew exclaimed, entering the sitting room, where he encountered Sabina's father heading out to investigate the commotion.

The two shook hands, then embraced as if they hadn't seen one another in a year.

"We are glad to have you back, my boy. We have been praying earnestly that nothing would go wrong."

By this time both Josef and Angela had appeared, the former from his workshop, the latter from the kitchen. After still another round of greetings, they all sat down in anticipation of Matthew's report.

"I did manage to locate my former governmental contact," he began. "Don't ask me how! It took three days. There's not really much he can do for us, though it is good at least to have reestablished that link, though he's had to go so far underground, he says, that his contact with the other side has been almost

nonexistent. His life is in constant danger. He's only now getting back 'in the hunt,' as he calls it. He says the wall's changed
the whole configuration of the spy game. In any case, I know
how to reach him if I have to, but there's not really much he can
do. He said the same thing Erich did earlier—that escapes are
just a private hit-or-miss affair. People try it . . . some of them
make it, some don't. You just have to come up with a good
scheme and hope you're two or three steps ahead of the *Vopos*,
the *Stasi*, and the KGB."

A few sighs went around the room.

"You don't sound overly encouraging, my boy," said the
baron.

"What did Hermann say?" persisted Sabina.

Matthew chuckled.

"You were right," he said. "He's a brusque customer. I had a
difficult time convincing him I was on the up-and-up, even by
telling him I knew his cousin, and with all the talk of roses, pet-
als, love, leaves, and fragrances!"

Sabina and her father laughed to hear their passwords spoken of in such a manner.

"But he finally softened," Matthew went on. "He had been
very worried about the two of you," he said, glancing at Sabina
and the baron. "He was visibly relieved to know that you were
safe. And when later I told him there was a good chance he
might see you again, his face actually lit up."

"The dear man!" said Sabina softly, with notable tenderness.

"Does he offer hope?" asked Josef.

Matthew nodded.

"In a manner of speaking, I suppose you could say so," he answered, then let out a long sigh.

"You do not sound very convincing," said Sabina.

"Hermann is involved—more involved than any of us realized. He has committed himself to helping as many people escape into West Berlin as possible. He has been involved in many
successful escapes. He has even led groups through the underground waterways and then come back home!"

"Amazing!" said an astonished Baron von Dortmann.

"He could have been free, and yet he returned?" exclaimed an
equally astonished Angela.

"Don't underestimate our friend Hermann. Beneath that gruff exterior burns a heart filled with passion. At present his passion is to outwit the Communists however he can."

"What does he suggest we do?" asked Sabina.

"He has not led or been part of an escape in over three months. Security has become just too tight. The wall is complete, high with barbed wire. Guard towers have gone up all across the city at regular intervals, making invisibility anywhere along its length an absolute impossibility. It's completely altered since the first months. All the storm drains were discovered quickly, and no one has gone out through them since October, according to Hermann. It is very, very difficult—and dangerous, he says. So, when you ask if he offers hope, on the one hand the prognosis is gloomy."

"But on the other?"

"On the other . . . there *may* be a way, he says."

The others inched forward in their seats, waiting for Matthew to continue.

"Hermann has a contact," Matthew went on, "an old fellow who worked in the drafting office for the city's Ministry of Works before the war. One of his responsibilities was to review blueprints for new construction. Now this man is himself trying to get out, and somehow he and Hermann have made contact.

"The fellow has been mentally reviewing every project he was associated with back in the '30s, and he and Hermann have come up with a daring, and risky, idea. But nobody's tried it yet—nobody's gone out this way, so they're not sure it will work. But right now, it's all Hermann's got up his sleeve."

He paused and glanced around the room. It was deathly quiet, and every eye was wide and expectant.

"Go on . . . go on," insisted Josef.

Matthew took in a deep breath and then plunged forward into the explanation.

"It's a variation on the storm drain route," he began. "There were many escapes through the rainwater canals until the Communists got wise and bolted the manhole covers leading to them. There was no way to get into the canals on the eastern side. But," he said, then paused for effect, "the canals *still* flow under the streets and to West Berlin, and they certainly aren't bolting them on the other side. So . . . *if* you could get into the storm drains, the underground route is still there. It's just a matter of gaining access on this side."

"And Hermann knows of a way?" asked Sabina.

"Possibly—that is, the other fellow may."

Again he paused before launching into the specifics of the scheme.

"A huge office and apartment building went up in the mid 1930s, which, as it happens, now sits about half a kilometer on the eastern side of the wall. There were two levels of basements, one a parking garage, the lower for storage and maintenance facilities, which, as the man recalls it, created a problem in the construction phase because during the winter months the lowest of these levels could occasionally find itself below the water table. Provision was made, therefore, for a large sump pump to keep the basement dry. A huge collection tank sat underground that gradually would fill with the draining groundwater. When it was full, the water was pumped directly into the nearest rainwater canal, which, coincidentally, ran directly beneath the street adjacent to the building.

"Anyway, the long and the short of it is this: If his memory is correct, the line leading from the building's collection tank to the rainwater canal is sixty centimeters in diameter—just big enough for people to squeeze through. Once inside, it would be a thirty-, maybe a forty-meter crawl until it opens into the city's storm drain. From there, it's a five-hundred-meter slosh until you're safely past Esplanadestrasse. Then all we'd have to do is find the next open manhole cover up and into West Berlin!"

Matthew stopped.

The expressions on the faces of his listeners did not register enthusiasm or confidence. However much they had understood of his detailed explanation, they knew it sounded difficult at best.

"There is much that could go wrong," said Josef at length.

Matthew nodded.

"Hermann was very clear about that also."

"What exactly are the risks?" asked Baron von Dortmann, his practical nature now asserting itself.

"For one thing, gaining access to the basement would be difficult. There are a few governmental offices on the lower floors, and all it would take was one suspicious and grasping clerk to make one phone call. The man doesn't remember for certain where access to the sump pump maintenance room is, so that would be an unknown. And once we made it into the maintenance room, presuming we could actually open and get inside the collection tank, we'd have to lower ourselves down into the water, and then crawl through the narrow pipe. If our timing was off and if somehow the pump activated when we were inside it, we'd drown before we could get out."

"Unless the force of the water pushed you through into the rainwater canal," suggested Josef.

"I suppose that is possible, but then we'd be in bad shape . . . and there could be injuries from falling at the end of the short drain, which is probably at the top of the canal. That brings up another point—he said there may be a sealed door at the end of the drain that is only opened when the sump pump activates, so as to prevent backflow from coming up into the building. If that door couldn't be forced open, we'd be trapped inside, unable to go forward without the pump active. Then the water flow would drown us."

Matthew let out a long breath.

"It's a risky plan, all right."

"What does Hermann say?" asked Sabina.

"The same thing—that it's risky."

"Does he think we could make it?"

"He says he's tried even more harebrained ideas and they've worked. But one slip-up and we'd be dead. Even if something went wrong and we got back out into the basement of the building, we'd probably be soaking wet and filthy. We'd be an obvious invitation for investigation by the first *Vopo* we met, and they're on every street corner in that part of the city."

"What does the other man think—the old fellow that knows about it?"

"Hermann says he's cautiously optimistic. He's doing the final preparations now, seeing what more he can learn about the layout of the place. Today, in fact, he was going to the building disguised as a maintenance man to see if he could gain access to the maintenance room and find out more about the pump, the sealed door, and anything else he could."

Sabina looked at her father with an expression of question, concern, and a hint of fear.

"If we want to go," Matthew went on, "Hermann will help us, but we've got to be ready at a moment's notice. He said he knew how to get in touch with Brumfeldt and he would notify us the moment it was on. But we'd have to leave for the city immediately, and we obviously wouldn't be able to take a thing with us."

Again glances of somber question went around the room.

"There is a great deal of prayer that must go into our decision," said the baron after a long pause.

"I want to go," said Angela. "I've been praying for any way to get to my husband again, and . . . I want to go."

∞ 30 ∞
Reserved Reunion

When Lola Reinhardt glanced back to see her boss walking into *Stasi* headquarters only moments behind her, a most peculiar sensation of detachment was her only reaction.

A year before, after so long a period of not seeing him, her heart would have been set to fluttering, and it would have been with great difficulty that she would have been able to concentrate on her work the rest of the day.

Now, however, after the first glance of recognition, she turned and continued on inside the building and up to the section chief's office. She was neither happy to see him nor unhappy. On the way up the stairs the question arose in her mind why she had reacted so differently, but even in facing the question she could mount no serious thought beyond lethargic disinterest.

Gustav caught up with her just as they were entering the office.

"Much to do, Fräulein Reinhardt!" he said, as if they had last spoken but ten minutes before.

She acknowledged his comment and continued into her office.

"You do not seem glad to see me today, Lola," commented Gustav with a raised eyebrow, pausing to remove his coat before going on into his own office, eyeing his longtime secretary and loyal assistant as he did so. He had within seconds noted a change in her, but was, for a thousand reasons, altogether incapable of identifying its source.

"I . . . I—of course I am happy to see you again, Herr Section Chief," Lola stammered awkwardly. "I'm sorry if it seems otherwise."

"You seem preoccupied, Lola," persisted Gustav, his years of training as an agent now unconsciously directed toward his own secretary, though he had no idea he had assumed the skeptically questioning tone.

"There is nothing, Herr Section Chief."

"Herr *Section Chief*? You haven't called me that in years, Lola." In reality it was what she usually called him, but on this day, for some reason it sounded to Gustav's ear stiff and formal and did not resonate well with the unease he had already begun to sense in the atmosphere of his office.

"I am sorry . . . Herr von Schmundt."

"Surely we have worked together too many years for all that formality, Lola," Gustav went on with a broad smile. "You may call me Gustav."

"I . . . I will try, Herr von Schmundt."

"There, you see—you have forgotten already! But never mind, Lola, as I said, we have much to attend to today."

He continued on into his office, threw his coat onto a vacant chair, and strode to his desk, where he stood a moment perusing the contents of its surface.

"Herr Galanov is back in Berlin," he heard Lola from the doorway.

He glanced up, then nodded with interest at the information.

"I see . . . good . . . yes, that will be very helpful," he replied slowly. "When did he arrive?"

"Two or three days ago, Herr von Schmundt. He asked where you were, but I—"

"Of course, you didn't know. I understand. Will he be in today?"

"He has come in every morning, Herr von Schmundt."

"Good. Well, while we are awaiting him, will you begin to accumulate all the files we have from the past several years on the underground activity we have been monitoring?"

Lola nodded, then turned back into her office to begin putting together the requested information. If only her boss knew that the most complete file of all was contained within the brain of one whom he saw nearly every day but had been completely oblivious to all these years. Even as she began to pull the folders from various files in both her and Gustav's offices, Lola could not help reliving her own private investigation and what had resulted from it. Not that it mattered much anyway. Section Chief Schmundt had discovered the girl alive even without her help. But that day, standing on the bridge above the river, had been a turning point for her nonetheless.

That a change had come Lola knew within the first hour of her boss's return. That her own heart now all of a sudden seemed so dead toward him was alarming at first. Like all timid natures who have spent their lifetime in a cocoon, she first interpreted a change as indicating something wrong within her. She could not yet realize that the change was caused rather by the great Right of the universe reordering her responses and reactions according to the straight, precise warp and woof of the heavenly grid rather than the disorganized jumble by which men of earthly outlook futilely attempt to weave the cloth of what they call their perspective.

The lines within that grid of response were tightening and straightening and coming into parallel within Lola, and suddenly Gustav seemed so much different from even just the few weeks ago when she had last seen him.

Petty and irksome he appeared to her now, and not nearly so handsome as she had always imagined him. His tone was peevish at times, arrogant and self-righteous at others. He carried himself with an altogether unbecoming swagger of feigned importance.

She had always considered him an important man. Now she wondered why. His position was important, it was true. But now all of a sudden he seemed so . . . so small in her eyes, so small in the ways of manhood that now suddenly mattered to Lola like they had never mattered before.

Meanwhile, Gustav went about his own search for every scrap from the old files he could lay his hands on.

His thoughts, too, centered around the change in his secretary, but now pursued far different channels of inquiry. The look in her eye caused a certain discomfort to stir within him. He didn't like change when he couldn't control it.

Suddenly it dawned on him.

He spun around and glanced through the door at his secretary busy in the office next to his. The other offices were now filling with operatives and agents and secretaries of his section, but she seemed oblivious to it all, with an expression of distraction upon her face.

Surely that was it! he said to himself.

The woman is in love with young Galanov!

He smiled at first, then with great effort had to choke down a laugh that wanted to burst from his lips at the idiocy of it.

She was easily fifteen years his senior and ugly as a cow! The thing was so laughable as to be absurd. What did the bubble-headed vixen think—that an attractive young man like Galanov, and a Russian to boot, was going to run off with the likes of a fool such as her!

Reining in the humor of the ludicrousness of it all, now Gustav found annoyance replacing it. He could not exactly have said why, but it irritated him that the woman—though of course he had never had the slightest interest in her himself—would find another man more attractive than she did him. If she was going to fall in love with anyone, he thought, why did she not have the good sense to fall in love with him? The fact that he would have shown her so little consideration if such had been the case—as it indeed had been, to his own self-preoccupied oblivion—in nowise precluded in Gustav's mind that one such as Lola ought to fall in love with him if she was going to fall in love with anyone.

He was unable to prosecute his tangled mental query further, however, for just then the second object of his thoughts entered the outer office.

∽ 31 ∽
Back on the Hunt

"Guten tag, *Herr von Schmundt!*" Galanov greeted the *Stasi* chief
with strong emphasis and a broad smile. "Hello again, Lola," he
added, still smiling, to the secretary. She nodded and returned
the smile.

The two men shook hands.

"Welcome back to Berlin, Galanov," rejoined Gustav, trying
to sound as upbeat as the young Russian, though with difficulty. "It has been many months since you were taken from us."

"The months have treated you well," said Galanov smoothly.

"And you," rejoined Gustav. "It would appear you are none
the worse for the unfortunate accident of last August."

"Fully recovered! I feel very good. And you?"

"Never better!" lied Gustav. He had, in fact, never quite felt
himself again, though he hid it admirably.

Gustav had observed the friendly exchange between Galanov
and his secretary, and it exacerbated his annoyance. He did not
like finding himself on the outside of a supposed intimacy and
shared relationship of confidence—especially right in his own
office.

His irritation mounted, directed now toward Galanov, who,
he supposed, must have done something in the last few days to
inveigle his way into the woman's affections.

Nor did it help that the young Russian seemed so bold, so
outspoken, so confident. It had only been three or four months
since he had seen him, but the fellow seemed to have added
three or four years to his stature. Gustav didn't like his new
bearing and manly carriage. He had half a mind to send him
straight back to Moscow!

His thoughts, however, were interrupted by the young KGB
agent.

"Well, I am anxious to be back under your command," now
lied Galanov in his turn.

Both men were skilled in two of the fundamental necessities
of Communist advancement—never divulge a weakness or an
emotion, and manipulate others to your own advantage at every

opportunity. Galanov, notwithstanding his years, was fast becoming a master at the latter and was destined to go far. He had determined to play the loyal lackey to Schmundt with even more servility this time around, hoping thereby to gain an even greater level of trust and thus in time give his uncle everything he desired. His uncle was the key to his future, not this bewildered fool of a German.

"Yes . . . uh—well, your arrival is . . . uh, well timed," replied Gustav, hesitating momentarily. He did need help right now, and the fellow had shown himself resourceful. He would send him back to Russia after he had Sabina in his clutches and the baron and McCallum in prison.

"How so?" asked Galanov, removing his coat and taking a chair. He knew far more than he was letting on, for he had been watching Schmundt's cat-and-mouse game with his prey for over two months.

"The American has made contact with the two Dortmanns," answered Gustav. "They were last seen in Magdeburg, and every indication is that they are heading this way; perhaps they are in Berlin even now, as we speak."

Gustav did not add that no one, least of all himself, had actually seen a one of them, nor that he had, in fact, lost track of them altogether and had been unable to uncover so much as a scrap of evidence in Magdeburg. He also failed to mention that he had nothing else to do but return to the capital and regroup his efforts. He hoped the fugitives were bound for Berlin, and in this particular case, Gustav's instincts happened to serve him well.

"It is imperative that we reactivate every file of all known underground activity in and around Berlin. They have led me on a wild goose chase these last months. But now that McCallum is with them, I have no doubt they are heading for the border."

"How do you think they will attempt to cross?"

"That I am not certain of. But we will interrogate every known associate with the underground. We will follow every lead. We will pressure all possible religious groups that may have some connection. We will rattle and lean and pressure until we learn what we need to. Something will turn up. We will outwit these people."

His inner vexation at the two now subsiding in the heat of the hunt, Gustav turned to Lola.

"Fräulein Reinhardt," he said, forgetting already the momentary closer approach, "In addition to what I said before, I want you to gather all the files and dossiers on anyone and everyone who might possibly provide a connection with these people: Christian groups, the Jewish underground, that network we heard about having something to do with a flower, the JDC, that fellow Hildebrand's organization. See, too, if you can discover anything where stamps might be a clue or a password. I got onto a network of traitors in Magdeburg that had to do with stamps, but I had no time to pursue it further. Bring everything to my office, and we will begin going through it all again with a fine-tooth comb. Somewhere in these files we will find the very individual the fugitives will contact—I know it."

He turned now to the young Russian agent.

"Galanov," he said, "I want you to go down to that region where we had our—*ahem* . . . our, uh . . . unfortunate accident. That region, I'm certain of it, is crawling with conspirators in this thing. What's the name of the village, Fräulein?" he asked, turning toward Lola.

"Grossbeeren," she replied. She caught herself immediately, realizing she could easily divulge that she knew far more about the so-called conspirators south of Berlin than either of the two men. She in fact knew every name that could possibly have any connection with the Dortmann escape whatever. But an inner reluctance held her back. Those people were her fellow countrymen, and she wasn't sure she was prepared quite yet to turn them over to the wicked devices the *Stasi* and KGB were capable of when they wanted information and didn't care what it took to get it.

Gustav, however, noticed not in the least her hasty reply to his question.

"Ah yes—Grossbeeren. Galanov, once the files are accumulated here—later today—you drive down there—tomorrow morning—and pay a personal visit to every name we have. Show some anger. Put the fear of prison into them. Rough up those farmers. I want information, and *someone* down there has it! Take a room. Call me the moment you are in place so that I will be able to reach you in case anything breaks here. Let your presence be felt. Spread the word that the *Stasi* is in town and will pay for information. Some lowlife will come forward. For a few marks those peasants would snitch on their own mother.

"Meanwhile, I will be busy here in the city. I will call upon all the old names from here. I have had an informant in place for some time who may still help us. And there is word about a man who arranges escapes. The *Vopos* have been zeroing in on him with an investigation of their own. I shall see what they have that might have links to the people in our files. It will be a good opportunity for the city police and the state police to work together. I might even garner some political benefits if we can crack this thing," he added with a smile, warming up to the prospects again after the recent string of demoralizing defeats.

He looked at the other two.

"So . . . are we clear?"

They both nodded.

"Then let's jump into these files. Go over every centimeter with care. Scrutinize every name and connection on the list. Use my office if you need to. I am going to pay a personal visit to the *Vopo* chief to see what he has on the fellow I mentioned."

So saying, he picked up his coat, then turned and left the building.

∽ 32 ∾
Neighbors

The familiar streets of the great German city sent more mixed emotions through Sabina's frame than she knew what to do with.

She had lived in Berlin so long and walked these streets so many times . . . back and forth to work on the other side . . . then the happy times last summer with Matthew, when these same streets took on such a happy and fairy-tale glow.

He had made her so happy, Sabina thought. How could one

person make another so happy! She had asked him—she had asked herself—that very question over and over.

Now it had all changed.

She had not been here since last August. Then she had been, if not exactly free, certainly free by today's standards. Every day she had walked over and back across the virtually invisible line separating East and West. Now that line was marked by a wall of division and death. Whatever freedom they had enjoyed back then was altogether gone now.

She walked on, the surroundings of streets and buildings and homes becoming increasingly familiar. This had been her neighborhood, although she had never taken much time to consider it such when she made her home here. It had seemed so cold and lifeless. Now it almost seemed inviting.

There it was, just ahead—the house she had lived in so long!

How drab it seemed now. It was probably unchanged, Sabina thought, yet during the past months of hiding out in one place after another, the old house in Berlin had seemed increasingly like a mansion in her memory.

It was a week after Matthew's return from the city.

Hermann had telephoned Erich late last night with instructions. The escape was set for today.

She was to meet Hermann near here, as she had so many times before, when they had exchanged furtive words in order to do their work helping others.

Now she and her father and Matthew were the ones for whom the daring plan had been devised.

With slow step she approached the house, paused a moment to take it in, unaware that inside her former apartment a set of eyes was observing her approach through a slit in the drawn curtains, and then walked up onto the veranda and knocked lightly on the door next to the one that had once been hers.

A minute or two passed.

Then she heard footsteps inside approaching. The door opened slowly, but only a crack, revealing a head crowned with pure white hair.

A gasp of pleasure sounded from inside.

"Fräulein Duftblatt!" exclaimed the occupant.

"Gerta!" said Sabina with a warm smile, "it is so wonderful to see you again."

"But what . . . oh—come in . . . please come in!" cried the astonished old woman, eyes already flowing with tears. "I never . . . I never thought . . ."

She could not complete the sentence.

Sabina followed her inside. She closed the door, but then, recovering her wits, and along with them her well-seasoned East German caution, she added: "But we must speak softly, Fräulein. The walls have ears."

"Oh, Gerta, are you all right? Are you well provided for?"

"I manage, Fräulein. But I have no one, you know—only my cousin . . . on the other side."

Sabina nodded.

"I can only stay a moment, Gerta. There are some people I must meet very soon. But I wanted to see you again, so that you would not worry about me . . . and to say good-bye."

"*Good-bye*, Fräulein?" said the old lady, repeating the words with questioning significance.

"Yes, Gerta. It is doubtful I will be back to Berlin again. I could not leave without seeing you once more."

Gerta smiled.

"You always were so kind. And . . . the young man? Did he find you?"

"Yes, Gerta," smiled Sabina. "He is well."

It fell silent. The visit had been far too brief, but Sabina knew she must go.

She embraced the old woman. Both wept. Sabina stood back.

Gerta's eyes sought and found hers, and in that instant she first understood.

"Fräulein Duftblatt, please," she said. "Please . . . take me with you."

"Oh, Gerta—"

"Please . . . I will come with you this instant as I am. There is nothing here for me to live for."

"Gerta . . . I'm sorry," said Sabina, heartbroken, "I am not the one who may say . . . there are others . . . it will be very dangerous."

She turned to go, sick at the fleeting hope of freedom she had aroused in the poor old woman's heart.

She opened the door, then turned back, tears still standing in her own eyes.

"Ask them—please ask them, Fräulein," implored Gerta one final time, "ask them to let me go with you!"

"I will ask, Gerta," promised Sabina. "I will ask."

The two women embraced again, and wept again briefly, then Sabina turned and left down the few steps quickly. Painful partings were of the fabric of life here. No wonder people wanted to get out any way they could.

As sad, lonely old Gerta Arnim closed the door behind her young friend and former neighbor and then sat down in her chair to weep softly at the hopelessness of her plight, through the walls—which, as she had truthfully declared, possessed ears of their own—in the apartment that had once been Sabina's, the occupant was already at the phone.

It took several minutes for the requested number to be reached.

Quickly and nervously she conveyed her message, then listened to a series of questions.

"I . . . I do not know for certain that it is the woman, *Herr Aufsichtsbeamte*—"

A rude expletive on the other end cut her short.

". . . those were the very words—'let me go with you.'"

A pause followed, while she listened.

"Yes . . . very close to the description you gave—"

Another question on the other end.

"Very beautiful, *Herr Aufsichtsbeamte*."

Another question.

"*Nein*. . . . I do not know where she went. . . . She was walking. . . . No, no auto. . . . Along the street. . . . I did not see the direction after that."

This time she heard no question in her ear, only the voice of command.

"If I locate her?"

A final command summarily ended the call.

The nervous stoolie picked up her coat and went outside,

timid to comply with the order she had just been given, yet terrified to disobey.

If only her husband were home, she thought. He would know better how to do this.

∽ 33 ∽
Hermann

It was ten minutes later when Sabina heard the heavy footsteps she recognized from many such meetings coming up behind her. In a moment or two Hermann was at her side, still staring straight ahead as if nothing were out of the ordinary.

"Where have you been, Karin? You are late," was his abrupt greeting.

Struggling to keep moving forward without showing her emotions too greatly, Sabina yet could not refrain from expressing them.

"Oh, Hermann . . . it's so good to hear your voice again!"

"Never mind all that—why are you late? Is something wrong?"

"No, Hermann, nothing is wrong. I stopped for a moment at my house."

"Why?" he barked, still staring ahead.

"To see it—to see Gerta."

"You should not have done that, Karin."

Sabina could not keep from smiling. Herman was so stiff and businesslike, but she knew a warm heart beat inside his chest, otherwise why would he take such risks for people he did not know? He had been doing so for years, all the while pretending to be a gruff and unfeeling man.

"She will say nothing," said Sabina.

"It is not the old lady I am worried about, but others. I have suspected for some time that there is a plant in that house."

"No—"

"It has all changed, Karin. The danger has increased many times over since two years ago. Where are the others?"

"Where you told Erich to take them."

"How many?"

"Four—just the three of us and Josef Dahlmann's younger sister."

"Dahlmann himself?"

"No, he wants to stay. Perhaps he is like you, Hermann—or will you be going all the way with us?"

Something in Sabina's tone arrested the steady lumbering stride of Hermann Lamprecht. Still moving, but with slower gait, he turned and at last glanced down at her. Sabina saw the conflict her question had caused within the big man's thoughts. It was a moment or two before he answered, as if he had to rethink a decision he had already made all the way through again.

"No, Karin," he sighed at last. "It is not possible for me to go. I must remain here."

He paused, and then a slight grin broke through, a rare occurrence that brought unaccustomed movements to Hermann's facial musculature.

"Even if I wanted to," he added, "I could not accompany you today—I could not squeeze through the pipe emptying out of that sump drain if my life depended on it . . . which surely it would!"

They walked on a while in silence, utterly unaware of the hastening pace of the nervous pedestrian behind them, who had seen them from a distance and was now trying to close the gap to make certain it was the same young lady she had just reported.

"I don't understand why you wanted me to meet you alone like this," said Sabina. "Matthew is the one who ought to—"

"Orders from the fellow who's masterminded this escape—the old fellow who worked on the building. He won't work with an American, he says. He says all this is the Americans' fault for giving us over to the Russians like they did. And he'd recognize your friend's accent for American in a second. He's got the whole plan worked out, but won't give it to anyone but a German. He doesn't mind if an American goes along, but unless he saw you and talked to you face-to-face, he said he wouldn't tell me how to gain access to the pump room and deactivate the sealed door at the other end of the sump pipe."

"Isn't he going to the West with us?" asked Sabina.

Hermann shook his head. "He doesn't want to escape—not yet, at least. He just wants to see if his idea will work."

Meanwhile, two or three kilometers away, a large green military truck wound its way methodically through the streets of East Berlin toward a certain office and apartment complex located approximately half a kilometer from the Berlin wall. Its engine ran with precision, owing to the fact that it had recently been overhauled by an expert mechanic in the village of Grossbeeren. It was, in fact, not military at all. Its owner had purchased it for little more than scrap, but had not had the chance to repaint it yet, and had brought it to Dahlmann to see what could be done for it. The mechanic had had it running in no time and now took occasion to bring it into the city for an extended test drive before notifying its owner.

The fact that he was carrying precious cargo was a fact he would likely not mention to the owner . . . or to anyone else.

Ten minutes later the truck was crawling through the door and down the ramped incline into the garage underneath the building, the door clearing by less than three centimeters the top of the green cab.

Once into the parking area, Dahlmann backed into position at one of the rear corners. He was glad no one seemed to be around, looking at his entrance with suspicious eyes. Now that the truck was in position and parked, no one would question it. It did not do to ask too many questions of the military.

Now all they had to do was wait.

∽ 34 ∾
Dropping the Net

In his office, Gustav von Schmundt sat brooding over the phone call he had just received.

It had been precisely the break in this thing he had been hoping for!

The thought that Sabina was so close—it *had* to be her, according to the woman's description!—set him to trembling again. It was all he could do to keep from running out and jumping into his car. He could be at her former residence— which he had discovered, to his chagrin, too late—in ten minutes. Scouring the streets, he just might be able to find her even if the woman wasn't able to follow her as he'd ordered.

But he'd allowed his emotions to overrule his judgment too many times in the past. He simply couldn't let it happen again.

Reason had to dictate his course.

Reason told him that McCallum and the baron weren't with her. The woman had said she was alone. To pick her up alone would accomplish nothing. She would never divulge the whereabouts of the other two. In that she would be just like her father, of that he was certain. She would sooner face prison for the rest of her life than give them away. All their stupid notions of sacrifice and self-abasement!

No, he had to entrap them all together. It was the only way complete success could be assured.

Besides, by the time he could get there, Sabina would be long gone.

He pondered the words the woman had overheard again— "let me go with you . . . let me go with you!"

An escape attempt was surely on, exactly as he had suspected. And probably set for today!

There was nothing to do but to wait by the phone and hope the woman managed to get on Sabina's trail. Eventually Sabina would return to her comrades, and then he would close in on them all. Meanwhile, he'd better make certain he had plenty of manpower available. If the woman didn't turn up anything within the hour, he'd send a hundred *Vopos* out to comb the area for any trace of her. But first he'd make sure he had plenty of men ready to cut off an escape attempt, wherever it happened.

Making sure his own private line remained clear, Gustav ran out into his secretary's office, grabbed up her phone, and was soon speaking to the chief of Berlin's police force, alerting him to a possible break over the wall involving a U.S. spy and an escaped prisoner.

"I want you to have at least fifty men standing by awaiting my orders," he barked into the phone. "And double your contingent at every guard post along the wall in the center of the city! I don't know where it's going to come, but I want your men ready. I expect to receive word at any moment."

Lola was listening to every word with trembling foreboding. Why did it suddenly feel as if she were one of those being chased and hunted? Why did she all at once feel more loyalty to the unknown fugitives than to her own boss? She had been working to help him track down the three individuals he was after, and yet she could not keep from hoping they would continue to elude him.

What was happening to her? she asked herself, trying to busy herself with the files she was still poring through, but altogether distracted by the drama she knew was about to take place somewhere in this city. She even found herself secretly wishing she could be there with them, whoever and wherever they were. *Oh*—the grandness of it suddenly struck her—*what would it be like to live in the West, where there was freedom and opportunity!*

Even as Lola was thus preoccupied with her daydreams, Gustav had retreated back into his office and now sat silent again, engaged in that most tedious, maddening, and nerve-numbing exercise called waiting for the phone to ring.

It did ring, but not for twenty or thirty minutes.

Gustav leapt out of his seat as he grabbed it.

"This is Frau Dietzel," the voice identified itself.

"Yes, of course I know who you are," snapped Gustav. "Did you find her?"

"Yes, *Herr Aufsichtsbeamte.*"

"You followed?"

"Yes. She was joined by another man."

"Only one?"

"Yes."

"Describe him."

"I saw only his back. He was a large man, very tall and broad."

"How old?"

"Forty-five or fifty."

Gustav thought for a moment. It was neither McCallum nor Dortmann. There was a similarity with a partial description he had received of the fellow said to plan escapes.

"Where did they go?" he asked into the phone.

"They walked for two blocks, then a third man joined them."

"Describe him."

"He was an old man."

Hmm, it could be Dortmann, mused Gustav.

"What did they do?"

"They continued to walk. The old man's hands were making gestures, and he did all the talking."

"Did you hear anything?"

"No, I was too far back. He seemed to be giving them directions."

"For what, in heaven's name!"

"I do not know, *Herr Aufsichtsbeamte.*"

"And then?"

"The old man left them."

"And the other two?"

"They went into the basement of the Stadtplatz Building. I then came to call you."

"Where are you now, Frau Dietzel?"

"Across the street."

"You can see the entrance to the basement of the building?"

"Yes, *mein Herr.*"

"But they have not come out?"

"No."

"Is there anything else I should know?"

"The old man was carrying something. When he left he gave it to the large man."

"What was it, woman? Don't play games with me!"

"I cannot be certain, *mein Herr*—it seemed to be a pair of waist-high fishing boots."

"And . . . what did he do with them?"

"The big man carried them with him . . . into the basement of the building."

Gustav hung up the phone. Now what was he to do?

He could seal off the building and search every room. But there would still be no guarantee McCallum and Dortmann would be there. Still, he smiled to himself, it would be high satisfaction to have Sabina at last.

Suddenly a great jolt ran through him.

He leapt from his chair and bounded to the wall where was mounted a detailed map of the entirety of Berlin. In an instant he located the building the woman had mentioned. His finger probed all around it, and toward *der Mauer.*

There could be no question . . . that had to be it! The building sat practically on top of it!

They were about to try for the Ragenwasser-Kanal under Esplanadestrasse!

He spun around, his brain spinning wildly.

But they had replaced every open grating in the city with bolted iron covers. There was no access to the rainwater drains from above.

Unless . . .

The building . . . the boots—

Unless there was access from inside the basement of the Stadtplatz directly into the underground storm drains!

That must be it!

What should he do? If they stormed the building, they might be too late.

He would intercept them in the canal itself!

"Reinhardt . . . Reinhardt!" he cried. "Get Public Works on your line . . . hold them for me!"

Even as he spoke he had picked up his own phone again and in a few moments again had the *Vopo* chief.

"Order those men I requested to stand by along Esplanadestrasse at the guard station!" he cried. "I will deploy them from there!"

He rushed out of his office and grabbed the waiting call from Lola's hand, issuing a similar order to the public utilities commissioner regarding the removal of the storm drain covers.

"No, tomorrow will not do, you imbecile!" he shrieked. "I will be there in five minutes and will expect your people there before I arrive. This is immediate priority; do you understand!"

He threw down the phone and stormed from the office, leaving Lola a nervous wreck. If the poor woman had known how to pray, now would have been the time to call upon that most elemental function of the human constitution. Though had she prayed, it would not have been for her superior's success, but that his enemies would somehow escape his detection.

That she did not know how to pray, however, did not prevent her heavenly Father from hearing the cry of her heart. He had already heard, even before that cry left her, and was already taking steps to give heed to it.

Flying from the building, Gustav thought briefly of the helicopter on the roof. He didn't like using it in the city, however. There were too many buildings and wires and towers.

It wasn't far. The car would be just as fast.

Besides all that, he'd almost been killed the last time he was in a helicopter, and he'd been afraid of them ever since.

⚮ 35 ⚮
A Wet Path toward Freedom

Josef Dahlmann was the first to see Sabina and Hermann walking down into the lower portion of the parking garage from his vantage point inside the truck.

He jumped out and met them as they approached.

"Anyone around?" Hermann asked, glancing about.

Josef shook his head.

"You two wait here with the others," said Hermann, handing Dahlmann the boots. "I'll go down to the maintenance level to make sure the way is clear into the sump room. The fellow says it's unmanned, but I want to make sure before we troop down there like sitting ducks."

He turned and disappeared through a door in the corner of the basement behind the truck.

Sabina and Josef stood out of sight, waiting.

Three minutes later Hermann reappeared, retrieved the boots, and signalled them to come.

Josef untied a cord and threw back a corner flap of the canvas covering the bed of the truck. Matthew jumped down, followed by Angela. He and Josef now helped Baron von Dortmann down to the floor.

"Follow me," said Hermann to the escapees. "Dahlmann, you'd better get this truck out of here."

"I'm staying until I know they're safe," replied Josef.

Hermann stopped and turned back.

"You and I won't know if they're safe. Once they're into that drain, they're on their own. There's nothing we can do for them then."

"But if something goes wrong—"

"If something goes wrong, my friend," said Hermann with a somber tone, "then all you're going to accomplish by remaining behind is to get thrown into prison with them. Get that truck out of here."

"I'm not moving until I know they're safe."

"Suit yourself," said Hermann. "But once I've got them on their way, none of you will see me again."

He turned and continued on, leading the small band—who were now far more nervous than before—down the stairs to the lowest underground level of the building, while Josef climbed back into the cab of the truck, then lay down on the seat so as not to be seen in case anyone did happen by.

They arrived at the maintenance level and, as expected, there was no one to question their presence. Within another three minutes they were inside the sump maintenance room.

"Bolt that door shut behind us," Hermann said to Matthew while he began the cumbersome process of climbing into the waist-high boots. A minute later he was unfastening the clamps that held on the iron lid of the collection tank.

He pulled it off with great effort and set it with a dull *clank* onto the concrete floor. Peering inside the great black cavity that yawned below, he said, "Well, my friends, there is your watery tunnel to freedom. Hand me that flashlight over there."

Matthew glanced around, located it, and did so.

Hermann sent the light downward. All five heads peered down in a semicircle to see the light dancing off the reflection from the top of the water.

"Tank looks to be about half full," said Hermann. "That should give you plenty of time to get out into the canal before it starts to overflow. Hold that light for me. . . . I'm going down."

Matthew took the light from his hand, and the next instant Hermann had disappeared and could be heard sloshing in the tank.

"Hold the light toward the pump here."

Matthew adjusted it.

"How deep is it?" asked Sabina, leaning her head over the lip of the opening.

"Just below my waist," came the echo of Hermann's reply. "The rest of you may get a little wet. But then once you get up on the other side, it won't matter if you leave a trail behind you. But I can't go walking out of here with boots and pants sloshing or I'll lead the *Vopos* straight to me!"

Everyone waited another minute or two.

"All right," they heard Hermann say. "I think I've got it. The pump should go on long enough just to loosen the hatch at the far end. Then I'll cut it off while the rest of you get through. McCallum, you'd better get going."

Matthew handed Sabina the flashlight and lowered himself down into the chilly water.

"Watch him, the rest of you," said Hermann. "Follow exactly as he goes. You don't have to come down all the way, just enough to ease yourselves into the drain line here at the top."

They watched as Matthew now scooted out of sight.

"McCallum," called Hermann, "call out when you've reached the door. You'll get doused, but get the door open, then get yourself out into the main canal. Then I'll send the others."

Four or five tense moments followed.

At last a muffled cry, as if from a kilometer away, could be heard.

"Hold your breath, McCallum!" Hermann called into the drain line.

He lifted the ball valve, and with a sudden great sucking sound the pump went on and a rush of water flooded the drain from below, nearly drowning Hermann as well as Matthew at the other end. It lasted less than a second before Hermann released it.

The sound of the pump went off, and the sloshing water in the collection tank jostled back and forth until it began to settle itself.

Again they waited.

"Got it!" they heard Matthew cry from the other end. "I'm in the canal . . . let's go to West Berlin!"

"All right, who's next?" said Hermann. "No time to lose."

"Papa . . . ?" said Sabina.

The baron glanced at his daughter. They both took in a deep breath of expectancy, then the baron climbed over into the tank of water.

"It'll be a difficult crawl, Baron," said Hermann, "and dark. But it's not long—McCallum's at the other end . . . he'll help you out. Next."

Sabina looked to Angela and nodded.

"Go ahead, Angela—your husband is waiting for you."

Angela smiled, then began her descent.

Finally Sabina climbed over the edge and into the chilly water. She paused only long enough to gaze one final time at her longtime ally.

"Thank you, Hermann," she said. "I will never forget you."

She bent over, kissed him lightly on the cheek, then turned to worm her own way into the round pipe behind Angela.

"Karin," said Hermann. "Take this."

He handed her the flashlight.

"I wouldn't want you to lose your way to West Berlin," he added. She knew he was smiling, and it warmed her heart. "Just follow the flow of the water once you're inside the main canal. When you see open gratings above you, try them to find out if they're open. If so, climb out and you will have done it!"

"Thank you, Hermann," Sabina repeated.

Then she turned and disappeared into the drain after the others.

ᘓ 36 ᘓ
Section Chief and Secretary

Gustav had arrived at the guard station near the street called Esplanade only moments after a transport truck had pulled up and two dozen green-uniformed *Vopo* troops of the city police poured out of the back of it.

With tires screeching, he half skidded to something less than a controlled stop, jumped out, and ran forward to take charge. Another truck was just pulling up, and within a few more seconds, *Vopos* were scattering in all directions—some to bolster the guard contingent at the wall itself, others stationed along Esplanadestrasse, and all instructed to take the prisoners alive if at all possible, but to shoot if it became necessary—but they were not to shoot the woman under any circumstances.

The engineers from Utilities had by then arrived and moments later had dispersed to the three nearest of the bolted drain covers. Gustav sent a half dozen men to each of the other two, took another half dozen with him to that closest the Stadtplatz, and in less than three minutes was lowering himself down into the wet, grimy rainwater canal that ran below the city.

Once his feet were firmly planted in the water at the bottom of the giant underground tunnel, he pulled out his flashlight . . . and his gun.

∽ᴗᴄ∾

Lola Reinhardt had watched her superior bolt from the office, then found her chair and sat down, staring ahead with wide eyes of disbelief.

What had become of her that she felt more empathy toward total strangers than she felt toward a man she thought she loved just a few short months ago?

What had become of Section Chief Schmundt that he could feel such hatred and desire such vengeance upon people whom, if what she had surmised was true, he had once been close to?

What had become of this country, that it could have allowed itself to sink to such depths that, at the very heart of its greatest city, countrymen killed countrymen upon orders from Russian strangers and interlopers? If they had ever been a superior race, as some maintained, surely the elite of the DDR now showed themselves inferior by such bestiality.

This had become a dreadful place, where guns and revenge and strangers ruled. There was no freedom here!

How could she not have seen it before! How could she have been so asleep to all this evil?

As she sat that day, Lola Reinhardt crossed a quiet threshold of decision. She was not sure exactly when the moment came or what had been the progression of her thoughts. But when she rose from her chair five minutes later, it was with the determination that, if opportunity ever presented itself . . . she would leave this place.

She did not know how, she did not know when, but henceforth she would keep her eyes and ears open.

Before she rose, however, she found her thoughts again drawn, as if by some deep spiritual magnet, to those individuals—whoever they were—who were now in such danger . . . more danger than they were even aware.

Without thinking of it, she suddenly blurted forth the words from her lips, *"God . . . keep them safe . . . help them get to freedom!"*

◦~ 37 ~◦
Underground Trap

Matthew stood in the blackness, shivering and soaked from head to toe, listening behind him to the sounds of the others whispering and squirming in the small pipe he had just left.

The brief discharge from the collection tank had thoroughly doused his body. But the brief activation of the pump had also released the lock of the backwash door. The moment he felt it give way, he shoved it open, scrambled through into the large cavity of the rainwater canal into which the sump pump regularly emptied its contents, and now stood holding the small door open for the others to crawl through behind him.

"Here we are, Baron," he said as he felt the baron's head now next to him. "Get your arms out of the pipe . . . good . . . now hold onto my shoulders—that's it . . . steady . . . here, take my free hand . . . it's about a four-foot jump down—I mean, a bit over a meter . . . easy . . . good—you're down."

"Not exactly how I envisioned spending my later years, my boy!" laughed the baron.

"This is no time for jokes," rejoined Matthew, laughing with him, feeling the exhilaration of the fact that, after all this time, they were only five hundred meters from freedom at last.

"Here, Baron," he said, "hold open this round door while I help the girls out. Hands up above your head . . . that's it. If it becomes too much for you, let me know—it's very heavy and is trying to close now that the pump is off. Here comes Angela!"

So saying, Matthew helped the young wife down, more easily, because of her weight and agility, than the baron. The next moment Sabina's light shone through the small door they were continuing to force open, and a few seconds later all four of the pilgrims were standing at the bottom of the larger canal.

"We've got to wedge something into that door to keep it from sealing shut again," said Matthew.

"Why?" asked Sabina. "We're not going back in there!"

"Just in case. I don't like the thought of cutting off our only escape route, and once this door is shut, it won't open again unless that sump pump is emptying that storage container of several thousand liters of water pouring through the pipe with such force we wouldn't stand a chance against it."

Matthew glanced around hurriedly, then in a swift motion ripped off his shirt.

"This isn't doing me much good all wet anyway . . ."

Wadding it into a compact mass, he stuffed it tightly against the hinge of the round door, then let the door go.

"Looks like that'll hold it—all right, let's go to West Berlin!"

With Sabina still holding the flashlight and Matthew leading the way, they began walking in the direction the ten or fifteen centimeters of water they were standing in was flowing.

The Ragenwasser-Kanal, one of several canals throughout the city that had led hundreds to freedom in the first months after the wall had gone up, was only four-and-a-half or five feet high, although in places it rose to over six, which necessitated walking stooped and watching out for one's head. The winter runoff in which they walked was only slightly above freezing, and before long toes and ankles were numb. It was dirty everywhere, and though it was dark and they couldn't see what a state they were in, all four were covered with mud and grime. They took consolation, however, in the fact that the smell of the place was not overpowering. At least it was not a sewer drain that must be used!

They had not gone far before Matthew suddenly stopped.

"Shh!" he said behind him.

"What is it, Matthew?" asked Sabina.

"Shh . . . quiet!" he whispered in a commanding tone. "Stay here. . . . Sabina, turn out the light."

He crept forward.

The canal made a long, gradual bend toward the right. Keeping close to its right wall, trying to see past it without being visible himself, Matthew walked on, quietly, out of sight of his companions, in blackness now, feeling his way along the rough right wall of the canal with his hand.

Suddenly he stopped.

His heart leapt into his throat.

Ahead, around the further bend of the tunnel, he saw fragments of light in the darkness, the unmistakable evidence of a jostling beam from a handheld lantern or flashlight.

Voices now began to echo in the distance accompanying it.

He turned and instantly began as hasty a retreat as he dared!

Without light to guide him, and with Sabina's light off, he nearly crashed into her two minutes later.

"Matthew, what is—"

"We've got company!" he whispered.

"Who . . . but—"

"No time—turn around, get going . . . back! Quickly . . . but quietly!"

The other three obeyed, and immediately they were sloshing back the way they had come, hearts pounding. Matthew took the light from Sabina, passed her, and now led his small band back to the wedged door through which they had just tumbled moments earlier.

Sending the beam of light frantically about the walls, Matthew at last located the door and stopped.

"I don't know who it is back there," he said, "but whoever it is didn't sound friendly!"

"Maybe it's other people trying to escape," suggested Angela.

"We can't take that chance. And it's unlikely. Back into the pipe, everyone! Sabina, can you try to hold that door open— take my shirt out of there—wide enough for me to help your father up?"

Matthew turned off the light, stuffed it into his back pocket, and made a makeshift step with his hands. The baron stepped and climbed up, and with some squirming on his part and shoving from behind, was soon spread out on his length inside the sixty-centimeter pipe leading back into the basement of the Stadtplatz Building.

Angela was right behind him.

Then came the most difficult part of all. Matthew knew that if they accidentally allowed the door to close, he would be trapped inside the canal with no way of escape. And the others would be trapped inside the pipe with no way to get back to him if whoever he heard did prove friendly to their attempt.

Once the trapdoor was shut, there would be no more movement through it in either direction. He had to keep it from sealing itself shut!

Holding the door with one hand, he did his best to help Sabina up and into the pipe. It was an effort, but at last she was inside.

Now he had to get up, without help . . . and without allowing the door accidentally to clang shut!

"Sabina . . . Sabina—can you hear me?" he whispered.

"Yes," came a muffled echo from inside the pipe.

"See if you can hold your foot against the door . . . keep it open while I try to get up."

She did so.

It was with great difficulty that Matthew scrambled up after her. He had nothing to hold on to to gain leverage or a foothold, and his hands and feet were wet.

"Scoot on a little farther," he said to Sabina. "I think I'm wedged into the door enough myself."

She did so.

Along the canal behind him, Matthew heard voices approaching now, louder and close.

Booted footsteps sloshing through the water were running.

Light shone behind him. . . . He heard yells and shouts.

Frantically grabbing at Sabina's ankles, he pulled with all his might and struggled up the rest of the way into the pipe, wriggling forward on his belly.

Matthew remembered, however, even in the midst of the

danger, that once the door was shut behind them, their route of escape to the West was cut off forever.

In the building Hermann would be gone by now. There were no second chances. Josef was probably gone from the garage too. If they could just wait out the danger, they could make another attempt.

So reasoning with himself in the seconds it took for him to climb into the pipe, Matthew inched forward, keeping his feet firmly against the trapdoor behind him, allowing the pressure of its automatic closing mechanism to close it all the way down to within one or two centimeters of sealing shut.

There he held it, barely unlocked, but hopefully such that it would not be noticed by whoever was now approaching them inside the canal.

All four held their breath.

In the canal where they had been only seconds before, booted feet now ran past. Matthew judged there to be five or six of them. An occasional voice sounded.

They seemed to go past.

It was silent a moment.

Now came more running footsteps. Just one man this time, it seemed to Matthew.

Voices . . . now the others that had gone on were returning this way. . . .

Crammed and wedged like sardines into the small pipe between reservoir tank and underground rain canal, the four would-be escapees were caught between two worlds and could go neither direction. Behind them, any retreat through the building or into the streets of East Berlin would be stopped by the first uniformed *Vopo* to spot them in their state. In the direction of freedom, however, sat a mechanized door that, if it shut the final two centimeters, would seal them off from the highway to West Berlin. Yet they could not open the door without revealing themselves to, Matthew now knew beyond any doubt from what he had been able to make out, guards who must have been waiting for them.

Suddenly an even more horrifying thought occurred to Matthew.

How long had it been since Hermann had climbed into the sump collection tank? How fast did it fill up?

If they lay here long enough for the tank to fill, the pump would activate and they would all be drowned like rats right here where they lay! Or had Hermann deactivated the pump once Matthew had the door open? Hadn't he said something—

It didn't matter! They couldn't take any chances. They mustn't lie here for long. They would have to make their move one way or the other.

Voices from the canal again interrupted Matthew's frantic thoughts.

No . . . How could it possibly—

He knew that voice!

He felt a tremor go through Sabina's body where his arm still touched her. She knew it too!

It was the voice of Gustav von Schmundt. He was standing less than two meters from where they lay!

Matthew had no time to reflect further, for the next instant echoed shouts told him they had discovered the trapdoor.

Lights shone in the crack his foot had kept open!

"Come out . . . come out all of you!" called Gustav's voice, clearly now. He was on the other side of the door calling to them. "We know you are in there! Don't force us to pry this open and shoot you."

It was silent a moment.

"Sabina . . ." called Gustav again, "Sabina . . . if you can hear me—give yourselves up and I will see that it goes well with you . . . Sabina, it is Gustav . . . you can trust me."

Matthew felt her shuddering, frantic with terror.

"Pry it open!" cried Gustav after waiting a second or two.

Matthew felt fingers attempting to wedge themselves into the opening at the bottom of the door so as to pry it open.

Freedom would have to wait! Their lives were more important than getting to West Berlin!

Bending his knees and gathering all the force he could muster, Matthew took a deep breath to summon every ounce of energy he had left, then with a great heaving effort shoved his feet with all their might against the round door.

He felt it crash against something, which then gave way.

For an instant the door was wide open. Light from the flashlights and lanterns behind them flooded the pipe for a split second. Had he been able to squirm around enough to see, he would have beheld Gustav's face gaping in astonishment.

But the next instant he let go with his feet and the door crashed shut—and with it their chance of freedom—with a loud, echoing, metallic clang.

Struggling to get hold of the flashlight, Matthew handed it up to Sabina.

"Sabina, get this up to your father! He will have to crawl out and into the holding tank. Tell him we are right behind him!"

Reaching back, she took the light and handed it forward to Angela, with Matthew's instructions.

"Make haste, everyone!" Matthew cried. "Now they know where we are!"

∾ 38 ∾

Close Getaway

What an unlikely place to meet Sabina again, thought Gustav as he traipsed along in the dark behind the half dozen or so *Vopo* guards to whom he'd given instructions and who were now sloshing along in front of him.

Under any other circumstances he would never have gotten down into this mess.

But this was one escape he was going to foil personally! He had been following them too long to miss out on the climax when he had them in his sights, and they all knew it . . . and had no way to escape.

He was shivering more at the moment in anticipation than from the cold in his soaking feet. He should have brought boots, but of course there had been no time.

Ahead of him, the *Vopo* patrol stopped.

"What is it?" Gustav asked.

"I thought I heard something, *mein Herr*," replied the leader.

"Like what!" barked Gustav impatiently.

"Echoes . . . steps . . . water sloshing."

"Then go after them, you idiots!" cried Gustav. "Get up there and stop them!"

The patrol turned around again and now began running around the wide leftward bend of the canal, with Gustav doing his best to keep up with them.

After another fifty meters or so they stopped again, and once more Gustav labored up behind them.

"What is it this time!"

"The tunnel is straight for many meters, *mein Herr*," replied the same man. "There is nothing to be seen. We have searched it with our lights—we can see nothing, and the sounds have ceased."

"What are you suggesting—that they escaped? They cannot have gotten out of the canal! They must be further on—keep going, I tell you!"

The patrol began to run off again.

Gustav's light fell upon the bottom of the tunnel at the edge of the right wall.

"Halt!" he cried after the others, then stooped down and picked up what appeared to be a folded-up man's shirt. Suddenly he found himself overcome with the same peculiar sensation he had had last year at that ridiculous ball the French had put on that he had attended.

The guards returned as Gustav searched up and down the walls of the tunnel with his light.

There it was . . . the door to a closed drain line, up at the very top of the wall.

He approached closer with his light, examining it all around the perimeter.

It wasn't closed at all! There was a thin slit along the bottom edge!

Suddenly the overpowering sense of Sabina's presence came over him. They were inside the drain . . . he knew it!

He sent the light of his flashlight into the crack. He could see the outline of a shoe!

"Come out . . . come out all of you!" cried Gustav into the opening. "We know you are in there! Don't force us to pry this open and shoot you."

There was no reply to his command.

"Sabina . . ." he said, "Sabina . . . if you can hear me—give yourselves up and I will see that it goes well with you . . . Sabina, it is Gustav . . . you can trust me."

Gustav waited another moment for a response. Then he stepped back and nodded toward the door to one of the *Vopos*.

"Pry it open!"

The man stepped forward, grabbed at the bottom edge of the door, and began to pull at it.

The next instant he was reeling back and crying out in pain from a punishing blow against his face and chest.

The guard staggered backward and fell. For the briefest of instants Gustav saw the open pipe with what was clearly the body of a man stretched out prone inside it. But the next it disappeared, and the Ragenwasser-Kanal sounded with the huge echo of the door's closing.

Gustav leapt forward, but one examination now told him it had been shut from the inside . . . to stay.

Spinning around, he dashed off the way they had come, shouting orders for the others to follow, heedless of the man who still lay dazed on his back in the water at the bottom of the muddy tunnel.

The traitors had only one route of escape now, and he knew exactly where it was!

~~~~~

Two minutes later Gustav was being helped from the open grating by which he had entered the canal, shouting orders to the guards who had remained above ground to seal off every door of the Stadtplatz Building.

Heedless of the mud and water dripping from his pants and shoes, he ran to his car and sped off toward the building.

He thought as he went.

Access to the drain line would be through the basement of the building. How would they hope to escape—did they have a connection inside the building?

All the exits would be sealed within minutes!

Now he remembered—the Stadtplatz had a parking garage

beneath it. He would go directly there and straight to the pump room. They couldn't have gotten far by this time!

Careening recklessly around a corner, Gustav accelerated toward the ramp down into the garage under the building, taking quick mental note of the two or three vehicles exiting it as he squealed in. As fast as he was able, he spun around the tight entrance, down the ramp, and toward the far end of the open garage, where the stairs and elevator were located.

Slamming on his brakes, he screeched to a stop, jumped out, and ran to the stairs. In a moment he was down a flight to the bottom basement. A blue-uniformed worker was walking toward him along the corridor, which ran the length of the building. Gustav ran toward him.

"This building has a sump pump, does it not!" he demanded.

"Yes."

"Where is it!" Gustav fairly screamed.

The man half turned and pointed back down the hall. "Last door."

Gustav was already gone.

He reached the door and threw it open.

One glance told him he was too late, but only by seconds. The hatch to the collection tank was on the floor. A pair of waist-high boots had been thrown in a corner. The floor was covered with water and mud.

He spun around, glancing about.

The muddy prints led across the corridor by which he had come and through another door.

He opened it.

Another flight of stairs up to the parking garage on this side of the building!

He flew up them, following the trail. This was going to be easier than he thought! He would track them by their muddy footsteps wherever they were bound. He was close behind them—they would have no time to change clothes no matter how many accomplices they had!

Arriving at the parking level once more, he stormed out the door into the garage.

They had been here all right—puddles and splotches of mud all about indicated they had stood right here.

Gustav glanced about.

But the trail *ended* in these puddles! There were no tracks leading away from here!

He sniffed the air.

He could still detect the faint odor of diesel.

There had obviously been an escape vehicle waiting for them! A truck, from the smell of it! They had climbed in right here, accounting for the puddles, and then had driven straight out of the garage!

He turned and dashed for his car, making the best imitation of a sprint he could, which wasn't much.

He had seen three vehicles a moment ago—a car, a large truck, and a delivery van. It had to be one of them! Most likely, from the diesel, one of the latter two.

Leaving what rubber on the floor of the garage his automobile's engine was capable of, he careened wildly back onto the street, turned in the direction both the trucks had taken, and shoved his foot all the way to the floor, now activating his siren and lights, honking madly at the rest of the traffic impeding him.

What were they—he racked his brain . . . a large truck . . . green—an army transport, that was one of them! The other was smaller . . . white . . . something written on the side . . . some business . . . a delivery service . . .

No! Suddenly it came to him!

It had been a bakery van!

Wild images spun through his brain—a helicopter chase . . . grenades, explosions . . . they had been chasing a bakery van on that day too . . . he could still see the writing on the side: *Bäkerei Meier!*

Gustav broke into a loud laugh.

It really was too foolish of them to use the same getaway ploy twice! Ha, ha! The bumbling fools! What kind of sap do they take me for?

There was the big green military truck lumbering ahead.

"Out of my way, you fool—don't you hear my siren!" cried Gustav as he passed it. He then bore down on the van about half a block ahead.

They were in his sights now!

Speeding ahead, he pulled alongside the bakery vehicle,

honking and gesturing for it to pull over. Then he sped ahead, pulled in sharply just ahead of it, and slammed on his brakes.

He had them!

It was only by sheer alertness and driving skill that the poor bewildered baker kept from crashing into the *Stasi* automobile altogether.

The section chief leapt from his car like a man possessed, eyes wide, pistol in hand, trembling in anticipation while the rest of the traffic continued past.

PART III

Ursula Wissen
April–June 1962

∽ 39 ∽
Many Fogs

A thin fog clung to the waters of the Havel, spreading its mist several hundred meters beyond its banks in either direction.

It had been a long walk this chilly April Sunday afternoon, but she had needed to get out of her apartment, to get away from the bustle of downtown Berlin, to sort out her thoughts.

This winter had felt longer than usual. Her heart would welcome the season of warmth and flowers again. Even the wintry bulbs she had planted in her flower box seemed a little stubborn about opening themselves to the pale sun, though it was easily two weeks past the time she should have seen their color. Their stalks poked through the soil, but their faces yet hid themselves within.

There had been a time when the spring's first daffodils brought gaiety and laughter to her soul. The unfolding of spring made her step light and her heart glad with the goodness of life.

It was different now.

This winter's chill had penetrated deeper. And not merely into the bones of her physical body. The raw numbness had gotten deep into her heart. It had begun to spread a layer of ice over the two characteristics that had seen her through the many difficult circumstances of the past fifteen years—her optimism and her sense of hope.

She tried to persuade herself that it was but the dreariness of winter getting to her. It got to everyone, she said. It would pass. The sun would come out and warm the land. As it did her hopeful cheerfulness would reemerge as well, just like one of springtime's flowers that perhaps needed a little extra coaxing out of its season of hibernation this time around.

But there was more. She knew it. And the coming of spring wouldn't change it.

For the first time in her life, Ursula Wissen was lonely deep in the core of her being.

She had brought a good supply of ready and available

arguments to her aid over the recent months in attempting to combat the admission of that fact.

She was doing important work, she told herself.

She was the Lord's handmaiden, and he lived within her heart.

The future was in God's hands. She had given it to him.

Most of all, she tried to convince herself, she *shouldn't* feel loneliness. She should not expect her life to be otherwise than it was. With the Lord at her side she had no right to be lonely.

None of the arguments helped.

Ursula was still lonely . . . and she was finally ready to admit it and look honestly at it.

Perhaps it was time to rethink some of the commitments she had made—commitments that, she knew, lay at the heart of her present loneliness. Though she had honored them, wanted to honor them, and would continue to honor them, Ursula was beginning to realize they needed to be given over into the Lord's hands more fully than perhaps she had yet done.

She sighed deeply and glanced once more at the filmy mists enshrouding the lake.

There was a similar fog spread upon this country and its people, she thought, though not so easily visible as this.

When she and Sabina had talked—before, when she had been with her friend more regularly—they had spoken of the fog that had settled over the people of the East. As the Communist cloud had grown suffocating, the steady deterioration of hope had been visible. A sad greyness had descended over those forced to live a life covered with a blanket of isolation. This had been one of the reasons she had begged and pleaded with Sabina to make the change she herself had made and come live with her in West Berlin. Ursula had even seen it gradually beginning to infect her radiant and buoyant friend of so many years.

But Sabina had her reasons for staying behind, just as Ursula had her own reasons for remaining unmarried all these years.

They were both women who honored their loyalties, no matter how much time passed—years that to many would have suggested it was time to stop looking back, but to the two of them only indicated that they must pray with more steadfastness of devotion.

Ursula missed Sabina.

It could not be denied that not seeing her smiling face for so long was a major contributor to the loneliness. In the last two or three years as the crisis over Berlin had grown tense, they had not seen one another as much as before, but just knowing they could visit now and then had kept the bonds of friendship as tight as ever.

Suddenly the wall had gone up. Now seeing one another was impossible. Though Sabina had managed to get a message to her before Christmas, she had no idea where her friend was and had no way to contact her. Ursula had not laid eyes on Sabina since before that fateful day last August, and the separation was beginning to tear at her heart.

If only she could have known that only days before she had come close to seeing Sabina once again. Perhaps it was best, in her present mood, that she didn't know the disappointing drama that had played itself out under the street called Esplanade on the other side of the wall.

Ursula stopped and impulsively picked up a small stone and tossed it into the water, listening to the splash and watching the ripples spread out from it. The water felt the disturbance, but the mist hanging above it was indifferent to the stone's flight through it, showing not a hint of motion.

There was a fog on this side of the barrier too, thought Ursula with pensive philosophical reflection as she continued on, though the very men and women who lived here were the most blind to it. There was a recklessness, as it seemed to her, with which they had been caught up in the rush and pace, the opportunity and wealth of that which they called freedom.

Everything was so different here than in the Poland she had known as a child and teenager. She supposed it was different everywhere since the war.

Even in the midst of the energetic life that made West Berlin everything it was, she saw in the eyes of its inhabitants a fog of a different kind. They were full of energy and liveliness, it was true. But they were no more free in the deeper ways that mattered than those imprisoned on the other side.

Bondage existed in more ways than in having restrictions imposed upon one's steps. There were as many walls within the millions of human souls on this side, keeping those souls from the freedom for which they were made, as there were individuals on the other side kept there by the one wall of bricks, cement, and stone.

The mortar holding all the walls together was Self. Its restrictive demon could either reign free, with all the bondages it imposed, or be shattered to bits—allowing freedom indeed to reign—anywhere on the globe.

Was life really so much worse on the other side? she wondered. It was not very often she saw freedom in the eyes of those she encountered here either.

Those in whom she did see it would have been free anywhere. For they were free in spirit. Their eyes were covered with no scales.

It was always the eyes Ursula looked for first.

It was the eyes she had first noticed in Sabina and her parents. Though she had been young at the time, she had seen it well enough . . . and knew there was a difference.

How well she remembered that day in Switzerland when they all knew Marion von Dortmann was about to die. She would never forget *those* eyes.

There was no mist covering them over!

Nor Sabina's. There had been many tears over the next days and weeks, but nothing to cloud the eyes and keep them from a visible clarity that was . . . different.

She knew her father had seen it too. He had never forgotten Baron von Dortmann and spoke of him often. She knew it had a lot to do with the vision that was so apparent in the baron's eyes.

She hadn't understood back then, at *Lebenshaus* or in Switzerland—at least not completely.

She understood now.

The look originated not in the eyes at all, but rather in the heart. When the transformation came to that lower, inner, hidden region, in time the light could not help but look out through those two transparent windows of the face that God devised to be so inextricably linked to the soul he created in which for his own presence to dwell.

It had been difficult for her family when she explained that

she would be going to Germany with Sabina rather than returning to Warsaw with them.

She and Sabina had become sisters.

How fondly she recalled the day she had knelt and, with only
Sabina to help her, given her heart to Jesus as her new Lord and
Messiah. After that, the bond between them had been as strong
as any family ties—stronger in many ways. She had matured in
her new faith, and they had grown together.

Her family had eventually found a new home in Russia,
though word soon reached her that things were scarcely better
there for Jews than they had been in Nazi Germany. She feared
for her family and what they might encounter. Thoughts and
prayers of them were always at the foundation of her work with
the network, helping others of their kind whenever and however they could.

She and Sabina had built a good life for themselves. They felt
needed and useful.

There had been many times, however, when Ursula almost
wished she had remained in the eastern sector. She had been
cut off from everyone she loved. What was the good of what the
world called freedom if that was the price?

Her family's sudden and surprising appearance last summer
put an end to those doubts. They were now safe in Israel, and
she knew she could join them at any time.

Somehow, though, she could not leave Berlin knowing that
Sabina was somewhere, out of touch and perhaps in danger . . .
on the other side of the wall.

∽ 40 ∾
An Ancient and Sacred Pledge

Ursula continued her leisurely stroll along the water's edge, a
slight afternoon's breeze now beginning to blow some of the
mist off its surface into the air.

She and Sabina had something else in common, she reflected.
They were both single, though in their mid to late thirties.

At least others considered them single. But they talked often
in their quiet moments of the ones they had loved.

As the years passed, Sabina spoke less and less often of him. She recognized how slim was the likelihood she would ever see him again. But Ursula knew her friend had never forgotten Matthew. Her relationship with him had been so strong, even though brief, that she seemed to be quietly satisfied with just the memory of it. The work they were involved in, meanwhile, consumed most of her time and energy.

It was different for Ursula. She had been betrothed. The little gold band on her finger reminded her of it constantly, and even as she walked she glanced down at it.

She was a Christian now, it was true. Yet her Jewish heritage and upbringing remained a vital part of her life and would always be an intrinsic part of everything she was as a person. Betrothal was not to be taken lightly. In betrothal was contained the commitment of marriage itself. It lasted a lifetime.

Her Joseph had said he would follow them out of Poland. But follow where? To Switzerland? To the new Israel? Or to Russia, where so many Jews had fled during the war, thinking there they would find safety?

How could he possibly have any inkling whatever where to find her? Berlin would probably never enter his mind as her likely new home.

If Joseph was even still alive at all.

She knew the facts of the Holocaust as well as any Jew alive. Not a great percentage had survived in this part of the world. Poland had been hit hardest of all.

How could she possibly continue to hold out hope of seeing Joseph again?

Even if somehow they did see one another again, surely he would never marry one such as she.

Some Christian friends told her she was not bound by the betrothal, that she was a new creature in Christ, and that old things had passed away. In all likelihood he was dead, they all agreed. But even if that were not the case, and even if by some miracle they did cross paths again, they reminded her that Joseph would certainly not be pleased—perhaps even offended and angry—to discover his betrothed a Christian.

She realized there would certainly be tension should such a moment come. And she had to admit, though she had grown to love him in her heart, she didn't know Joseph well. The marriage had been arranged by their two fathers. Still less did she know him now, know what kind of man he might have become through the years.

But if his namesake, Joseph of old, would risk so much to stand by his betrothed in the light of the public scandal brought on by the divine conception, surely her own Joseph would respect her and stand by her long enough to allow her to tell the story of her new faith.

As a young man Joseph had been, though strong of will and determined, a thinking and rational youth, and he had listened to those who encouraged the Jews to reach for more. Why would he not likewise listen to the reasons why she had chosen to reach for more in her spiritual life?

On her part, she had to honor the vow, even knowing that Joseph might "put her away," even as Mary's betrothed had thought of doing when he found her with child. Was not her having "forsaken" the religion of her youth an offense that equally allowed divorce?

Her thoughts went back to her Christian friends and the guidance and advice they had given her. Why, her friends asked, did she continue to honor it when he could not possibly want to marry her knowing she was a Christian?

They were more eager, it seemed, to talk her out of the commitment than see her honor it. It had been difficult to understand. Why did they treat commitment—especially the marriage commitment, the deepest and most lasting and binding of all earthly commitments—with such apparent indifference?

There were many aspects of her new faith that would always be difficult for Ursula to integrate with her upbringing. Her discussions with friends at the church she attended, and even the counsel she received from its pastor, over the matter of her betrothal remained the most troublesome for her. They seemed constantly searching for scriptural loopholes that they were desirous of seeing her take advantage of, rather than discovering ways to honor and obey Scripture's deepest principles and encouraging her to do likewise.

Sabina was the lone Christian friend and sister who

understood. Perhaps because she was half Jew herself. Or perhaps it was because she had a father who had taught her the
value of honoring commitments.

In any event, Ursula had made a solemn and sacred promise, a vow that could not be broken. She would wait . . . until
her own father, and the Lord himself, released her from it.

◇ 41 ◇
Fading Hopes and Fragrances

The sun, though not much warmth had been coming from it,
was thinking about its descent and had, in consequence,
turned a cold eye toward the earth it would soon leave in darkness.

Ursula shivered, pulled her coat up more tightly around her
neck and shoulders, and decided it was time to bend her direction for home. She would reach no conclusions about her
future or her fate on this afternoon, though she did feel
slightly better from the walk.

It was a four- or five-kilometer walk back to her apartment
near the hospital where she worked in the center of the city. As
Ursula made her way along, the persistent breeze, which had
by now kicked up into a blustery wintry wind, met her straight
in the face. Though a good tussle with the elements is usually
invigorating and stimulating to the soul's sense of well-being,
on this particular day and in the frame of mind she had been
in of late, the icy wind in her face accomplished just the opposite inside the downcast heart of Ursula Wissen.

It brought a return to the cold, sad, cheerless loneliness that
had prompted today's walk in the first place. She felt as isolated as anyone in the DDR, surrounded by an invisible wall of
her own aloneness.

On a day like this, she thought, it would be so nice to have
someone to go home to, someone to share cold days with . . .
someone to share life with.

Even though she had been young, she carried memories of
her own, as did Sabina, in her heart. . . .

Even as her thoughts began to drift back, she had to admit it was getting more and more difficult, on days like this, to find sustenance from the memories. With every passing year, the pleasant thoughts of Joseph faded further into the distance of her past. Neither they, nor her work, nor her hope, could keep the loneliness at bay.

Perhaps her Christian friends were right. How long, after all, could she hold out hope for a marriage that might all along have been impossible? Even her father last summer had hinted at the need one day to accept the inevitable—that they were never going to see Joseph again and that the betrothal should be broken. He had made extensive inquiries, he said, but they had turned up not so much as a whisper. He and his parents, as sad as he was to have to say it, had most likely died with the millions of others in the Nazi camps.

Reason told her it was the prudent way to look at it. And on days like this the loneliness spoke to her from a different quarter altogether, telling her that she was a woman in the prime of her life, who, if she did not marry soon, would probably not have many more chances.

She was thirty-five. There had been a few men who had expressed an interest. But she had shown them the ring, explained briefly, and closed the door in each case against further approach.

Now the human side of her wondered if the time had come to allow some of those doors to open again.

But she would not do so without the Lord's leading. No matter how lonely she became, she thought, quickening her pace unconsciously in the confusion of her thoughts, she must not break a sacred pledge.

Not unless . . .

Not unless the Lord showed her that the time had come, and that he wanted her at last to lay down the hopes she had cherished so long.

She would do so for him . . . but for no other.

An hour later Ursula reached her apartment, no nearer a resolution to her quandary than when she had set out.

She climbed the dark flight of stairs in the building to the third floor, meeting no one, opened her own door, and walked inside. It was as chilly in here as it had been outside. The gathering dusk added to the gloominess, for she had not left a light on.

The atmosphere of the place did nothing to alleviate the lump trying to gather in her throat.

She closed the door behind her, came all the way inside, stood a moment, then walked toward the small balcony outside her window that overlooked the street below.

Her eyes fell upon her tiny window box outside, and for a moment the sight took her breath away.

She had forgotten to look at it this morning!

A gasp of pleasure escaped her lips as she bounded forward.

There, staring up at her—as if it knew her mood and had come out just for her to say, "See, life has pleasures even in the middle of a cold day like this! I am your friend. Enjoy me . . . for I came to cheer you up!"—were the perfectly formed little faces of a lovely pink hyacinth, whose thick stalk had produced them so quickly she had not even seen them coming.

Ursula opened the glass door and stepped outside, approached the box with mingled wonder and gladness, stooped down, and gently let the wonderful fragrance fill her whole head with its aromatic messages of mystery.

She rose, a peaceful smile on her lips, her eyes suddenly flowing with an unexpected onrush of tears.

The flower had touched her loneliness.

She wept . . . and knew not why.

∽ 42 ∽
Memory of a Smile

The gloom of dusk had thoroughly infiltrated her apartment as Ursula turned back into it. From her kitchen she mechanically picked up a small knife, then returned to the balcony and carefully slit through the thick, fleshy stalk of the treasured flower. Holding it now by the base and weeping silently, she returned inside, closed the door, and walked slowly to her small sitting room, where she took a seat on the couch, still without turning on a light.

There, in the quietness of the late afternoon, alone with her tears and the fragrance of hyacinth slowly filling the room, Ursula allowed her mind to drift back to the day her father had announced her betrothal to Joseph.

She was twelve, he fourteen. Her father had chosen the Passover celebration for the announcement. It was a festive time, and many friends and relatives had gathered and, of course, Joseph's whole family.

Spring had come late that year too, though by then most of the bulbs were out and many of the perennials had also begun to bloom. Her mother had always loved flowers indoors and kept most of her bulbs in pots. During the Passover on that year, never had there been such a wonderful profusion of festive spring color in their home. The yellow of daffodils was everywhere, as were the varied whites and purples and pinks of hyacinths freshly broken out with their numerous delicate faces surrounding such stout green trunks.

The house had fairly reeked with the hyacinth perfume.

Ursula smiled and unconsciously lifted today's surprising wonder to her nose.

Then had come the announcement.

Oh, how embarrassed she had been to be the object of everyone's *ooh*s and *ah*s, smiles and congratulations. She was too shy to enjoy all the fuss, though of course she could not help smiling.

In the midst of it all, she found herself glancing shyly over at Joseph.

He was looking straight at her!

Her face had gone hot, and she had reddened immediately. But the downward glance of her eyes only lasted a second. She could not help looking up again.

He smiled, a shy and boyish expression of his own. But also a smile that said he understood . . . that he felt the embarrassment too. And it was a smile, though he was but fourteen, that appeared to her innocent eyes of twelve as an expression of calm maturity, as if he was saying that all was well and that the embarrassment would pass.

She looked away once more, and their eyes did not meet again that day. Young Ursula, however, stole two or three more glances in Joseph's direction through the course of the day. He wore a countenance of poise and intelligence. Even by the age of fourteen, he was a thinker and was admired by all the men of the synagogue, who declared him destined for great things for God. He had not yet become involved with the radicals. That came later. On that special day he was innocent yet already well on the way toward becoming a man.

During one of Ursula's quick peeks in his direction, it suddenly dawned upon her: *This man is going to be my husband . . . my husband!*

She was a betrothed young woman!

Joseph and she would live their lives together. They would talk and share about everything. They would have children together, walk with God together, and eventually grow old together.

It was with that realization, with the image of Joseph's animated face as he talked with some of the men—no doubt on some point of theology, she thought with a smile—when the seeds of love first entered the heart of Ursula Wissen for the man to whom her father had betrothed her.

And during the next few years, before the war tore them apart, she grew to love him steadily more deeply . . . in quiet ways . . . in the ways of love only a woman can understand when she looks upon the face of the man she loves when it is turned away, and beholds the *man* who resides beneath it.

She was not on intimate terms yet with hyacinths at the age of twelve. She had, like most men and women, not grown to love flowers until more pain had come to her life, along with the deepening of love's mystery, so that they were able to speak their soothing influences into deeper regions of the soul's hearing.

But ever after, at the faintest hint of the odor of hyacinth, her mind expanded with happy thoughts of that day . . . the memory of Joseph's youthful embarrassed smile struck her heart . . . and then followed the sadness.

It was a mysterious and melancholy perfume, filled with the enchantment of fairy tales, mingled with the exquisite pain of love that might have been, of youthful smiles left behind . . . and the dull ache of memories whose hopes had gone unfulfilled.

∽ 43 ∽
Prayer from a Lonely Heart

The apartment had grown nearly dark by now.

Still Ursula sat, the hyacinth in her hand, nearly forgotten now, though the evocative sensations from its bouquet were by no means diminished.

A quiet half-smile still rested upon her lips. It was a wet smile, for she could not stop the tears from above.

The memories had run their course, though they had accomplished no purpose other than to deepen the uncertainty of her loneliness.

What lay ahead for her? she asked for the dozenth time that day.

Sabina and Matthew had found one another, or, she realized, the Father of them both had led them together. Even if it had been for such a short time, at least they had been able to look upon one another again . . . and express their love.

Would the Father likewise lead her to Joseph?

She wanted to share that kind of love with someone too. Was it only the loneliness of her humanity, or did God at last want her to move on with her life, forward . . . and put the memories to rest?

As she sat, a quiet resolution began to steal over her.

There were not nearly so many escapes going on these days. Every potential hole in the border had been sealed up tight. She and a few acquaintances participated in helping refugees get settled, though the people of *The Rose* were only occasionally involved in such escapes. She would continue her work on this side of the wall with the network through summer, in hopes that another message would come from Sabina. If there was any chance to see her again, she would sacrifice anything for the opportunity.

Perhaps Sabina had finally found her father, and they had been forced to go deep into hiding. What else could explain that she hadn't heard another whisper from her? What if they couldn't escape—not now, not ever?

She could not remain here—isolated, alone, lonely—forever

holding out impossible hopes of seeing Joseph or Sabina. There had to come a change.

As she sat, a quiet resolution began to steal over her.

She would give it a few more months, hoping and praying for word of some kind, hoping that they would be able to contact the very *Network of the Rose* that their own sacrificial ministry to Jews during the war had begun.

But if nothing turned up, eventually she would have to leave Berlin. She would join her family in Israel for a while. Then she would diligently seek the Lord about whatever new life he had for her.

Suddenly another idea came to her mind.

She would try to contact Matthew, Ursula thought.

Though she had never met him, they were bound together by the common bond of love for Sabina. But, she thought further, how would she contact him? All she knew was where she had taken the rose for Sabina last Christmas. Surely they would be able to get her in contact with him there.

She would meet Matthew. She would let him know where she would be, so that if Sabina did one day get out of the East, he would be able to reach her.

Unconsciously again the hyacinth found its way to her nose, and the mystique of its incense brought new moisture, in the midst of thoughts of decision and change, to her eyes.

What about Joseph. . . ?

She could move from Berlin, she could go to Israel, she could start a new life . . . but still the gold band encircled her finger. Nothing could alter the fact that she was a betrothed woman.

"O God," she prayed softly, "*show me what you would have me do. You know the deepest places inside me. You know my loneliness, both as a Christian and as a woman. You know how I have honored and been faithful to the promises and pledges exchanged between my father and Joseph's. You know—*"

Her whispering voice broke, and she began to sob.

"*You know, Father,*" she said now, crying freely, "*that I love him!*"

Again she stopped, allowing the convulsing tears to flow and then gradually subside.

"*But, Lord,*" she prayed again, drawing in a calming breath, "*it *has been twenty years since I have seen Joseph. My heart is lonely, Lord. I'm sorry—forgive my weakness . . . but I am lonely, and tired.*

"Show me what you want me to do, where you want me to go. Show me, Father, if it is your desire that I remove the ring at last, and place my earthly hopes on the altar of sacrifice. I will do so, Lord, but only if you leave me no doubt that it is your will.

"Please show me your will, Father. I feel so alone that even your presence is difficult to remember at times. I don't know what you would have me do. Help me, Lord . . . help me."

❧ 44 ❧
Retreat and Regroup

The mood in the Dahlmann home was subdued.

It had been three days since the return from the aborted escape attempt. Most of that time had been spent in necessary recovery and in thinking through precautions that now must be made.

Following the initial elation of scrambling safely out of the drain line, running up the stairs and finding Josef still waiting in the garage, and making good their retreat out of the city, the realization had dawned all too clearly upon them that they had failed, and that it could be weeks, perhaps even months, before another escape route availed itself to them.

Their high hopes of early in the day, and the cheers of celebration—once they were several blocks away!—resulting from stealthy peeks through the corners of the canvas at a triumphant Gustav arresting the innocent baker, faded by the time they were back to the village into a more realistic and discouraging evaluation of the day.

The effort had taxed the baron, and he had been in bed almost continuously ever since. Matthew's arms, chest, elbows, and ribs had been badly scraped from the hasty and shirtless crawl through the pipe, and though the wounds were not serious, it had been a painful two days for him. Both he and Angela had, not surprisingly, contracted severe colds from the adventure as well.

Josef was more worried about the truck than a few scrapes and bruises. Though the license could not be traced—he had used one of his own manufacture for the excursion into Berlin—he was nevertheless concerned that the *Stasi* agent that had passed so close might have taken note of the vehicle. He remembered the *Stasi* car well enough pulling into the garage just as they were pulling out. The sigh of relief he had breathed was only temporary. When he heard its siren behind them not three minutes later, he was certain their goose was cooked.

The reprieve of the bakery van was but temporary, he was certain. If he had seen the *Stasi* car, then the agent had certainly seen the truck and would in time put two and two together. A search would be mounted, and it would be seen eventually, a condition worsened by the fact that it wasn't even his vehicle.

To return the truck to its unaware owner would only be to increase the risk. Josef had, therefore, made the owner an offer to repaint the vehicle as well as overhaul its engine, for a price that was too low for the man to pass up, and Josef had been carrying out that project now for two days. He was not yet finished, but at least the truck was far from easily recognizable as that which had been in the basement of the Stadtplatz Building on the day of the failed escape.

Dahlmann's anxiety was heightened by news of the fellow who had been snooping around Grossbeeren, a young KGB agent attached to the *Stasi*. He had come over a week ago, but then had disappeared after a few mostly harmless interviews. Now he was back, and his questions were more pointed and persistent. It was clear the *Stasi* was not about to let the escape attempt go by without a thorough investigation, and they clearly had reason to suspect Grossbeeren as its point of origin.

The reason was not hard to find, and Sabina was the first one to alert her comrades to it.

Gustav had been involved the previous August. He had been tracking Sabina and her father ever since. He was now closer than ever.

The facts were clear enough—Sabina, Matthew, and the baron were the reason the others here were in danger. Thus they knew they could not remain in Grossbeeren any longer than absolutely necessary.

What would become of their escape to the West they could not know. But they mustn't allow their presence to jeopardize the safety of their friends.

Erich Brumfeldt and his son Willy had ventured a visit and were now talking with Dahlmann, his sister, and their three guests.

"I am sorry, Kar—Sabina," Erich was saying, "that I have no contacts, no other alternatives to explore at present."

"It is not your fault Gustav learned of the attempt," sighed Sabina.

"The flow from here to the other side has dried up to such an extent I do not know what to suggest."

"How could he have known exactly where we would be!" said Angela, repeating the question every one of them had been asking for two days. In many ways the failure had been hardest on her. Even if Matthew and Sabina had to spend the rest of their lives in the East, at least they were together.

"That man has shown himself remarkably resilient, and uncannily shrewd at anticipating our steps—*my* steps, at least," said Matthew. "We may never know."

"Whatever we do, we mustn't stay here indefinitely," said Sabina.

"You are more than welcome," said Josef.

"We know and understand," said the baron kindly. "Your kindness is more than we can thank you for. But my daughter is right. We must not endanger you or the others here."

"They must suspect this region," added Matthew. "Otherwise why the close investigation? I've been thinking about it a lot these last two days, and I'm not sure I like my conclusions."

He let out a long sigh while the others waited. Then he went on.

"My theory on it is this: During all those months I was looking for the two of you—" he glanced toward Sabina and the baron as he spoke—"we know Gustav, and someone else some of the time too, was following me. Whatever else he is, Gustav is nobody's fool. He must have known I was looking for you. He also must have figured out what I was doing in trying to penetrate various undergrounds and networks and contacts that might know where you were. I'm sure his office already had extensive files on Christian and Jewish and such organizations and individuals. . . ."

He paused again briefly.

"Then came the prison-break incident," he went on. "They were right on our trail, somehow, and it all blew up right here, between Grossbeeren and the border. Gustav would have to have known we had help and that it came from here. So added to his previous files there is undoubtedly a Grossbeeren file, perhaps with all your names already in it.

"And then for two months what did I do but lead him throughout the whole DDR, to every possible contact I had, all the way to Magdeburg, where a man was killed because of my carelessness. By now Gustav probably has files bulging with names and contacts that he's accumulated . . . that I've led him to!"

"You can't blame yourself, Matthew," said Erich. "We all face danger in this business, and we've known it all along."

"Do you see what I'm getting at, though?" continued Matthew. "Even before the attempt a few days ago, he would have known a great deal about our contacts, and if he put his mind to it, it would only be a matter of time before he got onto our trail again. I'm afraid a lot of this is my doing. None of this explains how he knew we'd be in that rainwater canal, but it guarantees that none of us are safe while we're here—Gustav simply knows too much."

A knock on the door interrupted them.

Everyone went silent, glancing back and forth at one another.

"Angela . . . are we expecting anyone?"

"No, Josef," said his sister, shaking her head.

"Quickly, into the bedroom here," said Dahlmann, "Quietly! Angela, go slowly to the door and see who it might be. Erich, you remain seated," he added. "We must account for the coffee and biscuits."

They all obeyed noiselessly.

Angela opened the door.

"Good day, Fräulein," said a young man, showing his identification. "I am with the KGB. I am looking for a man by the name of Brumfeldt."

"I . . . uh . . ." stammered Angela in a terror of fear.

"His wife said he had come for a visit . . . here to your house," said Galanov forcefully.

"I am Erich Brumfeldt," said Erich, who had heard, now approaching from inside.

"Ah, Herr Brumfeldt—your name was given me as one who might have interest in Americans."

"I have no more interest in Americans than any man," replied Erich, fully aware that his manner and tone were being scrutinized by the agent.

"You are aware of no Americans in the area?"

"I have not heard so much as a word of English in longer than I can remember," said Erich, adding a light laugh that he hoped would convey just the right amount of unconcern.

"So," Galanov went on, eyeing him intently, "you are here . . . uh, for a *social* visit?"

"Josef and I are friends," replied Erich, his smile now disappearing, speaking graciously but without undue effort toward friendliness.

"With the, uh . . . the curtains drawn throughout the house?"

Now the master of the house also made his appearance.

"My sister is in mourning, *mein Herr*," he said, answering the question himself. "She prefers it dark in the house."

"In mourning . . . for what?" asked the agent, turning toward Angela, whose face had by now gone white as a sheet.

"For her husband," answered Josef.

"He is dead?"

"He is in the West, and she cannot go to him."

"So *he* is friendly with the Americans perhaps?"

"He is a German. He has no loyalties to the Americans. He happened to be there when you people built your wall, and now they are separated."

Josef's voice contained just the right amount of anger that Galanov believed him.

"A long time to mourn, is it not?"

"It is a long time for you to keep families apart with your wall," rejoined Josef boldly, now taking the offensive. "We are Germans here—loyal Germans. We have no more affiliation with the Americans than we do . . . with the Russians."

Apparently satisfied, Galanov nodded and turned to go. He was still young and learning his trade. He had been bettered in this encounter, but everyone in the house as they closed the door behind him realized that it was only a matter of time before the net closed around the fugitives.

Matthew was right—however he had accumulated the information, Gustav knew too much about the activities of the network in and around Grossbeeren for them to be safe here any longer.

Reemerging from the bedroom ten minutes later and hearing every word that had transpired repeated to them, Matthew and Sabina's faces were somber. They were fully aware of the implications of the interview.

"We must go," said Sabina when they had heard everything. "Immediately."

"But where?" asked Dahlmann.

"We cannot return to Magdeburg," said Matthew. "Everything has been compromised there too. Sabina is absolutely right—to remain here any longer will mean too great a risk to all of you. I already have to live with the poor man Fristch on my conscience. I don't want any more people dying because of me."

"I am willing to take the risk," said Josef.

"And we appreciate it," rejoined Matthew. "But I am not. We must go. I am now more convinced than ever that Gustav has far more information than we gave him credit for."

"Wherever you go," put in Erich now, "you must find means to remain in touch with us. Telephones are ordinarily safe. It may be that something will turn up, a way to get you over the wall. We do still maintain what contact we are able with our friends of *The Rose* on the other side, as sporadic as such contact is. But we must be able to contact you in case something should arise."

"And if something turns up for us," said Sabina, "we will do our best to contact you, Angela. We must all get out together . . . if we can."

"But where will you go?" asked Angela.

"I think I know," said Matthew slowly, his face now brightened. "There is a man who might be able to help us, perhaps even hide us for a while. There are no direct connections with you people here. But he has many resources and contacts in diverse directions."

"Where?" asked Dahlmann.

"It is best even you do not know," replied Matthew. "But Erich—and Willy," he added, turning toward the boy with a smile, "they will know how to reach us."

✷ 45 ✷
Consulate Request

It was with tentative step that Ursula Wissen entered the United States consulate for the second time in four months.

She walked to the front desk, not recognizing the lady who sat there but well remembering the interrogation she had submitted to during her previous mysterious errand last December.

"Yes, miss?" said the lady, looking up.

"I need to get in touch with a man who works for your government," said Ursula, in hesitant English.

Detecting her lack of fluency, the secretary now began speaking in German.

"Where does he work?" she asked.

"Here in Berlin."

"What department?"

"I'm sorry. I do not know."

"What is his name?"

"Matthew McCallum."

"Ah yes, Mr. McCallum—he is employed with the State Department."

Ursula smiled appreciatively.

"I won't be able to give out his address. If you'll wait a moment, I'll see if I can find out about how we might contact him for you."

"Thank you," replied Ursula.

The lady rose from her desk and disappeared down a hall behind her. Ursula stood waiting. The place was not nearly so busy as it had been a year ago at the height of the crisis, and she was at present the only visitor in the reception area.

Two or three minutes passed. The lady returned.

"I'm sorry," she said. "Apparently I was mistaken. I have just learned that Mr. McCallum is no longer with the State Department. In fact, he is no longer working for the government at all."

"But . . . but, there must be some way to contact him," said Ursula. "Do you have his address?"

"No, I really have nothing on him—he was staying at the Imperial Hotel while he was in Berlin. Then came the accident—"

"What accident?" interrupted Ursula.

"Oh, I assumed you knew. He was badly injured last August in an accident near the border. He was sent to Bavaria for several months of convalescence, and after his release there, apparently he resigned. I did not know that myself until just a moment ago."

Ursula thought for a minute, confused and bewildered by this new turn of events.

"Is there then no way to get in touch with him?" she asked again.

"I'm sorry," replied the lady. "No one here even knows where Mr. McCallum is. His father, Thaddeus McCallum, is still employed by the State Department, however."

"May I have his address?"

"I cannot give it to you. But if you would like to leave your name and address, I will see that he receives it with the message that you are trying to reach his son."

"If I bring a letter here, to you, would you see that it is passed on to Mr. McCallum?"

"Yes . . . yes, of course."

Slowly Ursula turned and left the building, new uncertainties filling her. It seemed every possible link with the past, anything she might be able to hold on to—even Matthew, whom she didn't even know—was being stripped away from her.

Surely it must be time for her to leave Berlin!

❦ 46 ❦
Brotherhood of the Heart

The farm of Udo Bietmann in the small village of Kehrigkburg, southeast of Berlin, was known only to Matthew, as he and his two loved ones and faithful underground comrade walked across the cultivated but bare field behind the barn.

Brumfeldt knew of Bietmann, but they had never met personally, and Matthew wanted the links between Kehrigkburg and Grossbeeren to remain as disconnected as possible, for everyone's safety.

He had also remained concerned about the Trabi, of whose existence he was now convinced Gustav probably knew. The little car, therefore, would remain out of sight with the mechanic Dahlmann until he could transform its appearance, should its services be required again. If not, eventually Matthew would inform Paddy Red as to its whereabouts. Not wanting any possibility of a neighbor recognizing any *other* automobile, Erich had driven them to within a kilometer of the house in the grey light of dawn of the morning following Galanov's visit of inquiry.

"Are you certain he will receive us, Matthew?" the baron had asked the night before.

"As certain as that you would have received any man or woman in need at *Lebenshaus*, Baron," replied Matthew. "As I have told you, this young man is a kindred spirit. One look in his eyes and I sensed the instant willingness to give himself, even die if need be, for his fellows. This is a man who knows the power of sacrifice. Yes, he will receive us."

They found entrance to the building where Matthew hoped to find the young man. The barn, however, was empty.

"You wait here. . . . I will go to the house."

Matthew disappeared.

He returned five minutes later, accompanied by a young man in what appeared his mid to late twenties, a beaming smile of welcome on his face.

Matthew introduced the two Germans.

"It is an honor to meet you, Herr Erich Brumfeldt," said

Bietmann, smiling and shaking the older man's hand vigorously. "I know of you."

"Your reputation is also one that has caused me to anticipate this day as well," replied Erich.

"Would that we had more time!"

"There will one day be time for all things."

"Amen!" rejoined Bietmann. "But now, Matthew tells me, there are more urgent matters. I am delighted you are here. My wife and I will do all we can to help. Please . . . come into the house. You must meet my Christa, and our new little daughter, Girdel."

In the background, Baron von Dortmann inwardly rejoiced in his spirit to see the two men of God gaze with such respect upon one another. Their manner of greeting confirmed what he already knew of the one and demonstrated what, before the day was out, he was to learn of the other: that both were kindred souls in that rare spiritual fellowship about which many talk but in which few partake—the fellowship of total and unreserved dedication to the Father's will above one's own. When one discovers himself among such individuals, and is one of their number himself, it is as fulfilling to observe the flow of common kinship as to participate in it directly. Thus was the baron fed though he said nothing.

Bietmann led the way out of the barn and inside, through the back door of the house, to a small kitchen. The smell of brewing coffee already filled the air.

The fellowship and discussion were rich, though serious topics were addressed as well. When Erich left an hour later, he knew he had discovered a brother for life.

He bid Godspeed to Matthew, Sabina, and Baron von Dortmann, promising to remain alert to anything that might help them with their dream of a life in the West, and then left across the fields to the wooded area where he had parked his car.

The three fugitives then began to discuss the more practical matters of their plight with their new host.

∽∾∾

That evening they were talking again. Once Matthew realized what had happened shortly after he and Bietmann had last parted, more than ever he knew how close Gustav had been during the latter stages of his quest to find Sabina and her father. Of this Bietmann himself said not a word. Matthew was well enough able to fill in the gaps, however, from the answers his host gave to his questions. Now he had to add the beating he was all but certain his friend had received to his conscience as well, a fact that did not offer much peace about remaining under Bietmann's roof any longer than he had Dahlmann's.

"You will be safe here," the young farmer assured him. "God will protect us all. And should your stay become lengthy, I think there is a place very close by where you could remain almost indefinitely and blend in with the surroundings very nicely. And," he added, "you would have the privilege of working for your bread."

"Now that sounds appealing!" said Matthew.

"I agree," added Sabina. "The worst of it is having nothing to do."

"That will not be a problem with these friends, whom I think might enjoy having you among them."

"Who are they?" asked the baron.

"Let me just say that they are friends among our local fellowship of believers. I think you will find them delightful brothers and sisters."

"What kind of fellowship is this you speak of?" asked Baron von Dortmann with interest. "A church, perhaps?"

"There are churches that many of our number attend. But no, when I speak of our fellowship, it is a loose group of individuals with whom we meet and pray and study the Bible in a deeper way than is usually possible in the more formal setting of a church service."

"I am intrigued. I have been out of touch with the whole world for so many years, I know very little of how God's people have fared under this new state they call communism."

"Here in the DDR," said Bietmann, "the government is not nearly so intolerant as in some of the others. Yet one guiding principle of communism is that no one must take anything *too* seriously. *Commitment* must be reserved for the state only. Anything perceived as dedication or devotion to any other cause is considered subversion. Therefore, people may go to church or write poetry or read books or discuss opinions, and no one minds. But let them begin taking their religion or their poetry or their books or their opinions too seriously, and then they *do* mind. Then you are in danger of being labeled a subversive against the communist state. That is precisely the point where we in our fellowship walk a precarious line between safety and danger. We take *our* faith very seriously."

"I am happy to hear it," replied the baron. "No faith but one taken seriously is worthy of the name. You do meet, then, I take it?"

"Yes. And we pray and we study the Word intently together. Because of that, we must exercise care. Though it is not widely known, there have been arrests, even here in the DDR, for no crime other than taking one's Christian faith too earnestly."

"It would be a privilege to meet some of your people," said Matthew.

"As I am certain you shall," rejoined Bietmann, "if you are with us for any length of time. But it is growing late. It is time we made you comfortable here in our humble home for the night. My wife, I believe, has everything ready for you. We shall see to your more lengthy accommodations later."

"We feel dreadful putting you at even more risk," said Sabina. "We are being sought by the *Stasi.*"

Bietmann laughed. It was a laugh intended to put their minds at ease, but clearly one with great depth and much experience behind it.

"You needn't worry," he said. "The Christian life is a life of risks, wherever you try to live it. The risks here may be of a more overt nature than some other places in the world . . . and still less than in others. But the moment one begins to take his Christianity seriously, he embarks upon a life of risk, and I for one would do nothing to lessen that risk if to do so means living what I believe with less passion. We are well accustomed to entertaining pilgrims. We have had many in our home such as yourselves. I am committed, along with the others I am in touch with, to helping those in need."

"What about the danger to your wife and your new little daughter?" asked Matthew. "Are you not concerned for them?"

"Of course. What man wouldn't be? But Christa understands

as well and is no less committed to what God has given us to do than am I."

Bietmann glanced over at his wife, who was sitting peacefully with their four-month-old daughter sleeping in her arms. Husband and wife smiled at one another. It was a smile that said they were together and that their commitment was a shared one.

"There are risks to being married to a man of God," said Christa. "Udo is such a man. But I would not trade my life with him for an easier or less dangerous life with any other man. I want my life to count in the kingdom of heaven, just as he does. Making a difference for God does not always come easily."

It was already late, as Bietmann said. Sabina and Christa rose to retire.

The discussion, however, continued energetically for several more hours between the three men. It was an evening none of them ever forgot.

✌ 47 ✌
Chilly Mountain Walk

Thaddeus McCallum stooped down, scraped up a large scoop of snow, wadded it into a snowball, and with a great heave let it fly overhead.

Maybe that would loosen some of the snow from the branches up there, he thought!

He waited several seconds, observing the trickles of white that filtered down, then retrieved his walking stick and continued on, trying to put to rest the demoralizing thoughts that had sent him outside half an hour earlier.

Ordinarily he enjoyed the cold and the snow. But Thaddeus had to admit that he had never spent such a lonely and despondent winter in all his life as the one just past. Though the work that came his way from the State Department was minimal, he had scarcely been able to keep his mind on even that.

Occasionally he would manage to lose himself in the writing

of his memoirs for a morning or an afternoon. It was an escape at best, however, and Thaddeus knew it. Eventually thoughts of Matthew would always intrude, and he would find himself drifting into morose holes of anxiety and self-pity all over again.

It was not like him. Since the death of Matthew's mother, he had normally been an even-tempered man. Never, he had thought, could anything again scrape so near the depths of emotion as had the loss of his wife. After that, no other crisis, no other situation, seemed important enough to cause him much emotional concern. But now he wondered.

It had only been four months since Matthew's abrupt and excited disappearance. He had been separated from him for longer periods many times. But Thaddeus, not usually given to such things, had a premonition that major change was about to come to his life, and he shuddered to think what that might be.

He knew well enough that his son, if caught behind the Iron Curtain—and beyond any doubt that's where he was—would be tried as a spy. The Russians had grown positively paranoid about spies these days. He didn't even want to consider the possibilities if Matthew got involved in all that! The U-2 pilot Gary Powers had just been traded for a Russian spy a couple months ago. But what if no spy was available for negotiations in Matthew's case? He wouldn't exactly be as important to the U.S. government as Powers!

He didn't like to think about it . . . yet he could think of nothing else. He was afraid.

But he *wouldn't* think about it, he had said to himself—not any more this morning, at least. It was time for a walk!

He had risen from his chair with sudden resolve, gulped down the last few swallows of coffee in the bottom of his cup, thrown on a coat and hat, caught up one of his several handmade walking sticks, and strode briskly out into the keen mountain air, where he had been doing his best for the last thirty minutes to boost his spirits, even to the throwing of snowballs into the trees!

Spring had arrived, yet in these regions overlooked to the south by the giant Alps of Bavaria, and south of them farther, Switzerland, it would be cold for another two months. The sun shone brightly on this day, glistening off the white residue of snow left over most of the ground from the fall last week. Around him the peaks of Krottenkopf, Alpspitze, and Kreuzspitze all showed thick blankets of snow from their majestic peaks to a distance halfway down their slopes. The Zugspitze certainly had more white than them all, but clouds, as they often did, obscured its heights. The owners of the ski resorts throughout the mountains would be happy, for it looked to be a prolonged season.

Thaddeus took in several great gulps of the bracing air and continued on toward the village of Obenammersfeld. He had taken the long way.

From the chalet, a glance downward to his right had revealed a gentle slope where patches of green were attempting here and there to show through the spots of snowmelt. Cattle would be grazing on this same slope within a month or two, but there wasn't much for them to find as yet. Toward the left, the hill rose toward a thick pine forest, which gradually steepened until it gave way to the alpine peaks.

It was toward this wood that the steps of the semiretired diplomat had taken him, along a path that had already been cut through the snow several times in previous days, where he arrived at length amongst the pines, on whose branches a good deal of snow still clung, though every now and then a faint *swishhh*, followed by a silent powdery descent of white, would indicate that some branch had tired of its wintry occupation and had at length relieved itself of the extra load.

It added to the excitement of taking the circuitous route to the village through the wood at such times, knowing that you must keep your eyes and ears open or be doused at any moment by one of these tiny unexpected snowstorms. And if the tired branch happened to be a high one, the release of its crystalline weight would set off many similar unburdenings on its way down, and the result on the head of the unsuspecting pedestrian would be a blizzard indeed.

It was chillier than Thaddeus had anticipated, and now, with his regloved hands still cold from the snowball, he gradually increased his pace.

The mountains were full of many challenges, thought

Thaddeus as he made his way now along the woodsy trail, and though several puff-trails of white descended around him, the worst he got from it was some flecks on his shoulders.

He was actually a little disappointed, accounting for his attempt to create a snowfall of his own. Yet he knew that one must not intentionally allow oneself to lose at the sport—where was the challenge in that! One must do one's best. But this was one game where to be abruptly and unintentionally bettered by one's opponent when you suddenly found snow all over your head could not help but bring a laugh of joy to even the most lonely of hearts.

By and by, Thaddeus had effected a large half circle, making his way to the top of the tiny village on the side of the slope, whence he turned downward, and thus found himself a few minutes later among the few quaintly constructed homes and barns and buildings of the place.

The tiny village, of which his chalet formed one of the outlying homes, was comprised of little more than some ten or a dozen residences, a small guest house capable of meal service to fifteen or twenty persons, and a bakery. The buildings were scattered over a four-hundred-meter-square plateau in the midst of this climb southward and upward out of the well-known German resort town of Oberammergau. Grasses and wildflowers grew luxuriant in the oasis surrounded by the pine forests through which Thaddeus had recently come. On the gradual nearby slopes the farmers of the village grew a few crops and grazed their cattle. Several individuals commuted down to the valley daily—when the snows permitted. A good number were elderly and retired. Thaddeus was the only foreigner, but he and Matthew—before the latter's departure—had already been welcomed warmly into the small Bavarian community, owing largely to the fact that they were both personable and spoke perfect German, even to a fair knowledge of the Bavarian idiom.

Indeed, the setting, for one who loved this land and its people as much as the elder McCallum, could not have been more a dream come true. During all his years as a United States diplomat, Thaddeus had enjoyed his tenure in Germany, having served before the war as assistant U.S. ambassador, more than any other location, and the Nazi scourge had done nothing to in any way extinguish his love for the place and its vigorous inhabitants.

Now, in postwar West Germany, serving in but a part-time and mostly advisory capacity, he found the pace to be more relaxed than in most parts of the BRD, and though skiing resorts and tourist towns surrounded them literally on all sides, the clamor of such activity did not intrude upon the peaceful life of Obenammersfeld—the village whose name meant "Field above the Ammer Valley."

The chalet was neither his nor was it owned by the State Department, which, however, paid the rent on it as part of its arrangement with the two McCallums. It was owned, in fact, by a woman whose husband, a retired German businessman, had passed away two years earlier. The lady did not want to remain in the large home alone, so far from her own relations, and had therefore relocated to München, some seventy or eighty kilometers to the north.

During their months together, Thaddeus had contemplated buying the home for himself and Matthew, if it should be available, even if it took retiring from the diplomatic corps and changing his citizenship to accomplish it. It was the perfect setting in which to retire and write, he thought, and there were really very few deep and binding ties calling to them from the States. The house was spacious, set on a large tract of land of its own. Its split-level design had been intended for a family of at least five. Matthew and Thaddeus, therefore, had each had a bedroom, an office, and a bathroom of their own. The nearest other home was some hundred meters away.

Now, however, changed as things were, Thaddeus found himself having to rethink his entire perspective on the future. He just could not get rid of the gnawing sense that enormous change was coming . . . and he feared for what it was.

If he received an official state visit, or an embassy pouch in the mail one day, with the news that Matthew was dead, he knew he could not remain here one week longer.

From the rear balcony of the chalet, Thaddeus could gaze downward upon grassy slopes, broken here and there by small lakes, cultivated fields, and pastureland; or straight out and upward, when the seemingly ever present clouds lifted for an afternoon or a day, upon the loftiest mountain peaks in all of Germany. He and Matthew had enjoyed entertaining guests during their all-too-brief few months together. Since the first of the year, however, owing more to his mood than to the occasionally prohibiting weather, Thaddeus had kept mostly to himself.

He walked now among the plastered, balconied, and ornately trimmed homes, enjoying the profusion of spring flowers displayed from window boxes and yards everywhere. Were ever a people more in love with flowers than the Swiss and the Bavarians? he wondered.

Greeting a few of the villagers as he went, Thaddeus made his way to the *Postamt*, where he retrieved his day's mail, then to the bakery, a favorite daily indulgence, where he bought a small bag of pastries and other goodies, visited a few moments with the owner and his wife—among the first friends he had made in the village, owing, in truth, more to their profession than to common interests—and then left for home.

He walked back to the chalet by the direct route across the open meadow, munching one of the delicacies of the baker's creation, thinking that perhaps this afternoon he would make another attempt to write.

∽ 48 ∾
Unexpected Correspondence

Thaddeus walked into the house, tossed his walking stick in a corner, and threw down the clump of letters on the table, glancing at them without great interest as he unwrapped from out of his coat.

As the various parcels and envelopes scattered slightly across the table, a letter marked "U.S. Consulate, Berlin" caught his eye.

A stab pierced his heart.

Unconsciously, the single word "Matthew!" escaped his lips.

Without even removing his hat, he grabbed at the envelope

and tore at its edge with trembling fingers. There hadn't been anything delivered here from the consulate since Matthew's peculiar Christmastime parcel!

Somehow he managed to work his fingers into the inner reaches of it, where they felt two pieces of paper. Further mangling the envelope, a second later he held in his hand a small note with an accompanying sealed letter in handwriting he did not recognize.

"Mr. Thaddeus McCallum," read the first. "The enclosed was brought here with the request that we deliver it to you." It was signed by the secretary of interdepartmental correspondence.

His heart still pounding, Thaddeus now picked up the blue envelope, slit its seal, more calmly this time, and with rising curiosity replacing the fear of a moment earlier, and still standing beside the table, he read the contents, which were written in English.

> *Dear Mr. McCallum,*
>
> *You will not know me. I have been a friend of Sabina von Dortmann's for many years. I know of your son Matthew, though I have never met him. I want to talk to him about Sabina. I have not been in touch with her for a long time because she is in the DDR. I may be leaving Berlin before long. I would like Matthew to know my whereabouts in case he hears from Sabina.*
>
> *Can you give me his location, or please ask him to contact me?*
>
> *I hope you can understand this. My English is not good. I asked a friend at work to help me with it.*
>
> *Sincerely,*
> *Ursula Wissen*

An address followed.

Thaddeus slowly walked to an easy chair, pulling off his hat and tossing it unceremoniously across the room as he did, and flopped down, still holding the letter. Even though the signature was from someone he had never heard of, somehow the words he had just read were as a message from out of the unknown, speaking to the depths of his own unknowing. The sudden realization that he now had another human being—a name only, not yet a face—with whom to share his distress, someone who would understand because she too had lost contact with one she loved, comforted his soul.

He read the letter through twice more, wiping at his eyes and having to sniff more than could be accounted for by the cold remaining on his face from outside, then rose and went to the room that was his office down the hall.

✤

The letter that Ursula received the following week, in near-perfect German, read as follows:

Dear Fräulein Wissen,

I received your letter with glad heart, and understood every word perfectly. You will understand, perhaps, why it brought tears to my eyes to hear from you, when I tell you what must be the disheartening news that I am unable to comply with your request.

The simple reason is this: I do not know where my son Matthew is. I have not seen him since the middle of January, nor have I heard a word from him.

He is, I am all but certain, behind the Iron Curtain, most likely in the DDR. He received a very strange parcel a few days before Christmas—a rose, actually, which he took as a clandestine message from your friend, Fräulein Dortmann. He was off soon afterwards in search of her, and I have heard nothing since.

My heart is afraid. But I pray, and do my best to remain hopeful.

It may interest you to know that I had some acquaintance with both Sabina and her dear father many years ago, before the war. Both Matthew and I were extremely fond of them both, and owe Baron von Dortmann a great deal in the way of faith.

I realize we do not know one another. I am more rapidly than I like to admit becoming an old man and have more time on my hands than, no doubt, you do. But it so cheered my heart to hear from one that, if I may be so bold, seemed like a friend, because of the intertwining strands of shared loves.

*In any event, it would gladden this downcast heart of mine
to see you and meet you. If you are a friend of Sabina von
Dortmann's, then most assuredly my son would consider you
his own friend as well. And for both their sakes, I would extend
that consideration to myself also.*

*It would honor me if you could pay me a visit here. If need
be, I would be happy to arrange for transportation from Berlin.
My duties with the government are not of great significance
these days, but I am still allowed to call upon the benefits of
my position from time to time.*

*We have a wonderful little guest house in the village, hardly
two stones' throw from my home. It would be such a pleasure for
me to have the chance to play "host" again.*

*Thank you for writing. I hope we may have the opportunity
to meet and talk face-to-face in the near future.*

Sincerely and appreciatively yours,

Thaddeus McCallum

Tears of joy were streaming down Ursula's face before she had
finished a third of Thaddeus's letter.

Any human contact at the deep point where soul meets soul
is an occurrence capable of suddenly shattering the dreadful
and oppressive sense of isolation that closes in when such contact does not exist for too long a period.

At last she understood more fully what she had done in complying with Sabina's request concerning the pink rose!

Oh yes—of course she would go see him in Bavaria!

What a joy it would be to know Matthew's father. Especially
since he knew Sabina as well!

It would be a way almost to touch her again!

∽ 49 ∽

A Community of Friends

Udo Bietmann's words could not have been more accurate.
Three days after their arrival at Kehrigkburg, he had driven Matthew, Sabina, and Baron von Dortmann—careful that they not

be seen by neighbors or townspeople—several kilometers out of the village to a small Mennonite community comprised of four families.

He explained to them as they went that it was a cooperative effort involving some twenty to thirty individuals. The four families had been allowed to retain their ownership of the land as long as the DDR received its share, because of the vastly superior efficiency of output the Mennonites produced. Officials even came periodically, ostensibly to inspect the premises, but in reality to get what information they could from the simple farmers whose methods obviously worked far better than those of the large Communist cooperatives that now made up most of East Germany.

Three full generations were represented, and an abundance of family ties knit those involved together in tight bonds of kinship as well as Christian brother- and sisterhood.

As they approached, they could see and hear machinery at work in the fields. Several tractors were ploughing the rich dark earth in preparation for the spring planting. Four houses, two large barns, and several other smaller structures made up the central cluster of buildings, out from which in all directions spread the rich farmland the farmers were now preparing for their crops.

Bietmann had already called on the elder of the community, Arndt Moeller, to discuss the situation. Their visitors, therefore, were expected.

The pacifist position of Mennonites in general, and those of Kehrigkburg specifically, prevented their involvement in what would be termed the politics of the world. They were neither anticommunist nor pro-democracy, nor vice-versa. They lived—more practically than many likewise laying claim to the theory in principle—the belief that since God's kingdom was not of this world, neither should be their allegiances or priorities. They were not, therefore, active in any of the underground activities in which Udo Bietmann played a prominent role. It was only rarely that he asked for their help and only in a situation such as this, where Christian brotherhood took preeminence over political loyalties.

Sabina, Matthew, and Sabina's father were all welcomed

warmly into the community and were each provided with one of the extra rooms in three of the four houses. All three, however, took their meals with the Moellers.

By day the baron romped about the place, talking with the older men and watching with fascination all that went on. Matthew went to work immediately with the men, first in completing the preparation of the fields for planting and, two weeks later, sowing the seed that would be tall and brown by harvesttime. Sabina spent her days with the women, mostly in the farmhouse with meal preparation, but occasionally with outdoor work as well.

It was a tonic to all three to be busy again and involved with the earth they loved so dearly.

On their third day, Matthew entered the farmhouse in the middle of the morning. There sat Sabina, her back to him, on a wooden stool across from Frau Moeller and two other younger women, a large pot on the floor between them. Her sleeves were rolled up, her hands wet to her wrists from the work as with her left hand she skillfully turned one potato after another, while with her right she plied a small sharp knife. Between her feet the curled remains of cutaway skins dropped into a pan, while the clean, white flesh of the inner potatoes was tossed into the water-filled pot in the center.

The vision that rose before his eyes was of a long-vanished time when the activities of a family were more tied to the earth and what it produced than was the case in this modern age. It reminded him of *Lebenshaus* and that peaceful era before the war.

Even more marvelous to Matthew's eyes was the speed with which chunks of peeled potatoes fell from the hands of the elderly woman and two younger daughters, plopping into the pot so rapidly that the motions of hands and fingers remained almost invisible, as were the deft movements of the knives they so adeptly wielded. At the same time a steady stream of conversation flowed between the four at nearly as brisk a pace as the knives sliced their way just below the surface of the potatoes.

Matthew had only a moment to take in the scene, for with his entrance all four heads turned toward him.

"Matthew!" exclaimed Sabina. "I thought you would be busy ploughing that field all morning."

"I came back to refuel the tractor," he said. "Have you seen your father? I thought he might want to go out with me."

"He was out and off with Herr Moeller shortly after coffee early this morning."

"You look like you're having fun," said Matthew, now also greeting the other women.

"Oh, you can't know! To be doing something productive for a change, without always having to look over our shoulders, feels better than I can tell you. It's been so long—well, since *Lebenshaus*—since I've had the feel of the agrarian life."

"You father said almost the same thing yesterday."

"When you grow up with the soil," said Sabina, "you can never escape it. Ever afterwards, life isn't complete when you don't have to do with the earth in some way."

"And speaking of the soil . . . I have a field of it waiting to be turned over," said Matthew.

"Are you having as much fun out there as I am in here?"

"I don't know, but it's probably close. If you see your father, tell him to come out and join me."

Matthew turned and left the kitchen, and Sabina resumed her peeling and the conversation that went with it.

∽ 50 ∽
Matthew 5:44

The evening had been quiet.

An undefined heaviness had gradually given way to a prayerful silence descending upon Matthew, Sabina, and the baron as they sat together in the sitting room. With one accord the thoughts had begun to revolve with unexpected compassion around their old neighbor, friend, and nemesis Gustav von Schmundt.

They had been at the Moeller farm a little more than a week. The warmth of summer was steadily approaching. With Matthew's help the preparatory stages had been completed a day or two earlier than anticipated, and now he and the baron had begun helping the men with the planting. All three found themselves more content with their accommodations than at any time for months, chiefly owing to the fact that they were able to work for their bread in the midst of the stimulating mental and spiritual fellowship of the Mennonites. The balanced diet of meaningful labor and invigorating intellectual exchange provided a full range of the sort of human nourishment they had been sorely lacking.

Their conversation late in the day had turned toward the attempted escape through the water canals. Enough time had passed since the incident that they found themselves able to talk about, and even laugh at, the closeness of the call, and had been explaining it to several of their new friends.

"When I heard Gustav calling my name, as I lay there in that pipe," said Sabina, laughing, "I nearly died from terror."

"I was so afraid he would poke the barrel of a gun into the crack I was holding open," added Matthew. "If they'd opened fire, the bullets would have bounced around inside that concrete pipe until we'd have all been full of holes!"

As the evening had worn on, however, their mood had turned more pensive with regard to their adversary. They had not been able to rid the sound of Gustav's voice from their minds, nor had Matthew been able to remove from his memory the sight of Gustav's face in the split second before the door had clanked shut, leaving them inside the blackness of the pipe.

Gustav had been so close to finally laying his hands on them!

Many emotions had surged through them in those frightful moments, all of which came back to revisit them on this evening as they thought of the incident from the perspective of gathering distance.

The dread of the voice, face, and motives that drove Gustav in this passionate search for them was a fear quite literally for their very lives. He whom Sabina and the baron had known all their lives had become a murderer . . . and their mortal enemy.

And yet . . . the very sound of Gustav's voice had sparked what they could only admit to be old sensations of compassion at the same time.

How could the two feelings intermingle? How could they love the very man who was trying to capture, imprison, and perhaps even kill them?

It was a spiritual quandary of enormous proportions, and the weight of it had been growing upon all three throughout the afternoon and evening.

It was Sabina who first gave voice to the confusing range of questions plaguing her. "I simply don't know," she sighed. "What are we supposed to think of poor Gustav, Papa?"

The baron smiled. "How else but as one of God's children upon whom we are commanded to look with compassion?" he replied.

"That's not easy when he is trying to do us harm."

"Nowhere that I can think of in the New Testament is the word *easy* applied to the living of the Christian life," said her father, smiling again, this time with a twinkle in his eye.

"Jesus said his yoke was easy," rejoined Sabina.

"Ah, Daughter," laughed the baron, "you indeed have me there!"

"What exactly do you mean by your question?" asked Matthew, looking at Sabina.

"I mean, is he our enemy or our friend?" answered Sabina seriously. "We're obviously doing everything we can to get away from him, but at the same time, as afraid of him as I am, I can't help but feel there's something more we ought to be doing . . . as a friend."

"You mean in the way of compassion, like your father said?"

"Perhaps that is it. I don't know. . . . It's all very confusing."

"There's certainly no doubt he is our enemy," said Matthew, who hadn't had the depth of relationship with Gustav to incline him toward an abundance of compassion.

"You know, however, my boy," said the baron, serious now and in the tone more of introspection than of offering counsel to either of the others, "that our enemies occupy a place of special significance in the life of the Christian. We are told to love them, pray for them, and do good to them."

"That is not an easy assignment," said Matthew.

"Not an easy assignment at all," rejoined the baron, his tone growing yet more pensive.

"But, Papa, how *can* we possibly do Gustav good when he is trying to do *us* harm?"

"I don't have a ready answer, my dear," answered the baron.

"I simply know the role between adversary and Christian is extremely important in the latter's growth. Jesus said that *anyone* can love those who love them in return. There is no distinguishing value in that."

Matthew and Sabina nodded their recognition of the basic truth stressed in the Sermon on the Mount.

"Perhaps its very difficulty," the baron went on, "indicates why it is, as I said, of such singular importance. It takes a depth of spiritual maturity and character to love and do good to those whose intent is just the opposite toward you."

"We're back to Sabina's question," said Matthew. "How can you do someone good whom you are doing your best to avoid?"

The baron did not answer immediately. His reflections sent him back to the seventeen years he had spent in prison at the hands of his own personal enemies—enemies whose reasons for keeping him there he still hadn't the vaguest notion of.

Both Matthew and Sabina sensed the depth of his thoughts and bided their time. They knew that the baron had, in a sense, earned the right to speak upon this most profound and even puzzling of spiritual directives—the command to love, do good toward, and pray for one's enemies. They were content to wait for his thoughts to collect themselves around words they could learn from.

It was several minutes before he spoke, but when he did, both his listeners recognized in his voice the tone that said he had spent many years thinking and praying his way around the horns of just this dilemma.

"The Lord said that by our obedience to this very command," began the baron at length, "will we be sons of our Father in heaven. I find *that* statement almost more shocking than the command to love one's enemies in itself."

"Why, Papa?" asked Sabina.

"Well just think of it! Imagine all the things Jesus could have pointed to that would be marks indicating deep spirituality—prayer, faith, righteousness, self-denial, fasting, spiritual knowledge, studying the Scriptures, expounding spiritual principles with deep insight for all to hear. But there's not a word of any of that here. If you want to truly be God's sons, says Jesus, even as I am the Father's Son, then this is what will make you a son—love your enemies and pray for those that persecute you, *so that you may be sons of your Father in heaven.* It is positively an astounding passage! It lends an entirely distinctive perspective to the view most Christians have of spirituality."

"Do you really consider it a new perspective, Baron?" asked Matthew.

"Not new. There have been many righteous men and teachers in the world who have proclaimed the principle of returning good for evil. But Jesus elevates the teaching to an altogether higher level when he so clearly bases spiritual adulthood upon it. For his followers, one of the great distinguishing qualities of behavior that will make them truly sons and daughters of God lies in one's response to those whose intent is to do you harm. It takes the attainment of spiritual maturity into such an intensely practical realm—a realm where most individuals, in fact, make no attempt to be spiritual at all because the command is so positively grating and vexing to the flesh."

He paused briefly, thinking as he spoke.

"Isn't this, after all, one of the things that so set Jesus apart from all other so-called holy men—that he so emphatically refused to defend himself against his enemies or speak against them. Just the opposite—he loved them and forgave them . . . even as they were putting him to death."

"But aren't we defending ourselves against Gustav, Papa," said Sabina, "by trying to get away from him?"

"Ah, Daughter," sighed the baron, "you have always asked the most difficult of questions!"

They laughed.

"I do not understand all of what it means to obey the command given in the Sermon on the Mount with regard to one's enemies. It contains depths into which my sight is incapable of seeing. When I was in prison, I prayed for my captors and did my best to love them. Nearly the only form that love could take was passive. I was in no position to do them any good, as the Scriptures say. So I contented myself with praying for them and for myself, that I would live in a constant attitude of forgiveness and compassion toward them. Yet it was always a constant struggle simply because of the facts of my circumstances."

"Did you find your circumstances conducive or hindering toward obeying Jesus' command?" asked Matthew with deep interest.

The baron sighed, then smiled.

"My heart's desire for most of the years of my adult life was to truly be God's son. After a year or two in prison, as I began to reflect with great prayer upon this passage, I saw that the Father had placed me in the absolutely *most* perfect environment in which for him to develop that sonship within me. Everything else was taken away. In a sense, nothing else was left except my enemies and my persecutors. Those are circumstances to either drive a man mad, or onto his knees that divine sonship may be cultivated in the depths of his character. I came, in time, to be deeply thankful for my lot. For there truly was nothing else I wanted but to yield to that sonship.

"And now, the facts of our circumstances seem to be such that we are trying to get away from those who would harm us. Gustav *is* our adversary, and we believe it to be God's will that we avoid him. So I do not know how we do good to him or love him. Perhaps only in our attitudes, in the forgiveness we allow to grow in our hearts toward him, even as we are seeking to remain out of his clutches. It is admittedly a quandary.

"There is, however, one thing we are always capable of toward any man, toward enemy or friend, whether we are in his presence or not. We are always capable of praying. That is perhaps the only outlet our obedience can presently take."

The silence that fell among them this time was prayerful. They were all three, by the very immediacy of the drama in which they found themselves, aware of the enormity of the command of the Lord in Matthew and of what laying down of hostility it required to obey it.

After a moment the baron slipped quietly to his knees. His action was followed immediately by his daughter and Matthew.

All prayed silently for some moments.

"*Father,*" said the baron at length, "*in what limited ways we are capable, and to the limited ways our finite minds are capable of grasping it, we do join our hearts and pray for Gustav, our onetime friend and now our enemy.*"

A whispered *amen* came softly from Sabina's lips.

"We do not even know what to pray, Lord," the baron continued, *"other than that our hearts would be clean of resentment or bitterness toward him and that you would love him and accomplish your will and your purpose in his life, whatever that might be. Even as we pray these things, however, we pray also for your continued protection, that you would blind the eyes of our enemies from finding us, as contrary as these two prayers seem to be."*

"I, too, offer Gustav into your hands, Lord," prayed Matthew. *"I pray that he would be capable of doing us no harm, yet that you would deepen love in our hearts toward him, the kind of love your Son, Jesus, commanded us to exercise toward him. We desire to fully be your sons and daughters, and we desire to obey your every command. Help us where we are weak."*

"Amen, Father," whispered the baron. *"Amen!"*

PART IV

Joseph Aviz-Rabin
July–August 1962

∽ 51 ∽
Joseph ben Eleazar

He hurried across the wide thoroughfare, on his way home, as night began to invade evening, after a day's work in a deep basement portion of the Kremlin.

Leon Tsankov—as he was known by day—was grateful for the job, and it had certainly provided dividends beyond the meager wage he was paid. During all those long years of exile, when freedom was a word whose meaning he nearly forgot, he had dreamed of moments like this, dreamed of having his old job back again, dreamed of walking along Moscow's quiet streets again.

But now that he was out, with much of the routine he had longed for reestablished in his life, he found that it was not a life worthy of dreams at all. It was tedious and boring, and he was tiring of it.

He had longed for freedom. But this was assuredly not it. He was no longer behind bars. But what freedom could this be called? Life in the Soviet Union offered no freedom anywhere, not in the Kremlin any more than in Siberia.

If such a commodity as freedom existed anywhere in the world, surely it must be a thing far different than this.

He did not stand as tall as he once had, nor with the same pride in his heritage as had fueled the fires of his youthful vision.

The Communist system had effectively destroyed the vitality in more than one youth's heart. Was it altogether destroyed in his? It felt nearly gone, yet he hoped there was still some life remaining . . . somewhere within him.

Prison robbed years off one's life, took the lilt from one's step, and stole the zest for living from one's spirit. He knew he looked old for his thirty-seven years, though what did it matter . . . now.

It was not prison, but rather the life he had tried to establish after it, that was now sapping him of what had driven him for so long—the desire to labor on behalf of his people against this dominating regime that had destroyed so much of what he loved.

Love . . . a strange word even to enter one's thoughts in this place, in this Russian capital called Moscow. How could love grow under a cloud that denied the existence of a supreme Good at all?

What did he love?

In his youth he had loved the idea of a country Jews could call their own. At barely fifteen he had joined with the Zionists who had secretly infiltrated Poland.

His father was appalled at first, though he grew used to the idea in time. As a follower of the venerable Ba'al Shem Tov, Eleazar Aviz-Rabin felt that the people of God gave God honor in their hearts—not through political causes.

Now, however, since his release from prison, he who was known late in night's lonely hours only to himself as Joseph Aviz-Rabin had been drawn more to the Hasidic community of Jews here in Moscow. They, like his father, found satisfaction in the more mystical elements of their faith. Indeed, Joseph found himself struggling more than he would have anticipated with conflicting pulls upon him—between the Zionism to which he had given so much, and for which he had suffered, and the Hasidism, which his father had gone to his grave believing in so earnestly.

Was there something more, something deeper, to it all than he had allowed himself to see, something the Hasidies had discovered? Did the religion of his heritage have anything to offer his tired and aching heart?

He was enough of a philosopher to realize that perhaps that was all one could look to religion for in Russia these days, a balm for the heart and mind. You were not permitted to possess much beyond your own thoughts—and those you had better keep to yourself.

Secrets of the heart. He had a few of his own, and they were speaking louder to him these days.

Whatever Zionism may have accomplished in Israel, there was not much it could do for him. On so many of these lonely nights walking home, what he longed for most . . . was a face to love.

He was not even free in his dreams. He could not be free from them, nor free to dream them.

He pulled his coat around his shoulders. A summer evening's chill whipped across the street, making him shiver. He walked on, unable to keep thoughts of the past from intruding unbidden into his mind.

Freedom . . .

It had been close back then. So close! But he had allowed it to slip away, and with it any hope for happiness.

He had relived the day many times in the memory of his mind . . . and his heart.

It had been the day of parting . . . the last time he had seen the face that had grown since to live in the quiet little home he had made for it, deep in the caverns of his innermost self.

Alas, it was no doubt the only part of himself he would ever be able to share with her.

∽ 52 ∽
Separations

His father had wanted him to marry the rabbi's daughter from the time he was ten or twelve. He had never been told the exact day or year when the two men had arranged it. He had known she would be his wife before even the hint of a beard began to show on his face.

It was not the way of all Jews during the changing times that both the twentieth century and the German Nazis brought to the Warsaw that was his home.

But it was the way of his family, for his father Eleazar was a Hasidic Jew, of the tribe of Judah—Hasidic and orthodox in family matters, as was the rabbi. Joseph was old enough at the time to find himself intrigued with the idea of marriage, and by the day the betrothal was made official he had to admit he approved of his father's selection.

The families had known one another, as did all in their synagogue, for years. But Rabbi Wissen was an important man, one of the most distinguished rabbis in all Poland. Joseph had never dreamed of marrying one of his daughters. Once his father made known to him, however, that he and the rabbi were discussing matters regarding the future of their son and daughter, he suddenly began to look at young Ursula in a new light.

Two years later, during one of the festivals in Poland when Jews had gathered from several villages at the big city to celebrate the Purim, he had seen her dance with other young maidens in their synagogue as part of the celebration. She was twelve by then, and he was amazed what a change had taken place, seemingly overnight—she was nearly a woman . . . and a pretty one too!

The betrothal was sealed shortly after that, and Ursula was given a small gold band to wear on her finger. The families began to spend holidays together, and the two young people saw one another more frequently. Ursula was a shy girl, but gradually she and Joseph learned to talk freely. As they did, he became more and more thankful for his father's wisdom. She was intelligent and able to talk about thoughts and ideas and the kinds of important things he was interested in.

He had not known it at the time, of course, but now in retrospect he realized that he had been growing to love her.

It was very soon afterward, however, that the Nazi net had begun to drop.

They had seen the persecution coming in Germany, but the moment Poland was invaded, everything changed. Whatever plans there had been for marriage were postponed. Both fathers agreed they must wait either until the war was over or until they could all get safely to either Russia or Switzerland.

The nightmare fell quickly upon Jewry in Poland. Suddenly everything was in turmoil. Names were changed. Many were arrested. Organizations such as the JDC began to help with emigration, though the difficulty in getting out grew every year.

It was during this time that he had himself become involved with the Zionists. Their political ambition of trying to establish a Jewish homeland in Palestine appealed to his sense of justice and idealism. Their fervor appealed to his youthful energy. Their willingness to fight, even die for a cause, appealed to the latent anger of all Jewish youths against the Germans for the persecution of their people.

At first he had tried to hide his keen interest in the movement, but in time it was impossible. An intelligent teenager, analytical of brain, sharp of wit, keen of tongue, it was not long before he and his father had engaged in heated discussion round about every angle of the Zionist cause. Aviz-Rabin, generally an open-minded man among Hasidim, after an initial negative reaction, in truth found many things to agree with and rather enjoyed the dialogues with his son. Of concern, however, was Rabbi Wissen's potential reaction to having a Zionist as a son-in-law.

The betrothal was set, however, and even such potential conflict would not cause a man of principle such as Rabbi Wissen to break it. He had grown, like his daughter, to love and respect the boy and prayed that in time the hot-flowing blood of youth would give way to a seasoned wisdom of years. Besides, like the boy's father, Rabbi Wissen hoped to live long enough to see an Israeli homeland in Palestine too and could not help hoping the Zionist cause would be successful.

Festivals were no longer public. Families kept to themselves. Most synagogues were shut down; many were destroyed. For the first years of the war Joseph saw very little of Ursula, though when they did see one another, the meeting of their two sets of eyes spoke of deepening love between them.

Rabbi Wissen, optimistic at first about remaining in Poland with his people, gradually began talking about escaping to Switzerland. He was concerned for his family, of course, but there were also certain valuable relics in his possession, he said, which he must *not* let fall into Nazi hands. There were ways, he said, that they could get out, a network of safe houses that would house them through Poland and Germany and south to Switzerland.

Then had arrived the fateful night when the rabbi had come to visit them. He was taking his family away from Warsaw, he said—immediately. He had made arrangements he hoped would see them safely to Switzerland.

Aviz-Rabin had been taken seriously ill, however, and knew he could not make the journey. At his request, the rabbi begged Joseph and his mother to accompany them. Eleazar urged them to go, but neither would leave him. Joseph said he would follow later and find the rabbi and his family among the Jewish congregation in Switzerland. He was torn between escaping with the family of his betrothed, his love for his father, and the loyalty he felt to his Zionist friends. Between the conflicting loves and loyalties, he had chosen the latter.

It was a decision he had questioned ever since.

It was but a short time later that the identity of his family, and others who lived in the same building, was discovered. A raid . . . screams in the night . . . angry shouts . . . fists beating on doors . . . Gestapo boots running through the building— the memories would live with him forever.

"Go, Joseph . . . flee!" cried his mother at first warning, pointing to the window of their small apartment.

A moment he hesitated, fear, uncertainty, confusion, question in his eyes—feeling so grown-up when talking boldly with his friends, now suddenly so young and afraid.

"Go, my son . . . obey your mother," came the weak voice of his father from the bed.

There was no time to think. For once he had to act upon impulse and obedience rather than by the inquiry of his reason.

Only a few seconds more he paused, still gazing at the two imploring him—like the few who had escaped the swords of Titus in Jerusalem in the year 70—to flee to the mountains.

Heavy-booted feet sounded in the corridor, coming toward them. Suddenly his own feet found themselves. He ran forward and kissed them both, unaware of the hot tears of anguished parting spilling down his cheeks.

"God be with you, our son" were the last words he heard.

In seconds he was on the fire escape and down to the alley . . . running . . . running, he hardly knew where. When he finally dared return to the building at three in the morning— where he had been for five hours he hardly knew—it was like a mausoleum. Every Jew in the place had been rounded up and taken away.

He cried the remainder of his tears, then took refuge with Zionist friends whose identities were still secret, doing what he could to investigate the whereabouts of his parents. All he learned was that everyone that night had been taken to the prison at Treblinka.

He could do nothing for them now. He knew that if they were not already, they would soon be dead.

At eighteen, Joseph Aviz-Rabin was an orphan, alone in the world. He had lost his chance to escape the Holocaust with the family of his betrothed . . . and now it was too late.

He had had no contact with her or Rabbi Wissen or anyone who had known them for nineteen years since, and it tore silently at his heart.

∽ 53 ∽
Call to Wakefulness

Joseph walked into the small, chilly apartment he euphemistically called home, sat down on the threadbare stuffed chair, which was the most comfortable piece of furniture in the sparse place—including the bed—and sat staring straight ahead.

The reflective walk home had put him in an even more somber and melancholy mood than usual. He had no energy even to find something to eat.

He had not always been so moody. His rational intellect and mental enthusiasm, along with an optimistic outlook, his vigor of personality and carriage, his thoughtful analysis of anything that came his way, had always served him well. He had even endured the years of his imprisonment with reasonable intellectual detachment from severe feelings of depression over his lot.

His was a cerebral, not an emotional, personality, driven by ideas, causes, and vision.

All that was slowly changing.

What more could he have asked for? Most dissidents and prisoners were not nearly so fortunate. Many lost their lives in Siberia . . . or were never heard from again.

Yet almost from the moment of his discharge from prison he had felt a gradually descending cloud of oppression coming over him, a suffocating sense of entrapment, instead of the jubilation he should have felt. What did *freedom* mean—there was that word again!

He had never felt less free than in these last two years. Nearly every friend from the old days was gone. The Zionist movement itself, now that so many of its goals had been reached, was not nearly so vibrant as before—at least in Russia. Those who had not been imprisoned by this time had found their way to Israel.

There would always be causes for concerned Jews. Like the matter of the photographs his boss had given him to smuggle out of the country. He had been glad to do it. If he could help his people, he would.

But somehow the zeal of old was on the wane.

He had fled eastward out of Poland into Russia with six other young men in 1944. They had established contact with Jewish communities in Russia, had studied hard to learn Russian, and had gradually been assimilated into the Russian system. He had become Leon Tsankov, a Polish Russian, with papers to prove it.

Unfortunately, after the war Stalin's persecution took over where Hitler's had ended. Out of the multitude of races in Russia, only the Jews were singled out for such brutal persecution. Only the Jews were required to have their race printed on their identity cards. The Hebrew language was banned. While other churches were allowed to remain open, synagogues were shut down. Thirty to forty thousand of the best intellects in the Russian Jewish community—poets, scholars, professors, writers, rabbis—were eliminated in the first wave of Stalin's silent postwar holocaust.

In his early twenties by then, with his new identity and working for Stoyidovich, Joseph became one of Moscow's leading underground Jewish political activists against these atrocities. He helped many escape from Russia, while making use of every contact he knew to attempt to learn the whereabouts of Rabbi Wissen. But to no avail.

Eventually his underground work was discovered, and he paid for it with eight years of his life. He knew he was lucky to be alive. Millions of his fellow Jews had not been so fortunate.

Happily, after Stalin's death in 1953 the persecution gradually lessened, though it continued still.

Now Joseph was out of prison, but time was passing. The years away had drained him of an essential vitality that could never be retrieved.

He had seen it in the eyes of nearly every Russian over the age of thirty with whom he was acquainted. He had always assumed it hereditary and, for that reason, that he would be immune to it's influence. But now he sensed it coming over him as well—a dull listlessness, a tired lethargy that was the result of nothing more nor less than giving up on life.

The Communist system killed people in many ways.

It killed the minds of its most creative poets, philosophers, and religious thinkers by sending them to Siberia. It killed Jews in the old-fashioned way Hitler had been so fond of—simply by eliminating them. And it killed its own obedient citizens by anesthetizing them to all that might offer them hope to reach out and live.

"Life" here was nothing more than numbness, a dead and impotent plodding on with whatever dull routine had been set before you. The vigor of youth was sapped and drained by the age of thirty. Every eye on all the sidewalks of Moscow bore the same empty, vacant expression—the look of the walking, hopeless, insensible, unfeeling dead.

The worst of it was that he felt the same anesthetic cloud of numbness settling over him as well. He could feel his own eyes glazing over as with an invisible narcotic of dreariness.

Yet strangely, he still possessed enough of what remained of his will not exactly to resist the process, but at least to observe that it had begun and say to himself, *I must somehow stand against this, or very soon I will become one of these listless, sluggish unmen myself.*

He knew that something was approaching upon which the future of his very being depended. Not exactly a crisis, for that would imply more alertness of foresight than his consciousness could at present claim to command. But certainly an offered fork in the road, which, if he did not take it, might be the last such that would come his way.

His will had grown sleepy, but it was yet, though barely,

conscious. With what remained of it he was doing his best to think about these things and summon himself back to full wakefulness.

What was wrong with him? He used to be so mentally vigorous. He had to get out of this rut. He had to *do* something!

Places were, in fact, coming alive within him in preparation for the change.

Yes . . . he could feel that a change was at hand.

The emotional half of his nature, for so many years walking in quiet subservience to the more active side of his intellect, was at last exerting itself, calling out to him from heretofore un-apprehended depths.

The season for the emergence of those inner wellsprings of feeling—to accompany and bring completion to his intellect—had come. All this time, even before he became aware of their more forceful assertion against the inner walls of his being, they had been carving out within him a reservoir which, now that he was becoming aware of its existence, and its emptiness, he longed to fill.

Joseph was lonely, and no cogitative analysis could make the feeling go away. It was not the first time in his life he had felt such an emotional reaction to his circumstances, but it was the first time he acknowledged it as such.

No longer was it enough to think and reason. No longer was it enough to fight for a cause. No longer could he force the un-pleasantness away from him.

From unseen depths rose the desire after something "other," something more, something that would allow him to say, "I feel, I am happy, I am alive . . . and life is good."

His normal way had always been to reason his way through the thicket of such personal quandaries. But he could not bring his mind upon them with sufficient focus.

In truth, it was not his own stirring emotions speaking this enlivening announcement of dissatisfaction. They had been sent only as messengers of wakefulness, to summon him to rise, and become a child. Out of those newly felt emotional reservoirs the voice of the Eternal was speaking to his soul and saying, "Come to me, my son. I have been waiting for you . . . and now it is time."

Into the heart of Joseph Aviz-Rabin, therefore, those words from the eternal Heart of the universe began to ring with newly tender reminders of his betrothed, beckoning him out of the loneliness, and forward toward a *life* that seemed too distant and vague to even hope for.

∾ 54 ∾
Lonely Resolution

When Joseph awoke, still seated in the chair he had occupied all evening, he was surrounded by the blackness of his small quarters.

He had drifted to sleep to thoughts of Ursula, and she had occupied his fragmentary dreams that followed as well.

He stared ahead into the darkness, hungry, still dressed, yet making no move to rise.

As he sat in the silence he felt something—something unusual . . . something that did not belong.

He brushed at his face unconsciously with his hand to swat away what must have been a fly.

His hand was wet.

Again it sought his face. It too was wet with tears.

Where had these come from! He had not wept in years. Even prison had brought no flow from his eyes.

The Voice continued to speak. The enlarging inner reservoir of emptiness was making its presence felt.

The will of Joseph Aviz-Rabin was engaged in the battle of its life—whether to allow the dreary Russian dullness of brain to overtake him . . . or whether to stand, exert himself, and fight.

Love . . . freedom . . . loneliness—everything that had drifted through his thoughts this day swirled about within him.

What was the use, said another voice. Give in to the sleep. You cannot fight it.

What was he thinking? said another voice. He had always been a fighter. Who was he to even think of giving up?

Ursula . . . Ursula . . .

Would she even remember? If she did, would she love him? What was the use of fighting for life—he would never find her anyway.

Perhaps it was best to leave her where she was, living in a corner of his heart, undisturbed. Was that not better to make a home for her inside himself than to search and search and never locate her, or to discover that she had died in one of the war camps . . . or that she was married to someone else?

The warm tears on his cheeks reminded him of her. He wiped at them again—why was he so powerless to stop the flow! They reminded him of springtime, of the fragrance of hyacinths and fresh grass and warm sunsets.

What was he doing thinking of such things! There were no happy sunsets in Russia, not for him.

But if there were none, why did he long so for those sights, those smells . . . for a life of happiness?

No, he would find out. He had to find out. He had to know what had happened to her.

There had to be something worth living for! He was not a Russian—he was a Pole, a Jew, with a proud heritage. The blood of the ancients flowed through him.

Hyacinths must still grow somewhere in the world!

Accompanying the urgings in his heart now came to his will the inner calling that it must rise, saying that it was finally time to follow his beloved and flee this place. If he did not act soon, it would be too late . . . and he would be asleep forever.

It was time to rise, to seek his future by more determined means than mere plodding forward. There was nothing more for him here.

He would find a place where flowers still grew!

It was time to leave Russia . . . or die trying.

He had helped enough others establish contacts with those who knew how to get people across the border and connected to undergrounds moving westward. He would now go to them on his own behalf.

He would begin making preparations tomorrow!

The instant the resolution came, Joseph rose to his feet. In the very act of decision, in the engaging of his will to live, had something snapped to attention within him.

He readied himself for bed and drifted to sleep more at peace with himself than he had been in weeks.

He awoke famished but refreshed.

He dressed for work and ate with an eagerness he now realized had been missing for nearly a year.

He had allowed himself to succumb for too long to the spiritless languor without even realizing it.

But no more!

ᘒ 55 ᘒ
The Three Communists

He had only been back in Berlin a few months, but Andrassy Galanov was finally tiring of this German assignment.

He could not help beginning to worry a little, too. Berlin could easily become a sinkhole to opportunity if he allowed himself to waste away ignominiously here.

All he was being given to do was investigate endless lists of names. He had knocked on more doors and asked more questions in the last month by far than he had in Moscow upon his uncle's quest.

And for what?

He hadn't uncovered so much as a whisper that could possibly connect the people they were looking for with the stolen photographs, nor with the rabbi his uncle so fervently sought. If he didn't turn up something soon, he was in danger of incurring Korskayev's wrath, and that would not be healthy for his career. He couldn't care much less about Schmundt's people, yet if there was a connection, he had to find it.

He'd questioned all the known Christians in the region south of the city near where last summer's accident had taken place. There were a few suspicious characters he'd run across, but he was reasonably certain they were hiding no one. Nor had he been able to tie them specifically to the escape attempt in the middle of the city six weeks ago. He had staked out both the Brumfeldt and the Dahlmann places for several days each and had seen nothing out of the ordinary.

The news had infuriated Schmundt, which was another thing Galanov was tiring of—the German's temper.

The secretary Reinhardt was more involved in knowing what was going on than he was. She was busy at all hours, sorting and categorizing reports for her boss. She seemed to be taking the investigation more personally than Galanov would have expected for someone in her position.

He and she had been talking just the other day when the distinct impression had come over him that she actually knew more about the potential movements of the fugitives than Schmundt himself or the fellow Schulte, who had been commandeered into action on the case as well.

He pondered it later, his curiosity mounting. What was it to him, he concluded in the end. He had no loyalties to either, though he felt a bit sorry for the secretary. She was a sad and lonely woman. He couldn't help think she would be better off away from the Schmundt fellow, who was so insensitive toward her.

What did he care anyway? She meant nothing to him.

∿⌒∿

Meanwhile, Gustav von Schmundt was doing his best to maintain some semblance of his own pride and dignity following the humiliation over the bungled affair at the Stadtplatz.

How was it possible that he could have been so close and yet had victory stolen from him yet one more time!

He was still holding the baker in a cell in Berlin, just out of spite, though he would have to release him eventually.

What an idiot, he chastised himself for the dozenth time! He had let the military truck drive right past him with all of them in it! Once he realized his horrendous mistake, nothing he had done had been able to gain any lead to locate the vehicle.

But he had both Galanov and his own loyal but slow-witted assistant Schulte on it and a dozen other leads. Every file from the past two years had been activated. He had his secretary working ten hours a day sorting through them all, making telephone calls, and whatever else she was capable of, while he tried to fit together the string of movements McCallum had made that had led them eventually to Magdeburg.

Pieces were gradually coming together. It was like a giant jigsaw puzzle, and eventually he would find the final connection that would put him face-to-face with his adversaries. When that day came, he would lay his hands on them! He would look into Sabina's face, hold her gaze, then smile in his victory. It would be a smile that would relish in the fear he would see in her eyes, a smile he would slowly allow to become an expression of benevolent kindness. Then she would finally see how foolish she had been to flee from him, that he alone could offer her salvation. She would approach him, begging for his help and mercy.

His pudgy lips broke into a smile just thinking of it. The one consolation after the recent mess was in knowing they were still in the DDR. He would crack their network wide open!

The failure to nab McCallum, Sabina, and her father—and such a mortifying failure, knowing they had outwitted him in the minutes following the close encounter in the drain—had effectively driven shut the doors of his conscience, whose faint creakings had previously set uncomfortable movements to motion in his thought processes. He had sealed out the annoying questions about what he had become. He felt foolish for being duped by the bakery van, and revenge now fueled his motives even more strongly than before.

Nothing can quell the humility so necessary for human growth more quickly than being made to look foolish in another's, or even in one's own, eyes. The immature man or woman immediately raises himself up to the full height of his pride and vows to have the better of it next time.

Whatever unpleasant thoughts had come to him in that hotel room—namely, that he had allowed himself to become a man whom Sabina never could admire—they were far from him now. If he chanced to reflect upon that day at all, it was only to laugh with disgust at the morose mood that must have come over him. When the time came that he had to put on whatever cloak of character was necessary to change Sabina's mind concerning him—once she had entreated him for compassion—he would do so.

Until then he would not worry about it . . . and he *would* have his revenge.

∽◠◡◠∾

Farther east, meanwhile, Emil Korsch continued his search for any trace left by the disappearance of the photographs. In this he was about to prove more successful than his two colleagues.

Inquiries had gotten him nowhere.

But somebody knew something! They had to. Nothing of this magnitude occurred without leaving behind a trail of sorts to follow. Korsch decided he needed to create a market for the crumbs. If they were turned into a sufficiently valuable commodity, somewhere in the city some lowlife would get wind of it, stoop down, realize what he had discovered, and attempt to profit by it.

He called one of his most skillful agents into his office.

"Kapp," he said, "I want you to see that a particular tidbit of information reaches the lower quarters of this city."

"I have ways to accomplish that, Comrade Korskayev. What information?"

"I want it known that the KGB will pay handsomely for information regarding traitorous Jews."

"Will the Committee condone such—"

"You let me worry about the Committee!" snapped Korsch. "It must be cleverly done, Kapp. There must be no tracing of it to this office. Do you understand?"

"Yes."

"I simply want to make it more profitable than usual for the pigeons in Moscow to bring us what they know."

"I understand, Comrade."

"Following that, make sure all your usual informants know it as well."

Kapp nodded.

"However, you mustn't pay them too easily, or their greedy hands will think we have become soft."

Kapp turned on his heels and left the office. While awaiting results from this latest maneuver, Korsch would continue investigating every Jewish connection he could lay his hands on.

Something would turn up soon, he was certain of it.

∾∾∾

Thus the quests of the three communists continued to converge. Unknown to any of the three, however, the scope of their search was about to widen to include a certain Jew from Russia . . . whose destiny lay westward.

∾ 56 ∾

Bavarian Retreat

The teakettle's merry tune rang with joy in the ears of Thaddeus McCallum and Ursula Wissen, who were seated at the table in the former's chalet, chatting while they waited for the water to boil.

It was the first time the whistling sound had felt happy in either of their hearts for months. They were acquaintances of less than an hour but seemed already to have been friends all their lives.

Thaddeus had picked Ursula up in Oberammergau and driven her the last several kilometers—over the mountain and to the chalet from behind—by horse-drawn carriage, which he had borrowed, including the horse, from one of his neighbors.

Even before they reached the house, the two had talked and laughed more together than had either in months. Never, they both declared later, had the simple companionship of another human being, one who understood, meant so much.

The sixty-three-year-old former ambassador and the thirty-five-year-old Pole were already fast friends.

Thaddeus rose to attend to the teakettle, but Ursula stopped him in his tracks.

"Please, Thaddeus," she said as she rose quickly, "let me."

"How can I play the host, young lady, if you will not let me serve you?" laughed Thaddeus.

"By allowing *me* to serve *you*," she answered. "You know the principle—the last shall be first and the first last. You will honor me by allowing me to be the servant in this case."

"I suppose I am unable to argue with your logic. You have turned the backwards spiritual equation at me."

"It has been so long," Ursula went on, her tone turning pensive, "since I have fixed tea for a man. You just can't imagine—"

Suddenly Ursula looked away, overcome with unexpected tears in the midst of her happiness.

Thaddeus rose and placed a gentle fatherly hand on her shoulder. He had never had a daughter, but he had had a wife whom he loved dearly, and his love for her went a long way to opening his heart to the sensitivities of the feminine disposition. More important to the deep knowing of women even than that, however, was his own sensitive, observant, and selfless nature. He had eyes to see, he understood, and his heart went out to Ursula with the love of the one true Father.

"You can't know how alone I've felt," Ursula said, finishing her sentence. "The tea . . . the smell . . . the sound of the teakettle—it all just suddenly overcame me."

Thaddeus McCallum knew people because he knew his own weaknesses. He loved others and put them ahead of himself. His eyes were therefore opened into the depths of humanity because his own Self did not obscure his vision.

"I understand, my dear," he said with compassion in his voice. "I, too, long to be able to serve those I love."

"My father so enjoys his tea," said Ursula, drawing in a long, steadying breath. "My mother and sister and I would take such pleasure in preparing it just the way he liked it."

She stopped and now turned toward Thaddeus, smiling again, though with a tear or two trickling out of her eyes.

"I'm sorry," she said. "Just the thought of tea, and suddenly I was overcome with so many things. It's just not the same fixing tea for yourself and drinking it alone."

"Well, that is what we are here for—to give one another someone to enjoy it with. I will be honored and blessed to allow you to serve me."

Ursula smiled again and set about measuring out the loose breakfast tea, placing it in a tiny wire strainer, and pouring the boiling water over it and into the teapot. Sugar, cream, and lemon slices sat on the counter in readiness once it had steeped the necessary three minutes.

"You are a dear man," she said, resuming her seat to wait. "If Matthew is anything like his father, then I understand why Sabina is in love with him."

Thaddeus laughed.

"How long has it been since you have seen Sabina?" he asked.

Ursula told him and went on to explain their history with one another. Then followed both their shared connections with *Lebenshaus*, such that, by the time the pot of tea was empty, they each had heard the other's story in detail. Thaddeus knew about Joseph as well.

"I am so glad you thought to write to me," said Thaddeus.

"I am grateful for your invitation," rejoined Ursula. "You can't imagine how good it feels just to talk about it all."

"Oh, can't I!"

"Come to think of it, I suppose it must be just the same for you."

The conversation continued, and thus the day passed more quickly than seemed possible. A walk through the woods to the village, another carriage ride—this time up the mountain to the village of Uelstenberg, where Thaddeus wanted to show her the quaint, centuries-old church with which he had made acquaintance—and much further pleasant conversation were all part of it.

They prepared a dinner together, which they partook of midway through the afternoon.

Evening came. It was warm, and they sat on the balcony overlooking the lovely downward slope of the hillside, sipping tea, and contentedly talking. Cows meandered about with their gently tinkling brass bells creating a random and yet wonderful mountainous xylophonic symphony.

A long silence came. Both had quickly grown so relaxed in the other's presence, however, that neither became uncomfortable with it, nor sought unnecessarily to fill it. It was a full silence, not an empty one, and therefore rich of nourishment for the soul. They drunk of its pleasures rather than endure its perceived awkwardnesses.

One of the singular marks of friendship must surely be the
capacity to enjoy silence together without feeling the need to
disturb it. Ursula and Thaddeus were by now friends and were
able to let the deep currents flow between them, though the
surface of the water showed no ripples of activity.

At length Ursula spoke.

"Do you mind if I ask you a question?" she said. Her tone
indicated that she had been thinking seriously already.

"Of course not, my dear."

Again it was some time before she continued. Thaddeus did
not press.

"How do you find a balance between being told to be content and thankful with what befalls you and, on the other
hand, wanting something to be different than it is—even
wanting something different because it seems the Lord must
want it different too?"

Now it was Thaddeus's turn to ponder carefully before
replying.

"Do you know what I am asking?" said Ursula.

Thaddeus smiled. "I think so," he said. "How can I obey the
command to rejoice and give thanks for all things when at the
same time I am praying fervently for Matthew's return and
feeling that the Lord must want his return too—is that something like what you are asking?"

"That's it," replied Ursula.

"If I am thankful and rejoicing, why would I pray for circumstances to be *different* than they are?"

"Exactly."

"And if I am praying for circumstances to change and for
some trial or hardship I am facing to be *taken away*, then does
that not imply a discontent with the way things are?"

"Yes!" agreed Ursula yet a third time. "I cannot honestly say
I *am* thankful for my lonely life. I try to be content. I try to *give*
thanks. But down deep, Thaddeus, I do want it to be different.
I *pray* for it to be different. Giving thanks is different than *being*
thankful. And I certainly have not been very rejoicing."

"Nor I," smiled Thaddeus. "Just the opposite. It has been a
very downcast and discouraging past few months for me."

"So how *are* we to obey when we are being pulled in such opposite directions? How am I to know what the Lord wants me to do about Joseph, being thankful for the separation on the one hand, and being so weary of it and wanting to find him on the other?"

Still another thoughtful few moments of reflection followed.

"Perhaps you put your finger on it a moment ago," said Thaddeus at length. "Perhaps the distinction we ought to draw is between *being* thankful and *giving* thanks, between *feeling* an exuberant joy and making the determined decision to say 'I *choose* to rejoice.' Maybe it is *not* always possible to feel rejoicingly thankful in the midst of painful circumstances, but perhaps we can still make that choice to say 'I give thanks to God for this in spite of its difficulty.'

Ursula thought for a few moments.

"You must be right. Sometimes it is impossible to command your feelings to change. Feelings and emotions seem to go however they want to go on their own."

"Yet if we are commanded to rejoice and give thanks, then it must be something we *do* rather than something we *feel*. We would not be given a command that our feelings could make us incapable of obeying."

"How do you mean?"

"If emotions operate in another realm than what we can control—if, as you say, what we *feel* at any given moment is a function of simply how our feelings happen to go—then the command must not be an emotional one at all, but rather one of the will, of the mind. Thankfulness must be a *choice* rather than something we either feel or do not feel."

"So we can feel the sadness, the loneliness . . . but still say 'I choose to be thankful.'"

"I think so. Now that I think about it, how can it be otherwise? Even though it sounds like a contradiction, I think we can even say 'I choose to rejoice,' though we may not feel what is commonly called *joy*. If it is not so, I do not see how the commands could possibly be obeyed. I have had no more success than you in commanding my feelings into submission. Perhaps some natures are able to exercise absolute authority over their emotions, but I have never been able to. The only thing I am absolute master of within myself, it seems to me, is my *will*.

Therefore, the will must be the seat of my obedience. If we are commanded to *do* things, how else than by our will can we do them?"

"What then about praying for circumstances to be altered?" asked Ursula. "If we choose to give thanks for our *present* circumstances, how do we justify praying for Matthew and Sabina and Joseph to be brought to us? Does not praying for a *change* mean the thankfulness is incomplete?"

"Hmm . . . that is a difficult one," said Thaddeus with a smile. "It would seem there is a contradiction of sorts."

"What else is prayer oftentimes," Ursula went on, "but asking God to alter circumstances. If we were truly thankful, why would we want him to change things?"

"The perplexities of your questions deepen! But," added Thaddeus, "something just comes to me. Consider Jesus' prayer in the garden. He asked his Father for the cup of crucifixion to be removed. There was certainly no feeling of thankfulness in his heart at that moment. He did not *want* to go to the cross, to such an extent he even asked the Father, if it was possible, to keep him from it. Yet he ended his plea with: *not my will but yours be done.* Perhaps therein lies the answer we have been seeking. In the flesh we will desire things and pray for things that we cannot know whether are God's will or not. Thus we pray, even for a change of circumstance, but always with the foundation undergirding those prayers of 'Lord, do *your* will,' and with the orientation undergirding the whole: 'I will choose to be thankful and grateful for your will, whatever it is, and will choose to rejoice in it however you may answer my prayers.'"

"It must be exactly as you say," sighed Ursula. "But that perspective is not an easy one to maintain sometimes."

"Not easy at all. Nor was it easy for Jesus. But then he had the advantage of knowing more intimately and deeply than we that the Father's ways are *always* best. That seems to be a truth very difficult for our stubborn, untrusting natures to learn."

A lengthy silence followed.

Dusk in the Bavarian Alps was well advanced, and a slight chill had crept down from the mountaintops to engulf the chalet and village.

"Will you pray with me, Thaddeus?" said Ursula at length. "I feel the need, yet again, to turn over my concerns to the Lord."

"It would give me more pleasure than you can know, my dear," replied Thaddeus sincerely.

They sat a minute or two longer in the quiet of the evening, then closed their eyes.

"God," prayed Ursula, *"I do give you thanks for the circumstances in which you have placed me, as lonely and disheartening as they can be at times. Help me, Lord, to be more thankful in my heart, and help me remember to give you thanks for all things in my mind. I do thank you Lord, right now."*

As Ursula's prayers fell silent, Thaddeus spoke.

"I, too, Father, give you thanks, as an act of my will," he said. *"I thank you for this time of separation from Matthew, even though with my next breath I pray that you would bring him back safely to me, along with Sabina and her father."*

"Amen," added Ursula. *"Protect them, Lord, and watch over them wherever they are."*

"And wherever Ursula's betrothed is at this moment, Father," prayed Thaddeus, *"if he is alive, we pray for your protection upon him, and that by some miracle you would reunite her with him. If he is with you or your will is otherwise, show Ursula what you would have her do. Make clear if the time has come that you would want her to lay the betrothal down and seek new directions within your will."*

Ursula quietly wept as Thaddeus prayed. She had not heard anyone pray for her in so long! To know another brother cared deeply enough to lift her in prayer before the Father's throne with such sincerity strengthened her immeasurably.

"Give us thankful hearts, Father," continued Thaddeus. *"Give us thankful wills and thankful hearts, even in the midst of the fleeting unthankfulness of our weak emotions. Above all, accomplish your will in our lives. Do your will, and we will give you thanks for it."*

They prayed quietly within their own thoughts for a time.

By now it was downright chilly, and after a few more minutes both arose and went inside.

"You sound almost like I remember Baron von Dortmann," said Ursula with a smile.

"Oh, my dear," rejoined Thaddeus, "how could you say such a thing. I am still such a spiritual infant alongside him!"

"Not in my eyes. It is clear the Lord has been at work within you for a very long time."

"Well, I shall take your words as a deep compliment . . . and with great humility. I suppose, as brief as was my encounter with him, the baron has been my mentor in spiritual things all this time. If a servant cannot be greater than his master, yet I suppose it is inevitable that a servant grows to reflect his master.

"But now, my new and dear friend, it becomes late. As much as I am loath to see you go, I fear the time has come that I must take you down to your lodgings in the village."

"Oh, Thaddeus," exclaimed Ursula, suddenly giving Matthew's father a great hug, "thank you so much for this day! I haven't enjoyed myself or felt so at peace for longer than I can remember."

"Nor I. And we shall have all day tomorrow as well. I shall fetch you bright and early and bring you back here for Eggs McCallum!"

"Oh, I can scarcely wait! Get me down to my bed so I can hurry to sleep and hasten the coming of morning."

"Are you up to walking down?" asked Thaddeus. "I think we shall have plenty of moonlight."

"Oh yes . . . that sounds delightful."

Thaddeus went to grab their coats. As they left the chalet, Ursula slipped her arm through Thaddeus's. From that moment on, as long as he lived, the elder McCallum considered Rabbi Wissen's eldest child his unofficially adopted daughter.

❧ 57 ❧

The Two Engineers

The nature of the interview was the last thing Friedrich Detmold had expected.

His trade involved buildings, not conspiracies. He was a contractor, not a spy.

Nor was he a man to take chances. He had not reached the pinnacle of his profession to throw it all away on some madcap scheme for a handful of people he had never heard of.

At first he had thought the two young engineers had been applying for jobs.

He had a personnel department for such things, he told them. They should submit their applications through channels.

They were not after jobs, they said—at least not right now. Their request was something only he could help them with.

"You own a small storage building, I believe?" said the young man who had introduced himself as Peters, who then went on to describe the building exactly, which was in reality not much more than a large storage shed. "We would like to make use of it . . . with your permission, of course."

"It is neither for rent or for sale," Detmold replied.

"We don't want to buy it or rent it, only use it for a short time."

"My company uses it for storage," objected Detmold. "I am presently engaged in a construction project less than a kilometer from there. I cannot allow—"

"Will you at least listen to the reason for our request?" interrupted the other, a fellow named Kohl.

Even though he was a prominent and wealthy businessman who had not gotten where he was by being a pigeon for other people's schemes, Friedrich Detmold prided himself on the capacity to listen to reason and to give every man a fair shake. He therefore consented to this last request and sat back to listen. He would throw the two out later if they didn't make any more sense than they had thus far.

Fifteen minutes later, the proud German contractor was visibly moved. It was a story no man who had ever loved a woman could hear without feeling anguish for the plight of these two who had come to him for help.

How could he not assist them when it lay so easily within his power to do so?

"I will think over your request," he said as the meeting had ended, shaking both men's hands. "Come see me again tomorrow."

The rest of the day and evening had been a thoughtful one for Detmold. He discovered within himself a long-dormant anger toward the Russians for what they had done to half of the once-proud German nation. His father had served during the war and had lost his life at the Russian front while trying to protect against invasion from the east.

And what had he died for?

The Russians had taken Poland and the eastern half of Germany anyway and now controlled half the globe! He had never liked them—he didn't like them now, and if he could help even one person get out from under the cloud of Communism . . . he would!

Kohl and Peters were putting their engineering training to shrewd use.

He *would* help them!

It would be his way to fight back, to avenge his father's death, to play some tangible role in protesting against the ugly Russian wall that was a mockery to freedom.

When the two returned the following day, they could not keep from showing their elation. They had been searching for a suitable site and a workable plan for months and had hoped the contractor would go along with it. But never had they dreamed the same man they had talked to the day before could be so enthusiastic today.

"Not only may you use my shed," said Detmold, "if you will allow me, I would like to help you carry out your plan. I have men, equipment . . . whatever you need."

Too stunned to speak, for a moment Kohl and Peters were beside themselves to accept his kind offer.

"There is still one difficulty in all this that we haven't been able to get around," said Peters.

"Name it," said the contractor.

"How will we be able to coordinate and time everything on the other side? We write, of course, but the letters are opened and scrutinized."

"I think I may be able to help you in that as well."

He went on to explain what he was thinking.

"Could you do that . . . so simply?" asked an astonished Kohl.

"Not simply. But certainly it could be done. I have many contacts . . . they would never suspect a thing. It will take a little time, of course. But I will get the arrangements under way this very afternoon."

The three agreed to meet again the following evening at

Detmold's home, where the two young East Germans would brief him on everything he would need to know.

∽ 58 ∽
A Peculiar Visit

The communication, when it arrived, was all the more mysterious in that there seemed no mystery to it at all.

All the proper restrictions regulating business dealings between the BRD and the DDR had been observed. The meeting had been cleared by several governmental agencies as well as the *Stasi.* The man's permit to enter East Germany for the day and then return to the western sector had been granted. Everything seemed so perfectly in order as to satisfy even the suspicious Communists.

The only question left unanswered was . . . *why?*

Why would one of West Berlin's leading building contractors want to consult with him, Josef Dahlmann, a simple and unpretentious East German mechanic?

Nothing about the request made the slightest sense.

Yet this was not a place where asking too many questions was healthy. He had been called on by the authorities. It had been explained to him that a request had come to their office for an interview, and they had granted it. The West Berliner would be brought out to his home—accompanied by an agency official, of course—in five days.

The only thing Josef could imagine, and during those five days the thought plagued him with mounting anxiety, was that something had been discovered in the matter of the escape attempt—the truck perhaps—and the supposed interview was but a ruse. Were they coming to arrest him? Had the *Stasi* uncovered the entire underground network?

The day arrived with no resolution to his angst.

But the good man needn't have worried. At midday the car arrived and the official of the DDR presented himself, then introduced Friedrich Detmold of the BRD to the humble village mechanic.

"Herr Dahlmann," said the contractor as the two men shook hands, "no doubt you are curious as to my reason for seeking you out."

Josef nodded, still half expecting to be arrested by some hidden *Stasi* or *Vopo*.

"I am a contractor, as I understand you have been told," Detmold went on. "I have a certain piece of large industrial equipment about which I need your advice."

"Please . . . come in," said Josef.

"I would, of course, be only too happy to help," he said, offering the two guests seats, "but how . . . how do you know of me? I repair mostly cars and trucks."

"And large farm equipment, if I am not mistaken."

"Yes . . . that is, uh . . . true, but—"

"You see, Herr Dahlmann," said the contractor, "I *do* know of you, and that is enough. You are considered—by those I have spoken with—to be an expert with regard to the machine of mine which is inoperable at the moment. Quite simply— that is why I have come: to seek your advice about bringing my project to completion."

"I still do not understand," said a bewildered Josef. "But . . . but of course, I will do whatever I am able to assist you."

"Good . . . excellent!" replied Detmold enthusiastically.

He looked around the room.

"Perhaps our, ah—our comrade here," he said, indicating his governmental chaperone, "would care for some tea or coffee while we discuss the technicalities of the matter?"

"Of course. Angela," called Josef.

In a minute his sister appeared. Josef introduced her to them. Equally bewildered, Angela could have no idea that she herself was the cause of this entire elaborate charade.

"Angela," said Josef, "would you like to fix the gentlemen some coffee and tea?"

She nodded, with an attempt at a smile, which betrayed more nervousness than hospitality, and went to the kitchen to comply with the request.

Detmold now pulled from his pocket two blank sheets of paper, on which he began drawing. Not a single mark made the slightest sense to Josef, but he did his best to follow the technical words that flowed until the tea and coffee were served.

As Angela filled their cups, the contractor continued to write. Now suddenly Josef understood something on the paper, as did his sister. Catching her eyes, Detmold pointed nonchalantly down with his pencil. There sister and brother read the words: "Ask him into kitchen."

A look of question came over Angela's face.

The almost imperceptible nod moved in the direction of the third man in the room, who was at that moment sipping from the cup she had just served him.

"Thank you, thank you very much, Fräulein," said Detmold, again with greatly affected good cheer. "Now, where were we?" he added to her brother, and continued with the same technical jargon from before.

"*Bitte, mein Herr,*" they heard Angela say to the official, "would you be so kind as to help me bring some cakes from the kitchen?"

"Uh, why . . . why, certainly, Fräulein," replied the man, taken momentarily aback but not about to deny opportunity to his sweet tooth.

He rose and followed her into the kitchen.

The instant he was gone, Detmold's voice lowered to a whisper.

"Pay close attention, Dahlmann," he said, barely audibly, "we do not have much time. I am working with Franz, your brother-in-law. The machine I am describing is for digging a tunnel—do you understand me?"

As he spoke, the pencil was flying across the page, and within seconds the lines he had been doodling with earlier took shape into the details of a map.

Eyes wide, Dahlmann nodded.

With furious haste, Detmold filled out the rest of the drawing, adding what details were necessary. In less than a minute, in addition to the map were indicated times, streets, and procedures his sister and her friend were to follow. In one corner, a strange, attempted drawing of a single stalk of plant with tiny leaves and flowers attached completed the page.

Hearing his sister and her unwitting companion finishing

their business in the kitchen, quickly Detmold folded the paper several times and stuffed it into Dahlmann's hand, then continued drawing on the sheet behind it, quickly fabricating a crude drawing of a large earthmover.

"I have arranged permission to contact you again. If there is a change in the schedule, you will receive a message saying that the machinery is not operating properly. Otherwise it will be as I have written it."

"There are others also," whispered Josef.

"They will have to wait," came the whispered reply. "If this succeeds, I will get word to you. Whoever they are, they must be ready."

∽ 59 ∽

Preparations — USSR

He wanted to tell Stoyidovich.

The old photographer had been kind to him. And they shared a secret no one else in the world knew.

For now, however, the old Jew would be safer, thought Joseph, if he knew nothing of his plans. When he did not appear for work one day, his boss would be as bewildered as anyone. If there were questions, he would be able to answer truthfully that he knew nothing concerning the disappearance of his assistant, Leon Tsankov.

Perhaps he could find some way at least to communicate his affection, even if he could not tell him all.

The young apprentice Paskov might be more troublesome.

He was one who had not given in to the lethargy of this land quite yet. Joseph had seen the look in his eyes. He recognized it well, though he had grave doubts about how friendly was the cause that inspired it. He knew the young fellow had been far from pleased when Stoyidovich had rehired him after his release, especially when the old man had immediately placed his former assistant above the younger apprentice.

He had not seen his coworker around for several days, however, and something told him it was just as well.

He was scheduled today to meet a man who arranged things for people in trouble. Joseph had worked with him before, though he knew no details of what the man did. He had never needed to know before. He hadn't wanted to know.

Now it was different. *He* was the one for whom the arrangements had to be made.

"You have . . . no objections to being sent through Christians?" the man asked after their preliminary arrangements had been taken care of.

"No, why should I?" asked Joseph.

"I know you are of Zionist leanings. You have told me so in the past. Some of your number are, shall we say, radical about matters of belief."

"I will take anyone's help who offers it," laughed Joseph.

"I am glad to hear it," replied the man.

"Besides, I am not nearly so radical in my own leanings as I once was. There comes time for reevaluation, you know."

The other smiled. "You will meet many individuals before your journey is over, some of them Jewish, but others quite different from yourself."

"Why did you ask about Christians?"

"There are many different routes and undergrounds and safe houses that can be used. What I have in mind for you involves a small group of Christian men in Poland. I think in your case they will be most reliable. I will get word to them immediately to see if they will be amenable to help."

"*If?*"

"They are somewhat peculiar in their notions. I have never actually spoken with them. I have another acquaintance who has means of contacting them. They are, as he puts it, rather finicky in whom they help. But I am confident they will have no problem in this case. And they are one of our best sources between here and Warsaw."

"After that?"

"Once you reach them, you are out of our hands. I have no idea what happens next. They make the arrangements beyond the Polish border."

"You have no contacts all the way to Germany?" asked Joseph.

"Oh, I do. Our own network has connections all the way to Berlin. But it is best to vary the escape routes used. The danger is much greater now since the wall."

"You still have never told me the name of your organization. Are you the JDC . . . or *The Rose?*"

The man smiled.

"Neither, I'm afraid."

Joseph waited, the look of interrogation still on his face.

"I have no organization," came the reply at length.

"But, I thought . . ."

"I am only a man, trying to do what he can to help all of God's children. If you should chance, however, to fall in with any individuals of the latter group you mentioned, you will be in good hands."

"You are connected with them?"

"Only distantly."

"Is it possible I will fall in with their number?"

"Of course. All such organizations, whether it be the Jewish Distribution Committee or *The Rose,* or whoever, have inter-connective linkages from time to time. Many safe houses operate freely to help several such underground networks."

"And you . . . what about you? In all the times we have met, I still do not know your name."

Again the man smiled.

"Care and prudence, Mr. Tsankov," he said. "It is for the same reason I do not know your real identity."

"Well, I will tell you," said Joseph. "I have to tell somebody before I go . . . I *want* to tell someone, and my senses tell me that you are a friend and that I may trust you. I am Joseph Aviz-Rabin. I am a Jew of the house of Judah. I hope, with your help, to reach the land of my people."

"I will pray that you will, Joseph," replied the other. "I, too, sense brotherhood with you. So you shall hear my name, and by God's grace perhaps you shall be led to pray for me, as I will for you. I am called Dmitri Rostovchev. I am a Christian, of the brotherhood of Jesus Christ."

He reached forward and took Joseph's hand and shook it vigorously and warmly.

"Will I see you again?" asked Joseph.

"Only on the day of your departure. Will you be ready four days from now?"

"I will be ready."

"Do you have an automobile?"

Joseph shook his head.

"We will have one for you, then. There is one we manage to take back and forth across the border as needed. It is old, but I think it will see you safely to Warsaw, where our contacts are usually told to pick it back up. I will also have all the needful documents at that time. You will drive into Poland alone."

"And if the Christians you spoke of choose not to help in this case?"

"Then I will make alternate arrangements for you. In either case, be ready and meet me here in four days. I have every confidence, however, that they will be eager to see you."

"Why?"

"Because I will get word to them that I think it is God's will for you to meet them."

"How can you know that?"

"I occasionally have a sense about these things."

"You are an intriguing man, Dmitri Rostovchev."

"That has been said to me before." Dmitri smiled.

"I am not at all sure I understand you."

"That too!"

"In any case, I thank you for helping me. I will meet you here in four days."

"Godspeed, Joseph."

∽ 60 ∾
Preparations — DDR

It had been with positive disbelief that Josef and Angela had pored over the strange paper that had been wadded into Josef's hand right in front of the Communist official.

Could they trust it?

What if it was some plot to entrap them? What if it all had to do with the previous escape, the truck, the network?

Yet . . . if she was ever going to be free, Angela said to herself, she would have to take risks.

Josef suggested they discuss the matter with Erich. They did. He too had reservations. On the other hand, how would Detmold have known so much about the two women's husbands if he had not actually spoken with them?

Most convincing of all was the drawing of the plant, and the eight words beside it which the contractor had written on the bottom of the sheet: "Franz says remember the walk in the *Heide.*"

"No one else could know about that day," said Angela, "certainly no official of the DDR. The message has to be from Franz himself."

"Are you willing to chance your freedom that this is his doing?" asked her brother.

Angela thought seriously for a moment, then nodded her head.

"What good is freedom if I am not with him?" she answered. "How free am I if I cannot be with my husband? Yes, I am willing to take the risk."

She paused, then smiled.

"It is from him," she added, looking down again at the paper. She was gazing at the drawing and thinking of that day she and Franz had spent. It was almost as good as if he had brought an actual stalk from the wiry shrub! This was Franz's doing—how could she have doubted it for a second?

Erich and her brother, however, were concentrating their attention on the drawing, the location of the wall, the proposed tunnel, and the instructions that accompanied it. It was certainly the most ingenious plan of escape they had ever heard of!

Daring . . . full of risks . . . but ingenious!

"The timing is everything," commented Erich. "Even a one-minute delay . . . hmm," he added, thinking. "Perhaps my cousin could help once they are in Berlin."

A smile broke over his face.

"If I know Hermann," he said, "especially after the last failure, he would be eager to participate in something so clever. To outwit the *Vopos* would give him extreme pleasure!"

Erich had put his finger directly on the greatest risk of all that was involved.

Everything would take place right within full sight of the *Vopos* border guards! It was so positively foolhardy, said Dahlmann after they had done their best to digest the details of the plan, that it just might work.

"It is not safe to keep this paper," said Erich. "I suggest we all three study it, discuss it so there can be no doubts as to what Angela and her friend are to do, and memorize every word . . . and then burn it. To keep it could be dangerous. We must not forget the KGB fellow who has been around and that we are still under surveillance."

The other two agreed, and by the end of the day, the paper was only a memory.

Her initial reservations quickly behind her, Angela was eager to visit Geoff's wife and tell her the exciting news. Then she had to go to Kehrigkburg and talk to her new friend Sabina. For if it worked, the contents of the mysterious paper they had just burned would involve her as well.

The two talked excitedly for some time. Sabina was thrilled for Angela. She well knew what it was like to be separated from the man you loved.

"I want to know what happened when you and Franz walked in the *Heide*," said Sabina.

"It was the day he asked me to marry him." Angela smiled.

"How romantic—was the *Heide* in bloom?"

"Everywhere! The wood was full of pink and purple. It was such a pretty day. We walked for hours and hours."

"Is that how you knew the message from the contractor had to be from him?"

"No one else could have known. But . . ." she added, "there was one other thing."

"What?" asked Sabina.

"Franz told me that day that if ever anything happened to separate us—he said in the DDR you never knew what might happen . . . it's almost as if he had seen into the future . . ."

Angela paused and sighed thoughtfully. Sabina waited patiently.

"He said that if anything like that happened to us," Angela went on, "we would send one another a stalk of heather as a reminder of our love. I think he was just being romantic at the time . . . but now we *are* separated, and then comes a strange message from a man we have never met . . . telling me to remember about the walk in the heather. How can it not be from Franz!"

Sabina smiled. She had similar memories of her own.

They talked a while longer, but soon it was time for Angela to return to Grossbeeren.

"You must get word to my friend," Sabina said as they parted.

"I promise," replied Angela. "She will be the first person I will call."

⤚ 61 ⤙
Bottom Crawlers

The business of betrayal in the countries within the Soviet orbit was one of the most widespread, lucrative, and hidden of the world's cottage industries. If free-market capitalism was not allowed here, the Communist system cultivated its own unique brand of devious socialist enterprise.

The stock-in-trade of this hidden industry was information. The only prerequisite for success was a ruthless willingness to betray the secrets of anyone in whom the authorities might take an interest. A cunning eye for untoward details and personal habits was also helpful.

Zam Paskov, twenty-seven-year-old photographer's apprentice, knew well enough what kind of information paid handsome dividends. He had been making extra money since he was sixteen by keeping his eyes open and his ears attentive. There were any of a half dozen low-level KGB agents and two or three other governmental officials who would take a call from him. If he said he had something, most would drop what they were doing to make time for a meeting with him. His was not usually the kind of information that commanded many rubles. But he was learning his trade well and lining his pockets with gradually increasing fees for what he had to sell.

It was a dangerous game, and Paskov knew it. In this part of the world there was only one fence and it had but two sides. Those on the one would never get anywhere, never amount to anything, and never have anything. That was no life for him. Those on the other were all like him—backstabbers and bottom crawlers. So if you wanted to exist on the side of the fence where opportunity lay, you had to watch yourself and be careful. You could get sold out yourself just as well as the man you were ratting on.

When word had begun to circulate last week that the governmental spy agency's ears were more open than usual, he had begun to give second thought to something that had happened at work. The more he considered it, the more he realized it might be precisely what the KGB was looking for.

Not only that what he had in his possession now just might be his ticket up to the next echelon, thought Paskov as he walked briskly along to the meeting he had set up last night.

This was a time, however, to walk with great care. It wasn't that bad a job, even if he did have to play low man to the Tsankov good-for-nothing. What if turning them both in put an end to it for him? Finding himself without a job at all would not be a wise exchange. He'd have to make sure they promised to keep him employed, and that he got enough to see him through any potential difficulty.

On the other hand, with the other two gone, he could be in line to move up, maybe even be put in charge of the whole darkroom.

With such thoughts to occupy his small and self-centered brain, he arrived at the entrance to Gorkogo Park, where he took his place at the prearranged spot. He did not have long to wait.

"You said you had information, Paskov?" asked a man bluntly as he walked up. There was no need to make a pretense of hiding their conversation, as would have been necessary had this been Washington, London, or even Berlin. This was Moscow, and the man was KGB. He had no fear of a lowlife like Paskov.

"What I have is important to your people, Kapp. It is worth a great deal."

"You will be paid, as always."

"I considered taking it straight to Korskayev myself."

"Ha!" laughed the other. "You would never get close to him. If you did, he would arrest you on the spot."

"Not for what I have, I think."

"You do not know Korskayev as I do."

"I must be paid handsomely."

"Don't haggle with me, Paskov, or I will slit your throat," spat the man called Kapp.

"How much?" said the young would-be spy, unconsciously taking a half-step back. It would not do to anger this man.

"Ten rubles."

"Ten! It is worth ten *times* that amount."

"So *you* say. I will give you twenty then."

"Agree to fifty," pressed Paskov. "If I have swindled you, then you may slit my throat. If it is all I say, then give me the hundred I ask for."

The agent eyed him skeptically but with the hint of a yellow-toothed grin. This lackey was bold, he would say that for him! For one so young, he was learning to think like the KGB itself. He was inclined to take his offer. He liked the odds.

"I'll agree to thirty," said Kapp.

"It may have to do with the photographs I know your people have been searching for," remarked Paskov with significant expression. "The *missing* photographs . . . of Jews."

"How do you know about those?" the agent snapped.

"I have my sources as well as the KGB," replied Paskov with even more significant expression. The fact of the matter was that he didn't have any sources whatsoever. But another individual, to whom he occasionally sold odd tidbits of information, had come to him, knowing of his job and his interest in such things, asking him to keep his ears open for anything to do with some photographs that might have been stolen by the Jewish underground. He had put two and two together and hoped there might be a profitable connection. Kapp's reaction told him he had been right and that the decision had been a wise one to bring it to him rather than the other, who wouldn't have paid more than fifteen rubles for it no matter what it was.

"If what you say is true," returned the agent, "I'll pay your fifty up front. Just remember the other half of the bargain you made."

"I remember well enough—another fifty if it is all I say."

"Don't be too shrewd for your own health, Paskov," rejoined the other. "It was the other half of the bargain I was referring to—what I will do if you have swindled me."

"Do we have a bargain?"

"We do."

"Let me see the fifty rubles."

Kapp pulled a handful of bills from his pocket. It was more money than Paskov had ever seen in one place in his life. It was with some difficulty that he kept his eyes from revealing his lusting astonishment.

He reached forward and took the money with a greedily trembling hand, stuffing it into some invisible place of concealment on his person.

He now pulled out a small scrap of paper and handed it to the man.

"What is it?" Kapp asked.

"Something I found in the trash where I work."

The man's eyebrows knit together in question, then he glanced up at his informant.

"What is this, Paskov—do you *want* me to slit your throat! This is only scratching and doodling from somebody's hand who had nothing better to do."

"It is in my boss's hand," said Paskov, as if that salient fact shed complete light on the situation.

"What does that have to do with it?"

"Don't you recognize that partial emblem there, on the right side?"

The man squinted again.

"A . . . star of some kind."

"A star of David," said Paskov.

"Hmm . . . yes, that is interesting," admitted the agent. "Yes, you have done well, Paskov. You have found your boss out, eh," he added in a sympathetic tone. "You think he is a Jew?"

"I think it is highly likely."

Suddenly the man's tone changed abruptly.

"So what if he is?" he nearly shouted, grabbing the little young man by the scruff of the neck. "Haven't you heard—Premier Khrushchev likes the Jews now. They are no longer being arrested. We are even letting them out of prison! You fool, what do you take me for? This is nothing! Let him be a Jew—no one cares! Give me back the fifty rubles this instant, and perhaps I will not slit your throat!"

"Please . . . please—that is not all," croaked Paskov.

Kapp relaxed his grip, still eyeing him angrily.

"Of course, I . . . I know it is nothing by itself," stuttered the apprentice. "But . . . but I . . . I overheard something a few days ago . . . I heard him talking with the other man who works there . . . they were whispering . . . they did not know I could hear."

"Other man . . . what is his name?"

"Tsankov."

"Go on, Paskov, . . . go on," said the agent, intrigued once again.

Relaxing, the young man took two or three breaths, then continued.

"I had not been at work for a week. When I came back the old man sent me to the darkroom. He is getting old . . . I think he forgot I was there. Then Tsankov—that is the other man who works there—a Jew if ever there was one, one like you say who was in prison and was released . . . Tsankov came in. He had been out. He did not know I was there. He began speaking . . . they were talking softly, but I heard him say that he loved Stoyidovich and would never forget all he had done."

"Why did he say that?"

"I don't know."

"What else?"

"There were more soft words . . . they sounded like words of parting, but why I do not know. There were no plans of change. And then the old man said—and by now I had crept toward the door of the darkroom and was listening carefully, so there can be no mistaking it . . . I heard him say, 'What about the photos?' Tsankov replied, but his back was turned and I could not hear. Then the old man spoke again. 'Did you get them into safe hands?' he said . . . 'Have you heard any more about them?'"

Paskov stopped. "That is all," he said. "I think Tsankov may have realized I was there by then and he said no more. They went about their work, and I snuck back to my place and finished the day's work. That was two days ago. I called you last night."

"Why did you not contact me immediately?" snapped Kapp.

"I . . . I tried," lied Paskov, "but I could not reach you." He had spent the day trying to decide which of his contacts would be likely to agree to his hundred-ruble gambit *without* slitting his throat.

The anger in the agent's eyes was gone. He realized what he had just heard might be exactly what his superior had been hounding them about for almost a year. If he was the one who could supply the missing lead . . .

His thoughts were broken by Paskov's voice.

"Is this information not worth a hundred rubles?" he said.

Kapp let out a long breath and looked down at him with mingled disdain and disbelieving respect.

"Don't worry, Paskov," he said. "If this leads us to the photographs, you will be paid the other fifty."

∾ 62 ∾
Father and Daughter

From the window of her room, Sabina had seen her father walking between the cultivated fields the moment she arose and looked out upon the new day.

He had always been an early riser in years past, but she had not seen him up so close to dawn since arriving at the Mennonite community.

She could tell, from one look, that he was deep in thought . . . and prayer. He may have aged, but many things about the man she loved so dearly would never change. When the ways of God weighed heavily upon him, she knew it instantly. His

countenance altered—somewhat, she liked to think, after the
fashion of Moses—when he was in communion with his Father
upon his own personal and inward Sinai.

He remained away from the others all morning and was noticeably detached at the midday meal.

Sabina knew she needed to talk with him and knew it was
something between him and her into which even Matthew
could not join. Midway through the afternoon, therefore,
observing him making slowly for the green uncultivated
meadow behind one of the storage barns, she begged permission from Frau Moeller to be excused and went outside to seek
him out.

"Hello, Papa," she said as she walked softly up behind him.

"Ah, Daughter!" exclaimed the baron with delight, turning to
greet her. "Is it not wonderful to have grass and dirt under our
feet again!"

"It is, indeed, Papa."

They walked on. The baron began chuckling.

"What is it, Papa?"

"I was just thinking of a walk you and I took many, many
years ago."

"We took many walks."

"I was recalling one in particular—one in which the subject
of dirt arose."

"I remember the day well," said Sabina, smiling at the
memory.

"What did I say?"

"That life and mystery are contained within the thing we call
dirt, that the commonest thing was the transmitter of life to
everything that grows on the face of God's earth."

Now truly did the baron laugh as in days of old.

"What a memory you have! That does sound like something I
might have said."

"Not something you might have said—something you *did*
say. Those were nearly your exact words, Papa. I have never forgotten that walk. You spoke to me of roses and dirt and egg
yolks and truth."

"It pleases me that you remember. More than that, you honor
me by remembering."

"I have always given *great* honor to your words, Papa. That is why I remember them. What I know of life and truth and our Father, I first learned from you. You have given me the most priceless gifts anyone can receive from another."

"What are those gifts, Sabina?" asked her father, his tone more serious now.

"Life . . . and truth. *God's* truth. The truth of who the Father is and how he grows his life in his children. Surely you know what I mean, Papa."

"I suppose so. But everyone gives different expression to such things, and I wanted to hear you say it."

"From you I learned to look inside every object, every circumstance, every flower, every sunset, every moment of time, even every tribulation, and especially inside every human face—to look for evidences of God's creative presence. The divine fingerprint, as you were fond of calling it."

They walked on a while in silence, each remembering the past in their own way. It was the future, however, that sat heavily upon both their minds.

"What have you been thinking about today, Papa?"

"What makes you think I have been thinking anything?"

"I know, Papa."

The baron smiled. "There is more and more of your mother in you every year," he said. "She could read me like a book."

Sabina smiled but waited. Though he was reluctant, the baron knew she would not be put off.

"Do you want me to try to answer my own question?" probed Sabina at length.

"Do you really know me so well?"

"You have enjoyed it here," said Sabina, not answering him directly. "These people we are with, the planting, having fields to walk in, dirt in which to run your fingers—something tells me you are having second thoughts about another escape attempt, Papa."

The baron sighed. She was indeed a perceptive young woman!

"This is my home, Sabina," he said. "The Germany of the east—this earth, these fields. I have not felt so much at home since that night we fled our beloved *Lebenshaus*."

"And you are thinking of staying, are you not, Papa?"

"What are the boundaries of political alignments to me? I know they are vitally important to Matthew. But I am an old man, Sabina. My life is nearly done. As long as I have my Father to love, I can be content anywhere on the globe. And . . ." he added, pausing briefly, "Arndt has offered to make a home for me right here, in their small community."

"I was sure of it, Papa," said Sabina.

"He says I will be safe, undisturbed, and that I may even have a garden plot to call my own."

"I am sure you would be extremely happy."

"I find my thoughts returning often these days to my old friend Bonhoeffer, who is now with our Father. I said to him during the war that I did not feel it my calling to involve myself societally or politically. I now find myself questioning whether, in faithfulness to that commitment, I ought to remain here rather than seek asylum in the West because it is more what is called politically free."

"I see, Papa. But it seems family now would come ahead of such a conviction."

"Perhaps you are right. To answer your question of earlier, this is what has been my struggle today—weighing these factors, of conscience, of commitment . . . of love."

Sabina nodded.

"Would you think it so very bad of me if I said I did not care about escape to the West?" resumed the baron.

"Of course not. Only it would be a sore trial for me."

"I know that, and therein lies my greatest agony."

"Even though you do not care about political freedom, Papa, the terrible wall they have put up parts people forever. How could I allow such a parting between us?"

"But, Sabina," said the baron, "*you* could not think of staying. Your place is with Matthew now."

"And also with you, Papa."

"A man and woman *leave* their parents, to become one with each other."

"I waited and searched for you too long to leave you now."

"Oh, Daughter," sighed the baron, "now you increase the burden of my decision manyfold! Never would I dream of

causing division between you and Matthew. You waited for
him even longer than you waited for me! It is only that I am
afraid—"

The baron stopped and turned away with a sigh. It was not
something he had intended to say. He knew what would be
Sabina's response, and he wanted to put neither her nor Matthew in that position.

"Afraid of what, Papa?" probed Sabina, sensing his reluctance. "You must tell me."

Again the baron sighed. He had hoped to make things easier
for the two young people, not add to their burden.

"Afraid that perhaps because of me," he said with resignation, "that . . . your plans for escape might be complicated, even
endangered."

"Oh, Papa, don't even think—"

"Please, Sabina," interrupted her father, "you are intelligent
enough to realize as well as I that two young people like yourself and Matthew will stand a much, much greater chance of
getting to safety on the other side without an elderly man to
worry about."

"That thought has not once crossed either of our minds."

"I would be surprised if it had. You are both kind and generous and completely unselfish and devoted to me. But the fact
that you would not think of it removes nothing from the truth-
fulness of my statement. You and Matthew would simply be
safer without me. You know I was the slowest one out of that
drainpipe, and if I had not been there, the military truck would
never have been seen. I cannot allow such a chance to be taken
again."

"And once we were on the other side, would we be *happier*
without you?"

"Perhaps not, but you would be free."

"What about you, Papa—would you be free?"

"I would miss you terribly, but I would be content . . . especially knowing that perhaps it was my staying behind that
enabled you and Matthew to live the rest of your lives free in the
West."

Again it was silent.

"Papa," said Sabina after a time, "you must make the decision you believe God is leading you to make. I would never attempt to convince you against your conscience. You know that I will love and respect you just as greatly if you choose to remain here. I know Matthew would feel the same. Yet we believe most strongly that your place is with us. We want you with us, no matter what the cost."

The times and decisions before them were weighty and contained no easy answers.

When Sabina spoke again, it was to remind them both of a morning that had forever burned itself into her memory with a depth of pain that always brought a stab to her heart. Yet there was also a realization that the same memory had shown her, perhaps as nothing else ever could, just what was meant by the message of the Cross.

"I watched you stay behind once before, Papa," she said quietly. "You sacrificed yourself for *Mutti* and me and all the others. I know why you did it. I know the love that prompted it. I honor you for it. And yet . . . yet I do not know if I could allow you to do it again. Perhaps the time has come for *me* to make the same sacrifice."

"What . . . what sort of sacrifice?" asked the baron. "You are not suggesting that . . . that *you* remain behind . . . either in my stead, or with me?"

"I don't know, Papa," said Sabina seriously. "Perhaps we all must reflect and pray further on the course that God has for us."

This was not what Baron von Dortmann had in mind at all. He had only been attempting to work out the dimensions of what sacrifice he might make for his daughter and her fiancé. That they might likewise desire to sacrifice their future, their happiness, even their freedom, *for him* . . . it was not something he had even remotely considered. When his daughter next spoke, it was to give voice to just that possibility.

"Perhaps," Sabina continued, "it is you who must allow us to make the sacrifice. If, as you say, your presence increases the danger, it may be that you will need to allow us to *face* that danger *for you* . . . as you faced the Nazis on our behalf back then."

The baron stopped, then turned toward his daughter.

"You make it easy for a father to be proud, Sabina," he said.

"Whatever you see in me, Papa," she returned, gazing up into the aged eyes that had not gone dim, "is only a reflection of you. You make it easy for a *daughter* to be proud."

A moment more they stood, then slowly embraced, wrapping their arms tenderly about one another. For several long moments they stood, Sabina leaning her head against the chest of the man who had given her life.

"I love you, my daughter," whispered the baron at length. "You are indeed a woman after the Father's own heart."

"And I love you, Papa."

PART V

Dieder Palacki
August 1962

❧ 63 ❧
Treason and Arrest

The investigation had been altogether too slow. Perhaps he shouldn't have sent his nephew back to Germany before they had cracked the network wide open on this end.

But at least it hadn't been a complete loss, thought Vaslav Korskayev—known to his former comrades on the other side of his ethnic schizophrenia as Emil Korsch—as he walked hurriedly and angrily down the lengthy corridor. They had finally located the trail of careless crumbs left behind from the photographs. He was positive now, as he had suspected for some time, that the men he had sent to Israel would find nothing there. He had been mistaken earlier. The photos were still on the continent, he was all but certain. But he would keep the men in Palestine regardless, trying to locate the rabbi.

His little ploy involving Kapp had paid off! Paying the pigeon would be worth every ruble.

The Jews, it seemed, had infiltrated everywhere, even the very basement rooms of the Kremlin itself.

This man had caused him no end of grief, and now that the KGB at last knew where the leak they had been searching for had originated, he would curse the day he had betrayed his country's leader for whatever misbegotten cause he thought he was helping.

Without so much as a pause he burst into the basement studio. Within minutes he had succeeded in destroying half the darkroom equipment of the place.

"Please . . . please . . . what is it you want?" implored the poor photographer.

"You will pay for your treason, you old Semite fool!" shouted Korsch, approaching the trembling man and grabbing him roughly by the shirt just below his neck.

"Please . . . please, my name is Stoyidovich."

"Bah! You were no more born a Stoyidovich than I was a Jacobs! Tell me where was their destination!"

"I do not know what you are—"

The back of Korsch's free hand struck with brute force across the man's cheek, knocking him stumbling backwards. Korsch managed to keep his fist clutched to the man's chest, however, and yanked him back forward to an upright position.

"Where are the photographs bound!"

"What . . . photographs?" whimpered the man, probably already realizing that he was as good as dead.

"The duplicate photographs that came from this studio last year, my good *Stoyidovich*, of some of your people—" as he spoke, an evil grin spread across Korsch's face—"who were, shall we say, in the same state you are presently going to find yourself . . . *if you do not answer my questions!*"

This latter was spoken *without* accompanying smile.

"I . . . I tell you . . . I do not know what photographs you mean. I . . . only process what they bring—"

The whack across his face this time was sufficient to loosen the poor old Jew from Korsch's clutches, but only for the purpose of sending him crashing to the floor.

Korsch knelt to one knee, nearly pouncing upon him with menacing threat.

"We know of the duplicates, whatever your name really is! You had a certain lackey who worked for you who found the offer of a few extra rubles too much to pass up. He knew what you had done. He tells of being replaced by a certain fellow of whose origins he was as suspicious as he was of yours."

"Tsankov was a capable assistant," said the man softly. "I . . . I hired him back when he returned to Moscow."

"Returned from where?"

"I . . . I do not know . . . he had been away."

"Away in prison!" cried Korsch. "For complicity in attempts to undermine the government."

He did not know this for certain, any more than he had known anything else about him thirty seconds ago. The facts on the man's assistant were sketchy, for the lackey who had brought them the information in actuality knew very little, except that he thought the man was a Zionist, apparently involved at high levels in the Jewish underground, and he had once overheard bits of a conversation in which prison was mentioned.

No sound came from the floor.

"Ah yes, my pathetic friend, we know all about your friend Tsankov, whatever his real name is. By the way, where is your assistant?"

"I . . . I have not seen him for several days."

"Of course you haven't—he is gone! And I want to know where!"

Again Stoyidovich said nothing.

"You gave Tsankov the photos, did you not?"

No sound.

A heavy-booted kick crashed into his ribs, evoking a cry of agony.

"He is a leader in this underground spy ring of yours, is he not!"

"We . . . we are no spies," came a whimper from the floor.

"No matter. I have a man on the way to his apartment even now. He will be arrested before the day is over."

He spun around and left the ransacked studio hastily.

Leaving the door ajar, however, Korsch paused upon reaching the outer corridor, then crept stealthily back, placing his ear to the crack he had left.

He could hear Stoyidovich crawling about, then struggling to his feet.

A moment passed. As he had suspected, the next sound he detected was the receiver of the phone being lifted.

Listening carefully, it only took a moment more, as the poor man croaked out the request to the operator, for Korsch to have the rest of the information he had come for—a telephone number of the residence, to complete the Tsankov file.

They had finally narrowed it down to the apparent kingpin of the Jewish underground. He would locate the precise address within half an hour! Smiling to himself, he turned once again and left the building.

Now he *would* have someone at the traitor's apartment, just as he had promised.

He mustn't forget, either, to send someone back to haul the decrepit Jewish photographer away.

∞ 64 ∞
Irate Call

The telephone conversation the following morning was terse on the one end, and the listener displayed no happy countenance at what he was hearing.

"When did this happen?" he said.

A moment of intense silence followed.

"You what . . . Kapp, you imbecile!"

The defensive voice coming through the receiver became noticeably more high-pitched and scratchy.

"You searched the place?"

A short answer.

"You had someone on him?"

A brief pause.

"Heading in what direction?"

He waited briefly.

"Have you alerted our people in that sector?" he asked with reserved passion.

Another pause.

"And then?" he barked.

The answer, though anticipated, sent him into renewed rage.

"Lost him. . . . I might have expected as much!"

A few stuttering words of attempted explanation.

"Where was he last seen?"

"You are certain . . . toward *Bialystok?*"

The pause this time was lengthy. The listener took in the new information with an initial bemusement indicated by a dark wrinkling of his black eyebrows, followed quickly by a new resolve that hardly displayed the seismic jolts now surging through him.

"There is nothing more?"

The answer was brief.

Emil Korsch threw down the phone in disgust. He was rapidly running out of patience.

All these fools had interfered with his plans for the last time! Why had he not taken the surveillance personally in hand? Just because the idiot Kapp had turned up one useful piece of information, that did not make him capable of conducting an entire investigation! He should have staked out the Jew's apartment himself.

It seemed neither the idiot Schmundt nor his nephew could lay their hands on the fugitives in Germany.

Now it appeared the Jew was making a break for the West as well, and his own people in Moscow had let him slip through their fingers!

He sprang from his seat and flew across his office to a cabinet of files, which he threw open with a venomous yank that nearly sent the entire drawer to the floor.

Hearing the unexpected name of the Polish city had set off a series of unforeseen tremors deep within his memory. He had encountered it once before, several years ago, in a file he had come across concerning the Polish revolt of 1956.

The report in question had been but a minor portion of the whole, a mere two pages, insignificant under any other circumstances. But his personal antipathies toward spiritual fanaticism of all kinds had caused him to glance over it with more interest than would most of his colleagues, and now suddenly the words at the top of the cover sheet rebounded into his brain:

Christian Organizations—Potential collusion in revolt.

There were lists of names, churches, various locales, mostly throughout Poland. It had been generally meaningless to him, and he hadn't even been looking for anything in particular.

But now suddenly, on this day, he recalled observing the name Bialystok on one of those pages. Was it possible . . . how could there be a connection?

And yet, he mused as he hastily flipped through the files to find the one on the events of 1956 and the Polish underground, he hadn't climbed to his present position without often being able to detect traces of clues that escaped less scrutinizing eyes.

There it was: *Polish Revolt.* Stamped across the top of the folder were the words "FOR KGB REVIEW AND ACCESS ONLY."

He tore open the file and scanned feverishly through the sheets, which covered everything from worker unrest to dossiers on all Poland's high-level governmental officials.

Halfway through the stack, his fingers stopped. He had located the one he'd been searching for. He grabbed it and the next sheet, pulled them out of the stack, and sent his eyes roving down the pages . . . there it was, just like he'd remembered—*Bialystok/Krynki!*

He slowed the pace of his overexcited search and read over the information deliberately.

It was sketchy and didn't offer a great deal to go on. But he had a sixth sense about these things. Something told him he had stumbled upon a major clue—if only he could unearth it—that would lead him to the Tsankov fellow.

"Small congregation of Polish Christians," read the entry, "suspected of links with Soviet Jewish underground . . . informant (See file: Grazinski, Ladislas) also suggests have assisted in two escape attempts into BRD. No known ties to revolutionary or nationalist groups. Not connected with any church. Implication in revolt: unknown and unconfirmed."

Several Polish names were listed: *Chmielnicki, Kervnov, Rydz, Laski,* and *Palacki,* as well as the Soviet officer responsible for providing the information: *Leonid Bolotnikov.*

Korsch was familiar with the Bolotnikov fellow, a distinguished young officer in the Soviet military who was on his way up the ladder rapidly these days. He had even picked up a rumor or two that Bolotnikov might be after *his* job.

He wouldn't worry about that at the moment.

Climbers and opportunists within the Soviet system were as numerous as snowflakes in Siberia. You had to prove your worth in this regime with more than desire. You had to be crafty, and experience usually won out over youth . . . as long as experience didn't grow cocky and complacent. He had no intention of becoming either.

If Bolotnikov knew anything more about what was going on among the Christians of Poland, Emil Korsch wanted the information!

He would get his nephew back here to help as well. He had been making a few inroads earlier in just this direction before leaving for Berlin. They hadn't pursued it then because they had been focused entirely on the Jewish angle. Perhaps the two groups were working together!

He strode back to his desk, papers from the file still in his hand, grabbed his phone, and barked into it.

While he waited impatiently, he glanced at his watch. It might be early enough in Berlin that he would catch him still at his apartment.

It took ten minutes for the connection to be made.

"Andrassy," he said without bothering with pleasantries. "Get the next flight to Moscow. I want you here immediately."

On the other end, Galanov spoke briefly.

"You can fill me in on everything—I may go to Berlin myself. But the case is breaking here. I have to have someone in Moscow I can depend on. I need you to get to the bottom of the Christian network—were you not moving in that direction before?"

Korsch listened to the response.

"Yes . . . yes, I thought you had made some initial contacts. It appears there may be more of a connection between them and the Jewish rabble than we thought. I want you to pursue the lead you mentioned."

Again Galanov spoke.

"Yes, that is true. I will likely be gone by the time you arrive. Work through my office as before. I will be in touch. I want you to find what you can about the Christian network in Moscow. I have no time myself—I must pursue another lead. We will coordinate our efforts. Be ready should I summon you at any time."

He put down the phone.

If there was a link to be found here in Moscow, Galanov would uncover it sooner than Kapp or any of the other incompetents he had on his staff.

Meanwhile, it was time for him to pay a visit to the fellow Bolotnikov.

He spun around, still clutching the two papers in his fist, grabbed his coat, threw it over his shoulders, and bounded out of his office.

With rising anticipation he sensed that what he had just discovered would enable him to intercept the traitor in Poland.

Then he would go to Bialystok himself . . . and all the way to Berlin if the trail led him that far!

∽ 65 ∽
Contact

He who had been known for a dozen years in Russia and Poland as Leon Tsankov slowed the car he had been driving across what seemed like half of Russia—from Moscow to Smolensk to Minsk, down to Brest, and now back into his own homeland, which he had not visited in years.

After crossing the border he had turned north again, though it seemed out of the way, and was now, with dusk descending, somewhere between Bialystok and the Belorussian Soviet border.

There had been someone following him at first, he was certain of it. How the car came to be back there, and who was in it, were questions he would never know the answers to. He had taken steps to elude them, though it had set him back an hour and involved many changes of directions and retracing of steps. Now, he was sure, he was at last alone.

He turned off the dirt road and approached what to all appearances was a deserted barn, glancing around for the tree with a broken limb. His instructions from Rostovchev had been sketchy, but this had to be the right place.

Yes, there it was.

He inched forward alongside the structure, easing toward the rear of the barn, then pulled in behind it, out of sight from the dirt byway he had just left. Leaving the engine idling, he got out and walked to the large door. It was unlocked, just as he had been told.

He pulled the heavy wooden slab toward him, opening a wide gap into the blackness inside. He climbed back into his car, pulled it into gear, and crept slowly forward while jamming the wheels to the right until the auto was safely inside.

He turned off the engine, got out again, and pulled the large door on its iron track until it clanked shut.

He was left standing inside, in near total darkness.

He stood for several moments, letting his eyes accustom themselves to the light, then felt his way back to the open door of his automobile, where he climbed in, sat back down on the seat, and waited.

After some forty minutes he heard the sound of a footstep outside. There had been no approach of car or other vehicle. A moment later the large door opened just wide enough to allow the figure of a man to show itself in the dimming light of evening outside.

"You there, Tsankov?" a voice said in Polish.

"Right here," he returned, stepping out of the car.

"My name is Vaclav. Come with me."

He obeyed, stepping outside while the other closed the door, locking it now, behind him.

"We'll be on foot for a while," said his guide. "Keep close; it will be dark soon."

∾ 66 ∾
Clandestine Business

Meanwhile, in a small converted basement room of a former dairy barn some ten kilometers away on the outskirts of the Polish city of Bialystok, a highly unusual and secretive meeting was already under way.

It was not the first such gathering, nor would it be the last. The group of men gradually assembling over the course of the afternoon and evening had been together for years. Arriving one at a time, by various means and routes, always different from those they had taken before so as to arouse not the slightest interest, suspicion, or even detection from neighbors or passersby, they had done this sort of thing for years.

As soon as it was determined that visitors were coming and that they would involve themselves, word went out secretly among them to begin making themselves ready for their guests' arrival. Usually the essential nature of the help required was known, and toward such were their preparatory efforts directed—whether food, clothing, shelter, money, transport, or other immediate necessity of dire or pressing circumstance.

The company of these committed men was not large. No financial or organizational backing undergirded their efforts. They were simple men, mostly farmers and all poor. What they accomplished, what they were able to give, the impact they exercised in the countless string of lives of those sent them originated in obedient faith and was sustained by prayer . . . and prayer alone.

That every individual was *sent*, and sent specifically to them for a specific purpose, which it was their solemn duty to discern and then carry out—of that foundational truth there was not the slightest doubt in a single one of their hearts. For such had their Lord and Master assembled them in the first place. It was in faithfulness to that calling that they so fearlessly, eagerly, yet unpretentiously laid their lives and their freedom on the line whenever it was required of them.

Both were indeed in peril at all times.

This was no friendly land to those of such radical spiritual persuasions. Most of these men lived within a hundred kilometers of the Soviet border, a constant reminder of the giant atheistic shadow that had engulfed their beloved Poland and the entirety of Eastern Europe.

Over the dozen or fourteen years of their activity, the most common need to which they had lent assistance was a simple and yet dangerous one: the sheltering and transfer of political and religious transients and sojourners, who, for a multitude of reasons, found themselves having to hide or flee from the oppression of Communism. Gradually their willingness to offer succor came to be known to many of the underground organizations within Russia, Poland, and Germany. Though connected organizationally with none, they were yet sufficiently in touch with others who could help more than they, and thus by their very geography were frequently contacted to function as underground "middlemen" between Russia and places further west.

They did not, however, allow any and all who called upon their services automatically to come. They were wary and protective of their secrecy, knowing that to jeopardize it could prove costly and detrimental to the Lord's purposes. They were workers in *his* eternal vineyard, not laborers in vineyards whose only purpose was the making of earthly wine. They would permit no tares to be sown in the fields he had given them to watch over and cultivate.

They had not allowed themselves, therefore, to become involved in the affairs and escape attempts of certain highly publicized political dissidents, occasionally to the great annoyance, even anger, of those individuals and groups to whose pleas they had to turn a deaf ear.

The reason for this perspective to which they held rigidly was one very few underground organizations understood: no political agenda drove their efforts, only a spiritual one. They would not compromise the latter for the sake of the former being imposed upon them by others.

An immediacy of "call" bound them together.

The older among them—who had been present from the beginning—as well as the younger—who gradually by the necessity of the passage of years took over more of the reins of leadership and responsibility—were linked together by the common vision of prayer-initiated evangelism.

They were evangelists every one, though theirs was an evangelism of servanthood, not primarily one of proclamation. None would have attached such a label either to themselves or to their efforts. They were servants only, in heart and deed. Out of such servanthood—though they knew it not—wide and far-reaching were the results of their prayers.

In the economy of the world's estimation, most of them would never be heard of outside a ten-kilometer radius from the places where they had been born, yet in the kingdom of God they were already recognized as mighty men. Their prayers were making assault against the very foundations of the strongholds surrounding their beloved land. Those strongholds would one day be toppled. Freedom would come—though the aged among them would not live to see it.

They came together in preparation to receive every new guest it pleased the Lord for them to entertain—and bowed both heads and knees in prayer.

No plans governed these seasons of intercession. From the very beginning they had been conscious that their chief duty was to open their hearts that the Spirit of God might pray through them according to *his* purposes, not theirs.

Thus, they approached their holy moments together as periods wherein they were called to listen more than to exercise themselves in petition and entreaty. They were unlearned men, they declared mutually. How could *they* possibly know the divine will? They merely opened hearts and minds and mouths to him who was their Master in all things, allowed him to pray *his* will *through* them, and then rose from their oftbent knees to carry out that will as they discerned he had revealed it.

No one, they believed, ever came to them except as divinely sent, for the purpose of receiving something that one of them would give, say, or do. Helping people move through their region, or escape from the authorities, was not their chief mission, but only the means whereby they were allowed opportunity to *give life* and *speak truth*, for the ultimate furthering of God's kingdom.

Their prayers, therefore, usually were in this wise:

"Lord, show us the need which you will call upon us to meet. Show us the physical and immediate necessities to which we must be attentive.

"Show us also the deeper need of heart to which you want us to give heed in sensitive and prayerful readiness with a word or deed fitly spoken.

"Give us merely and only the hearts of servants. Let us wash the feet of our visitor in all ways. Let us minister as to an angel unawares.

"Lord, prepare the heart of our coming visitor to receive the word for which you have sent him here. Protect him as he comes, and as he goes forth from among us. Protect and water the seed that is planted within him during his sojourn among us, and bring it to fruit in your time and in your way.

"Lord, bring freedom to this one for whom we pray—the freedom you intend.

"Bring freedom as well to this land. In your time and according to your chosen method, remove the yoke of oppression that has descended upon your people. We pray against the strongholds that defy your name. Remove the covering over the nations according to Isaiah 25:7, that your truth may be spread abroad among all people.

"Watch over your chosen ones. Protect them during these days of hardship and persecution.

"Make your truth known, Lord. May this land one day again be a land where your truth flourishes."

❧❧❧

Such were the prayers even now ascending on behalf of the Jewish pilgrim making his way over field and through wood. In the midst of descending dusk his silent guide led him, with no idea that he was the object of such concentrated prayer.

He could not know it yet, but after this night his life would never be the same.

❧ 67 ❧
Ladislas Grazinski

Though Emil Korsch's own heredity was as mongrelized as it was possible for a pedigree to become, he hated Poles nearly as much as he hated Christians, Germans, and Jews.

Hatred of anything *unlike him* was intrinsic to Emil Korsch's internal equilibrium. That he may well have had Polish, not to mention Jewish, blood flowing through his own veins was not a question he would have allowed to come nearer than a thousand miles of his consciousness. The fact that it was probably true only made him all the more resistant to it. There is a peculiarly devilish human tendency to resist a difficult truth concerning oneself with a force in direct proportion to the depth with which that flaw is ingrained within one's character. Devilish because of the origin of this blindness. The eyes of mankind are singularly ill-equipped to accurately assess its own strengths and weaknesses, in inverse ratio as those eyes are required for growth. This principle was alive and in full operation within Emil Korsch in the matter of his purity of breed.

He took a swallow from the glass of limpid ale in front of him, then glanced around the darkened public house.

Whoever this Ladislas Grazinski was, mused Korsch, he had better have a good reason for making him wait.

His thoughts trailed back to his interview two days ago with the Bolotnikov fellow. The officer was a powerful, handsome, and imposing young man. No wonder he had already caught the eye of the military elite in the Kremlin. Korsch had detected in the man's countenance that which made him wary instantly. Of a certainty, here was a fellow on the rise. He would have to be careful that it did not come at his own expense!

"I need information on certain Polish Christians," he had said.

"Why come to me?" asked Bolotnikov skeptically. He too was wary. Trust did not extend far in the Soviet Union, and in the direction of the KGB least of all.

"Your name was on a report that came to my attention," replied Korsch. "Filed after the uprising."

"I know very little."

"Why did you conduct the investigation?"

"I hate Christians."

"Why?"

"I have my own reasons," replied the young military officer evasively.

Korsch took in the information with dispassionate expression. He would divulge nothing, but here was a point of contact between them he might be able to exploit later.

"So you were assigned the case?"

"I volunteered."

"Have you made further inquiries?"

"I have not been back to Poland since the uprising. I keep files on Christian organizations; that is all."

"What about the Jews?"

"I have some information, not a great deal."

"There are connections, you know."

"I realize that, but it has not been my primary field of endeavor. I am a military man."

"What about the man called Grazinski?" asked Korsch.

Bolotnikov's face showed no sign of recognition.

"What about him? I know no such person."

"He is listed as an informant in your report—Ladislas Grazinski."

Now for the first time the young man's face showed a hint of a smile.

"Ah yes—a little Polish weasel . . . I remember now."

"What can you tell me about him?"

"Not much, really—only that for a price he would turn in his own brother. You know the type."

Korsch nodded. His KGB files had an inventory of just such individuals in nearly every city in Europe. Without the pipeline of information they provided, the KGB would be out of business.

"It is one of the reasons, however," Bolotnikov went on, "that I was suspicious of what he told me."

"Which was?"

"He had all kinds of stories about various subversives in his area—"

"Christians?" interrupted Korsch.

"Some were, not all."

"You did not believe what he told you?"

"I believed there were Christian individuals up to no good, though I could not substantiate their direct involvement in the revolt."

"Yes, your report indicated as much. However, times have changed. I have reason to believe they are involved in something equally treasonous. Can you put me in touch with the Grazinski weasel, as you call him?"

Bolotnikov had gone on to tell Korsch what he knew about the disloyal Pole, and now the agent sat waiting impatiently, sipping a beer that was becoming warmer by the minute.

A minute later the door opened. A small fidgety man walked in. Korsch recognized him instantly from Bolotnikov's description.

The fellow walked in, glancing nervously about.

"Grazinski," said Korsch in a low tone, "over here—I am the man you are looking for."

The Pole approached. Korsch nodded toward the chair opposite. Grazinski took it. Korsch showed him his identification.

If the little man was intimidated by the KGB, he did his best not to show it.

"I need information."

"Does the KGB pay well for what you want?"

"The KGB *gets* what it wants," rejoined Korsch with an expression conveyeing menace, as he had meant it to.

"My services are for hire," said the Pole, not to be cowed. His agitated weasellike demeanor did not accurately represent his inner resolve. It was clear the man had more guts inside his belly than Korsch had given him credit for.

"Relax, my little friend—you will be paid if what you give me proves useful. What I require is information on certain individuals, what you know of their current activities, and how they may be located."

"Do you have names?"

Korsch pulled out a slip of paper and shoved it across the table. Grazinski glanced over it, then nodded slightly.

"Yes, I know of several of them—Palacki, in particular, is becoming rather well known in some circles in Poland."

"Circles?" queried Korsch.

"Non-sanctioned church groups . . . possibly the Christian underground."

"And the others on this list?"

"I do not know every name. Palacki is the most troublesome to the authorities, but I believe the rest are similarly involved."

"Can you get me in touch with them?"

The dark eyebrows above the thin, close-set eyes rose slightly in greedy inquiry.

"I may be able to show you where to begin looking."

"I am not familiar with this country or this region. I want information as well as a guide."

Grazinski nodded, as if he had expected as much.

"Tonight."

"You mentioned . . . payment?" The tone of the voice was as weasellike as the expression on his face, thought Korsch. The Bolotnikov fellow had christened this lowlife with perfect accuracy.

"You will be given what you deserve," replied Korsch cryptically.

∽ 68 ∾
Ancient Words out of the Dark

The room Joseph found himself entering was dark, though he sensed immediately the presence of humankind within it. He could barely see the man who had been his guide for the last three hours, who now stopped, turned, and indicated for him to sit down on the floor.

Joseph did so, hearing the door close behind him.

The hush within the darkness was palpable. Joseph felt the air alive with the electric current of sheer silent Presence.

Fear sprang up momentarily within him. It was the same fear that people have of God when suddenly they feel he might be near in what they regard as his divine Awfulness. In truth they are only afraid because they do not yet comprehend that he is indeed awe-full, and that our only and proper response is to bow, *full of awe,* before him who is utterly and completely full of Love.

The first form in which Joseph's fear manifested itself was the dread feeling that he had been betrayed, and that the room was full of KGB agents. But such fear lasted less than a second and was dispelled instantly with the first sounds that came to his ears.

Only a moment more the silence lasted, then began to come voices softly out of the dark, speaking in a melodic but chantlike unison.

"He that dwelleth in the secret place of the Most High shall abide under the shadow of the Almighty . . ."

The deep, masculine chant, soft but forceful, contained the majesty and power of a chorus of angels, for what else could it be? It reminded him of hearing the rabbis, when he was a boy, slowly chanting the *Sh'ma Yisrael.*

"I will say of the Lord," the voices continued, *"He is my refuge and my fortress: my God; in him will I trust. Surely he shall deliver thee from the snare of the fowler, and from the noisome pestilence. He shall cover thee with his feathers, and under his wings shalt thou trust: his truth shall be thy shield and buckler. Thou shalt not be afraid for the terror by night; nor for the arrow that flieth by day. . . ."*

It was a moment or two before Joseph realized he was

hearing the words of the ninety-first Psalm, with which he was well familiar.

As the recitation continued, he joined in as best he could, although it had been years since he had memorized the verses and now found he had forgotten half of them, a difficulty added to by the fact that the translation being quoted, though in his native Polish tongue, was slightly different from that he had grown up on.

"A thousand shall fall at thy side, and ten thousand at thy right hand; but it shall not come nigh thee. . . . For he shall give his angels charge over thee, to keep thee in all thy ways. . . ."

By the time it was over, Joseph's fear had departed. The sense of awe, however, had only deepened.

∽ 69 ∽
A Strange Gathering

As the psalm drew to a close, again the air was silent. When the stillness again was broken, this time it was by a single voice speaking out of the darkness.

"Welcome, brother Tsankov. You are among friends."

The next moment a striking match sent light throughout the room. The flicker of a candle flame immediately followed.

Joseph glanced about.

He sat in a circle comprised of some six or eight men, in age varying from early twenties to something over sixty, and one boy looking to be ten or twelve. Like himself, all were seated on the floor. Not a piece of furniture could be seen. The room was small, though sufficient in size to hold probably twice the number present, some three meters by four. In the center of the small group, the lone candle that had just been lit stood in a simple clay receptacle resting on the floor.

"Welcome!" repeated the voice he had first heard. It came from a young man Joseph judged to be in either his late twenties or early thirties, who sat directly across from him. The young man now rose slightly and extended his hand around the candle and across the circle.

Joseph took it and the two men shook hands.

"I am glad you were able to join us in praying David's psalm for protection. I detected your voice among ours."

"I am afraid I had forgotten a good deal of it," confessed Joseph.

"Most of our guests have no inkling of it. But it is how we begin whenever the Lord sends someone among us. We take the promise of protection with the utmost seriousness and have not yet lost anyone."

"I am very appreciative for your helping me," said Joseph, glancing about. "But . . . who are you? I was told nothing, only where to go and that someone would meet me and lead me where to go next. I . . . I did not expect . . . I don't even know what to call it—a *gathering* such as this on my behalf."

The young man across from him, whom he took for the spokesman of the group, smiled.

"Yes, it strikes many of our visitors as unusual when first they meet us," he said. "You are not the only individual to pose that very question."

He glanced about the circle at his comrades, some of whom were nodding and smiling as he spoke.

"So I will explain," resumed the leader. "First, as to who we are—let me introduce ourselves. My name is Dieder Palacki. Though I am one of the youngest of our number, I am the pastor of a small evangelical group of believers in and about Bialystok, most of whom are not associated with this group in which you find yourself at present. Here, I am merely one of a handful of brothers sharing a common commitment to help persons such as yourself."

"Believers?" repeated Joseph uncertainly.

"Ah yes—forgive me. *Christian* believers. You are, as I understand it, Jewish?"

Joseph nodded.

"Please excuse me—I meant to imply no exclusion by the use of the term 'believer.' You are of course a believer in many of the same truths as we, in your own way, which we acknowledge."

"It is not usual to hear such a statement coming from the mouth of a Christian," said Joseph, with mingled skepticism and astonishment. "Nor do many of my Jewish background and belief hear you use the word *brother* toward us."

Again Palacki smiled.

"You are certainly right in what you say. Nevertheless, I spoke it intentionally. You will discover that our small fellowship is not in the habit of thinking in the same way as do many who share our system of belief. In any event there will be time enough for all that later. Let me continue to introduce my brothers."

The young pastor then proceeded from his left around the circle, each man in turn nodding to Joseph and offering a word or two of personal welcome and a handshake.

"Beside me," said Palacki, "is seated Michal Malik. . . ."

"Greetings to you in the Lord's name," said Malik.

"Beside Michal is my father, Andre Palacki . . ."

A nod and smile were exchanged.

". . . Kochow Rydz . . ."

"Welcome, brother Tsankov," said Rydz, clearly the youngest adult of the group, appearing twenty-three or twenty-four at the most.

". . . Karl Laski . . ."

Another nod.

". . . Jakob Kervnov. . ."

"Welcome."

". . . Vaclav Mikolajczyk, whom you already know, of course, as your guide here from where you left your automobile . . . Laszlo Gomulka . . . and finally Georg Chmielnicki and his son Waclau."

"Thank you, thank you all," said Joseph appreciatively. "I still do not know what this is all about, except that you have apparently come to help me and have welcomed me warmly."

"That is precisely our intent," said Palacki.

"I am very grateful. I must admit I have been isolated and alone since leaving Moscow. It has not been many days, and yet it feels good to be among friends . . . even if I have only just met you."

"Now that I have answered your question as to who we are," said Palacki, "let me ask *you* a question—are you hungry? Do you have other needs?"

"Now that you mention it, I suppose I am hungry," laughed Joseph, gradually relaxing. "I hadn't thought about it. More than anything, however, I think what I need is sleep."

Palacki nodded to the man called Kervnov, who rose. Palacki

blew out the candle. Joseph heard the door open and close. They waited in silence a minute or two. The door opened again, Kervnov reentered, again a match was struck and the candle lit. Kervnov again took his seat, placing in the middle of the circle a platter with a large loaf of black bread, a bottle of wine, and several glasses.

"Yes, it is late," said Palacki, resuming the previous thread of conversation. "We will not keep you long before taking you where you will be able to enjoy a long and peaceful night's slumber. But now, while we talk, please partake of our humble fare. It is not much, as you can see, but the elements you see before you have peculiar power to sustain both body *and* spirit. Jakob's rye bread will strengthen you, and his wine will warm your stomach and ready you for sleep."

"Thank you . . . thank you very much," replied Joseph with enthusiasm, the aroma from the wine and bread suddenly enlivening his hunger. He leaned forward and tore off a hunk from the loaf and then poured himself a glass of the dark red wine.

Several of the others likewise joined him, thinking and praying quietly to themselves over the significance of the supper they shared. They gave, however, not the slightest hint of their thoughts to their guest, for whom they were also in prayer. They would neither rush nor force the moving of truth. They had already prayed for the preparatory tilling of this man's spiritual soil. Now they would wait for the Lord to plant whatever seeds he desired.

They prayed for illumination from within and sought with no words to hurry its coming.

The Lord would be about the work of building up his body, even as they remembered the day on which he had broken it for them, in his own way and in his own time.

∾ 70 ∾
Inquisitive Eyes

Even as the prayerful congregation was lifting up its petitions to the Father, a more sinister but smaller gathering was taking place on the other side of Bialystok.

"Are you sure this is the place?"

"The Christians meet here," replied Grazinski. "I have seen them."

"Well, I have seen no one in more than an hour," growled Korsch.

"They are cunning. It will take patience."

"If I find you have led me here on a fool's errand, this will be your last assignment with the KGB . . . and quite possibly your last assignment of any kind!"

"There are other locations as well."

"Why did you not tell me that to begin with?"

"Because this is the most likely."

"Bah! There is nothing here."

"Relax. If they do not come I will take you to another. I am familiar with most of the ringleaders. If need be we will go to all the homes of the names I gave you."

"I've had enough of this place. Take me to the next one now!"

Korsch pulled out the list, illuminated it with a small flashlight, and squinted to see the names and locations the weasel had given him.

"If they are gathered tonight, we may need to visit every one of these addresses. We can't sit at every one for an hour. I have no more time to waste here!"

Meanwhile, to the west Gustav von Schmundt was scrutinizing a map and a list of names, running through his mind for the hundredth time the many paths and roads he had taken months earlier when tracking the McCallum fellow.

The hour was late to be in his office. But what did he have to go home to? The time would come when he would have someone waiting for him, but not until he got to the bottom of this puzzle.

He had gone all the way back to that day at the Dortmann estate and had successfully reconstructed every kilometer that had subsequently followed. He had drawn the whole series of movements out on the map he now had in front of him.

Wherever they were in hiding, there had to be a connection with the network of Christians in Grossbeeren. Of that much he was certain. Magdeburg remained a possibility, but he doubted they were holed up there. He and Schulte had both been back there in the last three weeks, and even their persistent and repeated visits to known associates of the dead postal man hadn't seemed to cause undue alarm. Galanov had been all around Grossbeeren itself. Confound them for calling him back to Moscow just when he needed him the most! His own man Schulte, though five years Galanov's senior, wasn't half as shrewd.

He glanced down at the map again.

Three locations stood out in his mind from months earlier. A sixth sense told him any of the three could perhaps be the refuge, even now, for the fugitives.

First, there was Niedersdorf itself. Though there could be no possible escape routes from that region, it was entirely likely that the desire to see his old estate would prove too much for Baron von Dortmann. It was also true that they might find, even after all this time, old friends willing to hide them.

He circled the site with the red pen he held between his fingers.

Secondly, he could not get out of his mind that horrid night he had spent in the flea trap in Kehrigkburg not far to the south of here. The farmer and his cows had annoyed him, though he and his cowardly friend had paid for their folly. But they had known about Magdeburg, and they might still know more than was good for them.

A second red circle went around the village named Kehrigkburg.

Then finally, there was Halle, further south, near Leipzig. They would be more difficult to trace if they were there, for Halle was a large city. But it was closer to the West German border than any other site of McCallum's earlier travels than Magdeburg, and McCallum had remained there longer than in most places, though he had lost sight of him temporarily. Gustav had the distinct impression a Christian underground network, similar to that he'd unearthed in Magdeburg, could well exist in Halle too.

A third red circle now was indicated on his map.

He had no choice but to get people to all three and to settle in to some long-term observation and surveillance. He would send a whole team of *Stasi* agents to Halle. It would take some time to get to the bottom of all the names.

He would send Schulte to Kehrigkburg to camp out in front of the two farmers' houses, armed with binoculars and plenty of coffee.

He himself would go to Neidersdorf. There were several informants he had been cultivating right here in Berlin, however, that were narrowing down the networks and possibilities that he couldn't afford to lose touch with. If by chance he was wrong about the three locations, or if they slipped back into the city, one of the informants was certain to hear of any new attempt being planned. He had to keep his lines of communication open with them.

He would see each and then be on his way to his own home village the moment he had everyone else settled on their assignments.

Satisfied, he turned out the lights and left his office for the night.

∽ 71 ∽
A Supper and Questions

As Joseph and his hosts partook, Palacki explained to their guest something of the nature of the gathering in which the fugitive Jew from Russia found himself.

"We are not an organization, as such," the young pastor explained. "We call ourselves simply a *brotherhood.* How we happened to come together is a long story. The connections between each of us have different roots."

"Is this all of you?" asked Joseph.

"There are others, but those of us you see here are what you would perhaps call the nucleus of the brotherhood."

"What is it you do?"

"Help and serve those in need . . . pray for our country and all lands oppressed under Communism . . . spread the Good News that God gives freedom to men in their hearts, in spite of the chains and walls with which men would imprison their fellows."

"You seem a small group to possess such lofty aims."

"Much is possible with God that of themselves men could never accomplish."

"What is the underlying purpose, then, of what you call your brotherhood?"

"To do the will of God."

"That seems an even *more* ambitious objective."

"Granted."

"I could say the same goal drives my Zionist friends, both in Russia, where I have just come from, and in Israel, where I hope to get to."

"The will of God is the purpose of many, many thousands, it is true. On one level, perhaps, it is ambitious. On another, however, but only when properly understood, it is in fact the most humble and *unpretentious* objective a man can have in life."

"How so?"

"Because there is nothing of the Self in it. There is no vain striving toward anything to call one's *own*."

Joseph thought a moment, trying to digest the simple yet profound truth. "If there are many thousands that seek the will of God, then, what makes you here unique?" he asked as he munched on the hearty piece of bread he held.

"I'm sorry—did I imply we were unique? I did not mean to. We do not think of ourselves in relation to anyone else. We began gathering some years ago—my father and a few of the older ones not long after the war, and we of the younger generation as the years went by, when it was obvious that religious freedom was being taken from our land and our people and that persecution was coming. We gathered simply to pray and to say to God, 'What do you want *us* to do?' We are unique only in that we happen to be *here, now,* in Poland, at a particular time. *All* God's people are unique in that same way, in that the Father will have a distinctive will for them to carry out specific to *their* place, *their* time, *their* function in his overall plan. In any event, it is that prayer—*'Lord, what do you want us to do . . . right here . . . right now?'*—that is the root of our brotherhood together and is the foundation for all we do."

"And you believe you have found the answer to that question?"

"We believe we are constantly in the process of discovering it. That is why we come together as now, with every new opportunity, with every new person he sends, that we may ask him what it is his will that we do."

"*Ask* him . . . how do you mean?"

"Pray, Mr. Tsankov—we have to pray and inquire what is the Father's will for us with regard to *you*. We have been together already more than an hour praying that very thing even prior to your arrival, asking God how most we can be of service to you and help you, what is your deepest need, what can we say to you, what can we do for you, that will address God's deepest purpose for you in *your* life."

Joseph took in the information with thoughtful expression. It was a suddenly humbling experience to realize this group of men had come together specifically and only for him.

He took a slow swallow of wine, pondering the implications.

"That was going to be my next question," he said at length. "What does all this about your brotherhood and the will of God have to do with me? It would seem you have answered my question even before I asked it. I must admit that, as deeply intrinsic as prayer is to the Jewish faith, I have never encountered it so personally directed."

"Yes, you are correct in your observation. We believe prayer to be supremely personal."

"How did that perspective come to you?" asked Joseph.

"It became obvious to us, as I said, years ago, that in this particular part of the world where we found ourselves, persecution against God's people was going to be heavy. I need tell you nothing of that, for your people have been more persecuted than any race on earth. And it continues, as no doubt you are aware."

"Of course," said Joseph.

"The Communists have made it extremely difficult for Christians as well," Palacki went on. "The government began confiscating Catholic lands as early as 1946 and has steadily extended restrictive controls over everything religious, which, unless it is pro-Soviet, they view as treasonous. Thousands of pastors, priests, and church leaders have been arrested through the years. We, therefore, as serious Christians, have had to decide upon a response."

"I take it, this . . . all this you do," said Joseph, gesturing around the room to indicate the gathering into which he had come, "is your response."

"Our response has been one of peaceful, prayerful, underground resistance to the sovietization of Poland's religious institutions," said Palacki, "as well as a commitment to help God's people wherever and however and in whatever need they come to us. The first objective we carry out by prayer alone. We will lift no hand and support no program against the authorities that govern. But we pray for the church, for God's people, and for freedom to triumph. As we have prayed, we have gradually found ourselves functioning in the provision of refuge for those in need who come or are sent to us."

"But why are you all here? I am only one man. Surely all this is not required. Why the bare room, the candle . . . and again, why so many of you, when all you need do is put me up for the night and send me on my way?"

"You ask many questions." Palacki smiled.

"I am intrigued."

"In your eyes, perhaps all that is required is to put you up and send you on, as you say. But we attempt to tune ourselves to deeper movements and divine motives. It may be there are more reasons you are here than only those."

"I . . . I am not sure I understand you."

"The will of God, Mr. Tsankov. It is his will we seek, not ours . . . or even yours."

"But why all . . . all this?" Joseph asked, glancing around again.

"As to the bare room and candle—"

Suddenly he stopped, then leaned forward and blew out the candle.

"There are footsteps above us," he whispered.

All was silent and still in the small room. The faint, muffled sound of someone walking across the ceiling under which they sat could be heard. It lasted but four or five seconds, then was gone.

"Papa?" whispered Palacki.

"I do not know, my son. It is late. There should be no one out."

For a minute or two they waited in utter silence until the sounds were gone. Then Dieder continued, still in darkness.

"As you see, we would have ourselves constantly reminded that we are pilgrims in an alien land. Danger is ever present. We take great precautions and always meet at night. Prying eyes are everywhere. God cannot honor prayers for protection if we are foolish and do not behave with prudence. We take nothing for granted, such as what has just taken place."

"I understand."

"Nor do we want to forget our ancestors—yours and ours—in Egypt. There is no furniture; there are no chairs; the floor is bare. It is our way of reminding ourselves, as the Lord said to the children of Israel when he commanded them to eat of the bitter herbs, that the season of bondage and exile is no time of luxury for the people of God. When your people come together every year at Passover, the young children ask the men what it all means. The answers are always the same: 'We must remember the bondage of Egypt, out of which God led our fathers.' We too consider it important to *remember*. Freedom is not something to be taken for granted. True, these may be external measures, and I assure you that the bed you will enjoy later will be most comfortable. But these reminders keep us focused upon the seriousness of our purpose."

"And the candle?"

"Again, a reminder of our predecessors in all ages who have been persecuted, of those who had to endure by candlelight in the catacombs under Rome, of those who, during the terrible war of recent times, had to hide in basements and attics and underground chambers."

Joseph recalled having had to hide in darkness and candlelight himself more than once.

"Most of all," Palacki continued, "the candle reminds us that the light of God's truth, though it will triumph over all darkness in the end, is precious and tenuous at present and must be carefully guarded and tended so that the darkness of the world will not extinguish it in such nations as this. The candle reminds us that we are but a small flame amid great darkness, and that we must therefore burn hot and bright."

"Your explanations make perfect sense, yet they only add to the mystery."

"Not all who come here are so desirous of understanding those things we make a priority—even though it concerns them directly."

"I have always been a seeker of truth."

"Many atheistic philosophers might say the same. Being what is commonly called a seeker of truth is but one step toward *ultimate* truth."

"I see you are a philosopher as well as a theologian," said Joseph, smiling. "Let me add, then, that I seek truth rooted in the Law of God and the Holy Scriptures."

Now it was Palacki's turn to smile. "I perceive that you are a spiritual man," he said.

"In my own way, I am in pursuit of the will of God just like you."

"It makes us all happy to hear you say it. If you truly want to know more about the mystery, as you call it, of what we are about, we would be most happy to tell you. But you did mention sleep before. The night is advanced, and we do not desire to tax you beyond what you wish. You had a lengthy walk and a long drive before that. And of course, we still must pray further, for that—to answer at least one of your questions—is the primary purpose for which we are gathered."

"I am tired, it is true. But I am also curious. I have been part of many undergrounds in Russia too, large and small. I am aware of such Christian organizations, as well as Jewish ones. But I have never encountered anything quite like this. So yes . . . I would like to know more. Sleep can always wait; sometimes opportunities cannot."

"Very well then."

Palacki paused, then glanced toward his father.

"Papa, would you like to explain the beginnings of the brotherhood to our guest?"

The old man nodded, then the room fell silent for several moments in anticipation.

❧ 72 ❧
A Late Call

The third name on Grazinski's list he identified as the residence of an elderly man and woman, whose only son, a factory worker, resided with them.

"This is the Palackis'," whispered Grazinski as they inched to a stop, lights off. "The young fellow is the pastor I told you of."

"You fool! Why did we not come here first!"

"He is usually seen elsewhere. Their church meetings are not held here."

Calmed momentarily, Korsch glanced around in the darkness.

"What is that building whose roofline I see faintly above, over there?" He pointed as he asked.

"There is a barn directly behind the house. This was a large dairy farm at one time."

"Its use now?"

"I know of nothing it is used for."

"An ideal place for meetings, would you not say? How is it entered?"

"I do not know. I have not had occasion to explore the place."

"Perhaps you should have, you fool," said Korsch. "I want to see it."

He got out of the car, quietly closing the door so as to make no sound, and stole carefully toward the house, then around by its side. Inside only one window was lit, but no sign of human occupation came from within. A moment later he was aware of Grazinski following at his side, though neither said a word.

They made their way behind the house, where now, even in the darkness, the large shape of the barn loomed before them only a few meters separate from the back door of the house, having been invisible from the street. They crept toward the large structure. Korsch removed the flashlight from his pocket, flipped it on, located the door, tried it, then walked carefully inside.

Pausing a moment, he breathed in, as if attempting to detect the prey with his nostrils, then sent the thin beam of his flashlight about the inside. One glance told him there had been no human activity in this place for years. Dust clung to every cobweb, and outmoded equipment stood rusting and silent. Late at night though it was, a yet deeper silence seemed to emanate from the very bricks and beams of wood.

Korsch took a few steps into the silent, spacious vault, stopped, glanced quickly about a second time, then turned back for the door.

"There's nothing in this old place," he said.

They walked back outside, around the side of the house, and toward the street. Grazinski opened the car door and climbed in. Korsch stopped and stood beside the car, surveying the quiet street, the house with a light burning in one of its windows, and the deserted barn behind it.

Methodically he pulled out a pack of cigarettes, stuck one between his lips, and lit it.

There was something here, he thought.

He didn't know what, but he could feel *something*. Obviously there was no meeting taking place, unless it was inside the house itself.

He had had this peculiar sensation before, and it unnerved him. It reminded him of his two encounters with Baron von Dortmann.

He took a long drag on his cigarette, thinking to himself.

"You stay here," he said into the open car window after a moment.

He turned and strode toward the house.

A few moments later his knock sounded on the door.

Inside, Mrs. Palacki nearly leapt with fright out of the chair where she had been dozing. Doing her best to calm herself, she rose, took several deep breaths, and then walked to the door.

"Good evening," she said, doing her best to mask her fear.

"It is late, Madam," said the strange-looking man on her doorstep, in broken but tolerable Polish, "yet you are still up."

"I . . . I have been reading."

"And your husband, does he read so late also, hmm?"

"No, he . . . uh, goes to sleep earlier than I."

As he questioned her, the man peered beyond her into the small dwelling, as if looking for something.

"You have a son, too, as I understand it?"

"That is correct," she answered, her anxiety growing for the men gathered in the hidden room beneath the barn.

"He too is, uh, early to retire, hmm?"

"Yes. . . . He works in the factory all day. Both my husband and son go much earlier to bed than I."

"But as I said, Madam," persisted the intruder, "it is late. You are expecting visitors, perhaps?"

"No . . . no, it was only that I could not sleep. I was reading, and I dozed off just before you came."

Still the man glanced about.

"Bring them to me," he said finally, in a tone of command.

"Bring . . . who?"

"Your husband and son, who else?" he rejoined curtly.

"But . . . but they are—"

"I am the KGB, Madam!" interrupted Korsch, beginning to lose his patience. "Bring them to me . . . now."

"They are sound sleepers. It . . . it will take me some time to rouse them and . . . and for them to dress."

"I will wait."

Trembling in terror, but arguing no further, Mrs. Palacki skillfully managed to close the door, leaving the dangerous man standing outside on the tiny front veranda, then hastened through the house to the back door, which she opened and closed behind her noiselessly.

As rapidly as she dared, and thankfully out of sight of both car and front porch, she flitted toward the adjacent side of the barn, lifted a large wooden door that was on the level of the ground and whose hinges were kept well oiled. Below was revealed a narrow set of earthen steps. She descended them quickly toward the ancient cellar, and rapped twice softly on the door.

When it opened, only blackness and the faint aroma of a snuffed candle met her senses.

"Andre . . . Dieder—come . . . *come quickly!* There is a man at the door—an evil man!"

∾ 73 ∾
Frightful Intrusion

"We are a people," the elder Palacki had begun his story minutes earlier, "not given to much moving about, a people of the land. Our families have been here in Poland for generations. We love this region, this nation. Thus how can we not hate what is becoming of it, what Hitler did to it, and now what the Communists are doing? But not merely doing to the Poland we love, but doing to her people—sucking the very lifeblood out of them by draining them of their spiritual vitality."

He paused, glancing slowly about the room, while Joseph listened intently.

"Some of these men here I have known all my life. This is no passing brotherhood of convenience. We are committed in every way and in all ways to one another. The bonds are lifelong. But I digress . . . my son asked me to explain the beginnings of our fellowship to you."

Again he paused, but only momentarily.

"Shortly after the war was over, several of us near Bialystok, farmers mostly, Christian brothers, chanced to be together. Dieder was only a boy at the time—"

"I was thirteen at the time, Papa," broke in Dieder, "and I remember the day well."

"Ah yes, thirteen," said the elderly man. "I fear my memory fails me. In any event, Karl was present that day—" he glanced over to Laski, who merely nodded—"Georg's brother, who is now unfortunately on the other side of the Russian border and unable to be with us, except rarely. There were two or three others who are now gone . . . let me see, Jakob's father . . ."

"And mine," added the young man Kochow Rydz.

"Yes, of course, Ernst Rydz—yes, I think that was all of us. In speaking of it later, none of us ever could say with certainty exactly why we were all together on that day. It was a Sunday. We had attended church and afterward were talking casually before leaving, and Ernst invited us to come to his home to continue our discussion. Do you recall the day, Kochow?"

"Only vaguely," answered the young Rydz. "My father talked about it often, up until the day he died. But I was only four or five at the time."

"Our wives went home, and then we gathered at Ernst's. I think even as we arrived we all began to sense something momentous at hand, that it was more than merely a Sunday-afternoon social gathering. There was a sense of being drawn, a sense of urgency, almost a sense of destiny about it. When we sat down together, it was solemn and silent between us for quite some time. We had all come, but suddenly there seemed no words to speak. The occasion seemed too heavy and portentous for words. After a while—"

His voice was interrupted by the sound of his wife's two knocks on the door.

The next instant the candle was again extinguished.

The two men rose immediately at the command from wife and mother, then followed her to the house.

"He is a KGB agent. He asks many questions," she whispered as they climbed the earthen steps. "He is at the front door at this moment. He thinks you have been asleep. Go into your bedrooms, rumple your beds, your hair, your clothes, and then come out quickly!"

The three stole softly into the house together through the back door she had left ajar. The two men obeyed her quick-thinking instructions, and about a minute later wandered, as if staggering out of a deep sleep, into the living room and toward the front door.

Mrs. Palacki opened it once again.

"So, the two sleepers arise from their slumber," said Korsch with the hint of a sneer. He was already half-angry with them, not only for being Christians, but for their apparent innocence in the matter of the Jew he was tracking. For both reasons, he enjoyed having the power to inconvenience them, an enjoyment heightened by the obvious fear in the eyes of the old Polish wife. The young man, however, displayed no such fear. His eyes looked remarkably alert for being awakened so rudely, and Korsch resented his self-confident and calm demeanor.

The Russian turned toward him.

"You are, I believe, the young pastor by the name of Palacki?" he said.

"Yes, my name is Dieder Palacki."

"Has your congregation conducted meetings tonight, or last evening?"

"No."

"I am looking for a man, a criminal, whom I have reason to believe may visit your fellowship."

"I have heard of no such man."

"There have been no unusual occurrences?"

Palacki shook his head. "I worked today all day in the factory as usual, as I did yesterday, and the day before that, and then came home."

"You have gone nowhere in the evening?" asked Korsch skeptically.

"Nowhere."

"You have had no guests, no meetings?"

Dieder glanced with truthful innocence toward his parents. All three shook their heads.

"There has been no one in our home but the three of us, for—" again he glanced toward his parents—"for more than a week. You are welcome to come in and search our home if you like. We have nothing to hide."

"Bah! I have no time to search your home, you young idiot! Don't you know that I could have you thrown in prison!"

"On what charge, if I might ask?"

"You admit to being a pastor!"

"The small group of believers I lead breaks no law."

"Enough of your insolence! You fanatics with your holier-than-thou innocence—you think you are above the law!"

Korsch narrowed the squint of his gaze in the dim light. His eyes met those of the young man he already despised. For a second or two nothing was spoken but the silent subtle exchange for supremacy between hatred and love.

When Korsch turned away, it was again with the uncomfortable sense of having been overpowered by a strength he could do nothing to counteract.

"You will be watched, young Palacki!" he barked as he backed down the steps.

He spun around and walked back toward the street, already vowing inside himself to find some pretext to throw the young rascal into jail.

The three residents watched him go, prayerfully thankful for having been spared, yet quivering to realize how close the danger always was and what price one must be willing to pay for one's faith in this region of the world.

Five minutes later the lone light in the house was extinguished. Sitting in the darkness, Mrs. Palacki kept watch through the window to the street outside.

When they were certain it was safe, the two men stole back outside along the invisible black corridor to the barn to rejoin their comrades.

∽ 74 ∽

The Brotherhood of Bialystok

After Dieder explained the cause for the interruption, their guest asked for a continuation of the story of their brotherhood.

"Kochow," said Dieder. "Would you go up and keep watch in the house? My mother will then be able to go to bed. Keep out all the lights. If you see anything, come to us immediately and we will disband. I doubt the man will return tonight, but we must not put our visitor at risk."

The young man obeyed and left the hidden room.

The elder Palacki then resumed his narrative from before.

"As I had been telling you, we found ourselves gathered together, and before we knew it we were praying. We prayed for more than an hour, scarcely knowing what came from our mouths. Though we were all simple and unschooled men of the earth, we prayed for our nation, for our people . . . and especially for God's people everywhere. We prayed that we might be instruments in God's hands for the taking forth of the gospel, into all the world, yes—but most importantly, into our small portion of it. We prayed that he would send us people in need of that gospel.

"We knew we could not fight the system called Communism, but we could be tools in God's hands to bring that greater freedom—freedom of the human spirit—into people's lives."

He stopped, breathing heavily in the excitement of the memory.

"I remember the day so vividly," put in the young pastor. "Even we two boys, Kochow and myself—were forever changed. None of us have ever forgotten it."

Nodding heads throughout the room confirmed the truth of his words.

"When we rose from prayer," now began Karl Laski, a man showing grey but several years younger than the elder Palacki, "we began to talk about the changes we could see coming. Many in our country were still caught up in the optimism of having the war over at last and fascism destroyed. But we knew the Communist threat was, in its own way, perhaps even going to be worse in its impact upon our freedom to worship. We spoke of many things that day. By the end of it we sensed that God had commissioned us for some purpose. It was a feeling, a commitment we all shared to a man."

He stopped and let out a deep breath.

"And that," now added the pastor's father, "was the beginning of the brotherhood."

"Did you start an underground organization?" asked Joseph, intrigued.

"No. We simply continued to pray that God's will would be done and that we would be shown our part in it to do."

"And you?" said Joseph, turning toward the younger Palacki. "You now seem to be the spokesman for the group."

"Only because the others defer to me," said Dieder with a smile. "I will always look to my father and Karl for spiritual leadership. Yet perhaps there is a sense in which I do represent the younger generation who have grown up under the hammer and sickle. My desire from a young age was to become a pastor. I lead a fellowship of twenty or thirty evangelical believers in Sunday worship in Bialystok, which, by the grace of God, the authorities have thus far turned a blind eye to."

Joseph was silent. The great dividing wall of difference

between himself as a Jew and the others as Christians had at last been spoken. Palacki sensed what he was thinking.

"When I called you brother earlier," the young pastor said, "I truly meant it. You and I have the same Father—Yahweh, the Lord God Almighty. That we differ on the status of our mutual brother Jesus—I call him the Christ; you call him rabbi—that excludes neither of us from God's family, it only means that we are brothers who are in disagreement."

"A rather serious disagreement, would you not admit?" asked Joseph.

"Perhaps. I cannot be the judge of that. Then again, perhaps not such a serious disagreement. Only God knows. In any event, perhaps our mutual Father has sent you to us so that you may come to know Jesus not merely as rabbi, but as the Christ, as we know him."

"I think I have been sent here so that you could help me get to Berlin," remarked Joseph, not with sarcasm but with wit.

"Granted, that is true," rejoined Palacki with a smile, yet not to be deterred from driving home his point. "Yet perhaps accompanying the purpose you are aware of is a deeper purpose that your Father in heaven has ordained for you—one you are unaware of at the conscious level, but which is in reality the most important purpose of all."

"You *are* outspoken," laughed Joseph.

Palacki chuckled. "So my friends tell me. They say it is bound to land me in prison one day. If not that, then surely it will get me in serious hot water with other Christians."

"Does the first possibility not frighten you?"

"You mean prison?"

Joseph nodded.

"I do not think so. We all live with the prospect hanging over us. It is intrinsic in the commitment of the brotherhood. There is a price to be paid to live one's faith boldly in Eastern Europe. You face the same prospect, no doubt."

Joseph smiled, though humorlessly.

"You are right. I have already spent eight years of my life in a Soviet prison."

The statement brought an immediate deepening to the already pensive prayerfulness of the gathering.

"In that regard, then, you wear a badge of respect none of us can claim. We honor you for it."

"It was far from pleasant. I claim no heroism. It virtually eliminated any possibility I will see my betrothed again."

"I am sorry. Is she in Israel?"

"I do not know. I have not seen her since during the war. So much time has passed that I have lost all contact with her and her family."

"Then we will make that a matter of prayer also, along with your safety . . . and that the *ultimate* truth will be revealed to your truth-loving heart."

A pause followed.

"I believe it is time for us to pray," said the elder Palacki.

Silently but as one, the entire group of men sat forward to arrange themselves on their knees.

"I know it is a peculiarly Christian custom," Andre went on, now addressing their guest personally, "but I hope you will do us the honor of allowing us to lay our hands upon you and pray specifically for you."

"Of course," replied Joseph, uncertain but without reluctance.

The others, old and young, now inched forward and each laid a hand gently upon Joseph's shoulders, back, knees, and legs, as they were able to reach him comfortably.

"*Our Father,*" began the elder Palacki, "*we commit the care of our friend and brother to you. Protect him, watch over him, guide his every footstep. Show us what is your will in how we may serve him and minister to him.*"

"*Amen,*" came two or three whispered voices.

"*Thank you for your protection this evening in the matter of the KGB man. Continue to watch over this brotherhood.*"

"*Amen . . . amen.*"

"*Honor the quest of our visitor's heart, Father,*" prayed Dieder. "*Lead him into the truth you have for him.*"

Around the room, all the other men prayed, some nearly inaudibly.

"*Let our hands be those of service, Lord,*" prayed Laski. "*In all things show us what to do, and give us courage and humility to obey you.*"

"We pray for those whom our friend Tsankov will meet in his journey," added Malik. "May his life touch theirs. May he be led to those whom you choose. May every encounter between here and his final destination be appointed by your will."

"Make straight his paths," said Mikolajczyk.

"Let him find his way to the Land of Promise for his people," added Gomulka. "Grant him safe passage into West Germany, though we know not yet what means you will devise for him."

"We ask that he be reunited with his betrothed," added Dieder. "By miraculous intercession, Father, open the way for them to come together, even after all these years. We pray for the young woman too, though we know her not, that you would stir her heart toward our new friend, her betrothed from long ago, that when they meet, the years of separation will fall away as if they had never been."

"We pray in faith for their marriage," now prayed Chmielnicki, "that it be a fruitful one in service to you, our God and their God."

They continued to pray in similar fashion, simply but vigorously, for twenty minutes.

When they finally arose, blew out the candle, and began one by one to leave the small room, with words of farewell and blessing, Joseph's heart and brain were so filled with new thoughts and sensations that he felt like one walking about in a dream.

He knew many faithful Jews who prayed, and he had participated in prayer services himself many times. But never had he witnessed anything like this, nor been the object himself of such an outpouring of petition.

When he lay down later in the bed, as had been promised, he lay wide awake for some time.

∽ 75 ∽
Prophetic Interview

While Joseph still slept the sun rose over Moscow.

Andrassy Galanov had only been back in the Soviet capital less than forty-eight hours, but he had been busy. He had every reason to believe this morning's meeting would complete the circle he had begun during his last stint in his homeland.

He had been annoyed the first time his uncle had so summarily summoned him home at the end of the previous year. But upon this occasion it brought a sense of relief. He even saw the action as complimentary on his uncle's part. Korskayev would never admit to such, but the words had been unmistakable: "I have to have someone in Moscow I can depend on."

It was a clear vote of confidence, though probably an unintended one. If he could perform to his uncle's satisfaction, it would mean his future would be secured. He had, whether wittingly or not, been handed an opportunity to prove himself. It would be all the better that he would not have his uncle's thumb on top of him. Korskayev had already put Kapp and two other agents—all three older than he—under his direct control.

His uncle's only suggestion was that he contact the officer Bolotnikov, who might possess information on the Christians. But he hoped he wouldn't have to bring anyone else into it. He wanted to handle this on his own. With his uncle himself not even in Moscow, it could not be denied that Galanov had suddenly found himself in a reasonably powerful position, and the more he could do without having to call in help, the more formidable that would make his resume in the KGB files.

He would bring that strength to bear upon the man he was following at this very moment.

He apprehended him in the next block.

"Comrade Rostovchev," said Galanov, taking rude hold of him and pushing him toward an alleyway, "let me introduce myself. I am Andrassy Galanov, with the KGB. I have been investigating the group of Christians with which you are associated."

"I am pleased to make your acquaintance, Comrade," replied the other, also a young man, though probably in his late twenties, with more kindliness, Galanov judged, than was appropriate under the circumstances in which he found himself.

He eased himself back, letting go of the man, then eyeing him up and down as if to say he had him just where he wanted him.

"You are," said Galanov with a voice of commanding triumph that sounded far older than his years, "the leader, I believe, of this little Christian labyrinth, whose treasonous plots I have been untangling."

"I make no such claim."

"You do not have to make the claim—I am making it for you!" spat back the agent, the power of his position and the superiority of his supposed victory intoxicating him with rude, youthful bravado. He did not yet hate Christians with the same venom as did his uncle, though the demon was on his very shoulder. But loose-tongued cowards like this man would make him feel the same way before long. "You do not admit to being a Christian, then?" he added sarcastically.

"I would *never* do that."

"Never do what?"

"Refuse to admit to my faith. I am most assuredly a Christian."

"A bold statement to make in front of the KGB. You would not deny it even to save your life?"

"Of course not."

"Hmm," reflected Galanov. "You are more a fool than I took you for, Rostovchev."

The other smiled oddly. He seemed not in the least offended by the remark. "I am aware of no treason we commit."

"You openly mock the Communist creed."

"I mock nothing," said the Christian, softly but no less firmly and decisively.

"You declare your belief in God. Our leaders say there is none. That is treason."

"Does your mother believe in God, Comrade Galanov?"

"That has nothing to do with your treason!"

"Perhaps not," said Rostovchev with a smile. "But it does show the impossibility of a government decreeing by law what people will believe."

"You are full of humbug as well as treason!"

"The silent faith of old people may have more to say about the truth than all the manifestos of your leaders put together."

"That is another treasonous statement, for which I could arrest you. But you still have not answered my question, and I grow weary of this debate."

"I am sorry. What is your question?"

"You said you make no such claim. Tell me, then, what claim would you not admit?"

"To being a leader."

"But you *are* a Christian?"

Rostovchev nodded.

"Who *is* your leader, then?"

"Jesus Christ."

"Bah! I do not mean some mythological figure!"

"Excuse me, Comrade Galanov. He is anything but that."

"Spare me your sermons, Rostovchev! I want to know who is the leader of your band."

"And I have told you."

"I mean your leader here, now—in Moscow, you moron! Don't play the simpleton with me. I know very well about your activities! What is your connection with the Jewish underground?"

"I have none."

"I do not believe you. Do you deny that you are involved with Jews?"

"Jews and Christians are often closely involved."

"In the underground!" rejoined Galanov angrily. He was losing his patience with this idiot.

The Christian did not answer.

"I have information that you—yes, *you*, Rostovchev!—have been involved in aiding traitors to leave the Soviet Union. Do you deny *that*?"

"I turn no man away who comes to me for help."

"Do you not realize that I could have you arrested on the spot?"

"I am aware of your position."

"Does that not frighten you?"

"Not in the least."

Galanov had never encountered such calm in his life. For a moment the words he had just heard stunned him. There was nothing in the KGB manuals or training procedures to prepare for such a complete absence of fear. It effectively removed his only weapon.

Suddenly he pulled out his gun and shoved its barrel against the man's throat.

"Not only could I have you arrested, you fanatic! I could kill you on the spot. You have openly admitted to treason! You are an enemy of the state."

"You will not."

"But I *could*. If the prospect of prison does not frighten you, perhaps the feel of my gun will drive some reason into that mush-filled brain of yours!"

"It only makes me pray for you the harder, Comrade."

"Pray for me! I want none of your cursed prayers! If you so much as open your mouth again, I swear I will pull this trigger!"

This interview was not going at all how Galanov had anticipated it! Before he could recover himself, with the steel barrel of his gun still jammed into Rostovchev's throat, he heard the soft whispered words from the mouth in front of him:

"Lord Jesus, I ask you to reveal yourself fully to this man, and to love him with a love that only you—"

"Shut up!" shrieked Galanov, pulling his gun away but clubbing the fellow alongside the head. The praying stopped, but otherwise the man made not so much as a peep at the blow.

He had had enough of this banter!

"I am looking for a man by the name of Tsankov," he said sternly. "I know he contacted you several days ago. I demand that you tell me what you know of him."

"I have never met a man whose name is Tsankov."

"You are lying!" shouted Galanov, taking a stride forward, his one fist clenching unconsciously, while the other still clutched his pistol. Rostovchev was a considerably taller man than he was, however, though only a year or two older, and he reconsidered. By now he should have known the man would not defend himself, yet some invisible force restrained him from further violence.

"He is thought to have left the country," continued the agent. "I demand you tell me what you know of the affair."

"I tell you in all truth," said the Christian, gazing straight into Galanov's eyes with a penetrating expression, "that I have absolutely no idea of the whereabouts of the man you seek."

In that moment, Galanov felt just what his uncle had felt upon several such occasions—a strength that originated somewhere deeper than any place with which he had personal acquaintance. The man held his gaze, and young Andrassy Galanov was powerless to pull himself from it.

"I am telling you the truth, Comrade Galanov," repeated

Rostovchev, still holding him by the eyes. "Now I tell you, in the name of Jesus Christ, whom I serve, to leave the search for this man, and to inquire about him no further. The God who made you loves you with the love of a Father, and I will never cease praying for your salvation as long as I live."

He turned and walked away, leaving the KGB agent in what amounted to a trance of submissive obedience.

When Galanov came to himself, the man was gone.

Suddenly the realization broke upon him that he had been vanquished by the mere will of another, and a Christian at that. With the realization, the demon of hatred climbed from the shoulder and entered into the heart of young Andrassy Galanov with such force that it would take the voice of the Lord himself, in direct answer to his servant's prayer, to eradicate it.

When next the two men laid eyes upon one another, both would have grown mighty in the service of their respective gods—Dmitri Rostovchev would be a man who walked with angels and kings, Galanov a latter-day Saul, given over to the persecution of God's people with yet more demonic abandon even than his uncle.

The two men's paths *would* cross again. Their destinies in the kingdom of heaven were intertwined. And the Maker of them both—he who hears prayers and answers them—had eternal designs upon them.

For the present, however, no more came to Galanov with regard to a certain Leon Tsankov's disappearance from the Soviet capital, and try as he might thereafter, he could secure not a single thread of evidence leading him either to the Jew or to the Christian whose eyes registered no fear.

There would be no assistance aiding his search coming to Emil Korsch from the direction of Moscow.

∞ 76 ∞

Shining Light on Inner Cracks

IT was midmorning before their guest emerged from the simple guest room of the Palacki home, which was in fact the room the unmarried Dieder himself occupied in the residence of his parents. He was greeted warmly by the elder two of his hosts, and it was explained that Dieder was at the factory where he worked and would not be home until evening.

"And the others?" asked Joseph, as he sat at the table while the pastor's mother placed a plate of sliced bread and cheese before him and poured him a cup of coffee.

"They were all back in their own beds during the night," replied her husband. "You will see young Kochow again. He will take you to your next destination, late tonight, in fact. We had hoped to keep you with us for several days. But after last evening's visit from the authorities, we must move you on without delay."

Joseph nodded. He spent the day in the house, napping occasionally and speaking with great delight to the two old people. Being with Poles again refreshed his spirit, though an undefined feature added to the interchange something he could not identify but found himself energized by.

Andre was careful throughout the day that Joseph not be seen. That evening, after supper and with shades drawn and lights low, father and son and guest fell to talking seriously again, as if the conversation from the previous evening had not been interrupted at all.

"I remain curious about something you said last night, just before you began to pray," said Joseph. "I wondered if you would mind explaining what you meant."

"Certainly, if I am able," replied Dieder.

"You spoke of the difference between seeking truth and finding *ultimate* truth. What *is* the 'ultimate' truth you speak of?"

"You indeed ask difficult questions." The young pastor smiled. "Are you quite sure you want me to answer you?"

"Why wouldn't I?"

"Many people ask questions and ponder issues in the area of their intellects, thinking that in so doing they may keep their findings at arm's length from their innermost selves."

"Not an uncommon fallacy in the human makeup," suggested Joseph.

"True enough. What I find intriguing, however, is that this

same erroneous tendency exists within those who call themselves 'seekers of truth' as well as in the unthinking masses."

"How do you mean?"

"They mostly think of what they call *truth* as being an intellectual system."

"You do not see it as such?"

"Not at all."

"How *do* you see truth, then?"

"As an intellectually consistent system of belief *that can be lived by* and that *is* lived by. If the truth one says he believes does not alter how that one lives and behaves and thinks, then I cannot call such a one a *true* truth seeker."

"How does that view apply to what you were saying before?"

"We were talking about asking questions regarding truth. What happens when truth is probing and pointed and personal? Those whom I call *untrue* truth seekers find it unpleasant, even offensive. They then proceed to attack the deliverer of truth rather than examining that at which, within their own character, the light of that truth is shining. I call them 'untrue truth seekers' because they are seeking so-called intellectual truth but are not seeking to *be* true within themselves."

"Perhaps I should ask, then, what in your opinion makes a man or woman a truth seeker?"

"A *true* truth seeker is looking for cracks and flaws within his own character most of all. Devising an intellectually consistent system of belief is vastly subservient to that primary goal. A truth seeker has to begin within his own self and discover what is true regarding his own weaknesses. No intellectual system of belief can be erected unless that foundation is taken care of first."

"Many would disagree."

"I have learned over the years that people are sometimes not as open to such personal truth as they think they are."

"I take it you have been attacked as a deliverer of truth."

"Upon many occasions," replied Palacki, smiling once again.

"Why?"

"The Lord has given me eyes to see things."

"And you tell people what you see?"

"When I perceive that to do so will be eternally beneficial."

"A rather bold determination for one man to make with regard to another, especially one as young as yourself."

"Granted. But one must be true and faithful to the gifts and callings God places upon him, even gifts that are not wrapped in pretty packages that make the recipient happy."

"Do you not worry about your own flaws, perhaps even your own pride, hindering your accurate vision? The rabbi Jesus, whom you so esteem, said: 'Do not judge.'"

"Indeed he did, by which he meant not to *condemn*. He also declared that he *could* judge, because, he added, 'My judgment is true.'"

"You believe you can say the same of yours?"

"If it is from God, yes. Jesus is not the only one to whom God gives true judgment. I believe, in fact, that he wants his people walking so selflessly that they possess the capability of such discernment, so that when it is required it may be judiciously exercised. I do not say this is always so in my case, nor that pride and my own flaws, as you say, do not occasionally interfere with the process."

"I think I see, at least partially, what you mean."

"I am," Palacki continued, "like all men, a broken and incomplete vessel. But even a jar with a crack is capable of carrying water, and that water is just as capable of accomplishing the purposes God intends as that from a pure mountain stream. For a man with *need* of water to disdain what comes to him in his thirsty condition because the jar has a crack seems to me the height of foolishness."

"I take it, then, that you continue to distribute water to those around you?"

The young pastor nodded. "It would be equally foolish of me to still my tongue because of my own flaws. If a man must be perfect to speak the truth, very little truth would get spoken in the world. I do not *look* for things to say, I can only say I am *shown*. More often than not I resist saying anything until the Lord impels me with such force I can do nothing else."

∾ 77 ∾
Unusual Insight

During the thoughtful lull in the conversation that followed, Joseph glanced over at Andre Palacki, who was listening with attentive silence.

"Are you comfortable with what your son says?"

"Completely. I trust what he sees because I know him better than anyone else. I have watched him grow from his youth on up. I know what manner of spirit pulses within him. I know that the keenness of his analysis and the searchlight of his prayerful heart are constantly turned upon himself more than anyone else. Therein lies the basis of his unusual insight. He *knows* himself. It is the one aspect of my son's character very few others allow themselves to see. It is what, in the midst of such boldness, keeps him humble with respect to his *own* walk of faith."

Joseph nodded in understanding.

"Yes, I trust him," added the father. "All the more in that whenever the slightest word comes to him, from whatever quarter, concerning some need within his *own* soul—and as he has grown through the years, often they have come from me—he is on his knees *the next instant*, praying for God to root out of him whatever does not reflect the man God would have him to be. Yes, he is my son, and yes, he is still a young man, but I have rarely seen one so hungry to grow and so without motive of self in relation to others."

"You must admit such a response from a father to be somewhat unique. You know what the rabbi Jesus said about the honor of prophets in their own home."

"It is not so in this home. We highly honor God's work in our son."

Joseph took the information in without comment, then turned again to the younger of the two men.

"Why do these opportunities you speak of with people come to you? How do they originate?"

"I am involved with people. God sends men and women with needs my way. And I *love* people. I hunger after growth. I yearn to see men and women become all they can become, all God desires them to become, all he envisioned for them when he made them."

He paused briefly, then added, "And there is another reason."

"Which is?"

"I pray for people. I pray for everyone I meet. I pray to be used in people's lives. I am evangelistic about the perspectives God has given me, about growth, about truth, about God's fatherhood. Therefore, God sends people to us—people such as yourself—and I am constantly asking him what he would have me do and say and be in relation to them. No encounter occurs by chance, and I take every encounter, every relationship, as an opportunity ordained by God to speak truth, that the kingdom of heaven may be expanded and deepened, and thereby exercise a more expansive influence throughout the world.

"He may give my voice opportunity to speak my mind to thousands one day—" He paused. "And who knows," he added with a humorous smile, "perhaps find them offended by my outspoken boldness. He may choose, on the other hand, that I serve him, as have others, in a Communist prison—it matters not. I will continue to pray for and communicate the truth he gives me to proclaim, whether it be happy and pleasant, or painful and convicting."

"In *my* case, do you feel a reluctance to speak your mind?" asked Joseph.

"I don't know—should I?"

"If I ask, as I did earlier, what you mean by ultimate truth, I ought to be open enough to hear your reply."

"What if my answer is more personal and pointed than you anticipated? What if—"

They were interrupted by the pastor's mother.

"Andre, Dieder," she said, "I think someone may be watching the house. I have seen a man pass by along the street several times."

"In a car?" asked her husband.

"No, on foot. But he is walking slowly and seems to be looking this way."

"Can you tell if it is the same man from last night?"

"It is not him."

The two men thought for a moment or two.

"Let us move into the bedroom, as a precaution," said Dieder. "Mother, will you watch again and tell us when he is not in view, so we may move without giving off any shadows."

She returned to her vantage point, peeking through one of the drawn shades, and signaled them that the coast was clear.

A minute later they were seated, not quite as comfortably but out of sight, in the larger of the home's two bedrooms.

"Is danger always so present?" asked Joseph. "As a Jew, I am used to it, but I must admit I did not realize it was the same for Christians."

"It is not for all Christians, and there have been times when we have enjoyed relative peace to worship as we please. The political landscape changes without warning. I have the feeling, however, that this present danger involves you and the man who was looking for you last night. It is good that you are leaving soon. Hopefully he will lose sight of you after tonight. I am only sorry that we may have brought the danger closer to you."

"It is I who am sorry," rejoined Joseph. "If the man has been following me, it is I who have brought the danger to you."

"It matters not. We will continue to pray for protection, and the Lord will be faithful to us all."

It fell silent.

"I hope this will not cause you to discontinue what you were going to tell me a few minutes ago," said Joseph.

"It will not . . . . if it is your desire for me to continue."

"It is."

"But, as I was saying, what if in you I see things that even you do not see? Painful things, perhaps a word you need to hear— but it is an unpleasant word?"

"It would seem I have no right to ask you for insight into your words if I am not prepared to be man enough to listen, wherever your response might lead."

"You speak the words of a wise man."

"Then speak forth. Shine whatever light you believe our mutual Father has revealed to you. Shine it as probingly as you feel you ought. If eight years in prison accomplished anything in me, I hope it gave me courage, and a little mettle and toughness of manhood besides."

"Well put!" rejoined Palacki heartily. "Then I will take you at your word and proceed."

Joseph nodded his assent.

❧ 78 ❧
Doors of Resistance

"For every individual," began the young pastor after a lengthy pause, "the word *ultimate* carries different specifics. Is there such a thing as *ultimate truth*? It is doubtful, except of course that in God is contained all truth, but that is not exactly how I am using the phrase."

He paused, thinking.

"Let me put it this way," he went on. "There are doors within each of us which we unknowingly close against the entrance of truth. We are masters of self-deception. We assume that we are open to all that is good and closed to all that is not. I doubt that ever a man looked at himself in the mirror and said, 'I am a closed-minded man.' We are *all* self-deceived at that point. Would you agree?"

"It is not something I have considered, but for the moment let us say that I agree with your premise."

"As there are perhaps many doors of blindness within each one of us, I would go on to say that there are one or two large doors we keep more tightly shut than all the rest. They exist at very deep, subterranean, and usually unseen subconscious places within us. They wall off regions within our characters at which we do not want to look, holes of darkness where we most persistently do *not* want to let the light shine.

"It is these very places that provide the key to personal growth. Those are the *very* doors through which light and truth must enter if we are going to become whole and complete men and women. The *deepest* truths must flow into us through the *deepest* cisterns. If we would know the deepest truth, and come to know the deepest intimacy with God, we must open the deepest and most tightly locked doors through which flow our thoughts, attitudes, emotions . . . and through whose circuitous channels truth will enter."

Again he paused, eyeing their guest carefully, praying silently to know how far to extend the discussion.

The elder Palacki had by this time leaned back in his chair and was, to all appearances, asleep. In truth, he was praying diligently for this eager Jewish man, praying that the seeds being planted at this moment of his receptivity would sprout and bear fruit, in the Father's time, thirty, sixty, and a hundredfold.

How could Andre know that even the silent prayers uttered from his motionless lips were themselves responses in the spiritual realm to prayers prayed by another nearly two decades earlier, a brother he would never know in this life, one whose heart moved in like love for the bonds of unity felt with his Hebrew kin.

The ways and purposes of God move according to no byways the eyes of man can discern. Neither do the prayers of man always germinate in the directions they have pointed them. Every prayer, coming from the lips of the loftiest-thinking theologian, to the simplest child praying for the Lord's eye to watch over her while she sleeps, to the despairing cry lifted from how many millions of beds in the midst of how many sleepless nights, *"Oh God . . . help me!"*—all enter into the heart of God, are heard, and are responded to according to the divine plan.

But God is not bound by the aim of man's prayers. His ends are higher. Occasionally, to fulfill those purposes, he bends the flight of man's prayer-arrows so that they strike hearts unintended and unseen. The petitions accomplish no less mighty and miraculous ends in that they pierce the spiritual flesh of others whose need *God* knew, though the prayer from which they were launched apprehended nothing of their final destination.

The words and thoughts of men's prayers are as ascending mists, which God gathers together in great clouds of his design, then to blow them over the face of the earth to see where they are needed. When a human seedling is bent low from the parched hot wind of circumstance, or when the seed in some human garden is stirring about in readiness to sprout, he sends down the moist, ministering dewdrops of life, though those same prayerful dews of love may have been offered heavenward at some other place and some other time by one of his faithful children who knew not where their ministry would finally water the earth.

And now—by that miraculous multiplicity of divine vaporization and condensation—flowed down the gentle rains of God's voice, those precipitating droplets created by the heaven-directed words intended by Baron von Dortmann for his Jewish guest and friend so many years before—raining down into the heart of the rabbi's lost would-be son-in-law, through a brother the baron would never meet. How could the German have known that his prayers would swirl about in the heavenly clouds, awaiting this day when, joined by new love-vapors from an aging Pole, God would slowly release them upon the earth . . . to nourish the seeds of eternal life.

～ 79 ～
The Second Red Circle

Earlier that same day, while the fugitive Jew yet slept, and at nearly the same time as the drama between KGB agent and Christian was being played out in a Moscow alley, Lola Reinhardt unlocked the Berlin offices of the *Stasi* section chief and walked inside to begin her day's work.

The discovery she made in the next five minutes, and what came of it later, would change her life forever.

The door to the section chief's inner office stood open, though she knew he had not yet arrived this morning. Absently she wandered in, without motive other than to open the blinds as she usually did and turn on the light.

There lay the open map on the desk he had been using as a worktable. Slowly, still absently, she approached, glancing over the black lines that zigzagged throughout the DDR, Czechoslovakia, and parts of western Poland, with notes and reminders scrawled here and there. She knew he had been attempting to reconstruct the moves of the American, for they had spoken of it just yesterday.

What were those three red circles? she wondered. They were new since the time she had last observed Herr von Schmundt poring over the map.

She bent down to look at them more carefully . . . two villages and the city of Halle. The northernmost she knew well enough to be the site of the former Dortmann estate. The other village as well was known to her, though she had never been there. Her own private research had brought it to her attention, and now a sudden premonition seized her heart regarding it.

Without any piece of concrete evidence to substantiate it, she knew that her boss was nearly on the threshold of locating the fugitives.

Hearing the door to the outer office open, she turned quickly away from the desk and walked briskly out of the office. Why did she feel so nervous all of a sudden, as if she had discovered the clue to a great mystery and mustn't be found out!

"Good morning, Herr Section Chief," she said, doing her best to sound cheerful amid the turmoil of thoughts in her brain.

Gustav responded coolly, then asked if Schulte had yet made an appearance this morning.

Lola replied that he hadn't. She felt a redness in her face and cheeks. She hoped he didn't notice!

"Well he'd better get here soon," growled Gustav. "I have an important errand on which to send him. I will be gone again myself for a while, Fräulein Reinhardt," he added.

"Where are you going, if I may ask?" she said, breathing deeply, trying to sound casual and collected.

"Poland. I may be away a week or two. There will be important surveillance going on in various parts of the country, Fräulein. If any messages come for me, you must contact me immediately. I will leave word with you how I can be reached. Extremely urgent matters are at hand."

"Yes, Herr von Schmundt."

Judging from his tone, Lola concluded that the fugitives had not been located yet.

Still she was worried.

Did *he* know, she wondered, all that *she* knew about the red circle on his map that had drawn her attention?

She thought through the implications of her discovery all the rest of the day, and when she went to bed she lay awake long into the night pondering what to do.

∾ 80 ∾
The Freedom of Ultimate Truth

While Lola attempted to sleep, the earnest conversation, meanwhile, was continuing between Polish Christian and Russian Jew. "When I said I would make it a matter of prayer that the ultimate truth would be revealed to your truth-loving heart," Dieder went on in a sincere and quiet tone, "I meant nothing more nor less than that you would come to apprehend the full destiny and culmination toward which your religion, your history, your race as a people points. It is for this purpose that I believe our Father sent you here, that you might respond to the challenge to come the rest of the way—all the way!—into the family to which you are already so closely bound."

"You continue to amaze me with your straightforward manner. I cannot say I was not warned!"

Palacki smiled.

"I have been the subject once or twice," Joseph resumed, "of what I believe some of your people call witnessing. It has always been a most unpleasant experience."

"An unfortunate Americanized version of evangelism that has spread even to our part of the world in spite of Communism. Yes, I know what you mean."

"I feel more the object of condemnation and judgment than the love which they say is their motive."

"Speaking for myself," relpied Palacki, "I have no desire to *convert* any man to my or any way of thinking. You cannot imagine a man less desirous of proselytizing than I."

"Yet you say evangelism is your vision."

"Yes, so that men may be *free*—free to understand the truth, free to know themselves, free to know their Father! That is a far different mission than the gaining of so-called converts. Nothing could interest me less than that."

"What do you consider freedom?" asked Joseph.

"A perceptive question . . . and an important one."

Dieder thought for a moment. "Freedom is probably one of the most sought-after commodities of all history. All men of all times have wanted to be free. Yet curiously, earthly freedom does not seem one of the things foremost in God's mind. It is a different kind of freedom he would give to men. He wants them to be free, yes, but *in their hearts*, whatever may be their outward circumstances."

"What is freedom of the heart?"

"Freedom from the bondage and tyranny of their *selves*. The human Self is the most ruthless of all possible masters, a dictator from whose hand happiness can never be received."

"Are men wrong, then, to desire earthly freedom?"

"Of course not. We help people to escape the injustices of Communism when we can. You are attempting to get to Israel, where you will be free. But in spite of these efforts, we never lose sight of what true freedom is, at the deeper level. A man may be free politically, yet still in chains to the mastery of his own self. And speaking for myself, though I am not free to travel out of Poland or to preach God's Word as freely as I would like, I am yet a *free* man. No earthly system can enslave me. They could imprison me for the rest of my life, but nothing can take away my freedom. Do you see the difference?"

Joseph nodded.

"I consider it no coincidence that God's people, the Jews, have been wandering without a homeland for much of their history. God promised them freedom, he promised them a land of their own. Yet in the world's eyes neither has been fulfilled. It is because the freedom he has to give is not, at the foundation, political freedom, nor is the land of milk and honey the land of Palestine, which we now again call Israel. He may want to give them those too, but they do not represent the ultimate truth. No, the freedom he wants to give is the same freedom he desires for all men."

"Which is?"

"Freedom from Self, and thus freedom to enter into intimate relationship with him."

"A revolutionary concept for a Zionist."

"No doubt. God's agenda is not a political one. The intimacy I speak of, for the truly *free* man, can be enjoyed in chains, with or without a homeland, and in your case, whether or not you find your betrothed. It is an intimacy, for the *free* man or woman, that can be entered into no matter how bleak, how painful, how sad may be one's earthly lot.

"That intimacy with him is the freedom into which he would lead us. *That* is the land of promise—intimacy with God our Father! For such did Moses lead the children of Israel out of Egypt—to give us a picture of the bondage God wants us all to escape out of . . . the bondage of Self, out of which the Deliverer, the Messiah, to whom Moses pointed as a symbolic foreshadowing, has come to lead us.

"The Messiah has come, my dear friend, to lead us to the land of promise . . . to freedom. Freedom within ourselves, freedom to join ourselves in intimate relationship with the Creator who made us!"

Joseph pondered these words for several moments in silence, then spoke again. "How am I as a Jew to respond to what you say?"

"There is a grave danger in approaching matters of spirituality from a cultural and social and political vantage point," replied Palacki, not answering Joseph's question directly. "All religions do this to some degree, and thus all suffer weaknesses as a result."

He paused, then went on. "The Jewish religious system is peculiarly vulnerable to this danger," he said, "because it is so deeply cultural, historic, ethnic, and societal. These features give it its strength . . . yet, as I said, make it vulnerable to a loss of the personal spirituality that must always remain at the foundation.

"Since the war, the rise of Zionism has only made it more political in its orientation, without the foundation of individual spiritual roots."

Palacki paused briefly.

"Now I have arrived at my very personal answer to your question," he went on. "I realize I often take the long way around to get to my point. But for a thoughtful man such as yourself I feel it is important to lay the foundation for what I have to say. So finally I will tell you how all this applies to *you*. I fear that the political aspects of your faith have made religion for you a

political, racial, ethnic, cultural, and historical *system*, but not
an intensely personal way of life in which you walk in fellowship with God."

Joseph was silent, looking down. The words stung, and yet he
knew they were coming from a heart of love.

He also knew they were true.

"I perceive," Palacki went on, "that you have been one who
claims to value truth, but who has seen truth as a thing external
to your own being. You have not turned it upon your own character, to ask what sort of man God would have *you* to be. Your religion has been for you, though meaningful, a 'religion' rather
than a personal experience in growth toward intimacy with God.

"What else is religion but that? If there is no experience of intimacy, then it is no religion at all, or a false one. Not necessarily
false in its precepts, but false in its reality in a man's heart.

"If this is true—and only you can make the determination
whether the light of my words is being accurately focused—then
you will never know the *ultimate truth* nor the *full freedom* you
seek, whether you are successful in your escape to the West or
not."

⤳ 81 ⤳
Intimacy with the Father

The silence that followed the young pastor's probing and
challenging words was long.

By now the night was well advanced. Mrs. Palacki had
retired, and only the light of one dim bulb shone in the small
room. The elder of the two hosts still sat with his eyes closed,
but wide awake of spirit, praying vigorously, with joy in his
heart.

It was their Jewish guest who at long last broke the pensive
and personally contemplative silence.

"How is this intimacy you speak of achieved?" he asked.
"Men and women the world over, and throughout all time, have
questioned how to attain intimacy with God. But very few have
succeeded in achieving it."

"Because very few have sought Jesus as the Christ to show them the answer. That is where your own people have erred. Not erred, as I said before, by deception, but erred from incompleteness. Jesus was sent by God, to *you*, to the nation and children of Israel.

"To be a full and complete Jew requires entering into the intimacy with God as your Father that Jesus came to bring the world. Without that intimacy, God remains but the Old Testament judge and lawgiver, mighty and sovereign, but not an *Abba* with whom you may enjoy intimacy.

"Yours remains, therefore, an incomplete relationship with him. That is why Jesus is unique, why he is the Messiah, because he came to lead us into the intimacy of which the Old Testament Scriptures offer only a faint and distant portrait."

Again there was a pause. Once more it was Joseph who first broke it.

"You do not, then, consider that I as a Jew believe something that is *not true*, such as I would say of the Buddhists, for example?"

"By no means. If I have conveyed such, forgive me. I have spoken, not against the untrue, but rather against the incomplete." Palacki paused. "Yet it may be that one of the doors of resistance within you that requires opening is the door with Jesus' own name on it."

Joseph received the statement with a slow nod, but said nothing for a moment.

"That is why I began at that point, in fact," added Palacki, speaking of the doors of resistance, "because for Jews that is precisely the door they must enter—that of Jesus' being the Messiah."

"Now . . . today, however," Joseph said after a moment, "even though I *am* a Jew, yet you have called me brother. Many of your fellow Christians would call me many things, but surely *brother* would not be one of them."

Palacki acknowledged the truth of his statement with a smile. "Paul," he said, "the first-century Pharisee and persecutor of Christians turned spokesman for the very movement he tried to stamp out, wrote a letter to the young Christian congregation at Ephesus in which he addressed the mysterious linkage that existed then between the Jewish and Christian faiths. He called it a mystery, and I happen to believe that same linkage exists today."

"Go on . . . explain."

"Paul was attempting to decipher to new Gentile Christians the peculiar relationship between Old Testament Judaism and *fulfilled New Testament Judaism.* He said that in the old times there was separation between Jews and Gentiles. Jesus came, he said, to make the two one—to unite all men, to bring Gentiles into the Abrahamic covenant.

"Paul calls it a mystery—a mystery kept hidden through past ages, but now fully revealed . . . but—and here is the great stumbling block for Jews that keeps them from apprehending this full revelation—it is a fulfillment of truth revealed *through Jesus.*

"Listen to Paul's words: 'This mystery is that through the gospel *the Gentiles are heirs together with Israel,* members together of *one* body, and *sharers together in the promise* in Christ Jesus.'

"'*Sharers together in the promise!*'" he repeated with enthusiastic emphasis. "What else can he mean but the promise, the covenant made to Abraham—*brought to completion and fulfilled now in Jesus.*

"If those words do not speak of a brotherhood intrinsic within the Jewish-Christian relationship, I cannot imagine what else they speak of!"

"I see your point," laughed Joseph lightly.

"So you see, my friend—and brother!" Palacki went on, "Judaism and Christianity are not separate and distinct religions. They have the same foundation and grow out of the same soil. Judaism, as a religious 'system,' however, simply doesn't go far enough with it. God planted the seed with Abraham, and in the four thousand years since, it has grown into a towering and mighty tree. Jews simply need to look up and behold the *whole* tree of God's making rather than continuing to be satisfied with the incomplete memory of a transitional stage in the tree's growth.

"Christians are Jews in the spiritual sense. We are all Abraham's offspring, children of the covenant. Jews, likewise, must be Christians, that is, followers of Christ—Jesus the Messiah, himself a Jew, the complete Jew whom God sent, God's very Son—in order to be *complete* and *fulfilled* Jews.

"There is no right or wrong between Jews and Christians. *Christians are Jews* because we have been grafted onto the plant that is God's family and have thus become—by spiritual means—sharers in God's covenant with Abraham. *Jews must also be Christians* in order to fully partake of the fulfillment of that covenant.

"It is all a wonderful harmony of design and purpose that God intended to flow among us. Paul's words sum it up with such glorious precision—*heirs together* with Israel, *members together . . . sharers together* in the promise.

"Don't you see," Palacki went on excitedly, "you have an opportunity that a physical Gentile like myself will never have—the opportunity to be a *full* Jew and a *full* Christian both, a fulfilled and complete man of God in every way.

"I envy the possibility before you, even though I am in no way dissatisfied with my own lot. I envy you the opportunity to be a leader among your people who truly apprehends how broad and wide and deep is the covenant for which your race was chosen to be the mouthpiece to the world!"

∾ 82 ∾
Next Stage of the Journey

Kochow Rydz, the youngest active member of the brotherhood, arrived through farmland at the back door of the Palacki home at 1:30 A.M.

His charge was ready. The discussion with Palacki had broken up shortly after 11:30, and Joseph had napped until time for his departure. Now, after heartfelt exchanges of farewells and blessings, he took his leave and embarked upon the next stage of his pilgrimage toward freedom.

The young Christian and sojourning Jew walked eighteen kilometers on foot through the middle of the night. At their destination, strange to tell, Joseph found the same automobile awaiting him that he had abandoned at the barn a day and a half earlier on the other side of Bialystok altogether.

It had a fresh tank of petrol, Polish plates in replacement of the Russian, and in a bag on the floor he discovered a container of hot coffee, two apples, and a fresh-baked loaf of bread.

"How . . . but, where did—," he stammered in amazement.

"Everything is provided," said his young companion.

"But, I thought your brotherhood was small . . . that I had met nearly all of you."

"The brotherhood has many friends. Now, you must drive to Warsaw by small back roads in case they should know the car. We usually use other means, but since you grew up in the area and came by auto, this is the way the arrangements have been made in your case. You still must be cautious. There is a map, if you have forgotten or lose your way."

"Why should I not just drive all the way across Poland and into Germany?"

"What would you do then?" asked Kochow. "How would you keep from leaving a trail behind you? Where would you stay, how would you obtain German money and German identification papers? What if you encountered trouble? The KGB is close behind you; of that we are already certain from what happened the other night."

"Yes . . . of course, you are right."

"Most of all," continued the young man, who, in spite of his youth, had clearly been involved in many such escape plans and showed a thorough command of what was required, "what would you do once you actually arrived in Berlin? If your goal is to reach Israel, then you must get to the West. That has never been more difficult or perilous . . . nor is it something one can successfully accomplish alone."

"How *am* I going to get to the West?" asked Joseph, the enormity of the road ahead suddenly dawning upon him with greater clarity than before. He had at first been so preoccupied with just getting safely out of the Soviet Union that now suddenly a whole new range of difficulties rose before his mind's eye.

"I do not know that," answered Rydz. "None of our fellowship does. We are, as Dieder explained, only connected fragmentarily with other underground organizations. We are mere middlemen who will put you in touch with others and who, from this moment on, will uphold your journey in prayer."

"Why don't I simply drive across Poland and then contact the underground people on the other side of the country?"

"You have been involved in the underground in Russia. You know how things work, that links are kept short for everyone's safety. These things cannot be rushed. It may take you a week or more, though it is a mere four or five hundred kilometers, to reach Berlin. There may be dangers we know nothing of. You may have to remain hiding in one place for a season. Great care must be taken so as not to compromise the safety of other organizations or individuals."

Joseph smiled. He did know, of course. Even in Moscow itself he had been unable to establish contact with anyone who knew the rabbi personally because of the cloak of protective secrecy surrounding him.

"In order for trust to be established, you have to move along the underground channels as they determine, not for your own convenience. It is the only way during these times. Before you reach Berlin, you will pass through the hands of perhaps three or four such groups as ours, linked in the desire to help only, but knowing very little about one another."

"Do you know nothing of how I will be assisted in reaching the West?"

"There is a network we have heard of that may be involved in your case. There is word of an escape attempt involving an important man—"

"A rabbi?" interrupted Joseph, with sudden hopefulness.

"I have heard nothing such as that. A Christian man, I believe, a political prisoner for some years. In any event, whether this is accurate or not I cannot say. But we suspect they may take you across with him."

"*They* . . . who do you mean?"

"They who are making those arrangements—who, specifically, we do not know."

"You hear things?"

"Word occasionally comes to us about a loosely knit network in Germany that has ties to the West."

"You know nothing about them?"

"Only that they go by the name of a flower."

"What flower?" asked Joseph, wondering if by some remote chance . . . he had heard rumors in Moscow too.

"Only a flower," replied Rydz. "That is all I know, my friend. It is now time for us to part. Godspeed."

"Shalom. Greet your brothers for me, and thank them!"

"You will be in our prayers, our brother!"

∽ 83 ∽
KGB Revenge

In truth, the KGB was closer behind than even Kochow Rydz knew when he spoke the words of warning to Joseph as they parted.

Even as the young Rydz was returning by foot to Bialystok, Emil Korsch was driving once again to the home of a certain Dieder Palacki, whom he suspected of knowing more in the affair of the fugitive Jew than he was telling. All Korsch's reports indicated Bialystok as the man's destination after crossing the Polish border. There were no other likely Christian organizations between the border and Warsaw. And both Bolotnikov and Grazinski confirmed Palacki as a daring and outspoken Christian leader.

He knew something all right!

It had been gnawing on Korsch all day as he followed the weasel-like Pole around, chasing one fruitless lead after another. Even after Grazinski's surveillance at the house had resulted in nothing out of the ordinary, he remained suspicious.

Finally, Korsch determined to raid the place the following morning.

If the pastor wouldn't tell him what he wanted to know, then he would pay for his obstinateness with his freedom!

The fist of Emil Korsch beat on the door, this time without the thin veneer of kindness he had shown the traitor's mother two nights previous.

It had not been light more than an hour. The young fool should still be at home.

It was two or three minutes before the door opened, during which time it had been nearly beaten down by the agent's angry hand.

"Get out of my way, you old biddy!" cried Korsch, shoving Mrs. Palacki aside the moment the door opened a crack and storming inside, brandishing his gun threateningly in his hand. "Where is he!"

The poor lady was too terrified to speak. It hardly mattered. Her son came forward from the living room, dressed in his work clothes in preparation for the day, to meet the intruder stomping toward him.

"Palacki!" shouted Korsch. "I demand you tell me what you know in the matter of the criminal I am seeking."

"I told you previously," answered Dieder calmly. "I have not the slightest knowledge of any criminal."

The elder of the house now approached.

"Please, sir, my son knows nothing. Perhaps I might be able—"

A clout from the back of Korsch's hand both silenced him and sent him sprawling to the floor at once.

"There is no need for violence," said Dieder, stepping forward, doing his utmost to suppress the emotion of retaliation that surged suddenly through him. He was no coward and would have expended his very life for his father. But his parents had taught him according to an inverted pyramid of values that Emil Korsch could never fathom. He knew revenge was no answer . . . and that it would accomplish nothing but evil toward all parties in the end.

He thus stood, silently praying for guardian angels to protect his mother and father, while he awaited his own fate.

Korsch saw the flash that erupted in the young man's eye, and well knew what feelings of revenge he had stirred. He had encountered it before, always with religious types who were too cowardly to prove their manhood by letting their anger rage openly.

A thin grin came to his lips, a smile of devilish temptation and cunning.

"You would like to repay me with your fists for hurting your father, I see? Who is to stop you? You are young and strong; I am aging. You could easily overpower me . . . perhaps even shoot me, hmm?"

Palacki stared forward, giving no reply.

Again their eyes met, as they had two nights earlier. As before Korsch saw a light shining in his adversary's, but he mistook this second light for the momentary anger of the first.

He stretched out his hand and gave Dieder a rough shove, causing him to stumble backward.

"What is to stop you, Palacki?" he goaded. "Come, save your parents. I am but one man—"

Again he pushed him backwards, more forcefully this time, his own anger roused at the other's reluctance to fight him fist to fist, man to man.

"Are you afraid, young Pole!" he taunted, hitting him now, first in the stomach, then kicking at him as he doubled over. The kick finally sent him down to the floor on his back.

"Stop! Stop!" screamed the horrified mother, rushing forward and grabbing Korsch's arm.

The next moment she found herself tossed backward like a rag doll, toppling over a chair that collapsed over upon her. Her husband was at her side in an instant.

Dieder was now on his feet, eyes flashing once more.

Had Korsch taken one more step toward either his father or mother, he would have found himself hard pressed against the righteous anger that had finally been kindled into full flame within the courageous young man.

Korsch saw the change, thought better of culminating the confrontation, and rose up to what there was of his height, turning his pistol toward him.

"As I thought," he said with cold cynicism. "You are a coward through and through. A Pole and a Christian—I cannot think of a more ideal combination for cowardice. Now come with me, you young hypocrite and fool! You are under arrest!"

He stepped forward, grabbed Dieder brusquely by one arm, yanked him forward, and led him from the house, leaving behind only the sounds of a mother's agonized weeping and an aging father's scarcely audible prayers for the son and man of God whom he loved.

∽ 84 ∽
Husbands and Wives

The dirt-splotched face and grimy clothing could do nothing to diminish the radiant smile on the face of Angela Peters when she emerged from the darkness to see the face of her husband staring down the hole at her.

"Franz!" she cried in a near hysteria of joy, reaching up to grab his hands. Then, scrambling up out of the very pit he had dug just for her, she fell into his arms.

"I *knew* it was you . . . the message of heather . . . the—"

She could not say another word, but broke down sobbing, as he kissed her about the lips and cheeks, the latter of which were now being made mud from the rivers flowing down them.

Behind her, Kohl's wife and then Kohl himself were now crawling the last few meters to safety, where they would complete the brief reunion they had begun in the cramped underground grave.

Watching it all with satisfaction and pride was the third member of the rescue team, Friedrich Detmold, who had not felt so pleased about anything he had been associated with in years. This was far better than building skyscrapers, he said to himself. He just might go into the excavation business full-time!

Now first Angela noticed the contractor who had paid the strange visit to her and her brother weeks before.

"Herr Detmold!" she said, now running over and embracing him, still crying liberally. "Thank you . . . thank you!"

"You must have been able to interpret my messages," he said laughing. "I'm afraid I'm not much of an artist."

"Oh yes, we understood everything perfectly."

Angela turned back to her husband, to see him pulling the rope in from out of the hole.

"Is everything securely back in place, Geoff?" he said to Kohl.

"Our friend Brecht will never be suspected of the slightest complicity until his services are required again."

"Good . . . then let's show our wives West Berlin!"

"Oh, that reminds me!" exclaimed Angela. "I've got to call someone."

"Who?"

"Someone a dear friend of mine asked me to call. I've got to get a message to her friend . . . that she hopes to see her soon."

∽ 85 ∽
Expanding Friendships

Ursula had sensed a change coming for nearly a week now. Strange promptings descended upon her during quiet times alone with the Lord. She found Joseph and Sabina both in her thoughts almost continuously.

But pray as she might, she could not discern what the Father might be attempting to say. On the one hand a hint of anticipation seemed rising within her breast. At the same time a feeling of relinquishment was pressing itself upon her consciousness, as if the Lord was about to require some sacrifice of her, something she was going to have to lay down . . . something she would be called to place on the altar and give over to him.

She had picked up the phone three or four times to call Thaddeus but had then thought better of it. What would she say?

She sat down to write him a letter once or twice too, but neither had that proven any more successful. Maybe she would drive down to see him next weekend, she thought.

Ursula rose from her small kitchen table, where she had been eating a light supper. The evening would be warm, and it would be light for several more hours.

She would go out for a walk.

She left her apartment, descended the stairway, and emerged from the building into the street, then began walking in a careless fashion, heedless of direction.

Half an hour later she unexpectedly found herself approaching the Friedrichstrasse checkpoint station between East and West Berlin. She stopped, glancing first to her right, and then to her left, along the expanse of concrete and wire that stretched out in both directions as far as she could see.

For some time she stood, thinking of nothing in particular, gazing upon the wall, then peering through the checkpoint toward the other side, a side which seemed now so dreary and barren.

Where was Sabina? she wondered. What was to become of her?

Ursula continued to stand, as if caught between two worlds, caught between East and West, oppression and freedom, the past from which she had come and the future toward which she was bound.

But what *was* her future?

Where was she—Ursula Wissen, daughter of Israel but still without a homeland of her own—where was she bound?

Here she stood, at the dividing line between all things, the barrier that bisected the entire world into two humanities— one slave, one free—even as the great wall of truth divided the world into two humanities of spirituality—one lost, one saved, one bound for hell, one for heaven.

Ursula felt as if she was standing in the same sort of no-man's-land upon which she now gazed, unable to go *forward* into life and freedom . . . until some revelation was given her that allowed her to fully resolve the past.

And yet . . . she could not see beyond the wall of the present, even as her eyes at this moment—

"Can I help you, miss?" a voice sounded beside her.

Startled, Ursula turned. There stood an American soldier, the border guard who had spoken to her.

"Oh . . . oh, no," she replied. "I . . . was just thinking."

She turned and walked off, wondering what inner compulsion had brought her here on this night, and what it had to do with the strange things she had been feeling for two or three days.

Dusk had by now begun to descend over the city.

Ursula still felt like walking. Her steps slowly took her away from the checkpoint and toward the bustling center of the city. Before long she was walking along Kurfürstenstrasse. Surrounding her on all sides were people and noise and activity of the Berlin night, hardly diminished though it was now half past nine. She felt out of place in the midst of it, like a foreigner, though in a strange way at the same time, the movement and bustle of strangers of her kind gave her a peculiar feeling of belonging she had not often felt during her years in Berlin.

How long she thus walked, Ursula did not know. Many were the thoughts and sensations that came to her throughout the hours, most of which she could never have put into words. Though confusing in its own way, incorporated into the evening was almost the sense of bidding farewell to the city that had been her home for so many years.

Wondering if the Lord was readying to take her away from this place, Ursula did not arrive back at her apartment until shortly after eleven, full of more questioning anticipation of spirit than when she had set out.

She had just stepped out of the bathtub, still in the midst of a perplexity of thought and prayer, when her telephone rang.

The conversation was brief, ending with arrangements to meet in person. Ursula hung up the phone with an exhilaration surging through her she hadn't experienced in months. Suddenly all the evening—all the last several days!—made sense.

God had been shaking her up, getting her ready for this!

It was too good to believe, hearing from Sabina at last!

She had not actually heard from her in person. But being in some contact again was, at least the way she felt right now, almost as good.

The telephone call from Angela Peters was like a telephone call from heaven. It was truly an answer to the prayers that had been going about inside her all day.

And now, said Angela, Sabina might follow!

But what of the other half of what she had been sensing, thought Ursula as she lay excitedly down in bed. What was there to be laid down? Was that the part of it that had to do with Joseph?

She wouldn't worry about that just now, Ursula said to herself. This turn of events was too thrilling, and she wanted to relish in it.

Now she *would* call Thaddeus—first thing in the morning! She couldn't wait to tell him the news.

➶ 86 ➷
Refuge Penetrated

Matthew, Sabina, and Baron von Dortmann had been engaged for over three months now in that most difficult of all exercises of the human spirit—patient waiting.

They could not have found an environment more to their liking in which to pass the time. The contact with farmers and men and women of the earth again, and devout Christians besides, had energized Baron von Dortmann and brought renewed vigor to his brain. Many an evening he and Herr Moeller, who was what amounted to the patriarch of the small community, sat late into the night deliberating points of theology, examining common views of Christian noninterventionism, or discussing their favorite growing things.

As the weeks had passed gradually into months, Sabina and Matthew had spent as much time talking about the implications of the baron's contentment as the baron himself had spent praying about the quandary he had placed them all in.

"I'm an American," Matthew had said when Sabina had first told him of her talk with her father. "I don't like knowing Communism controls this place. It gives me the willies, and I don't want to spend a minute longer here than I have to."

The thought of any of them being separated from the others was untenable.

They still had come to no final resolution. All three had reached the point of saying to the Lord that they were willing to do whatever he instructed. They only had to discern what that will was.

Such was now the object of their prayers.

Their friend Udo Bietmann had sent out many secretive inquiries in all directions throughout Eastern Europe, in hopes that one might produce a breakthrough. Until now no word had returned to him of any escapes being planned that the three fugitives might be part of. His inquiries, however, did have the fortuitous result of alerting the loose Christian network in Poland of his search. Hints of it, in fact, had spread as far to the east as Bialystok.

When help finally did arrive, it was from the very source they had anticipated earlier—their friends in Grossbeeren.

The visit from Angela heightened anticipation that made the final stages of waiting all the more difficult.

Bietmann, unaware that he had been the object of *Stasi* scrutiny for the past week, arrived at the Moeller farm six days after Angela's call. They immediately knew from his expression that his drive out was for more than just a friendly visit.

"Erich Brumfeldt called me today," he told Sabina. "Where are Matthew and your father? We must talk."

"I'll take you to them," she replied. They left the house together and crossed the yard toward one of the barns, from which all four emerged, talking, a few minutes later.

"Dahlmann's sister made it out four days ago."

"Oh!" Sabina exclaimed, "that's wonderful!"

"You must be ready yourselves at a moment's notice. It could be the next day; it could be another week. He said Dahlmann is waiting for contact from a fellow on the other side, a contractor. Everything is already being coordinated with the people there."

"We'll be ready," Matthew assured him.

All were so absorbed in the discussion that none noticed the stealthy figure that had parked several hundred kilometers away and had drawn closer alongside the edge of a small pinewood that bordered the land of the community.

In his right hand he clutched a pair of binoculars, which, once he had a clear vantage point of the Moeller house, he raised to his eyes, just as the man he had followed knocked on the door.

The second Sabina came into view, he knew his patience had been rewarded!

Neither he nor the innocent and beautiful object of his vision would ever know how eerily reminiscent the moment was of that time long ago when his own superior had sent *his* gaze silently down upon this same lovely face from his secret wooded vantage point. How little had the years changed. Still Gustav was trying to gain sight of her from a distance beyond what his eyes could descry. And still the protective angels that watch over the Father's children stood guard over this precious one of his daughters.

There could be no possible mistaking that face, the lackey said to himself. He knew it instantly from the description he had been given.

With his eyes he followed the two to the barn, and when they emerged a little later with the other two men, his ecstasy mounted to nearly the bounds of what he could contain. He was sure to receive a promotion for this!

He had located them at last!

He turned and hurried back to his automobile and was soon speeding back toward Berlin.

∼ 87 ∼
Burning the Past's Bridges

The moment agent Schulte strode happily into the office, Lola knew he had big news.

"Where is Section Chief Schmundt?" he said. "I must see him immediately."

"He is, er . . . he has been away," answered Lola evasively. "Have you found them?" she added, by her tone presuming upon a greater degree of influence with their mutual boss than at the moment she actually possessed.

"Yes—yes, I have!" the assistant answered triumphantly. "I must talk to Herr von Schmundt! He will want to arrest them immediately. There is yet time today."

What occurred over the course of the next few minutes was not consciously premeditated, yet still less was it accidental.

To say that it simply seemed to *happen* would be, in a manner of speaking, to view it altogether incorrectly. In reality Lola had been tending toward just this point for some time. That it happened without the calculation of the moment in no way removed Lola's will from being the active and causative force behind it.

The direction in which we point ourselves will produce results that may appear at first glance accidental. They are not haphazard, however; nor do they merely "happen." Most incidents in life are in some way traceable to the orientation of mind and heart and attitudes one has chosen. The sharpest arrow point of determinative direction results from one's *alignment of will,* out of which will's multitude of large and small choices flows the progression of life's occurrences.

In later years, Lola would look back upon the ensuing brief conversation with Schulte, questioning within her conscience the ethics of what she had done, debating whether lying was a justifiable price to pay for freedom, either her own or that of others. If deception was required to obtain it, could one's conscience truly *be* free, notwithstanding that other more fleeting forms of freedom might be brought in as part of the bargain?

It was a dilemma she would never resolve.

Especially on this day did she not resolve it. She did not even think of it! Before she knew it, the lies had begun, and once they were done, though she was trembling with terror for what would happen if she were found out, she could yet feel no remorse for the sin of having allowed untruths to flow out of her mouth.

Now did all the progressive and invisible movements of her will reach a climax. All at once the floodgates of decision burst open, and by the time Schulte left the office a few minutes later, all the bridges to Lola's past were going up in flames behind her.

Assuming in an instant the former carriage of the section chief's authority which had served her so well, Lola turned toward the young and unremarkable assistant with a confidence of command to which he immediately succumbed. She would never have been able to pull off such a charade had Galanov still been attached to the office.

"Wonderful, Herr Schulte!" said Lola exuberantly. "I will get word to Herr von Schmundt immediately. He asked me to contact him the moment I heard from you."

"But should I not—," began the young agent.

Lola cut him off before he could finish.

"Do not worry about a thing. Herr von Schmundt and I will be speaking very soon. You located them in Kehrigkburg; is that correct?"

"Yes," replied Schulte.

"With the man Bietmann?" said Lola with a calculated

gamble. If she was mistaken about Schulte's information, she could betray the fugitives herself.

"Why . . . why yes—that is, not exactly, though near there. But he knows everything. I did not know you were so familiar with the details."

"Of course. I have been working on it from the beginning. When he returned to the city last evening," Lola went on with the lie, "Herr von Schmundt said he was now certain it was Kehrigkburg. He said he would go out there this afternoon to meet you himself, but that if you returned with anything before then, I was to get all the details from you and then send you down to Halle to join the others there."

"The others . . . what are they looking for?"

"For the rest of the Christian network, of course—didn't Herr von Schmundt tell you?" rejoined Lola with an annoyed tone. "Now give me the details, Herr Schulte. The section chief will not want to be kept waiting with this news!"

The young agent briefly filled her in on the site of the group of farmhouses to which he had followed Bietmann.

"Good . . . you have done very well!" said Lola. "There may well be advancement for you in this, once the traitors are brought to justice. Now you must be on your way to Halle immediately. They are shorthanded. Ornsberg is waiting for you. He's at the Lenin Hotel."

Still somewhat mystified, but finding no reason to question the secretary's forceful orders, Schulte left the building.

Once she was certain he was gone, Lola turned out the lights, glanced around with a deep sigh, then locked the office and left.

Important business lay ahead.

∽ 88 ∾
Joseph's Flight

Across the Poland of his birth flew the fugitive Jew, seeking the freedom of the West.

Upon the inner doors of his heart the persistent knocks continued their awakening call to his consciousness to seek yet another freedom. This latter was that spoken of by the friend of Bialystok and his brotherhood, whose fate at the hands of injustice Joseph could not possibly know. How quickly came the call prophesied by the young pastor, when the mettle and fortitude of his own faith would be tested in the soul-furnaces of Egypt's mud pits. By the lash of his Russian taskmasters would it be determined whether he himself indeed possessed the inner freedom he had spoken of to the Jew he had, in faith, called *brother.*

As for Joseph ben Eleazar, he found himself passed from person to person, through fragments of fellowships and networks unnamed—sleeping . . . eating . . . walking . . . riding . . . never knowing from one moment to the next where his pathway would lead.

Never had he been in a position of having to trust others so blindly. He had always been the one helping others. Now he was the bewildered pilgrim, awakened by voices in the middle of the night telling him to dress in haste and follow. Now *he* was the one sleeping in barns one night, soft beds the next, with his every need provided for, if only he did as he was instructed.

As the days passed, however, the sense gradually stole over him that his way belonged neither to him nor to his many helpers to guide, but rather that he was being watched over by an unseen providence. Never had he so unmistakably felt the *presence* of God in his life.

More and more as a result of that Presence did the words of Dieder Palacki come back to his memory, haunting him, working upon the deep places of his being with a whole new orientation toward the Almighty than had been his way of thinking of him before:

To be a full and complete Jew requires entering into the intimacy with God as your Father that Jesus came to bring the world.

Yours remains an incomplete relationship with him. . . . Jesus the Messiah came to lead us into intimacy, of which the Old Testament Scriptures offer only a faint and distant portrait.

He felt the intimacy closing in around him.

Yet he did not know what to do, how to respond to it. There was nothing in his Jewish experience to fall back upon, nothing to grab hold of that would explain what was happening to him and tell him what ought to be his reply to the beckoning calls of the great unknowable yet suddenly so knowable I AM.

Ever was the question before him, a question raised up into the gristmill of his intellect by the searchlight of Dieder Palacki's words: Was he a *true* truth seeker—one prepared to seek truth about himself, about his own flaws, about the cracks within his own belief system?

He was an astute enough thinker to know where such questions led. But was he man enough to look them in the face?

He knew the encounter with the brotherhood of Bialystok boiled down to one and only one thing insofar as he, Joseph ben Eleazar, was concerned: What if . . . *what if Christianity was true after all!*

If he was merely an *intellectual* truth seeker, a distinction he had never observed before, then such a question, whatever the answer, would not carry with it implications of great import.

But if he was a *true* truth seeker, a distinction from the former that Palacki had raised, then upon the answer to that question hung the very universe!

If he answered yes, it would immediately be followed by the inevitable imperative: *How must I then live in consequence?*

Thus as he traveled, seeking that which the world judges freedom, the pilgrim from Russia, a Pole by birth, a Jew by blood, and a child of God by destiny, was hounded by the inner call of Fatherhood upon his searching heart, drawn toward the intimacy of a different freedom. The mettle of his manhood was tested in cauldrons of doubt and question, where, by slow degrees, it was made ready to be molded by the refiner's fire into the shape that had been the fortune of his divinely created personhood since the beginning of time.

❧ 89 ❧
Help from an Unforeseen Quarter

Far to the west, in the German DDR, help was about to arrive to other of God's children from a source as unforeseen to them as Palacki's had been to Joseph.

Lola Reinhardt had been following Gustav's moves more carefully than he realized. Gradually over the course of his search, though she had never seen any of the fugitives, both from his comments and from what she had learned on her own, the sense had grown upon her that in the young woman the section chief sought she might perhaps find a friend.

How could Lola have known what forces were at work within her? If anyone had attempted to explain at this inceptive stage of her budding life about the movings and promptings of God's divine Spirit within the human spirit of man, it would have only bewildered her. Nonetheless, however, were those heavenly promptings now exerting their influence upon this daughter whom the Father desired to draw near to in a special way.

When she realized what Gustav was about to discover the instant he and Schulte again spoke, she realized the moment of decision had finally come. That they would speak was certain. Her forestalling maneuver was temporary at best. How much time it would give her she could not know—two or three days . . . maybe four at the most.

She could attempt to follow Schulte's directions. Yet she knew the man whose identity and involvements she had been aware of for some time was sure to be involved.

She would go straight to him.

The first moments at the doorstep of Udo Bietmann were awkward, though more for Lola than for the young farmer. Even after she identified herself, no fear rose up within him to quench the love he had felt at first laying eyes upon her.

"Herr Bietmann?" she had begun.

"Yes, I am Udo Bietmann."

"You do not know me," Lola had continued, "and please . . . do not . . . be afraid for what I am going to say."

She paused, again nervously. How greatly had her demeanor changed since the previous year, when she had been acting in the authority of her office. Even her interview of this very morning with Schulte had been carried out with great trepidation. Now that she was acting in the authority of the truth, the humility such a change brought to her countenance was readily visible.

"I am secretary to *Stasi* Section Chief Schmundt," she said. "It is urgent that I contact people that are hiding here."

"I am hiding no one," returned Bietmann, truthfully enough.

"I do not mean here. They are at the farm outside the village."

Bietmann took in the information with interest. The woman knew a great deal.

"Please, you must trust me," implored Lola. "I am here on my own. Herr von Schmundt would have me arrested if he knew. I must speak to them. He will be here himself soon—tomorrow, perhaps the day after."

"What makes you think I know the whereabouts—"

"Please," interrupted Lola, "I am not here to betray them . . . but to help them. They are in great danger. I want to help them so that he will not find them."

Bietmann sought the woman's eyes.

It only took a moment more. He knew she was telling the truth.

"Come in, my dear," Bietmann said at length, smiling. "I sense the urgency in your voice. But please, before I take you to them, have some tea with me and tell me of the danger you speak of. Then I will know what is best to be done."

∾ 90 ∾
Lola and Sabina

An hour later Udo Bietmann appeared at the Moeller farm with a woman none of them recognized. He knew that in the world's eyes he was taking a tremendous risk. But he trusted their Father to see to it.

He immediately sought Sabina.

"Sabina," said Bietmann, "I would like to present Fräulein Lola Reinhardt. Miss Reinhardt . . . Sabina von Dortmann."

The two women shook hands and smiled. She was indeed beautiful, thought Lola. It was no wonder her boss had once loved her.

"Please, Fräulein," said Lola, "do not be alarmed."

"Why would I be alarmed?" said Sabina cheerfully.

"Because . . . I am the secretary of one I believe you are acquainted with."

"Oh?"

"My boss's name . . . is Herr von Schmundt—Herr Gustav von Schmundt."

Sabina's face went white as a sheet. She glanced at Bietmann in terror, with a look of betrayed question in her eyes.

"Have no fear, Sabina," Bietmann said. "Fräulein Reinhardt and I have spent the last hour becoming very well acquainted. She has come to help you and your father."

Sabina glanced back to Lola, some of the color returning to her face.

"Herr von Schmundt knows—or he will know soon—where you are," said Lola, speaking again and with urgency in her tone. "You and the others must leave this place quickly . . . today."

"But . . . but how do you know all this . . . how do you know all about us?"

"It is a long story, Fräulein Dortmann," said Lola, with a sad smile that pierced Sabina's heart.

"But . . . but where will we—"

"You shall come to my house again," began Bietmann.

"No," said Lola imperatively. "No, you mustn't return to Kehrigkburg. He knows your name most of all. He knows your house. He knows your very face, Herr Bietmann. You and he have met before, outside the village."

Bietmann remembered the incident with Micka's cows.

His friend had regretted the day ever since. Perhaps the day had come for him to redeem himself and now give the help he had been unable to offer that day.

"We will have to get you to Dahlmann's again," said Bietmann, thinking even as he spoke. "Then you will be ready when the final call comes."

"What about you?" Sabina asked. "You will be in great danger."

"You are probably right," mused Bietmann.

He thought a moment.

"I shall take my wife and daughter eastward, to friends, for a time," he said. "That will be best. I must not place them in danger. The community here will be safe once you are gone. They

are in favor presently, and I do not think Herr von Schmundt
will be able to upset that."

"Gone?" repeated Lola. "What call?" She glanced at them
both, and suddenly the one piece of the puzzle that she hadn't
known fit into place. Her eyes widened as she knew to what
Bietmann referred. All at once she realized the full implications of what she had but briefly considered before, that she
could not go back.

"Please," she said, her voice trembling with sudden anticipation, "please . . . take me with you!"

Now it was Sabina and Bietmann's turn to glance at one
another with question and wonder.

"But, Fräulein—your boss, how would you—," began Bietmann.

By this time Lola was too agitated even to listen to the rest of
his question.

"Please," she implored, "I will go with you—now! I do not
need to go back. I need nothing. Oh, take me with you. I too
want to be free!"

About that moment Matthew and Baron von Dortmann,
who had seen the arrival of Bietmann's car, approached. Bietmann saw them, and the three men shook hands and
exchanged greetings.

Years of reserve at last about to break through the shell of
her feminine humanity, tears were already welling up inside
the eyes of their official guest. Sabina saw them. Gently she
placed a hand about Lola's shoulder and began leading her
toward the house.

The mere feel of human touch, the outgoing expression of
love from one woman to another, was all the catalyst her inner
reservoir needed. Before they were well inside, Lola was weeping freely.

Bietmann explained the reason for her appearance to the
other two men. The baron took in the information with sober
countenance, realizing what consequences for the safety of the
Mennonite community were contained in the revelation
Gustav was soon to come upon. Before the discussion between
the three men was over, the decision he had been wrestling
with was behind him.

Other decisions must be made too . . . and there were many good-byes to be said.

Meanwhile, in the house, the two women were seated side by side on the couch, speaking softly and freely, allowing their mingled tears of compassion and loneliness to flow.

Within the hour Lola had poured out everything to her new friend. And Sabina had told her of him in whose wide and expansive heart all the sorrows of the universe are swallowed up in tender, compassionate, understanding love.

∽ 91 ∽
Toward a New Life

By now Joseph was far removed from his contact with the brothers at Bialystok, yet ever did the same spirit pervade the ministering hands and voices of those to whom his care had been committed. By learning to trust them, he was invisibly being prepared for the greater step of trust that would ultimately be required of him.

Ever closer to his goal he drew, though slowly.

He was a week in Lodz, two days in Legnica, before crossing into East Germany and to Dresden, where he was hidden for another three days. The accommodations in a converted storeroom behind a butcher's shop were adequate, and he was amply provided for with everything but human company.

All he could do was think, and that he did.

As he had trekked across the ancient land of his parents, grandparents, and great-grandparents, and finally across the last border save one that stood between himself and the freedom of the West, word had spread throughout the network carrying him (a network about which he still knew very little) of the need for an escape attempt across the wall.

Word was therefore sent in return to a hulking man, a certain resident of Berlin with whom many of their number had had association over the years that, if possible, one was coming to him that might be included in the plans, if and when anything came of them.

Even as Joseph was reaching the final stages of his journey, having finally been rescued from the Dresden butcher's, north of him the small automobile of a certain Kehrigkburg farmer by the name of Micka was speeding toward the village of Grossbeeren squeezed full of a cargo of far greater worth than the cattle for which he was responsible in the fields back home. The driver had been so feverishly excited by Bietmann's call that he had hurried over almost instantly.

"There may again be danger," cautioned Bietmann.

"Then I will face it with more courage than last time," replied Micka.

And now, having met the three fugitives and the *Stasi* secretary, Micka had poured out the story of his past failure, his remorse over the incident, telling them that he had been praying ever since for an opportunity to make up for it.

The sad tale went strangely to Lola's soul and planted itself there along with much Sabina had said on the Moellers' couch. In a short time, there were already sown many seeds in the garden of her heart, where they were even now being watered and warmed by the sunshine and rains of love flowing within the tiny group of fugitives of which she had suddenly become so deeply a part.

Where they were bound, and what was to become of her, Lola scarcely knew.

But for the first time in her life she felt cared for by a love she had never before encountered. Within that love were swallowed all other passing concerns.

There was *life* here with these people. She would, therefore, follow wherever it led!

∽ 92 ∽
Wrathful Revelation

The two telephone calls came within twenty minutes of one another. Gustav knew the instant he concluded the second that they were inextricably related.

The first came from his assistant Schulte.

"Herr Section Chief," the assistant had said. "I thought you would be back from Niedersdorf by this time."

"Why should I be back?"

"I returned to Berlin, but no one was in the office, so I thought to try you there."

"I told you to stay at your post! And you still have not told me why I should be back."

"To apprehend the criminals. I thought you would have—"

"How would I have apprehended them?" interrupted Gustav.

"In Kehrigkburg, where I told you I saw them."

"You what!" exploded Gustav.

"I saw them in Kehrigkburg. That is why I returned to Berlin then, to notify you immediately."

"I have not spoken to you in a week and a half, you idiot! What do you mean notify me? When was this!"

As he listened to the answer, his face went various shades of red.

"Three days ago!" shrieked Gustav. "I'll have your head, you fool! Why did you not apprehend them?"

"Naturally, I assumed you would want that honor—"

"You assumed! You are an agent of the *Staatssicherheitsdienst* as well as I am, you moron! What have you been doing ever since!"

"I have been in Halle, *mein Herr.*"

"Halle!" screamed Gustav in a passion of fury. "You are a greater idiot than I dreamed! What were you doing in Halle?"

"Helping the men there."

"Helping the men what, you moron, if you had already located them! Why did you go to Halle?"

"Fräulein Reinhardt said you had ordered it. She said the message concerning the fugitives would be passed to you immediately."

"The hag!" cried Gustav. "I shall have her head along with yours! You told *her* of your discovery and not *me!* You loose-tongued simpleton!"

"I assumed that she spoke—"

"Don't make another move until you see me!" cried Gustav in a rage. "Where is Reinhardt?"

"I have not seen her. Apparently she has not yet come in to-day."

"Bah, I will see to her later. On second thought, you drive back down to Kehrigkburg immediately. We must ascertain if they are still there. I will be there within two hours. Telephone me at the office and you may fill me in on everything then!"

He threw down the phone in a fit of wrath, as bewildered by the perplexing turn of events as he was livid.

Tossing his few things together, he was in the lobby checking out of the only excuse Niedersdorf possessed for decent accommodations when the second call came through. It was from one of his most reliable Berlin street informants. He took it in a private booth.

He listened calmly for perhaps thirty seconds.

"Is there nothing more specific as to time? . . . What about location? . . . Is the source trustworthy?"

Again he listened.

"I am returning to Berlin immediately. I will see you this afternoon. If you are correct and it is tomorrow, we will maintain constant contact throughout the entire day."

The question that followed on the other end of the line was a brief one.

So was Gustav's answer.

"Yes, my slimy friend. If you provide me the missing piece that leads to their arrest, I will put the two thousand marks into your hand."

He paused a moment, thinking of the two morons in his own office who had as good as betrayed him, then added, so as to augment the payoff and ensure its success with a healthy dose of fear: "But, my friend," said Gustav, "if I should find you have misled me when this is all over, you shall find *yourself* the fugitive until I put my hands around your throat and throw you in the same prison that awaits the others!"

He set down the phone, more calmly this time.

The fury brought on by the first call was by now partially mollified by the second. He would, of course, have to get rid of the idiot Schulte, and perhaps even his fool secretary too for her dim-wittedness in the affair.

What could possibly have gotten into the vixen to make her say such things!

Yet it was still apparently not too late, as long as the break didn't come within the next two hours.

He would be back in Berlin by then, standing by his phone. Once he had the three in custody, then he would decide what to do with Schulte and Reinhardt.

The two numbskulls! They had nearly succeeded in blowing a whole year's work!

The second call confirmed that the idiot Schulte would find nothing more at Kehrigkburg. It was too late to nab them there. He would have to make the arrest when the fugitives made for the West.

∽ 93 ∾
Sincerely, Detmold

The atmosphere in the large home was charged as with a current of electric anticipation. The fear that could not be prevented from intermingling with it only heightened the overall tingle of expectation.

Even Baron von Dortmann, content as he had been at the Moeller farm, and even reluctant as he had been to, as he considered it, impede and possibly endanger the others with his presence, found himself walking about the place in mounting eagerness to be on with it.

He, more than all the others, was aware of the significance of lives about to be left behind, for he had spent all of his sixty-eight years here. He had no regrets, however. His eyes shone with the sparkle of youth. Once the decision had been made, the normally patient man was restless to cross the river into whatever new land of promise his God had for him.

He had even had to come to the point of personal relinquishment, of realizing his need to be willing to leave behind his treasured journals and his more-treasured Bible. His own writings, and the Lord's, were all he had brought out of prison other than the clothes he wore. And now, with those Matthew had retrieved from the hidden dungeon of *Lebenshaus*, they comprised the closest approach to worldly possessions capable of tempting the aging saint toward greed after the temporal.

Heinrich von Dortmann was under no illusions about their value to others. He knew well enough that they were destined to the dust along with all passing things of the earth. It was not for any external value he treasured them, but because they were *him*. Within their pages lived his soul. They represented his quest after and his life with his heavenly Father. In that, therefore, their contents were of eternal significance and worth.

Matthew came upon the baron two days after their arrival back in Grossbeeren, seated pensively alone, with the books and ancient Bible in his lap. He knew immediately what the baron was thinking. Sabina's father had, in fact, been reflecting upon the most effective disposition of the volumes among the few of God's men he now knew. He had nearly left them with Arndt Moeller two days before and had now concluded that he must make some arrangements for Dahlmann to get them back to the faithful Mennonite brother.

"Don't concern yourself too greatly, Baron," said Matthew. "Your journals will be going out with us."

The baron glanced up. He had been so lost in thought that he wondered if he had heard correctly.

"But . . . there will not be—"

"Baron," said Matthew, "they *must* accompany us. Even if *you* had decided to remain behind yourself, I would have insisted upon taking them! They are more valuable to Sabina and me than I think you have any idea. Your life is a legacy that must be preserved, and I intend to make it my business to preserve it."

The baron was speechless. He glanced up at the young man he loved, tears flooding his eyes, unable to find a single word to speak.

Sabina also had but few possessions. Nothing could be taken more than what could be easily held and concealed within the folds of their clothing. All she cared about were tokens of sentimental memories and a special book or two.

Matthew had walked into the DDR the previous January with nothing of his own. Now the only possession he treasured, other than the baron's journals, was the china box he had also retrieved from its hiding place beneath the ancient House of

Dortmann. He and Sabina both agreed they must find means to keep it with them as a lifelong token and remembrance of the love God had caused to grow between them.

Each of the four knew the stakes and that once they embarked upon this final stage of their adventure there could be no turning back. A door would close behind them, perhaps never to be opened again.

Lola Reinhardt knew it most of all.

The qualms within her heart had no bearing on possessions left behind, but upon the change all this represented within her being. She had gone to Kehrigkburg to warn these new friends about Gustav. Out of her role as a *Stasi* agent, suddenly she had stepped as into a fairy-tale world, the outcome of which she could not possibly foresee.

They were all so kind, so warm, so gracious, and seemed to *care* about her so deeply. The tears that came often, and so unexpectedly, as a result had been her constant companion since arriving here.

But now that three days had passed, she could not help new anxieties beginning to mount. When would Herr von Schmundt find out about her duplicity? Surely it would not be hard to trace them from Kehrigkburg to here. How long would it take before he arrested them all—herself along with the others!

In the midst of her thoughts, a knock sounded on the outside door.

Lola nearly leapt out of her skin in fright.

Their host was into the room in a moment, swiftly and silently motioning Lola and the others toward the back of the house.

They all rose noiselessly and tiptoed from the semidarkened room, while Dahlmann waited, then himself slowly approached the door.

He opened it to the sight of a uniformed official of the DDR government, sent down from the same office by which he had been contacted earlier.

"Herr Dahlmann?"

Josef nodded.

"Communication for you from Berlin," the man said, handing him an envelope.

"From whom?" Josef asked.

"I do not know, Herr Dahlmann. It was cleared through our office, and I was instructed to bring it to you."

Josef thanked the man, then returned inside.

Once he was certain the man was gone, he gathered his four visitors to show them the brief message he had received.

It read:

Dahlmann,

    Machinery working perfectly. Set to try on job site on 6th. By sunset should know if efforts have been successful.

    Thank you again for your help in the matter. Will contact you again only if necessary.

    Sincerely,

    Detmold

They all glanced around at one another. Every one of the five knew perfectly well what the message meant.

Today was Wednesday, September 5.

PART VI

E. Brecht
September 1962

∾ 94 ∾
Laying Down the Past
September 5—7:30 P.M.

Ursula Wissen had never been so nervous and afraid—in the midst of an excitement she could hardly contain—in all her life. She remembered the danger of her family's escape to Switzerland during the war. But that was a long time ago, and somehow the terror of it—borne more by her father and Baron von Dortmann—had faded through the years.

Now, however, other people's lives—people she loved, people she would die for if it came to that—depended on *her*.

Only her and two others!

One false move, one tiny slipup, one miscue in the signal, and the whole escape plan would be undone and all of those on the other side caught and imprisoned . . . or worse!

She would die for them, but she was terrified that some misstep on her part might cause one of *them* to die.

That she *wasn't* willing to have happen!

She reached the end of the street, paused, and turned left along the adjacent sidewalk.

There was the wall, just ahead. She had walked along here many times, never dreaming she would be involved in anything like this. The day had finally come. For better or worse . . . at least it would all be over.

So would the years of her own personal doubt.

She had been awake half of last night, thinking and praying it all through one final time.

The decision had actually been reached some time before. She couldn't pinpoint it exactly. Probably a few days ago, maybe shortly after the long walk she had taken through the city, followed by Angela's telephone call. A sense had gradually stolen over her that it was time to cease the inner fight, to end the quandary of doubt, that the answer had arrived, and that peace of mind was finally at hand.

"Lord, what is it you are trying to tell me?" she began to pray two

or three nights ago, with even increased urgency now that she felt an answer had been given to her many previous years of prayers.

The only words that came to her in reply were these: *Trust me, my child . . . all is well. Trust me.*

In the middle of last night she had known what the words meant. It was time to lay it all down. The moment had come to put away the past—with all its hopes, and even its commitments—and give them once and for all into the hands of her Master . . . then to look forward.

The decision was no easy one for a nature like Ursula's.

She had sensed the change coming for months. Everything on the other side of the wall that she had held dear, that she had lived for—that season of her life was drawing to a close.

By the day after tomorrow it would all be gone.

Her past life, her heritage, even her identity as an individual, was no longer linked to the Poland of her childhood. She was a German citizen now. Most of the Polish Jews they had known were gone— either killed in the camps or gone to continue the perennial Jewish pilgrimage elsewhere.

As of last year her family was no longer behind the Iron Curtain but now safely residing in Israel.

Her only remaining links to the past were Sabina and the baron. By tomorrow, if all went well, they would be here with her.

There was nothing more for her over there.

It was time to lay down her hope of seeing Joseph again. If he still lived, he surely had forgotten her by now and had remarried. No man could be expected to wait all this time. He would most certainly think her dead. Why would he not marry another?

As soon as Sabina was in her arms, safe in the free West, with the baron beside her, Ursula would take off the ring.

It would be her sign that she had given her future, and whatever marriage plans he might have for her, into the Lord's hands.

She would, as of that moment, consider herself free from the betrothal to which she had remained faithful for so long.

The decision was a painful one. She was sure to shed more

than a few tears. But there could be no mistaking the added words she had sensed the Lord speaking to her over the past few days: *Trust me for everything. I have a future for you—a wonderful future. But to enter into it you must lay down the past . . . and trust me.*

She *would* trust him.

He, the Lord, was her bridegroom. It was time she transferred her betrothal in her mind from Joseph to him.

It would be difficult, but she would remove the ring as soon as her friends were through to safety . . . and freedom.

∽ 95 ∽
West-Side Preparations

Still occupied with her thoughts and the decision she had made, Ursula arrived at the storage shed where she had been scheduled to meet the three men who were making this all possible. The four of them had made all the arrangements, and this was the final dress rehearsal before tomorrow's carrying out of the daring plan.

Tonight they would check everything again, especially that the two guards were out of direct line of sight at 8:20 from the man known to posterity as E. Brecht.

Two of the young men had dug the tunnel over the past month and, only last week, had safely gotten their wives to West Berlin. The plan was feasible. But could it be depended on with a group of eight? What if the *Vopos* had discovered it in the meantime?

So many *what ifs!*

Ursula was the first to arrive. The men would be here shortly. Even in West Berlin they had to take precautions. Too many people moving too suspiciously, even on the free side, could arouse the ever-roving eyes of the tower guards on the other. Angela had desperately wanted to come—Sabina was her friend now too, she said—but her husband had prevented it. She could wait at the car. He had been without her so long, he said, he wouldn't take any chances on anything going wrong that involved her close by.

Ursula and the men would take different routes and come to the rear of the storage shed separately.

Ursula looked around, then took a seat on a crate.

There was certainly nothing to look at here. It was just a shed with a few odds and ends kept in it from the construction site nearby. Its owner had agreed to the plan when he was approached by Kohl and Peters.

Detmold had not only agreed, he had become an intrinsic part of it himself, even committing a few workmen and whatever equipment was necessary to the task. Once Fraus Kohl and Peters were safe, the tunnel was anyone's to use, and now, a week later, it was about to be put into service once more.

Dusk was scheduled again, both for the dim light and for the likelihood of a greater number of bereaved paying respects to their loved ones.

The only thing of interest inside the shed, thought Ursula, was the visible end of a rope that disappeared down a black hole in the ground. Everything depended upon that rope.

She opened the small bag she had brought and pulled out the single flower inside it. She lifted it to her nostrils and took in a long, satisfying breath. Did ever an aroma contain such an enormous mingling of wonderful yet melancholy sensations as that!

She looked at the delicate blossoms, already beginning to fade. She had been lucky to find it, she thought, even at a florist. This was hardly the right season.

But she had found it, and now this fragrant flower would be a symbol, with the removing of her ring, that the past was behind her. When everything was behind them, twenty-four hours from now, she would toss the bloom into the tunnel, in the same way that she would be burying her past. It would serve as a reminder that though her love would live on, she had buried any remaining hopes for them in the tomb of God's heart.

She held it to her nose again and smiled, allowing herself one last pleasant interlude with her memories of long ago.

With her thoughts to keep her company, Ursula passed the next thirty minutes until the first of her associates arrived, carrying a pair of binoculars under his coat. In another twenty minutes, the third and then the final member of their team entered the shed.

When they were next assembled like this it would be for real. All they would have to do then was wait for the mourners to arrive on the other side.

∾ 96 ∾
Inner Wall to Freedom
September 5 — 11:30 P.M.

Joseph ben Eleazar, pilgrim Jew from Russia, had reached the final stage of his inner pilgrimage.

The very day he left the brotherhood of Bialystok, he had been a marked man. Voices from on high, and the prayers of many who loved him, had his soul squarely within their heavenly sights.

He had never been one tolerant of inconsistency. Above all he believed that a man must *live* by the creeds he adopted. How astonishing, then, to have the creeds of his own Jewish belief thrown back at him and the question of his own consistency raised.

Neither Palacki nor anyone else had done it.

His intellect had thrown them back at himself. His own integrity demanded that he look afresh at everything . . . most of all himself.

Across Poland and East Germany, for every day, every hour of these past weeks, he had not been able to dislodge Palacki's forceful words from his brain.

You have been one who claims to value truth, but who has seen truth as a thing external to your own being. You have not turned it upon your own character. You have not asked what sort of man God would have you to be.

He could not argue. Palacki was right. He had never even thought to ask such a question. What did religion have to do with the sort of man he was?

Suddenly it had *everything* to do with it!

Your religion, though meaningful, has been for you a 'religion' rather than a personal experience in growth toward intimacy with God.

More words that pierced his very soul. Again . . . Palacki had hit the mark dead center.

If this is true—and only you can make the determination—then you will never know the ultimate truth nor the full freedom you seek, whether you are successful in your escape to the West or not.

He could have gone on, perhaps for the rest of his life, content with what he called his "system of belief." But once the challenge had been raised he could never forget it, never dismiss it from his considerations.

He had to know.

He had to find, then *live*, the truth.

He realized the night before he was scheduled to enter Berlin that the moment of truth had come. It had almost ceased to matter whether or not the escape to freedom was successful.

This moment of truth concerned the freedom of his soul, not the freedom of his body.

He knew the wall he had to cross was an inner one, a wall higher and thicker and more impenetrable by far than that erected by man through the center of the German capital.

It was the wall between his reason and his passion.

It was the barrier between what the intellect of his mind had conditioned itself to *say* was true, and what the innermost feelings of his heart by now *knew* to be true.

The latter had been crying out for weeks, longing to proclaim their independence from the former. The tears he had wept on many nights—inexplicable, unsought, warm, soothing, yet acrid tears—spoke to him of truths deeper than the shapes he could contrive by which to explain them in his intellect, truths that came wrapped in scents, sunsets, dreams, and memories.

Yet the wall between the two existed, standing between his soul and freedom, awaiting the moment when he took hammer in hand to smash its bricks into powder.

The dual paths toward truth were never so apparent in a man—the intellectual and the intuitive—as in Joseph Aviz-Rabin as he stood gazing upon their convergence at the base of the inner wall between his heart and brain.

How was he was to scale its height? Where was the instrument that could topple it?

How could he fuse the two into one? How could he bring his reason and his emotion into a single entity of being that he could joyfully and happily call *himself*?

He was a tormented man. But it was no longer the torment of living under Communism that hounded him. It was the tormenting struggle within his brain and heart between everything he had always believed, everything he had been taught, everything he had so thoroughly accepted . . . and the startling reality that *perhaps Jesus really was the Messiah!*

That reality made him alive to sunsets and hyacinths, made him look deeper into the eyes of those who served him, made his heart leap at the tiniest pleasures, made him think more often of Ursula with a newer and even deeper longing of love than before.

No mere rabbi could effect the change. Surely it took the Son of God to account for the transformation within him.

The reality of the Christ made him weep . . . and he knew not why.

∾ 97 ∾
Prayer of Capitulation
September 6—1:50 A.M.

The night was black.

It was late, but Joseph could not sleep. He had been lying awake for hours in a safe house in East Berlin . . . thinking. Tomorrow, he had been told several hours ago, he would meet the man engineering the escape attempt he would be joining.

Some inner compulsion told him he must come to terms with his personal battle now . . . tonight.

He could put off the moment of climax no longer.

What if he lost his life tomorrow? Then it would be too late. And if the attempt *were* successful, he wanted to start his new life in the West free in all ways, not merely free of body and still enslaved of soul to the doubt.

Adding to the torment of decision was the inescapable fact that this change—for wherever it led, there could be no longer any doubt that he was a *changed* man!—would utterly reorient whatever possible relationship might exist in the future between him and his betrothed.

What if he did find Ursula?

Her father would scarcely condone a marriage to one who was entertaining such scandalous notions as he now found occupying his thoughts! His own father had been worried about his affiliation with Zionism earlier. *This* would surely make his father turn over in his grave, wherever it was, and cause Rabbi Wissen to put him away with a writ of divorce instantly! At least Zionism had been Jewish. But this . . .

He couldn't even finish the thought.

What of Ursula herself? Even if it were not for her father's inevitable objections, what would *she* think?

Even if she were *not* married, even if by some remote chance she *had* honored the betrothal all these years, and even if by some remoter chance she still loved him, the moment she learned that he was questioning whether Jesus might be the Messiah after all, would *she* not immediately request her father to break the betrothal, whatever stigma might be attached to the action?

Surely she would never marry one such as he!

Where would he place the relative balance—if it came to that—on the scales between a future with Ursula and committing himself to what he felt—no, what he knew!—was the truth?

If it came to a choice, what would be his?

He already knew. What kind of truth seeker would he be, what kind of man would he be, if he was not willing to sacrifice for what he believed? Was that not the mark of courage, the willingness to die for one's convictions . . . for honor, for integrity, for belief?

He had to be willing to lay down even that which he had longed for more than anything—a future with Ursula—for the sake of embracing what he now knew was truth. As dear to him as that had become, as greatly as he hoped it wouldn't come to that and that she would understand, for the first time in his life he realized there was One he had to place above even her.

This was no moment of jubilation. Rather had come a moment of sacrificial acknowledgment.

No motives of gain stirred in his brain, no awareness of what he might *receive* in consequence of this action, no ambition that across the threshold at which he stood lay promise of happiness.

There was only the sense of relinquishment, of giving in, of laying down a hope he had cherished for more than half his young life.

Slowly Joseph slipped from the bed in which he lay, to his knees on the floor. There were the tears again! He had lost nearly all ability to control them.

He had been taught to pray as a child. He knew all the formulas, all the words of rote memory. But lately had been bubbling up from unseen places within him more personal expressions of intimacy with his Maker than he had been taught man had a right to expect or enjoy.

And now on this night, in a hidden corner of Berlin, unseen of any but the Eye that sees all, tearful and reluctant yet without reservation, the utter childlikeness of that intimacy at last broke forth in abandon, holding nothing more back, and Joseph admitted that Jesus was the Christ, saying that—if Father and Son would have him—he would henceforth give his life in service, not just to the former, but to the latter as well.

"God," he whispered, *"I will give all to you. I will lay down my claims on the past, my hopes for the future. If you require it of me I will lay down even my love for Ursula. I want to know the truth, no matter what it is, no matter where it leads me, no matter what it demands of me. Take me, I pray, as I am. Lead me where you want me to go. Do with me what you will. If Jesus is your Son, then teach me to ally myself with him as I have never given thought to before. As I have thought of myself till now as a son of Jacob and Judah, make me now your son, and teach me to call you Father."*

His lips fell silent, though his spirit continued to groan in expression of the inexpressible.

The hammer had been taken up, and the first blows were falling against the wall.

Freedom was nigh.

‿ 98 ‿
Uneasy Sleep
September 6—3:45 A.M.

Joseph's was not the only night troubled with sleeplessness. That which caused the ceaseless disturbance to the bed of Gustav von Schmundt, however, though from the same originating cause, was to lead to a much different result.

A man or woman's conscience can disturb him for either of two very opposite reasons. One who is *seeking* the truth, but has not yet altogether laid hold of it, may find himself restless of mind until he abandons himself to the peace that passeth understanding, and declares his search at an end.

One, on the other hand, who is *running* from the truth will indeed find himself eternally restless of mind until he one day turns and faces his conscience and allows it to do its purifying work, or, never turning, runs and runs . . . until the moment death overtakes him.

Once Joseph had risen from the posture and decision of submission, he slept the rest of the night like a baby. His mind at peace, his body was capable of the most childlike slumber.

Gustav, however, rolled and tossed all the night long and awoke in a foul temper, despite the breakthrough that was at hand. He knew the day would be one of significance, though he could not foresee toward what end.

In truth, it was not really his conscience that had bothered him all the night long, but rather his dreams.

They had been filled with Sabina, and he had hardly been able to get through the night without going mad.

At one moment she seemed altogether changed, smiling at him, even beckoning him to come . . . then the next intruded ugly scenes and shouts and angry voices—he could not tell whose—and when he next looked up, Sabina was gone, gone forever, disappeared where only a moment earlier her face had risen on the horizon in beautiful answer to a lifetime of dreams.

He threw his damp featherbed from his perspiring body, rose, went to the toilet, then doused his face in cold water. He had to get some sleep!

He lay back down on his back, staring straight toward the black ceiling of his apartment.

He knew well enough what had brought on the dreams.

In all likelihood he would see Sabina tomorrow. In the midst of the frustrations of recent days, and the idiotic machinations of his two moronic assistants, the final pieces had nevertheless begun to fit together.

His informant's information seemed correct, that an escape attempt was on. Another informant had learned—though the cur wouldn't tell Gustav how—that someone important, an escaped prisoner he thought, was going to be arriving in the western sector of the city. The fellow had a contact over there, he said, who knew of people who were abuzz over a long-anticipated arrival. He didn't know exactly when or where the escape was to take place, but he hoped to find out. There was an indication it might again be through some connection to the storm drainage system, but that had not yet been confirmed. Another clue said something about a funeral parlor. He had the incompetent Schulte scheduled to check all of the city's funeral homes tomorrow, to make sure there were no caskets bound for the western sector. He was not so stupid as to allow himself to fall for that one!

He had two other informants working around the clock on the street, trying to locate any additional clue that would pinpoint the precise location. All the evidence indicated the attempt would come tomorrow.

Though the dreams had roused up all the same feelings from the past, now that he was fully awake, the thought of seeing Sabina no longer thrilled him in the same way as before.

Another element had entered his considerations, a darker and more sinister factor. For years he had allowed himself to pretend that if he could just see her and explain all he could do for her and her father, everything would fall neatly into place.

But it was a fiction.

At last he knew it.

It had always been a fiction—who had he been trying to fool?

Even if by some wild change of heart—impossible hope!—she should consent to give in, there were still the raw facts of the case. Even though he had been searching for them all this time, at the deepest part of his being he had successfully shut out those facts, conveniently ignored their intensely personal demands upon his ultimate loyalties.

But how could he ignore them now?

The facts were straightforward enough, and as he lay sleeplessly staring into the darkness, never had they seemed quite so stark as they did at this moment: Sabina's father was an escaped prisoner who must be brought to justice. Matthew McCallum was an American spy.

And Sabina herself was an accomplice to both.

All three—*including* Sabina!—were fugitives from the authorities of the DDR, and it was *his* duty to apprehend them. Failing that, should they try to escape, his orders were clear enough. He had passed on those very orders from the highest authority in the land: Escapes are to be prevented, with bullets if necessary.

The orders were: *Shoot to kill.*

He could pretend no longer.

If he did see Sabina tomorrow, he knew very well what the circumstances would be. She would be attempting to escape.

His orders did not now concern impersonal faceless criminals. They did not merely concern the baron and the McCallum fellow. He would have no qualms about stopping either of *them* dead in their tracks.

But his orders also concerned Sabina.

This was the deep reality of his quest he had never allowed himself squarely to face.

Did he love her? What *could* he do for her now? She had made her choice. It was too late to help . . . even her.

What if he found her at last, what if their eyes met . . . and then she turned and made a last madcap dash for the West, in spite of his cries, in spite of all he might do to protect her from recrimination, to save her, to keep her from prison or death?

What if . . . ?

Where would his final loyalties lie if it came to a split-second decision between past fantasies and the need to keep *himself* from being indicted as having aided an escape as he watched her running in full flight away from him?

To hesitate at that moment could well result in a charge of treason—with prison to follow—*against him!*

He remembered the fearful anxiety he had experienced driving to *Lebenshaus* that night so many years ago, knowing they were about to arrest Sabina's father. Then the next morning when they had faced the band of refugees on the lonely country road. . . .

He knew Korsch had looked upon him as a coward ever since, for hesitating when he ordered him to shoot the baron.

Gustav had been a mere boy. Had he really changed in all the years since? He had killed, it was true. But could he, even now, look Sabina's father in the eyes and kill *him*?

Worse, could he look Sabina in the eyes and . . . ?

He twisted over in his bed, shaking his head to rid it of the horrendous thought.

He could not even think it!

Did he have the courage to fulfill his duty as a *Stasi* chief?

He would have to decide.

He was experienced enough to know that indecision was the most costly enemy of all. A moment's hesitation in the heat of battle and all could be lost.

Gustav drew in a deep sigh and let it out.

"Sabina, Sabina," he murmured with sad, lingering dismay, "why did you let it come to this? Why did you not let me help . . . before it was too late for you all?"

He rolled over again and closed his eyes in a desperate attempt to force sleep to come.

It was no use.

Gustav was a man ill at ease with his prospects for the future, and there was no rest to be found for his ailing soul.

∽ 99 ∽
Readying for Flight
September 6—4:50 P.M.

The gathering in the apartment building that fronted the street called Fischer late that Thursday afternoon was solemn. All knew that more than just their futures were at stake.

The events of this night would determine whether there would be any future for them to anticipate at all.

The tiny congregation was not large, though before the night was over, Matthew knew probably better than any of them that a great deal would be demanded of each one. Sabina's father was the eldest of the group, at sixty-eight. Matthew was more concerned, however, about Sabina's former neighbor Gerta Arnim. She was a few years younger but appeared frail. He had already seen her step falter twice just moving about inside the room.

The child was most worrisome of all. A five-year-old would have plenty of stamina. But it was an age when sounds could not always be controlled. Any peep from that innocent mouth at the wrong time, any whine of fatigue or blurted question could spell death to all the rest. The assurances of the lad's mother were vehement concerning his ability to obey unquestioningly and to keep silent as a mouse, but Matthew couldn't help being concerned.

Sabina was a trooper, he thought, watching her bustling about among the nervous refugees, tending to every need, cheering every flagging countenance. He and she had hardly managed three words together all day they had both been so preoccupied with the others.

Matthew glanced down at his watch.

The go-ahead was scheduled for 8:23—three and a half hours from now.

The small group of pilgrims had arrived at different times, entering the building as innocently as they could manage, and, using the elevator or stairway and different corridors, had all eventually knocked on the door of apartment 11-D on the eleventh floor. It had been rented only yesterday by their long-faithful comrade Hermann. He had worn a disguise and given a fake name, and even if any suspicious neighbors reported the strange goings-on, by the time this night was over the apartment would be vacant of any trace and Hermann would never return to pay another installment on the rent.

Getting the props necessary for their upcoming charade into the building had taken some doing. But over the course of the past twenty-four hours, a few concealed deliveries, overstuffed coats, with here and there a large shopping bag, had brought in all they would require.

The first of them would leave two hours and forty-five minutes from now. The baron would go first. Then Gerta ten minutes later. They would arouse the least suspicion. Old people frequenting cemeteries were nothing out of the ordinary. They would each be holding a small bouquet of flowers. Under his arm but concealed beneath his coat, the baron also insisted on carrying his fair share of the load of journals. Matthew would manage the remainder.

Matthew himself would go next.

Sabina had argued strenuously against it from the first.

"You will be the most in danger of us all," she protested. "They are always suspicious of young men. You should remain in the building until the last possible moment."

"If there is any possibility of something going wrong, I want to be out there to spot it," he had replied. "Besides, there have been just as many young women, and old men *and* women, making escape attempts as young men."

"I know that, but the *Vopos* are still bound to look at you more closely."

"But remember, I do one of the best slumped-old-man imitations in all of Germany!"

In the end, he had not exactly convinced her, but since his mind was firm, the plan was set to go as he had said.

Lola Reinhardt, the mother and her young boy, Sabina, and the new arrival Hermann had informed them of when they had seen him yesterday—if he got here at all—would exit the building at 8:00 to become the black-clad funeral procession.

Matthew continued to be anxious about the boy. One chance slipup—a word to one of the others whom he wasn't supposed to know overheard by a loyal Communist sympathizer—and one shout to the *Vopos* would end it all.

Sabina would lead the small party to the grave marked E. Brecht, 1905-1946, at precisely 8:22. He would converge from the other direction and, the moment the signal came, would get the lady and her son through first.

By then the baron and the old lady would have arrived at the site . . .

Matthew sighed, sat down, and tried to doze as the others were doing.

He had run the plan through in his mind a hundred times. Yet his heart continued to pound inside his chest.

He was more than just a *little* nervous—his knees were shaking!

Where was the fellow Hermann said the underground was sending?

There had been no more word all day. If he didn't get here, they would have no recourse but to go on without him. Once the momentum for a plan like this was in motion, there was no turning back without greatly increased danger to everyone involved.

What seemed like the next moment a soft knock sounded on the door.

Matthew glanced at his watch. An hour had passed—he must have dozed off.

He was on his feet and to the door in an instant.

∽ 100 ∾
Clues Leading West
September 6—5:00 P.M.

It was uncanny how the years could evaporate when you suddenly found yourself traveling the byways from some long-past era.

So it was as Emil Korsch, a.k.a. Vaslav Korskayev, worked his way methodically across Poland, the faint whiffs from a bygone trail of deception guiding his diabolically clever steps.

Jews had always left the odor of their presence upon whatever they touched, and Korsch would know it anywhere. Now the Christian smell was becoming more and more recognizable to him as well. There were different subtleties involved, different modes of expression, different hints to watch for, different looks in the eyes. But he was learning rapidly to know their kind.

Most maddening of all was their absolutely ridiculous notion of treating their enemies graciously, even praying for them. Whenever he sensed an extra measure of kindness being spent upon him, he knew he was in the presence of some moronic Christian.

It made him hate them all the more!

When his requests were greeted with impassioned annoyance and disdain, he knew the people were likely telling the truth. But the mask of goodwill and cordiality made him suspicious immediately.

But they would pay for their idiotic kindness!

It only made his job the easier. Thinking to mask their deceptions with the charade of geniality, the fools only gave themselves away!

It was admittedly a complex and cleverly conceived matrix of concealment they had woven throughout Eastern Europe. But by isolating its threads one at a time, and giving here and there an appropriate tug, bringing just the right pressure to bear . . . watching, waiting, listening . . . in time the connections and linkages began to reveal themselves.

The years had taught him how to use the power of the KGB with skill and precision. Fear was a potent device for extracting information, and whatever smiles to the contrary they plastered on their simpleminded faces, deep down the Christians were just as afraid as everyone else. Perhaps more, because they had something to hide.

A chance word from a child or a frightened wife, a hastily delivered message to a neighbor after they thought he was gone, bribes to greedy informants (for even the Christian circles had their gossips and deviants who would betray their compatriots for a price), greetings between individuals and groups sent in code—all these and a dozen more ploys he had put to insidiously crafty use since leaving Bialystok, with the result that, as his Mercedes now sped toward Berlin to meet with Schmundt, he was confident they were at last about to lay their hands on the Jew Tsankov, who had stolen the photos, *and*—if Schmundt did not lose them in the next twenty-four hours—the German baron who would lead them to the rabbi!

The young pastor he had imprisoned at Bialystok had been utterly recalcitrant. Not a speck of information had he divulged in spite of repeated beatings, nor did he implicate any of those whom Korsch had learned to be his closest associates.

But others of his so-called congregation had been persuaded to talk, for the sake, they thought, of getting the rabble-rouser Palacki released.

Ha, what fools! They had talked, and still their idiotic young leader sat in prison! How long he would keep him there, Korsch hadn't yet decided.

The information he had obtained at Bialystok had pointed toward Warsaw. There he had found himself crisscrossing leads and names from nearly twenty years before when he had been tracking the rabbi.

He had flown hastily back from Warsaw to Moscow, retrieved whatever files the KGB had on Polish Jewish and Christian underground activity, spoken again with Bolotnikov, brought himself up to date on the few findings his nephew had uncovered having to do with the Rostovchev fellow, and then had returned to Poland. Armed with the available information and calling upon his own memory of places and events from before, he gradually began to pick up the trail of Tsankov since leaving Bialystok.

He had come to Warsaw, that had been certain, then Lodz, and to Legnica, where Korsch had almost caught him.

But always he seemed just a few days too late.

When the trail grew warm again, it had crossed into the DDR. A border guard remembered him at Görlitz.

The fool had not even bothered to change his name. He was still traveling as Tsankov! He did, however, have a valid DDR passport, the guard assured him, which indicated that somewhere prior to that time he had had sufficient assistance to have arranged new identity papers.

"Where was his destination?" asked Korsch.

"Dresden, *mein Herr*," replied the guard.

"Was he traveling alone?"

"*Ja.*"

"Auto?"

"Trabi."

"Color?"

"Red."

"License?"

The guard consulted his records and gave the number to Korsch.

Korsch wrote it down and stuffed the paper inside his pocket. He doubted it would accomplish much, but he would alert the *Vopos* and *Stasi* to trace the car in any case.

In Dresden the trail had grown confusing.

It was there suddenly the past had come back to haunt him. Without warning the words *Rheinsdorf* and *Fürstenburg* had surfaced again. They were the very clues that had sent him off on his wild-goose chase to Switzerland twenty years ago! And now here he was in a direct line between Poznan and München.

Could the same Swiss escape network, he wondered, still be in place after all this time? He knew of escapes through Czechoslovakia, ending in both Wien and München.

Was it possible this was Tsankov's route?

If the rabbi's holy box had made it to Switzerland earlier, and Tsankov was connected to that plot as well as the smuggling of the photos, it would all fit.

Yet a nagging uncertainty still hounded him, the uncomfortable memory that the southern ploy had failed him on the earlier hunt.

Something told him, despite appearances, that Berlin was the destination, not Switzerland.

He had been too long in Dresden, Korsch chastised himself. They would not make him run around chasing his own tail this time! It was time to act.

He called Schmundt.

Were there any new developments?

Yes. He had gotten wind two days ago of an escape attempt that was being planned by the Christian underground. Gustav failed to mention the botched Kehrigkburg affair.

Where? asked Korsch.

Right in Berlin.

Involving the escaped prisoner they were seeking?

Schmundt was certain of it. Contacts in West Berlin had confirmed today as the day. He had not been able to unearth the precise location yet, but he had three informants working on it and expected a breakthrough any moment. Likely a funeral procession of empty caskets, though perhaps an underground storm drain. He was literally standing by his phone, ready to move.

That had to be it! Tsankov was making for Berlin and was part of the same plot! Empty caskets! Ingenious! Too bad they would interrupt the rite before they could be driven through the checkpoint!

How soon could Korsch be there, Schmundt asked. He might need help in order to entrap the entire network.

Korsch looked at his watch. It was five o'clock now. He would be in Berlin by eight.

By then he should know the site of the attempt, said Schmundt. It could come momentarily. He suspected some-time tonight.

He would be there without delay, said Korsch.

Good, replied Schmundt. They would be there together and arrest them all.

Korsch hung up the phone with an exuberant thrill of lusty triumph such as he had rarely experienced.

After twenty years, he was about to obtain his long-awaited revenge on Baron von Dortmann!

Without even bothering to check out of his hotel, he ran to his car, sent the engine roaring to life, sped out of Dresden, thrust his foot to the accelerator, and flew northward toward the German capital.

∽ 101 ∽
Unknown Acquaintance
September 6—6:00 P.M.

The man whom Joseph had just left had given him his final instructions with the words "You will need a code to be admit-ted. At this stage of an escape attempt, more precautions need to be taken than in all your journey till now. Your German is not the best, but it will have to do. Now listen carefully."

He had then proceeded to go over the memorized phrases with him several times, which, as he now walked toward the tall building in the next block, he repeated over and over to himself.

But he was distracted and could hardly keep his mind on it.

He wanted to talk to somebody, but the fellow called Hermann seemed too gruff for the kind of question he had to ask. The code phrases he had taught him, however, filled him with hope that the people he was about to meet might be willing to listen and help him. He had heard things about those connected with *The Rose*, and with his whole heart Joseph now hoped the rumors he'd heard were true.

∼✸∽

One look at the fellow standing in the hall and Matthew knew he had more on his mind than the impending escape. His first thought was that it couldn't be the man he'd been waiting for at all, and that he'd knocked on 11-D by mistake.

The first words out of the man's mouth, however, set that worry to rest instantly.

"Haben Sie vielleicht Rosen?" came from his mouth in halting German.

Matthew's response was immediate. *"Nein, das is nicht die Jahrezeit für Blüten."*

"But for those . . . those who love . . . even the leaves smell . . . are fragrant with perfume," added the man.

"Good, come in," said Matthew.

"I'm Tsankov," said the new arrival.

Matthew nodded, pulled him quickly inside, and closed the door. Everyone was assembled at last!

"All right, sit down everyone," said Matthew after he had made the brief needful introductions. "As you can see, Mr. Tsankov, the floor is the best we have. Now that all eight of us are here, I want to go over every detail of the plan once again. Mr. Tsankov," he said, turning toward Joseph, "we will have to converse in German—you are, as I understand it, Russian?"

"Polish," corrected Joseph.

"Ah . . . well," said Matthew, "your German sounds good enough to enable us to communicate readily. But if there is anything you do not understand, speak up."

Joseph nodded, and Matthew went on with his explanations.

It was all Joseph could do to keep his mind on the urgencies
at hand. Ever since last night he had known something more
was necessary—something he needed to do but didn't know
what. If he didn't talk to these people, here and now, he would
probably never see them again, and who could tell when he
would meet others who would . . .

But how could he talk about such deep matters to people he
didn't even know? Yet they must be Christians if they were connected to *The Rose*.

An inner voice told him this was something that had to be
done now, during this last hour before the attempt. He didn't
know why, but it couldn't wait. An inner urging compelled him
to ask these people what he ought to do.

The old man had been looking strangely at him, smiling
oddly whenever he would return his gaze. It was an expression
he recognized.

It reminded him of the brotherhood at Bialystok.

At last Matthew concluded with his instructions.

"Any final questions?" he said.

No one spoke.

"All right, then," he added, glancing at his watch, "we have
about an hour and ten minutes before the first departure. Let's
all rest and use this last hour in prayer."

He moved toward Sabina at one corner of the room and sat
down beside her.

Almost immediately he saw the new man rise from the
opposite wall and approach them.

"Do . . . do you mind if I talk to you?" he said, kneeling
down.

"Of course not, Mr. Tsankov—what is on your mind?" said
Matthew.

"In, uh . . . private. Is there another room?"

"I think so . . . sure," replied Matthew, glancing at Sabina
with a look of question. "Did you want to talk to me . . .
alone?" he added.

"She is welcome too," replied Joseph, "if she knows about
roses."

Matthew smiled. "She is intimately acquainted with them. As, too, is one other of our number."

"Good," said Joseph. "I . . . I have a question about a spiritual matter. I was given to understand that the people who knew about roses were . . . that perhaps they could help."

"We will be only too happy to if we are able," said Matthew, rising, then helping Sabina to her feet.

Matthew led Joseph into a small adjoining room in the apartment while Sabina went to her father and knelt down and whispered a few words in his ear.

He too now rose, and in two minutes the four were seated on the floor together in a small circle. Matthew, Sabina, and Baron von Dortmann waited expectantly for the revelation of their new arrival's unusual request.

∾ 102 ∾
Final Peace

Joseph made but scanty introduction to his request.

He told them he was a Jew who had of late, with the help of Christians whose paths he had crossed, found himself examining for the first time the potential reality and veracity of the Christian faith.

His journey—both physical and spiritual—it would seem had culminated simultaneously on this day and at this very spot. Without going into the details, which would be too numerous to recount in the short time they had together, he found himself, he said, at the point of desiring to confess his allegiance to what he now considered the truth—that is, Christianity.

He assumed they were Christians because he had heard of the spiritual inclinations of persons connected with *The Rose*. That was why he had been so bold as to request to speak about such a personal matter to them.

In short, he wanted to become a Christian, but—he was sorry to be so ignorant in such a matter involving his sister religion— was uncertain what was to be done. Was there some ritual to perform, some rite, some prayer? He knew about baptism, he said, but obviously he could not be baptized here and now. Beyond that, whatever was to be done, he wanted to do it before the escape attempt. He could not explain why, nor what was the urgency, for in all honesty he did not know himself. But he felt he had been led to them, and it seemed he must ask for their help.

"In short, I want to bring fulfillment to the faith of my fathers. I want to become a complete Jew, an acknowledged believer in the Messiah that God sent."

Before he was halfway through with his speech, which was difficult in other than his mother tongue, Joseph noticed that the elder of the two men had closed his eyes and bore a look strangely akin to that of Andre Palacki while he had been speaking to his son.

On Baron von Dortmann's part, what joy it would have brought his heart to know that it was in no small measure his *own* faithful prayers for another through the years that had drawn this very young man to the throne of grace. The baron's prayers for Rabbi Wissen had continued to ascend, and before him now sat—though neither knew it—the divinely appointed messenger to carry the glad tidings of gospel joy to the rabbi himself.

"We would be happy to help," said Matthew.

"What then shall I do?" inquired Joseph with the innocence of the child that he had become.

"If you are in search of, as you say, some ritual, some rite, some prayer that will turn you into a Christian, so to speak," said Matthew, "there is none. Christianity is probably the most ritual-free religion in the world."

"Is there nothing to be *done*, then?" asked Joseph, somewhat bewildered.

Matthew smiled. "I did not say that. There is *everything* to be done."

"I am afraid I do not follow you."

"The following of some ritual or the performing of some rite would make it easier than God intends," said Matthew. "It would make it too simple a matter to perform the Christian ritual without truly *being* a Christian. That is why there is none. To be a Christian, you simply have to . . . *be* a Christian. Do you know what a Christian is, Mr. Tsankov?"

"One who believes that Christianity is true," he answered, though with the inflection of uncertainty in his tone. "In my case, a great deal of that would depend upon an acknowledgment that Jesus is the Messiah, the Christ."

"It is, of course, helpful, perhaps even necessary, to believe those things," rejoined Matthew. "But believing them will not make one a Christian."

"What *is* a Christian then?"

"The word means nothing more nor less than one who is a *follower of Christ.* The very first Christians were Peter and Andrew, James and John, to whom Jesus uttered the very simple command: *Follow me.* They performed no rite, they merely got up and followed."

"What then is the *everything* you speak of?"

"Following Jesus is not so much a system of belief as it is a way of life. To be his follower means to live by his example— think as he taught his followers to think, behave as he taught his followers to behave, speak as he told his followers to speak. In other words, Christianity is a very *unreligious* sort of religion, if you understand me. It is all about *living,* not about believing a list of precepts or carrying out religious rituals. It is about becoming people of a certain kind, the kind of people Jesus expects his followers to be."

"That is very different from what we learn our Judaism to be."

"It is very different from what many Christians are taught as well," said Matthew. "Nevertheless, such is the essence of the Christian faith—following Christ in *all* ways, in *every* thing."

There was a pause.

"I think I understand," replied Joseph. "To tell you the truth, you speak very much like the other Christians I mentioned. It is this very idea that has been at the center of my thoughts, and my prayers, for some time. I want exactly what you say. I have reached the decision that I do not merely want to say I believe Christianity is true . . . I do indeed desire to become his follower."

"I could not be more delighted!" exclaimed Matthew.

"We are pleased that you have asked us to be with you at such

a special moment," added Sabina, speaking now for the first
time.

"I echo my daughter's words," added the baron, opening his
eyes and smiling broadly. "You do us a great honor, Mr.
Tsankov."

Joseph now laughed lightly. "I have been so preoccupied
with all this, I completely forgot—Tsankov is not my real name.
I don't suppose at a time like this there is any need for the charade any longer. You may call me Joseph, the name my father
gave me."

"It is a name worthy to be worn by a Jew *or* a Christian!" said
the baron.

"But now, please," Joseph went on with persistence, "we do
not have a great deal of time. You have explained what it means
to *be* a Christian. But how does one *become* a Christian?"

Matthew glanced over at the baron, ready and willing to defer
to the wisdom of his years.

"You are doing as well as I could, Son," said the baron, in a
soft voice that sounded ready to give way. "Go right ahead." In
truth, the old man's heart was so full at hearing Matthew so lovingly and delicately leading their new friend into the Lord's
presence that he could not have spoken more than a few words
without breaking out in spontaneous prayers of praise.

"All right, Joseph," said Matthew, "here is what I would say.
You become a follower of the Lord by doing what Peter,
Andrew, James, and John did—getting up, leaving your nets, so
to speak, in other words your former way of life, and falling in
behind the Lord as he walks . . . following him wherever he
goes. After that, it is a matter, like the disciples had to do, of
learning to live according to his teaching and example."

"That's all there is to it, just . . . *following* him?"

"That's what a Christian is."

"Hmm," replied Joseph. "Perhaps I was trying to make it
more complicated in my mind than it really was."

"It is helpful to verbally acknowledge your decision to follow
him. It helps set you on the road. You have done exactly that by
telling us of your decision. And it is helpful to pray to your heavenly Father also, telling him of your decision and asking for his
help as you now try to live as a follower of his Son."

"I have been praying rather regularly through all this," confessed Joseph.

"I thought probably you had."

"I would like to pray again, with the three of you, if you do not mind. I want to cement in an official way that on this day I have chosen to give the allegiance of my heart and mind, the actions of my hands, and the steps of my feet to Jesus, the Christ . . . Israel's Messiah."

"We would be honored," said Matthew solemnly.

All three bowed their heads and began praying silently. Baron von Dortmann was the first to speak.

"O loving Father in heaven," he prayed with soft earnestness, *"we are so grateful to you for sending Joseph, our brother, here that we might participate with him in this moment of liberation in his life. God, bless him, and make his life fruitful for you and full of the joy of knowing intimacy with your Son as he learns to walk with him day by day."*

It was quiet a few moments.

"God," prayed Joseph in his native tongue, *"I tell you here and now, in front of these friends and brothers and sister, that I am today becoming a follower of Jesus, whom I now accept as my Messiah. I ask for your help because, as I have prayed all my life long, I want to serve you with all my heart, with all my soul, with all my mind, and with all my strength. Help me to be a complete and fulfilled Jewish son of Abraham. Show me what I am to do. Show me how to live as a Christian. Show me where to go as I follow Messiah Jesus' steps. Help me to learn, as my new Christian friends all seem to do, and as I know Jesus taught, to call you my own Father."*

When he stopped, the baron, who was the only other one to have understood the words of the Polish prayer, glanced up, his wizened old cheeks glistening with tears.

"Bring our new brother into a deep walk of intimacy with you, Lord," prayed Matthew. *"Reveal yourself to him. Fill his heart with your love."*

"Protect him, Father," said Sabina softly. *"Watch over him in every way. Guide the steps of his future according to your perfect will."*

"And now," prayed Joseph, again in Polish, and so softly that neither the baron nor either of the other two heard his words, nor recognized the name he spoke, *"I offer to you my first request*

as a Christian. I pray, Lord God, that in some way only you can possibly know, that you would lead me to Ursula, and that you would give me words to be able to tell her what I have done . . . so that she will understand."

The small room fell silent again.

There would be many more prayers, but for now it was enough.

The time was nearly at hand for them to raise up the staff of the Lord's deliverance against the dividing Red Sea that stretched through the great German capital and entrust their passage to freedom under it into his hands.

Yet a few moments more they remained, with eyes closed, each exulting in his own way in the thunderous silent roar of the toppling of bricks and mortar and clay.

The inner wall had become dust. The final peace of created childship had replaced it.

Freedom had come to the soul of Joseph, son of Eleazar, of the house called Aviz-Rabin.

❦ 103 ❦
Waiting
September 6—6:30 P.M.

The day had brought no resolution to his quandary of soul between present professional duty and past personal passions.

Gustav had gone to his office, expecting the triumphant culmination of years of investigation, as a man rather on his way to the gallows. Some intuitive sense told him this day of destiny would bring him no joy. The victory he had so long sought had already grown empty. For Gustav von Schmundt on this day, there would be no peace.

Even had he wanted to, however, the momentum of events was already beyond his control. He could not have stopped them had he tried.

On top of the fatigue from the night and the frustration brought on by its cause, Gustav's annoyance was heightened by finding that his worrisomely rebellious secretary had still made no appearance at the office. He had not seen her since arriving back from Niedersdorf. Neither could she be reached at home. It was not like her. Lola Reinhardt had not missed more than three or four days' work in ten years.

This was going to be inconvenient. There was a great deal going on today. He needed her to answer the phone, relay messages, and who could tell what else. This was no time for her to disappear.

He tried her apartment yet again. No answer. Could something have happened to her? He asked a few others on the floor. Nobody had heard a thing. She'd said nothing several days ago about being gone.

Gustav took the news with irritation. He had neither Reinhardt nor Galanov to assist him! Only the idiot Schulte!

He walked with agitation about his office.

He went out at 10:30 to meet a contact. Yes, as far as he knew it was still on for today, probably tonight. He was going to see someone who knew of two women who'd disappeared last week. Rumor was the same route was going to be used.

The fellow would call Schmundt at his office when he found out.

Gustav checked out two or three leads of his own. Nothing new.

Another meeting with one of his informants. No, all the storm drains had been sealed off. That couldn't be the route.

He went back to his office. Two messages. One from Schulte. There was a delivery of a corpse scheduled to be sent by hearse to West Berlin, but there was only one casket. He was on his way to investigate nonetheless. Gustav returned the other call. Nothing helpful.

Late in the afternoon he fell into an uneasy sleep.

Suddenly he jolted awake in his chair. The phone was ringing. It was Korsch. Yes, he expected the final piece of the puzzle any moment . . . how soon could Korsch get here.

"Good," said Gustav. "Yes, I am certain that before the night is out we will be able to drop a net and arrest them all."

Gustav hung up and looked at his watch.

Five o'clock.

He'd better hear something soon.

If Korsch got here from Dresden before he knew anything, he would have to suffer one of the man's screaming tirades again, and he didn't think he had the stomach for it.

Sometimes that man drove him to the brink of insanity.

Gustav picked up the phone and made two or three calls. When they were over he sat back in his chair, thinking. He had to remain here. He had to be by the phone from here on out. He would order something to eat and have it delivered.

He picked up the phone again, placed his order, then again sat back . . . to wait.

The food came. Gustav ate in lonely silence.

∽ 104 ∽

Escape — Not over a Wall, But up a Stair

September 6—7:15 P.M.

"It is nearly time for us to go," said Matthew, addressing the assembled group in apartment 11-D of the eleventh floor of the building across the street from the Fischerstrasse cemetery. "Before we begin to set out, we need to commit our way unto the Lord, who alone will protect us. We have each come by many different pathways to arrive at this point here this evening. Only God knows those pathways, and only he can guide these few steps we will take together once we leave this place."

He paused and glanced toward Sabina's father.

"Baron von Dortmann," he said, "as the elder member of our expedition, and our *elder* also in the spiritual sense, would you please pray on our behalf and commit our way unto the Lord?"

"It would be an honor," replied the baron softly. "First I would like to share a brief poem," he went on. "It was written by the old Scotsman of whom I am so fond. I had so little to read during my years in prison that I occupied myself in trying to recall some of his writings from memory. When I did, I jotted them down.

"They say the human mind never forgets anything that goes into it. I do not know if that is true, but I did find it remarkable over the years how much I managed to remember, sometimes only adding one word at a time. There were occasions when, perhaps after not thinking of a certain passage for over a year, a line or a phrase would pop to the surface of my brain, and I would quickly grab up whatever writing instrument I had and make note of it.

"So this poem was particularly meaningful to me, and I have been fiddling with it during the last month, in anticipation of this day, adapting it as the old poet might have written it were he here among us.

"I give it to you now as a reminder that the freedom we all seek is not a freedom we will achieve by climbing over a wall made by the hands of men. It is a higher destiny we seek, where freedom is gained by climbing a stair to the heavenly places where our Father dwells.

"Here is my adaptation of the old poem."

> *"Traveler, what lies over the wall?*
> *Tip-toe high, tell to me:*
> *Peer across, and back to me call,*
> *Because over it I cannot see."*
>
> *"My child, a valley green lies there,*
> *Lovely with trees, and shy;*
> *And a tiny brook that says, 'Take care,*
> *Or I'll drown you by and by!'"*
>
> *"And what comes next?"—"A little town,*
> *Then a towering hill again;*
> *More hills and valleys up and down,*
> *And a snow-capped peak now and then."*
>
> *"And what comes next?"—"Blue sea, a moaning tide,*
> *Forests, meadows, flowers all round;*
> *Then more streams, lakes, rivers deep and wide.*
> *It is a wonderful land—freedom abounds!"*
>
> *"How do I get there, over the wall?*
> *It seems such a pleasant place to be.*
> *Come, let's climb over, though we mustn't fall;*
> *I want to be free!"*

"No, no, I have not told you the best,
I have not told you the end;
If you want to escape, away in the west,
You will see a stair ascend,

"Built of all colors of lovely stones,
A stair up into the sky
Where no one is weary, and no one moans,
Or wishes to be laid by."

"Is it far away?"—"I do not know;
You must fix your eyes thereon,
And travel, travel through thunder and snow,
Till the weary way is gone.

"All day, though you never see it shine,
You must travel, not turn aside,
All night you must keep straight as a line
Through moonbeams or darkness wide.

"There freedom lives—truly it is so!
Let us journey, not over but up, with open eyes.
He who to the old sunset would go,
Starts best with the young sunrise."

"Is the stair right up? Is it very steep?"
"Too steep for us to climb.
To gain freedom, you must lie at the foot of the heap,
And, patient, wait your time."

"How long?"—"That I cannot tell.
In wind and rain, in cell or frost,
It may be so; thus it is well
That you should count the cost.

"Pilgrims from near and from distant lands
Will step on you lying there;
But a wayfaring Jew with wounded hands
Will carry you up the stair."

The small room fell silent.
The moment had come. It was time for each of them to seek
the stairway to his own freedom.

The baron's voice rose once more, casting a spell of quiet calm over each heart.

"*Our Father,*" he prayed, "*we humbly and confidently place ourselves into your care. We ask, in the name of Jesus your Son, for your protection, that your angels would go before and behind us, that you would guide our every step according to your promise. We ask you to blind the eyes of those who would do your children harm. And we ask that you would bring us, each and every one, into the freedom that only comes as we enter your presence, and give ourselves in joyful abandonment to you. Thank you, our Father, that you love us, and in all things bring goodness into our lives. Amen.*"

Quiet *Amens* sounded throughout the room.

∽ 105 ∾
The Final Piece
September 6—7:45 P.M.

At 7:43 Gustav's phone rang again. After a moment or two his eyes widened as he listened intently.

"No . . . it can't be!" he said in quiet astonishment. "But . . . there is no checkpoint . . . the processional . . . how will the caskets . . . ?"

At last he stopped interrupting the caller, then continued to listen, absorbing every word with an amazed interest, unconsciously picking up a pencil and scribbling down the single message of the call on the pad beside the phone. It was the final piece of the puzzle he had been waiting for—the location!

The call lasted but another few seconds. He was already rising as he hung up the receiver.

He glanced hurriedly at his watch.

It seemed Korsch was too late. But he couldn't wait for him.

It was too bad, thought Gustav with a wry grin. This was one major arrest the KGB was about to miss out on!

He checked his gun to make sure it had a full cartridge, shuddering unintentionally as he did so.

He could not stop to think what he was about to do.

This was no time to think at all.

He had given himself to the Communist system, and now he had to prove it.

That must be his decision in the end. There really had never been any alternative.

Gustav hastened out of the building and ran to his car.

∼ 106 ∼

The Mourners

September 6—7:45 to 8:00 P.M.

The sun had been set for some time, though dusk, even at half past seven this September evening, had prolonged visibility well to this hour.

A full moon had begun its nightly climb, behind scattered clouds, into the sky, already hinting at the soft, pale-grey glow it would send abroad over the land to replace the ebbing reds and violets of the fading sunset to the west.

Cemetery plots had always been taken more seriously by Germans than by many peoples. The postwar generation of survivors, on both sides of the wall dividing them, had more dead loved ones to hold in its memory with flowers, shrubs, and tidy tombstones than any generation ought to have to thus remember.

In this they were all Germans together, and no cold war between East-West superpowers could make it otherwise: Those who had spent their lives and were now gone—be the passing a natural and peaceful one or a result of the terrible conflagration their own past leaders had brought down upon them—must not be forgotten, and their resting places must be honored.

The quiet hours after sunset were traditionally those chosen for widows, sisters, fathers, and an occasional child accompanying his mother, to visit the graves of those who had shared life with them. The subdued mood of dusk seemed to suit the quiet atmosphere that everyone knew the dead preferred.

On this particular evening, the Fischerstrasse *Friedhof* seemed even rather more busy than normal.

Several small clusters of individuals of all ages were engaged throughout it, weeding, sweeping, plucking off dead blossoms, planting new ones.

A mother, draped in black, held the hand of a young boy, following a man in a black top hat and two other black-clad and veiled women in an apparently grieving funeral procession. The four adults carried wreaths, the three women clutched at handkerchiefs that made regular passes between their eyes and noses, clearly struggling with tears brought on by the solemn occasion.

The quiet display of grief went on with seeming oblivion to the watching East Berlin policemen who paced back and forth at the western border of the cemetery, which, by an accident of postwar diplomacy, had been rudely cut through by the border between Soviet and Allied sectors, and, a year earlier, had seen a wall go up across it. In one of the strangest and surely most bizarre twists of fate this city had seen, a man's body had been separated from his wife's by the ugly grey barrier. Stories had immediately begun circulating about the unrest this occurrence occasioned the ghosts of the two departed Berliners, who were said to haunt the wall, offering their assistance to any and all who braved to cross it, until the wise government of the DDR dug up the woman's body and graciously allowed her to be buried with her husband on the West Berlin side—a free woman at last. Their courtesy, however, did not extend to the departed couple's grandchildren, who were never again allowed to pay graveside respects to their ancestors.

None of this, however, was presently on the mind of the three *Vopo* guards patrolling the area as they did every evening, all night long, and throughout the next day, twenty-four hours a day, seven days a week. Neither was it on the mind of the small procession that was apparently mourning some fortunate individual laid to rest farther inside the DDR boundary in a less controversial and troublesome location, though not far from the cemetery's west wall, which was, in fact *der Mauer* of Berlin.

Twenty or thirty meters away, an old man stood, head bowed, reflecting with obvious emotion upon the passing of a dearly beloved wife. Whether he was actually reading the headstone could not be determined from a distance, though the tears of memory were real enough.

Other parts of the cemetery had gradually filled too. An elderly lady stood alone, white haired and bent with years.

A stooped man strode by, pausing now and then at one of the markers, but always continuing on, effecting a gradual circle and then returning. He was a curious mourner, and though his face was concealed by a hat, it was clearly an observant countenance. He appeared elderly, though a close examination of the face would have revealed that he was in truth much further from the age of most of the permanent residents of this place than his attire and walk signified. He also appeared to be carrying something under his coat.

Though he concealed it well enough not to be noticed by the *Vopo* guards, the man glanced about regularly at all his fellow mourners, as if taking mental note of everyone who had come that evening to the Fischer Street cemetery.

∽ 107 ∽
Chase by Air
September 6—8:19 P.M.

Emil Korsch had been in Berlin less than an hour before he realized he may have already been too late.

Cursing and blaring his horn every kilometer of the way, he got through the traffic of the city and to the *Stasi* headquarters at 8:09.

Screeching up in front of the building, he left the Mercedes in the street and ran into the building, flashing his KGB credentials at the guard and without even pausing ran up the two flights of stairs to the chief's office.

His identification again gave him instant access to the guard in charge of the floor. Korsch demanded that he open the section chief's office.

With keys jingling from his trembling hand, the guard complied.

Korsch burst through the door.

Schmundt was gone. His *Stasi* office was quiet as a tomb.

Korsch stormed throughout the room, glancing feverishly

about. He ran back out, shouting a brief interrogation to the guard. No, he had not seen Section Chief Schmundt.

Hastily Korsch returned to the office, trying to remember everything Schmundt had told him.

He expected the attempt to be tonight . . . he was expecting to learn the location any moment . . . he was literally standing by the phone ready to move . . .

Standing by his phone! The words exploded like a grenade in Korsch's ears.

He ran to Schmundt's desk. There was a pad next to the phone. He grabbed it and tore off the top sheet.

It contained only a single word: *cemetery.*

It only took a second or two for Korsch to think through the implications.

Glancing hurriedly around again, his eyes fell on the large street map of Berlin on the opposite wall. He bounded to it and was scanning it with intensity but a second later.

The index finger of his right hand located the wall, then began tracing its serpentine route through the center of the city, as his lips murmured to themselves:

Friedhof . . . friedhof, hmm . . . what cemetery might make a likely place for—

"Aha!" he exclaimed.

There it was! There could be no mistake. Exactly against the border, even partially bisected by it . . . out several kilometers from the city center.

That was where the attempt was taking place!

Within four minutes he had commandeered the helicopter usually reserved for the section chief and was speeding away from the top of the building in the gathering dusk, shouting out orders to the German pilot.

∞ 108 ∞
The Signal
September 6—8:22 P.M.

From the vantage point where he had positioned himself, lying prone, on top of the storage shed, Angela's husband possessed a clear line of sight to the patrol of *Vopos* nearest the cemetery. He had been watching them for five nights now. He had their routine and the movements of their steps memorized.

Sometime within two or three minutes of 8:20, the tomb of a certain E. Brecht should be utterly out of their line of vision.

He glanced at his watch.

It was 8:19, and the two night guards had made their turn exactly as they always did.

8:20 . . . now 8:21 . . . they were just about far enough . . .

He squinted to make absolutely certain they were beyond the marker he used as a reference point at the far end of the cemetery.

Now!

Ursula Wissen and Friedrich Detmold heard the faint but urgent tapping on the roof above them. Ursula's heart was pounding, and she was sweating in mounting fear. It was the sound she had been expecting.

The moment had arrived!

She had been waiting with both hands poised. As Detmold stood by, Ursula now gave a great tug at the rope that descended into the blackness of the hole down through the earthen floor. Then a second tug to make sure the leg of Kohl, their fourth companion, felt the signal clearly.

There could be no delay!

The eight funeral mourners, who had by some coincidence congregated in front of E. Brecht's resting place to lay their wreaths, now beheld an eerie sight. The engraved stone upon the ground suddenly disappeared. Silently a human hand reached up from the grave, and a finger urgently beckoned the mourners to come.

The curious, observant cemetery wanderer had by this time joined the five clad in black, as had the lone elderly man and the white-haired lady. The pretended stoop of the young man had vanished, and he displayed a sudden energy as he knelt beside the strangely open vault into the earth below.

"Come . . . step down—quickly!" whispered Matthew, helping the little boy down first, then his mother. In the blackness of the earth, their hidden West Berlin accomplice already had the child in his arms and was exhorting him with great vigor to follow him, crawling through the tunnel as quickly as he could.

"Mama . . . ?" questioned the youngster.

"*Shh* . . . yes, dear. Go with the man! I am right behind you."

Baron von Dortmann and Matthew were already assisting Gerta down, and on all fours she now struggled slowly on behind the others.

"Sabina," said Matthew urgently, even as he let go of the old lady's hand.

"I will *not* go until the others are safe," she replied with as definite a whisper as it is possible to imagine.

"Papa!" implored Sabina in the next breath. *"You must go!"*

Every instinct in the poor old man's being resisted. The most natural office in the world, that for which every atom of his being lived, was that of servant. He would go last. It was only right, fitting, and proper. There was no other position with respect to his fellows he desired to occupy than to be last of all and servant of all. How could he put his own safety ahead of anyone's?

These thoughts passed through his brain in the scarcest of a second. He looked into Sabina's eyes, the eyes of the daughter he loved, with an imploring look, as if she had just asked him to do the impossible.

Only an instant he hesitated.

Then from some deep reservoir within him, he apprehended that the moment had come for him to pass on the privilege of sacrifice to his daughter and her own young man. They were children no longer, but a man and woman of stature in the Lord's service. It was their right to command him, and he would obey.

With only the hint of a tear in his eye, he turned and stooped, following Gerta's white hair down into the long black cylinder of life.

Next Matthew reached out his hand to help Fräulein Reinhardt, who was already kneeling down on the heels of the baron.

∾ 109 ∾
Convergence at the Place of Death
September 6—8:23 P.M.

He could not have known, as he drove up Fischerstrasse, slammed on his brakes, and leapt from his car, that the figure he saw in the distance was the very one he had been searching for in vain for more than fifteen years.

Neither could Gustav von Schmundt know that the cemetery had mysteriously lost several of its mourners, though none had exited the gate toward which he now ran shouting out orders, across the expansive area of green, to whoever might hear him.

Suddenly the screaming blades of a helicopter whirred overhead.

Gustav glanced behind him to see his own vehicle careening recklessly down to the ground.

There was no time to pause to question what it was doing here and who had conscripted it into action against his orders.

Probably Galanov, he thought, though how could he have known? He was an enterprising young man. He had figured out the escape route at Teltow a year ago. Perhaps he had figured this one out as well.

No, what was he thinking—Galanov wasn't even in Berlin!

He ran forward into the cemetery, firing two warning shots into the air.

Scurrying figures ahead confirmed everything!

He had arrived just at the high climax of the escape plot! His deductions had all been on the mark!

"Stop!" he screamed. "Stop in the name of the *Stasi* of the DDR!"

Two more shots echoed through the night.

In the name of . . . what was Lola . . . ? He knew nothing of a gravesite of any loved . . . how did she come to be here?

"Lola . . . Lola," he cried with injudicious jubilation. "Reinhardt, stop them—they are all traitors!"

The next instant, to his bewildered consternation, his faithful but unnoticed secretary of so many years had disappeared before his very eyes.

But he had not even an instant to ponder the metaphysical complexity he had just witnessed. For that very second, as if in Lola's place, a face rose before him, bathed in the soft glow of moonlight, such an eerie luminescence clinging to the beautiful features he had so often dreamed of that for several seconds his dumbfounded eyes and stupefied brain thought they were beholding a spirit risen out of the grave.

He had expected it, he had dreamed of it, he had anticipated it all last night and all day long, but in the reality of the moment he lost all command of his senses.

Poor Gustav was undone.

His running steps came to a halt. Chase all but forgotten, pistol, hand, and arms dropping suddenly limp at his side, he stood transfixed as Lot's wife, though not quite yet a pillar of salt.

"Sabina!" he murmured.

∽ 110 ∽
A Moment of Remembrance

The deep truths of creation hide themselves in the most inverted of spiritual pyramids.

Truly are the principles of highest life foolishness in the eyes of the world. To achieve greatness requires servanthood. To be first requires putting others ahead of oneself. And highest truth of all: *To live one must die.*

The mathematics of earth's systems are incapable of solving equations of divine origins. For the plight of man's sin, his Creator devised a heavenly remedy, invisible to the eyes and incomprehensible to the equations of man.

The remedy was a crude, ugly, nail-scarred, blood-smeared wooden cross upon which only the worst of criminals were executed. Upon such a despised instrument of death would almighty God offer *himself* as a sacrifice of love, to bring all creatures of his making back into fully restored childship with him, their Creator.

What intellect of man can fashion rational explanation for the *why* of such a thing?

Death of Creator yields *life* to all creation.

Those who loved the divine Son laid him in a tomb. There was the battle with Death waged. And there was Death defeated, not merely for a chosen few, but eternally vanquished unto everlasting, that the intent of God might be fulfilled, and every knee bow in chosen submission to his Son.

By the empty tomb will all things be restored to their triumphant purpose within the heart of God. Into the tomb must all venture, that they may find, each one, that Death no more exists inside it.

In the empty tomb is life, victory, and the restitution of all things!

At the Fischer Street gravesite where no body was to be found, an empty sepulchre was bestowing life, freedom, and newfound joy to a small band of God's children, as the empty tomb in a hillside outside Jerusalem gave life and freedom to all the world nineteen centuries before.

Half their number were now through the tunnel of life that made its way under the resting place of the dead.

"Lola, you must go next," said Sabina with urgency in her voice. "He has seen you . . . hurry!"

Lola did not argue. She had already tasted enough of the life these people knew that she never wanted to go back. Without hesitating, or even once glancing up in the direction of her former superior's voice calling her name, she slipped away into blackness, baptized into the death of the grave, that she might rise to new life on the other side.

Joseph, though he was loath to take a place ahead of a woman, had seen Matthew's nod of command in his direction, and now likewise began his descent without questioning why Sabina tarried.

For each involved in this exodus, the symbolism of the grave carried different significance.

For the baron, it represented the primal cause and raison d'être of his entire consciousness. No more fitting climax than this could be imagined to a life, in very truth, lived that he might learn to apply the eternal lesson of the empty tomb more fully into every corner of his being.

For Lola, the grave signified the promise of life to come.

For Joseph, now came the baptism for which he had longed to seal the pledge he had made to his Messiah—the death of the old, the birth of the new. For the old man is crucified with Christ, buried with him, that in new birth we may rise to life eternal!

As he approached the yawning black hole, quietness engulfed him. His senses slowed, and in the submissive act of kneeling down, all the past fifteen years passed through his brain as if in preparation for this one instant of time.

Indeed was new life about to break forth into the life of Joseph Aviz-Rabin, with more glorious wonder than ever he could imagine. His prayers *had* been heard, every one, and moments later he was crawling through the dirt and blackness toward the unsuspecting face of one of their answers.

Yet two of them remained in harm's way.

Sabina had known the voice instantly.

The dread that smote her at its sound, however, could not prevent her lifting her head toward it. The pull of onetime childhood affection inexplicably drew her.

She glanced up. Gustav filled her gaze some thirty-five meters away, his running step suddenly faltering to a standstill.

In that instant, she knew he had the power to kill both her and Matthew.

The gun dropped to his side.

Even in the moonlight she saw his lips move. A shudder coursed through her frame. Instinctively she knew the word he had spoken.

He was whispering her own name.

Sabina had no leisure to meditate upon the moment, for the next she heard another voice screaming through the night, a voice she also recognized from long ago, a voice that struck terror to the very depths of her soul.

She knew his was no step that would arrest itself at the sight of her face. Nor would his gun delay its discharge.

At most a second had passed.

Suddenly she became aware of Matthew beside her yelling at her in command, no longer making even the slightest pretense of attempting to keep quiet.

"*Sabina . . . go!*" he cried.

The next moment she was in blackness, falling to her hands and knees, crawling into the unknown void ahead of her.

∞ 111 ∞
Final Fury
September 6—8:24 P.M.

The shrieking voice of Emil Korsch, as he vaulted from the helicopter and ran out from under its slowing blades and forward into the Fischer Street cemetery, was not one filled with remembrance of the past or passion for the present.

The fury of vile imprecations filling the air as the echoes from Gustav's gun died away manifested an evil wrath venting itself on the gods for what Korsch could see unfolding before his very eyes—the colossal defeat of his life.

Even as he had been screaming out orders to the terrified pilot to land the lurching machine, he had divined the whole truth of the drama being played out below him—that the men he had been seeking, the only two men remaining in the Eastern bloc who were capable of leading him to what his greedy brain had lusted after for so long, were quickly disappearing down a hole not twenty meters from the Berlin wall itself!

"Schmundt!" he shrieked as he sprinted forward. "Stop them! Kill them, you fool!"

But the simultaneous sight of Sabina's lovely face in his eyes and Emil Korsch's maledictions in his ears finally stretched the convoluted brain of Gustav von Schmundt beyond its breaking point. He had been dangerously close to it for some time.

Suddenly came the snap.

He turned, slowly, toward the voice, a zombielike dispassion on his countenance.

Without even enough warning to slow his steps, the KGB agent suddenly realized that the *Stasi* pistol of death had been raised against him!

The Fischer Street cemetery rang out again with repeated explosions of gunfire.

With disbelief and horror at the awful sight, but thankful neither Sabina nor the baron had witnessed it, Matthew hesitated on his knees but an instant more. He realized with irony that, in the end, they all owed their freedom to none other than Gustav von Schmundt. Then he scrambled down the hole after Sabina, pausing only to replace the tombstone above him that read "E. Brecht."

Everything had happened so quickly, with most of the mourners gone from view before the first warning shots had been fired, that the *Vopo* guards who now came running saw only a man in the familiar *Stasi* uniform standing stock-still, warm gun clutched in the hand that hung by his side.

Ten or twelve meters beyond, the dead body of Emil Korsch lay sprawled on the ground, warm blood still pouring out of the six or eight holes through his chest.

Gustav stared forward at the scene, as one struck dumb, eyes wide . . . but in them was only the look of emptiness.

PART VII

Escape to Freedom
September–December 1962

∽ 112 ∽
Freedom

At the sound of the shots, Sabina's heart failed her.

She gave a cry, stopped, and did her best in the dirty blackness to squirm around. Only a moment or two later the tunnel went black.

"Matthew!" she cried in terror.

But the next instant she felt Matthew scrambling against her from behind.

"Get going!" he urged, half laughing to find her stationary there, but with still an imperative and frightened tone.

"Oh, Matthew, I thought—"

"I'm safe, I'm safe . . . we're *all* safe! But let's get out of here!"

Sabina wriggled around again. With no light from the open grave behind them, they crawled forward until the dim light ahead gradually began to light their way.

Sabina's pause had allowed the others to get ahead.

∽∾∽

In the storage shed, Kohl was just emerging from the tunnel, rope still tied to one foot, as the contractor Detmold was helping the young boy up and out, when Ursula heard the first volley of gunshots from the other side.

An involuntary scream escaped her lips, but there was no time. The boy's mother was scrambling up now.

God, O God . . . bring Sabina through safely! whispered Ursula to herself.

Shouts were now coming from the other side, angry shouts. Something dreadful must have gone wrong!

∽∾∽

Joseph had heard the shots from the middle of the tunnel. He did not know that Sabina was no longer right behind him and continued to crawl forward behind Lola Reinhardt.

There was the light ahead . . . could it really be light coming from the western side of the wall!

He had no time nor was he inclined to pause to analyze it. Lola was now standing and scrambling up with the help of many hands reaching down from above.

Now Joseph had arrived at the end of the tunnel.

He lifted his hands off the ground, now stretched his knees and stood . . . hands were clustered downward, reaching, stretching, grasping at him . . . sounds, voices, congratulatory celebrations reached him. He took several of the hands and struggled and pulled his way up to the floor of the storage shed that had made possible such a daring rescue right under the collective nose of the *Vopos,* the *Stasi,* and the KGB.

A swarm of eight or ten people of all ages excitedly stood about, helping, encouraging, cheering him as he emerged into their midst, most of them begrimed with dirt and mud over their recent funeral attire, just like him.

There was the little boy and his mother . . . the old man, the lovely lady's father, who had prayed . . . the white-haired lady—they had all made it!

Exultantly he greeted his new friends . . . handshakes . . . slaps on the back . . . glances all round . . .

Suddenly a great shudder swept through him like a chill of death and a bolt of hot lightning.

Who was that woman . . . why was she staring at him so? Her face was white as a ghost. Where had he—

But . . . but he had seen that face before . . . long ago.

～～⌒～

There was scarcely time for Ursula's prayer for Sabina to grow silent on her lips before the refugees were coming. The mother and her boy first, now an elderly woman whose pale face had splotches of dirt all over it. She was so exhausted she collapsed on the floor the moment Friedrich had her up.

Ursula knelt to speak a few encouraging words in her ear, then returned to the top of the hole down to the tunnel.

There was . . . yes, it must be the baron! She hardly recognized him. He was safe!

Oh, Sabina . . . Sabina!

Baron von Dortmann turned on his knees the moment he was up—not seeing or realizing that his own escape had been made possible by one who had sought refuge in his own house so many years ago. Ursula reached down with the other hand, calling out encouragement as a middle-aged woman she didn't know now grabbed at whatever she could, a smile of relief on her face.

She was up now.

Ursula bent down again, amid the growing clamor in the small shed. *Where was Sabina?*

She reached her hands down . . . a man's head came into view, crawling to the end of the tunnel. He stopped and rose.

Suddenly Ursula staggered back from the open hole, clutching her breast, her face gone clammy and white.

O God, it couldn't . . .

They were hauling the man out now . . . voices and shouts . . . everyone was still looking down into the hole . . .

The man had seen her. He stopped. Why was he standing staring at her with such a shocked look on his face? He was moving toward her now . . .

God, it couldn't . . . it couldn't be!

He was approaching. Everything was so changed . . . he looked different. It had been so many years!

A smile, faint at first, broke out on the man's lips.

She would know that smile if it had been a hundred years! It was! *O Lord . . . how did you . . . ?*

He was standing in front of her now, a look of mingled disbelief and ecstasy dawning upon his face.

Her voice, when it came, was scarcely more than a whisper.

"Joseph . . . ?" she said, in questioning exclamation.

"Ursula!" was his only reply.

Then they were in one another's arms.

∽ 113 ∽
For Love of Hyacinth

As Sabina led Matthew the remainder of the way through the tunnel under *der Mauer* of Berlin to freedom at last, neither had any idea of the incredible drama being played out within the little storage shed above them.

Neither, in fact, did the baron or Lola or any of the others who were now clustered anxiously about the hole awaiting the final two refugees, the leaders of their escape to freedom.

The delay had only been a matter of a few seconds. But those who waited had all heard the gunfire on the other side, and thus could not help but be anxious when only blackness met their collective gazes after Joseph's emergence out of the tomb of life.

If, behind them, *Stasi* bullets had cut the number of their group short, they could not possibly know it until now. They all turned back toward the way they had come and waited nervously.

But now came sounds . . . then appeared Sabina's blonde head. She glanced up, flashed a radiant smile, stood, and took two of the many hands reaching down to her.

A second later Matthew bounded up after her, and a great cheer went up inside the small building.

They had done it! All were safe and in West Berlin!

The baron took Sabina in his arms and gave her a long embrace.

"Oh, Papa!"

He released her, then extended his hand to Matthew.

"Well done, my boy!" he exclaimed. "You said when you found us hiding in Magdeburg that you would get us out, and indeed you did!"

"Not without the help of a good many of your people," laughed Matthew.

"Not *my* people, Son, *God's* people."

Sabina was already greeting the rest of those in their party, as if the separation had been a month rather than five minutes.

"Gerta . . ."

"Thank you . . . thank you, Fräulein Duftblatt," wept Gerta.

Sabina hugged her warmly, then found Lola.

"Oh, Lola," she said. "How can we ever thank you?"

"It is I who will spend the rest of my life in gratitude to you for everything," replied Lola, tears standing in her eyes.

The two women embraced.

"But, where is Joseph?" Sabina suddenly exclaimed, realizing he was the one member of their daring band whose face she still had not seen.

Almost the same instant, she remembered Ursula. *Where was Ursula!* Even with all the commotion, how could she have forgotten her friend!

Hurriedly Sabina glanced around, scanning every face and every centimeter of the small shed.

When her eyes fell upon the wondrous sight off to one side from the tumult surrounding the tunnel, the astonishment and confusion registering upon her face were evident in every feature. She took two steps forward, then stopped, bewildered.

There were Ursula and Joseph . . . together . . . in each other's arms in a manner that no mere excitement over the escape could account for.

What could it all mean!

She tried to urge herself forward, but was suddenly shy to intrude.

Some momentous thing was at hand, but what could it be!

At last Ursula saw her from the corner of her eye and released herself from Joseph's embrace. She approached Sabina, eyes full of tears, the most radiant smile imaginable upon her face.

The two friends of so many years fell into each other's arms, sobbing for joy.

They stood for what seemed minutes but was only seconds, before Ursula broke the holy silence of friendship.

"Sabina, how did you know?" whispered Ursula.

"Know what? . . . I *don't* know—what does all this mean, Ursula?"

"How did you know to bring Joseph? How did you find him?"

"We did not bring him. He came to us. But how do *you* know him? We only just met—"

"Sabina, don't you understand? This is Joseph . . . *my* Joseph!"

At last the truth broke over Sabina's consciousness. As they parted, Joseph now approached, a sheepish grin on his face. He and Sabina embraced, and as they stood back, Sabina still shook her head in disbelief.

Matthew and the baron now walked forward, further introductions were made, and soon everyone had been made aware of the astonishing reunion only God could have masterminded.

"It appears we have more to thank our Father for than any of us had any idea," remarked Sabina's father.

"Far more!" added Joseph.

"It would seem he has answered our prayers a bit like he multiplied the loaves and fishes in the hands of his Son's disciples!" added the baron.

The baron's reference to the miraculous feedings of the Galilean crowds suddenly reminded Joseph of the dramatically altered situation between him and Ursula. He now turned back toward her and spoke softly, out of the hearing of the others, who gradually backed away so the two could share a few moments alone.

"You are still wearing the ring," he said, smiling down and taking her hand in his.

"I have been faithful to our betrothal," she replied quietly.

"As have I," he said. "But—," he continued, then paused uncertainly—"but we have much to talk about. I . . . I am not the same person I was back then."

"Nor am I," rejoined Ursula.

"I am not even the same man I was a week ago. I have . . . there is much I have to tell you."

"There is a great deal you must know about me as well," said Ursula.

"We shall have time to tell each other everything!"

Beyond her, suddenly Joseph's eyes fell upon the flower that would never make its final grave in the tunnel after all.

"What is this?" he said, walking slowly toward where it lay on an overturned crate. "I thought I smelled something! How did this lonely pink hyacinth get here . . . and out of season?"

"I brought it," answered Ursula, picking it up tenderly.

"But . . . but how could you possibly know? It is my favorite of all the flowers in the world!"

"I had no idea."

"Then why did you bring it?" asked an incredulous Joseph.

"It is a long story," said Ursula with a smile. "I will tell you, along with all those other things you need to know."

"But . . . but why here, now, today?"

"I can only tell you this," said Ursula, "that the fragrance has always reminded me of you."

"It is just the same for me! How could you possibly . . . ? I have never smelled a hyacinth and not thought of you! Yet . . . yet you could have had no idea I would be here today. You could not have brought it for me!"

"My reason for bringing it had to do with you, it is true," said Ursula. "But that reason no longer exists. I am just happy that I am able to share it with you and to give you this hyacinth as a gift of welcome to West Berlin."

She held it out to Joseph's face.

He inhaled a long and contented breath. Ursula now bent forward, and they partook of its aroma together.

Henceforth would hyacinth contain yet *more* mystery for each of them. But for now its melancholy was swallowed up in the scent of gladness.

It had become again the fragrance of fairy tales!

∽ 114 ∽
Another Reunion

Come, come, everyone!" Ursula called out above the continued din. "It is late in the evening and will be dark soon. You are all dirty and must be hungry and exhausted. Arrangements have been made for your every need. For tonight at least, you are honored guests. You will be fed and bathed, and a sumptuous feast is already awaiting you."

"But where, Ursula?" said Sabina. "Surely your small apartment—"

Ursula laughed. It was a merry laugh that reminded the baron as he heard it of his own daughter's laugh of childhood. None of those present could possibly have known how long it had been since just such a joyous laugh had sounded from Ursula Wissen's mouth.

"My apartment would be much too small!" she replied. "No, your benefactor has made arrangements for all of you at one of Berlin's finest hotels."

"Our benefactor?" repeated several voices at once.

"Yes, a mysterious well-wisher!" said Ursula, laughing again. Her heart was so full of joy she could not help herself. "Now come! The automobiles are waiting!"

She led the way out of the shed, Joseph beside her, the hyacinth between them. There, on the curb of the adjacent street, stood a van of the Detmold Construction Company, as well as the cars brought by Kohl and Peters. Beside the latter stood another friend, feverish with tearful anticipation.

"Angela!" cried Sabina, rushing forward.

Now still another unexpected reunion took place, as Angela greeted her former comrades of the rainwater canal.

After another minute or two, the passengers proceeded to pile into the three cars and were presently en route single file to the World Towers Hotel. Angela and her husband, their friend Kohl, and Detmold accompanied the troop as chauffeurs for the celebration.

For Matthew and Ursula, the ride was one of great joy and fulfilled happiness. Baron von Dortmann saw very little of the way, for his eyes were closed for most of it. Sabina cried. Joseph was too stunned to pay much attention to the streets as they passed through them. The others, however, beheld the opulence of West Berlin for the first time, and were amazed. They had heard it was much different from what they had become accustomed to in the East, but never in their wildest expectations could they have anticipated the bustling metropolis that now met their wide-eyed stares.

Poor Lola! Tears streamed down her tired face. She was happy enough to cry, but not quite happy enough to keep from worrying about what would become of her now. She felt

suddenly inferior and out of place in this strange, bright, viva-
cious new world.

Surely Lola Reinhardt was in the care of the Father's hands
as securely as was her new and only friend in the West, Sabina
von Dortmann. The Father would not abandon her now, after
going to such lengths to woo her into his presence, that she
might share a home in his heart.

Arriving at the hotel only heightened their stupefaction.

No sooner had they stopped than uniformed attendants
appeared, opening the doors and leading them inside.

Was this truly a hotel?

Now was Joseph awake, and Baron von Dortmann too. It
looked to the eyes of the easterners like the mansion of man-
sions! The baron remembered places such as this from days of
old. But never had Joseph, Lola, the mother and her boy, or
white-haired Gerta with the dirty face, who clung to the
baron's arm as they entered—never had they beheld such
glories.

Ursula began to hang back.

She could not prevent the smile that was indeed so wide it
threatened to do physical hurt to her cheeks if it grew wider,
and she would not give away the surprise prematurely.

The doors opened, and in the pilgrims walked to the spacious
and brightly lit, carpeted, wide, warm lobby of the World
Towers. They had reached the end of their journey at last.

Ursula was just passing through the large double doors
when she heard the exclamation she had been anticipating.

"Dad!" cried Matthew.

Running footsteps followed.

The young and the old were lost in one another's arms in an
instant, standing in front of friends and sojourners, as well as
strangers and hotel staff altogether, for several long seconds.
Spontaneously the observers broke into a happy applause.

Now indeed was it time for the weeping to be revealed that
most resembles the rains that fall from the eyes of God—the
strong, joyful, unashamed, virile weeping of the Father's
mighty men.

Matthew and Thaddeus stepped back, cheeks wet, both

shaking their heads as they both probed one another's eyes for expressions that would not come.

There were no words. They could find none. They needed none.

Behind his son, Thaddeus now beheld he whom he had prayed for an opportunity again to lay eyes on for more than twenty years. The baron had changed far more than had Thaddeus. But nothing had changed in the love and respect each felt for the other.

They approached slowly, and their hands clasped in a tight, manly grip as their eyes met.

"Thaddeus," murmured the baron.

"Heinrich, I . . . I—"

Neither now were there words.

An embrace followed. The two men clung to one another without shame.

In the kingdom where Love reigns, there is none.

∾ 115 ∾
The Strange Fate of Gustav von Schmundt

Meanwhile, on the other side of the wall, an altogether different drama was unfolding.

As the *Vopo* guards rushed forward, and the giant blades of the helicopter gradually slowed, and the innocent cemetery mourners scurried from the scene in terror, and the echoes from his murderous gunfire died away in the night air to the sounds of a few shouts and barking dogs in the distance, Gustav von Schmundt stood over the dead body of his onetime comrade and mentor in the ways of evil with a blank expression of finality and relief.

There was no remorse in his eyes for what he had done. The only stab that began to intrude upon his heart after a moment or two was the reminder—forgotten in the few seconds that the explosions sounded from his hand—of what he had just seen.

Sabina had been there . . . just a few dozen meters away!

He had beheld her face, gazed into her eyes. She was more lovely than he had even allowed his memory to imagine. The renewed thought of it—along with the image of McCallum's face beside her, which he had hardly noticed at the time—brought fresh agony to his being. The knife of selfish unlove slashed through his brain to the core.

She had seen him, and then had turned away . . . disappeared. She had *rejected* him and was now gone forever.

Somehow, though, Gustav's brain was not so seared by the sight of Sabina and the treacherous deed his hand had done as to lose sight for more than a few seconds of the precariousness of his own position.

Who could tell what backup might be following Korsch even now, or what would be the ramifications should the dead man's identity be learned?

Gustav had not only failed to stop the escape, but his hesitation had, in fact, been *responsible* for the successful escape of an American spy and an escaped prisoner! He could easily have killed both Sabina and McCallum and, now that he thought of it, probably two or three others if he'd jumped down into the tunnel and opened fire—perhaps even Baron von Dortmann himself.

Yes, Gustav realized, he had placed himself in a delicate situation indeed.

This was no time to wallow in the loss.

A misstep now, and he would be in prison *himself* before morning!

All this raced through his brain in but a second or two. Then suddenly Gustav seemed to come to himself.

"I am *Stasi* Section Chief Schmundt. Examine that tunnel there!" he called, pointing toward it, to one of the *Vopos* as he ran up. "See if the traitors have left any clues to their identity. Then post a guard beside it until we can get it filled in."

Quickly he then turned to the other.

"Get this man's identity off him!" he shouted. "I think you will find that he is a KGB agent by the name of Korskayev. He is the traitor who planned this escape, in collusion with the Americans. Luckily I uncovered his little plot in time at least to stop *him* from escaping himself, although it would seem we are too late to have kept his friends, whoever they are, from getting through."

Now he spoke to the third man.

"It appears also that he managed to steal a *Stasi* helicopter," he said. "Notify your superiors of what has happened. Watch the body. I will send a detail for it to be taken to the morgue. Meanwhile, seal off this cemetery. I will return to headquarters to see what more we can learn of this plot."

He spun around and ran to the helicopter, quickly recounting the same information, followed by a ruthless tongue-lashing, to his pilot for allowing the traitorous KGB double agent so easily to dupe him.

Putting aside his own fear of the unstable machine, a minute later they were in the air, circling up and around the site where, on the one side of the ugly grey barrier jubilation reigned, while on the grassy expanse of the other the corpse of the man who had brought such cruelty to so many had already begun to cool.

As for Emil Korsch, he was already far, far away, in another world, having entered that fiery place about which most who think of it make one of two miscalculations—making too little of it, or too much. Those who understand the ultimate designs of God's Fatherhood fall into neither error.

The papers of East Berlin the next morning were filled with headlines of the affair.

A high-level KGB agent, secretly in Berlin from Moscow, had been discovered to be a double agent masterminding a major escape attempt through a tunnel into West Berlin. *Stasi* Section Chief Gustav von Schmundt, long an associate of Korskayev and suspicious of his loyalties, had uncovered the scheme in time to prevent the renegade traitor from making good his getaway to the West, although an undetermined handful of others apparently did slip under the wall. As the attempt was made to apprehend him, the KGB agent resisted and was shot at the border by Schmundt.

Comments by the section chief were not yet available, but an interview was expected in tomorrow's paper.

Comment was not available for the simple reason that, after filling out his report and notifying the newspaper and all necessary departments as to the disposition of Korsch and the sealing of the tunnel, Gustav von Schmundt had gone home to his apartment and proceeded to get drunker than he had ever been in his life. When he finally passed out about three in the morning, he had managed to convince himself that getting rid of Sabina was the best thing he could have hoped for and wondered why he had persisted so long with his foolish fantasies.

When he awoke the next day around noon, he was too sick to think about anything.

The scheduled interview was forced to wait for another day.

By then, however, Gustav was in good form and added still more detail and insight to the events that had transpired, including when and how he had first discovered the deception at such a high level within the KGB.

The overall effect of the incident, the interview, and all that followed was to make Section Chief Schmundt something of a hero within the DDR for a short time, which resulted about six months later in a major promotion into the upper echelons of the Communist bureaucracy.

There began to be talk eventually of an elected position of even higher prominence.

∿⌒∿

When the reports reached Moscow, Andrassy Galanov did not believe them for a moment.

He knew too much about both men, and what they each wanted, to be taken in.

It did cause him to reflect a good deal about what ought to be his own response. In the end, he concluded that there was little to be gained by exposing Schmundt as a liar. What proof would he have anyway? He had to admit, upon further reflection, that the German had proved more cunning and resourceful than he had given him credit for.

If the German had bested his uncle, perhaps it would be best to leave well enough alone.

Galanov remained in Moscow, therefore, and continued his upward climb through the KGB. Though he did not exactly come to occupy his uncle's former office, he yet became a very powerful and feared agent indeed.

∽ 116 ∽
Hot Baths and Clean Sheets

Are you our mysterious benefactor?" exclaimed Matthew to his father the moment the two older men had completed their greeting.

"I don't know," laughed Thaddeus. "What did she tell you?"

Ursula now joined them. Thaddeus stretched out his arm to her. They hugged and exchanged a warm smile.

"You two know each other, too!" now exclaimed Sabina in astonishment.

"There is no end to the wonders of this day!" added the baron with gleeful, boyish delight.

"Oh, Thaddeus!" exclaimed Ursula, "you'll never believe who came through the tunnel just before Sabina—Joseph, my betrothed!"

She now introduced Joseph to Matthew's father.

"It seems there are more reunions than we can all keep track of!" remarked Thaddeus. "But now you all have to come with me!"

"So you *are* our benefactor!" said Matthew, falling in beside his father as the elder McCallum led the bedraggled troop toward the stairs.

"In a manner of speaking," said Thaddeus. Then he lowered his voice and added, "But just between you and me, I am going to have a little help footing the bill."

"Who from?"

"Let's just say I let the State Department know you might be returning over the wall and bringing some people with you. Word got back—very hush-hush, you understand . . . not through official channels—to a certain source who got a message back to me saying to spare no expense, roll out the red carpet, and that Uncle Sam would pick up the tab."

"The president!" exclaimed Matthew in a loud whisper.

"You know the old expression we diplomats live by:" replied his father with a grin, "'I'm not free to comment on that.' However, off the record, I think he will be very happy to see you."

Thaddeus led the way to the second floor, where two suites

and two smaller rooms awaited them. Gerta Arnim and the mother and her son each had rooms of their own. Sabina, Ursula, and Lola would share a suite. And a spacious two-bedroom suite would house Matthew, Joseph, Thaddeus, and Baron von Dortmann.

Thaddeus led the way into the larger of the suites, where a magnificent feast was spread on a table in the center of the sitting room—breads, cheeses, meats, pastries, coffee, tea, wine, cold drinks.

Thaddeus proceeded to explain the room assignments.

"I realize it is late," he concluded, "but if the rest of you feel anything like I do myself, I doubt sleep will invade this excited brain of mine for many hours to come. So feel free to have something to eat now, or else you may go to your rooms, bathe, shower, change clothes, and then return to our suite here to relax."

He glanced around at everyone, then to Ursula.

"You women, Ursula is your hostess. She has seen to fresh clothing for all of you, as I have for the men. You will find what we hope is a suitable change for all of you on your beds and clean sheets inside them to enjoy later, when the fatigue of the day finally becomes too much for you."

More exclamations of wonder went around, followed by much thanksgiving.

"Before you disperse to your rooms, we need to thank the three men who dug the tunnel by which your freedom was gained—Friedrich Detmold, Geoff Kohl, and Franz Peters!"

A great cheer went up in the room, followed by clapping and many appreciative words.

"I am sorry we could not allow you to come with our wives," said Franz. "We were too worried that something might go wrong. We had to know if the plan would work."

"They wanted to use their wives for the experiment!" put in Angela.

Laugher followed.

"We are happy you are all here," added Franz. "It makes all that digging even more worthwhile!"

"We are going to let you all get your rest and visit one another," said Angela as she and the three men readied to leave.

More thankful expressions of parting followed, while Sabina and Angela made arrangements to meet again in a couple of days.

As the others slowly dispersed, Thaddeus turned to the young mother.

"Your husband, as I understand it, is in Hannover?"

She nodded. "But he does not know. I could not get word to him."

"Would you like me to try to telephone him for you? Then we will arrange transportation for you and your son tomorrow."

The woman nodded, but was unable to speak for the tears of gratitude that welled up in her eyes.

"You have a cousin here in Berlin, Frau Arnim?" he asked, now speaking to Gerta.

"Yes, she is expecting me."

"I would be happy to send someone for her," said Thaddeus. "Or if you would prefer, we could take you to her tonight."

"If . . . if I could perhaps speak with her by phone?" suggested Gerta.

"Certainly. I will have someone attend to it presently."

Thaddeus now stopped Lola also.

"Fräulein Reinhardt," he said. "I want to speak with you a moment. As I understand it, you have no one over here in the West who is expecting you."

Lola nodded, a look of anxiety passing over her face. Were they going to send her back? "I . . . I have an aunt in Hamburg . . . but she does not know."

Thaddeus saw her anxiety and instantly tried to alleviate her worry. "Please, do not be concerned," he said. "Tomorrow I will take you to meet a man who will, I am certain, be able to find you a job. You speak English, do you not?"

"Yes."

"Good. There are a couple possibilities he and I have spoken about, perhaps in one of the governmental agencies here or in Bonn. Have no anxiety about anything. I will take care of anything you need. Also tomorrow we will make certain you have a small supply of cash for your personal needs."

Lola turned to go and left the room on Sabina's arm, weeping quietly in mounting disbelief. For her the fairy tale remained woven throughout with melancholy, though containing none the less wonder.

Thaddeus closed the door behind them, then turned back to the other three men.

"My goodness, Dad," exclaimed Matthew, "you have every possible detail accounted for. How did you possibly know everything?"

"*The Network of the Rose* is very thorough," laughed Thaddeus. "Ursula had been given minimal information on most of those accompanying you, so I simply called upon my diplomatic background to fill in where there were needs."

He glanced around the room, then laughed again.

"What?" said Matthew.

"Now that I think of it, I don't suppose I had *every* detail accounted for!"

"How so?"

"Neither Ursula nor I knew about Joseph. We were expecting a fellow by the name of Tsankov, a Russian I think. Whatever happened to *him?*"

The other three now broke into a hearty laugh.

"A long story!" said Joseph.

"In any event," Thaddeus went on, "I had something all lined up for Tsankov too. Now it looks like he won't be needing it!"

"One never knows!" laughed Joseph.

"I don't know about the rest of you, but I'm ready for that shower!" said Matthew.

∾ 117 ∾
Catching Up on the Months
. . . and Years

It was past eleven before everyone was assembled once again in the large parlor of the suite occupied by the four men. But the lateness of the hour in no way diminished the exuberant atmosphere once they were all together again.

Hot baths, clean clothes, tasty food and drink, combined with the anticipation of a night spent between fresh sheets in a cozy warm bed, and most of all the reminder growing upon them steadily as the night progressed that they had made it safely into *West* Berlin—these and a thousand other things flying through the minds of those assembled on the second floor of the World Towers Hotel on the night of September 6, 1962, prevented sleep and made of the gathering a carnival.

Most of the tears had been attended to. Now it was time for celebration.

There was more catching up to do than could possibly be completed in one evening.

Matthew and Thaddeus, and, when Matthew was otherwise occupied, Thaddeus and Baron von Dortmann, as might be expected, spoke with one another almost feverishly. The few months they had been apart might, to all appearances, have been years the way father and son carried on. And the years since they had seen one another made of Thaddeus and the baron children again. The baron became giddy with delight several times. Sabina could not contain her mirth, for she had never seen him behave with such childlike abandon.

Laughter and dialogue permeated the air like a charged current.

Sabina and Ursula rambled on like teenagers, as the latter had been when they had first met at *Lebenshaus*. Never in all their years of friendship in Switzerland, and then later living and working together in Berlin, had such an unabashed happiness flowed between them. They felt the unusual experience not granted to many of being allowed to get to know one another all over again on a new level. They had worked together, shared vision, shared life—and loved one another. But in the matrix of loneliness that comprised the worlds in which each lived, never had they truly been *happy* together. Too much had been missing.

Now all at once they had their men, their freedom, and each other!

Not every emotion in the room was one of exuberance. The incredible event of the escape drew out other feelings as well, some from deep personal reservoirs whose contents had never previously been tapped.

Lola found herself alternating between contentment and new anxieties. How could she not feel different and still isolated and alone amid such joy of reunion as was all around her? Here were family, friends, lovers, fathers, sons, daughters—but she was alone.

What was to become of her? Would her aunt and cousin even remember her? Matthew's father was kind, it was true, but his assurances could not alleviate her very practical worries. She was not well acquainted with either people or a society where the keeping of promises ranked high as a priority.

Yet sadness is not nearly such an inhibitor of personal growth as most think. It is, in fact, not a constraint at all, but rather one of the best and most needful nutrients for the development of spiritual personhood.

Lola's new life had begun. The roots of that life would extend down into the soil of new relationships such as these she was presently forming. Even now, her Father was caring for her. The quiet joy that would gradually replace the melancholy in her heart would never match the ebullience of Sabina's. Lola had been given a different road to walk. But the joy the Father purposed especially for *her* would come in time because she would then be walking with *him*.

Both Baron von Dortmann and Thaddeus McCallum were keenly sensitive to Lola's unique position in the fellowship that evening. Each in his turn took extended opportunities, as did Sabina, to sit beside her and talk and listen quietly, drawing out the lonely woman from East Germany in a way that reassured her that she would never be alone again. Thus they did their part to establish the foundations of friendships she would need to depend on in the coming months and helped ease her through the first of many transitions she would face.

Others, too, besides Lola found emotions other than excitability at work in themselves.

As much as they had prayed, as many years as they had waited, as deeply as they had hoped for this very day, both Joseph and Ursula discovered themselves in some ways altogether unprepared for it. An unexpected yet somehow delicious shyness enveloped them while the night wore on, as they began to draw toward one side of the room alone together.

Now—and so suddenly and serendipitously!—these two *hearts* that had belonged to none other for more than twenty

years found themselves awkwardly facing the joyous but timor-
ously embarrassing task of having to get to know one another at
the *surface* level. This they had scarcely begun when the war tore
them apart. Through the years of their separation, their hearts
had deepened in their mutual love and commitment to one another, yet their bodies, their hands, their faces, their glances,
their modes of expression, and all the other thousand ways by
which people become acquainted—in these expressions of personality they were yet strangers.

Many, therefore, were the uncompleted sentences, the shy
reddenings of neck and cheeks, the downward glances, the half
smiles, the faltering laughs, the stumbling attempts at conversation. How could a man of thirty-seven, thought Joseph, behave
so much like a timid schoolboy!

When each later retired, happier than they thought they would
ever be, both yet felt strangely inept and immature. Ursula fell at
last to sleep wondering if Joseph thought her uncomely and inex-
pressive. On Joseph's part, sleep finally came to his brain amid
thoughts of chagrined self-consciousness for how foolishly he
was certain he had deported himself.

In this, however, had the evening's conversation between the
two been successful: As they parted for the night, each knew
that everything between them had changed. It had been Joseph
who had spoken first, briefly though with definite emphasis, of
his new acceptance of the truth of Christianity. He had been so
solemn and serious through it, with such a determined expression, that Ursula had grown fearful that what he had to tell her
was that he could not honor the betrothal.

The moment the light dawned upon her of what he was attempting to relate, she broke into immediate quiet sobs that she
was positively powerless to still for more than two minutes.

Such a reaction could only indicate to Joseph her absolute rejection of this new direction in his life, and likewise a rejection
of him as a result. Even as he maladroitly attempted to comfort
Ursula through her tears, his inner mortification over what he
was certain would be her first words in reply was profound.

How unprepared was he then when, at last lifting her face
again to him, through the abating flood of tears, he beheld a
smile of great joy and relief.

"Oh, Joseph!" she said, quietly and still weepily, "you . . . you cannot know . . . how happy you have made me."

Bewildered and confused, the stupefied expression on Joseph's face was all the reply he could manage. Once again, his tongue was mute.

"Joseph," Ursula went on, seeing clearly enough that he didn't understand her, "I have been a Christian myself for years! I was so afraid you wouldn't understand."

Suddenly, for the first time since the shed, they found themselves briefly in one another's arms. Tears were now in their eyes.

The embrace lasted only for a moment.

The awkwardness resumed, but a great threshold had been crossed. They talked more easily and freely the next day, and with still greater ease the next, until, in less than a week, the twenty years of separation were already fading rapidly into memory.

∽ 118 ∽
Kleines Lebenshaus Süd

The gathering at the McCallum chalet in the hilly countryside south of Munich was, by any estimation, an unlikely assortment of individuals.

It had been two weeks since the escape.

The mother and her son had been joyfully reunited with husband and father in Hannover. Gerta was with her cousin, who could not have been happier to see her.

Angela and Franz Peters were settling into their new married life together in West Berlin. Both Franz Peters and Geoff Kohl were working for the construction firm of Friedrich Detmold. None of them could have been happier. Nor could Detmold. Ever since the adventure the contractor had been on the lookout for an opportunity to employ the services of his company in another similar project.

Lola Reinhardt had been placed in an apartment with two other single women also employed by the Bureau of Statistics

in Berlin. She would work at the post until options of reloca-
tion could be explored, probably to Hamburg, Frankfurt, or
Munich. Lola was tending toward the former. She had already
been to the great northern city, where she had been successful
in locating her aunt and cousin and with whom the renewing
of familial ties had proved unexpectedly rich.

As for Joseph, he was residing for the time in Berlin, in a
house with several Christian young men—three Germans, an
American, and a Scotsman—three of whom taught at the
Berlin Evangelical Bible Academy, where the other two were
students. Ursula was well acquainted with two of the men
from her Christian contacts and knew the environment of the
place to be exceptional for the nurturing of belief.

They saw one another every day, and quickly the deepening
relationship found the right channels and began to flow
smoothly. They had hardly been a week in one another's presence before both knew beyond any doubt why God had
kept them for one another all this time—they loved one
another!

Once the inevitable timidity had given way to easy conversation and comfortable sharing, the talk turned to the matter of
their betrothal. Though both recognized the change brought
about by the fact of their Christian commitment, the desire in
both their hearts was to proceed with the marriage as quickly
as possible. They must, however, speak with Ursula's father
before anticipating anything further.

Plans, therefore, began to get under way almost immediately for a trip to Israel toward that end.

Sabina and her father were, like Lola, those most clearly
without a home or roots of any kind in the West. Since the
baron's escape from prison, they had literally been on the run
from one place to the next now for thirteen months.

From the first night in the hotel Thaddeus had convinced
the baron that the only natural and proper place for them was
with himself and Matthew in Bavaria. They had an abundance
of room, he said, and he had already made every possible
arrangement for their comfort.

"We shall see, Thaddeus," the baron said repeatedly. "We
mustn't put you out."

"Put us out! Don't be preposterous! We will be grief stricken if you do not come with us."

Inwardly the baron could not have been more delighted, but he was loath to make commitments before the will of God could be known, and that was a thing that took more time to discern than men generally give it. He was a grown man, he said. But every year of his life he realized all the more what a child he was. He must consult his Father on the matter.

At first Sabina thought to stay with Ursula until her own wedding arrangements could be finalized, but the thought of a further separation from either her father or Matthew was more than she could bear. She must accompany them to the south.

The boarding house in the village was mentioned.

"That will be perfect!" exclaimed the baron. "Sabina and I will make a home for ourselves there."

"Nonsense," rejoined Thaddeus, not realizing toward what implication his statement would lead, "there is no reason for *you* not to be at the chalet with us."

"I will be fine at the boarding house by myself, Papa," said Sabina. "Thaddeus is right."

Now it was Matthew's turn to step in with an objection.

In the end it was Matthew who took up temporary night-time quarters in the village, while Thaddeus, Sabina, and Baron von Dortmann shared the chalet.

"Besides," Matthew concluded. "I will be all the closer to the bakery!"

And now, several days after their return from Berlin, the other members of their fellowship of friendship arrived in Obenammersfeld for a weekend together, away from Berlin, to talk and visit in a more peaceful setting, and to pray together concerning their collective and individual futures.

Joseph and Ursula had driven down from Berlin, bringing Lola with them. Joseph would occupy a room in the boarding house with Matthew. There was abundant room for the two women at the house.

They had been talking freely for some time as the seven sat around the dinner table, during which time Joseph had shared at length about the brothers at Bialystok and the many things

Dieder had told him that had set his thoughts moving in new directions.

"Your brief stay with the brotherhood there sounds like it had exactly the same impact as Dad's and my first visit to the baron and Sabina at *Lebenshaus*," said Matthew. "Doesn't it, Dad?"

"Exactly," added Thaddeus. "There is no substitute for seeing the life of faith lived out in daily practical ways by a Christian who, at the same time, is prayerfully ready to speak challenging words—even bold words at times. For twenty years I have been grateful to you, Heinrich—" he turned his head and nodded toward the baron—"for having the courage to challenge Matt and me to think more personally about God than we had. Those challenging words changed our lives. It sounds like our brother Palacki did the same for you, Joseph."

"I will always be in his debt, that is for certain. I only hope somehow I will be allowed to see him again one day, shake his hand, and tell him that face-to-face."

"I'm sure that would not be difficult for the Lord to arrange," said Matthew, "if he could bring all of *us* together!"

They all laughed.

"He sounds like the kind of man I would like to meet as well," Matthew added.

"Perhaps we shall meet him together one day," said Joseph.

There was a brief silence.

"And so, our Jewish Christian friends, what does the future bode for you?" asked the baron, glancing toward Ursula and Joseph.

"We are going to be married, if that is what you mean," replied Joseph. "We do not exactly know when yet."

"We want to speak to my father," said Ursula. "We are trying to make arrangements for a flight to Jerusalem as soon as possible."

"Have you spoken with them?" asked Sabina.

"Oh yes! I'm afraid I will have a dreadful telephone bill! They are all so excited!"

"Have you told them . . . about Joseph?" asked Matthew. "The *new* Joseph I mean?"

"Not yet. That is something we want to do in person," answered Joseph.

"What about you?" Ursula asked, turning toward her friend.

"We don't know yet either," said Sabina. "Perhaps next month."

"That soon?" said Joseph.

"The sooner the better!" said Matthew. "We've been waiting for each other for what—let me see . . . we left in 1939, that's— we've been waiting for twenty-three years! Yes, that soon—I'm going to marry this lady before I lose any more opportunities!"

They all laughed.

"Wouldn't it be wonderful, Sabina," exclaimed Ursula, her face lighting up, "if we could be married on the same day . . . together?"

"But . . . your family?" said Sabina. "I can't think of anything more delightful, but . . . surely you will want to be with them."

"You're right. What am I thinking?"

"The important thing is that we get all four of you married as soon as possible," now put in Thaddeus. "Heinrich and I cannot wait much longer, and I imagine your father feels the same, Ursula! If my vote counts for anything, I say let us proceed with a double wedding with all possible dispatch!"

"I couldn't agree more!" added the baron with gusto.

The conversation moved in other directions by common consent out of respect for Lola.

"What about you, Lola?" said the baron at length. "Tell us about your new job."

"It is not the most interesting of work," Lola said, but with a smile. "Even in the wonderful, free BRD, statistics can be dull and dry. And there is much to learn, of course."

The baron laughed, delighted to see humor at last emerging from her. The stunted flower was beginning to open to the sun.

"But I am blessed and grateful," Lola went on. "The people in the office are so kind to me, as are the women I am living with. Already I am seeing such a multitude of ways in which life is different over here. It will perhaps take me a long time to feel comfortable. But I certainly am content and very pleased with where I am for the present."

"And how is your new spiritual life?" asked Thaddeus, with the warm tone of a friend. It was obvious the two had already spent a great deal of time together on the subject.

Lola smiled and thought for a moment. The expression on her face was one to warm the hearts of all those who saw it and who had been, in their own way, holding her up in prayer to their mutual Father. It was a smile of peace.

"I am finding," Lola answered after a moment, "that I have more to accustom myself to, in the way of looking at things differently, even than I do in reorienting myself from the DDR to the BRD. It is just as you have told me, Thaddeus. In this too, in thinking of God as a Father who is with me every moment, and who loves me . . . I find I have so much to learn."

"So do we all, dear," replied Thaddeus tenderly, "believe me, so do we all."

There was a long silence. It was Thaddeus, speaking again, who broke it.

"There is one thing I still do not understand," he said. "Why, if the tunnel was there and the plan was apparently going to work, didn't some of the other people you told me about come too—the fellow Brumfeldt and his family, and Angela's brother, or the man Hermann in Berlin?"

It remained silent. No one seemed inclined to attempt an answer.

"In Brumfeldt's case," said Sabina at length, "his wife, a dear but anxious woman by the name of Clara, would never have come. Erich is a contented man. He is one of the rare ones, like Udo Bietmann and Dieder Palacki, who will be free wherever he is."

"The other two?"

"I'm not quite sure about Josef," answered Sabina. "I halfway expected him to accompany us. But then they have important work still to do on the other side. God's people need help there just as much as here. That is their home. And yet . . ." Sabina smiled as she paused to think. "I cannot say it would surprise me," she went on, "to see Josef Dahlmann on this side one day."

"What about Hermann?" said Matthew.

Now Sabina's smile broke into laughter. "Dear Hermann! I'm not even going to try to understand what he is thinking!

"On the other hand," she added after a moment, "it would not surprise me to see him over here some day either!"

∽ 119 ∼
The Photographs

As they sat on the balcony that evening, enjoying a warm, peaceful sunset, the conversation turned to the photographs that had been such an important but invisible thread in the drama involving each one. Thaddeus and the baron knew nothing about the pictures, but all the others had been involved around such different edges of events as they had unfolded that a multitude of diverse perspectives was present. Before long, they began attempting to piece together a history of what had happened for the benefit of the baron and Thaddeus.

"Where did these mysterious photographs come from in the first place?" Thaddeus asked.

"I worked as assistant to a photographer in Moscow," replied Joseph. "He was a Jew, like me, with a false identity. How he was chosen for the job in the Kremlin in the first place I never did know. I suspect he learned the trade during the war and followed it as an occupation later. When I became associated with him, he was from time to time given delicate film to process for the military or the government. The darkroom where we worked was in the basement of the Kremlin itself. Can you imagine—two Jews, one of them a Zionist, developing the Kremlin's pictures!"

"Incredible!" exclaimed the baron with a hearty laugh.

Joseph went on to explain about his own imprisonment after his affiliations were discovered, what Stoyidovich had done while he was gone, and that the old man had come to him only a year and a half ago and told him of the photos, asking him if he could get them into hands where they would be made public.

"He never told me exactly why he made the duplicates. I suppose something came over him that maybe someday he would be able to use them to help his people. He exposed the paper but kept them undeveloped for several years to avoid any chance of discovery. However, after I came back to work for him, after my release, he told me about them, and then, when I said I could help, he developed them and turned them over to me."

"But how did they possibly wind up in my father's hands?"

asked Ursula. "He told me about them when he was in Berlin last summer. If only we'd known it was you who had placed them in the underground in the first place."

Joseph smiled, but it was not a smile that contained much humor, for the realization of how close he had been to the rabbi was an irony that still carried a certain amount of pain when he thought of it.

"It's nearly impossible to convey to any of you who haven't been there," replied Joseph after a moment, "how secretive and fragmented everything is in the Soviet Union and how frightened everyone is—Jews and Christians more than anyone. The Communist regime has literally exterminated hundreds of thousands—some say millions—of Jews. Informants and traitors exist everywhere. One false step, one misspoken word, and for a handful of rubles someone will tell what he has heard to the KGB. So even within the Jewish and Christian communities there is suspicion, and most remain tightlipped. There are many underground organizations, linked but loosely, with caution guarding every movement. I had heard about the people of *The Rose* and that they were the likely ones to get the photographs out of Russia. So I arranged a meeting with a fellow who was supposed to be able to put them into their hands, met him late one foggy night in the middle of the Kamenny Bridge, and turned them over to him."

"That is when they came into my hands," said Sabina, picking up the tale. "After they reached him in Moscow, Rabbi Wissen and I met in Warsaw. He was disguised, and I knew he was worried. I was to take the photos back to Berlin and get them into Ursula's hands in West Berlin. She would then see that they were given to the proper authorities, who would know how best to use them."

"But you didn't!" now put in Ursula, laughing. "She became so secretive herself all of a sudden," she added to the others. "I didn't know what you were up to!"

Sabina laughed with delight.

"You see what effect you were having on me, Matthew?" she said. "As soon as I saw you again, I didn't know what to do about the photographs. Then before long, everything got crazy with the prison escape and the terrible accident."

"The one thing I want to know is," said the baron, "has anyone actually seen these photographs to know why they are so important and why they would have been so incriminating to the Communists?"

Joseph nodded. "I saw them. It was not a pretty sight, though I have to admit, I did not see why they would undertake a chase across half of Europe to retrieve them."

"I presume, then," added Thaddeus with a questioning tone, "that the photographs were lost or destroyed or left at your old home in Berlin?"

"Oh no," replied Sabina. "I finally gave them to Matthew before we went to rescue Papa."

"Wait a minute!" exclaimed Matthew suddenly. "Here we've been sitting here talking about them, and I am the one who's had them all this time! Sabina did give them to me, and I ought to still have them!"

Like a shot he was off to the basement, where the last few boxes still remained unpacked from the Imperial Hotel in Berlin of a year ago.

He did not return for perhaps ten minutes. Gradually the openmouthed silence around the table created by his abrupt departure gave way again to further dialogue between those remaining.

When he reentered the room from the hallway, Matthew's step was slow and heavy and an ashen look was spread over his face. He had clearly found the fatal photographs among his possessions and had just looked at them a moment earlier.

He sat down heavily.

"I'd never seen them before," he said. "Sabina just handed me an envelope and told me to put them where they would be safe. I never looked inside it until a moment ago."

He now passed them to Sabina's father, who recognized two of the faces at first glance. His countenance also went pale as death, as he in turn passed them to Thaddeus as they made their way slowly around the table.

Stunned, sickened silence was the inevitable and only possible reaction. A few gagged at the unmistakable sight.

A heap of naked bodies lay as high as the three men's heads who stood beside it, some of the victims so thin it appeared they had not eaten in months, all of them obviously dumped where they lay in grotesque readiness for their final burial. To one side sat a small bulldozer, and an open pit yawned ready to receive them behind. A road sign in the distance indicated that Moscow lay fifty-seven kilometers away. A single word, in Russian script, had been written across the bottom of the negative. The three men standing beside the pile with their rifles all wore grisly and hideous smiles.

The second photo was a close-up of the men who had apparently with pride and satisfaction committed the heinous deed. The one, clearly recognizable even with slightly more hair and a trimmer figure, was Nikita Khrushchev. The man beside him none knew. The third—recognized faintly by both Sabina and Lola, who had each seen him only a time or two, but whose evil grin was known instantly by Baron von Dortmann—was Emil Korsch.

"What is that word down at the bottom?" asked Matthew.

"*Jews,*" answered Joseph softly.

The silence that followed in the chalet lasted for several minutes.

What was there to say? Three of those present shared the blood of the victims. And the rest, as children of God, shared their heritage. Their fate was the global scourge of the century.

"It all makes sense now," sighed Matthew at length. "These photographs on the front pages of the world's newspapers would positively destroy Khrushchev's public relations propaganda about tolerance within the Soviet Union."

"What will you do with them, Matthew?" asked Sabina.

"I don't know," he sighed again. "I don't see that I have much choice but to turn them over to the State Department or take them to the president personally. They did come into my hands when I was employed as a representative of the U.S. government, so it seems I have that obligation, as well as a responsibility to the people who sacrificed so much so that the plight of Jews in Russia could be known to the world."

"What about the other men?" asked Thaddeus.

"Emil Korsch," murmured the baron, a shiver passing through him.

"Where does he fit in?"

"I saw him once in our office in East Berlin," commented Lola. "That was several years ago, and that was not the name he used."

"My path and his crossed twice—many, many years ago," sighed the baron. "Neither was a pleasant encounter."

"Does anyone know what's become of him since?" asked Thaddeus.

"I'm all but certain I heard his voice in the cemetery the night of the escape," said Sabina.

Matthew recalled the gruesome scene at the cemetery and the subsequent news release indicating the killing of a KGB official, but it had not been a name he recognized. He wondered if there could be any connection with Korsch, but he said nothing.

The unraveling of the trail of the long-sought photographs was now nearly complete. The mystery of the rabbi's treasured box, however, remained. Alas, Emil Korsch would never see it, nor get to the bottom of that mystery.

That would be reserved for others who, in the fullness of time as appointed by God, would again lay eyes on the holy stones of Jewish antiquity.

❦ 120 ❦
New and Sacred Vows

A warm autumn sun shone down brilliantly over the grassy expanse of meadow next to the two-hundred-year-old church in the picturesque Bavarian village of Uelstenberg.

The Alps towering behind the cluster of quaint homes, farmhouses, barns, and shops contained snow throughout the year, and now, as winter made its approach, had received several new blankets already. The days were shortening too, but the midday sun yet held warmth enough for the very special occasion taking place in the village today.

Matthew and Sabina had decided to hold their small wedding ceremony in the side yard of the small but agedly magnificent building, the nearest church to the McCallum chalet several kilometers higher up the mountain slopes. The moment she had beheld the setting on their first horseback ride, Sabina had declared to Matthew that this was the spot she wanted to be married.

"Why do you think I brought you here!" he had said, with a smile. "I'd been thinking the very same thing."

As the few guests and new village acquaintances now began to seat themselves in the few rows of chairs that had been set in a semicircle facing in the direction of the mountains, they beheld a most exquisite panorama that no sea-dweller could imagine—augmented by sounds and fragrances found exclusively in the midst of such pure mountain air—to accompany the holy and happy event.

To their right stood the church, behind which rested in peace the mortal remains of the villagers who had gone on to their reward. The grave markers of these faithful, along with the clear antiquity of the stone-and-timber church, lent a solemn quietness, more from ambience than from actuality, to the occasion, notwithstanding the tones from the bell tower overhead and the reminder that the sacrament of marriage was deeply rooted in spiritual truth and in the most ancient traditions of men.

Toward the left rose the mountains, their outlines of white showing clear against a gorgeous blue expanse of the noon sky. A few stray billows of cloud, as if mirroring the snowcapped peaks, floated leisurely around overhead, showing no purpose in their motion, however, for there was little wind. Had it been July, the heat would have been great. In late October, the temperature could not have been more ideal.

The music from the mouths of the last few birds of autumn made chorus with a few barely discernible high buzzes of insects. In the distance, the far-off tinkling of the soprano and alto bells that hung from the necks of wandering grey alpine cattle mingled in appealing dissonance with the tenor and bass clangs now sounding from the resonant chimes in the tower above the church.

A subtle aroma invaded every nostril that paused long enough to reflect upon it, though the ones raised in the place could not have detected it had they tried, for it was the only air they had ever known. It was the clean odor of highness, the fragrance of mountain atmosphere. It was actually an overall *sense* more than a smell, a feeling of cleanness, of open space that lifted to the very heavens, of purity. Of such must surely have been the air God gave his man and his woman to breathe in the Garden of Genesis, oxygen from the King's Fountain, where life originates.

The most overpowering sensation of the day, however, was something only a few of those present would have been capable of affixing a name to. It was an awareness as equally undefinable and equally ethereal as the fragrance of purity—the intuitive perception that God himself, the Creator of mountains and fragrances, birds, music, love, and snow all together, was himself the presiding Presence over this small ceremony.

Those four in particular—the bride and groom and their two fathers—who were most keenly cognizant of it radiated a light of peace from their very countenances, which could not have derived from any other source than this divine Presence which was not only *over* all on this day but *in* them as well.

Indeed, in this setting beneath the clouds and the snow, under this air of purity, and in the midst of this holy Presence, only the color white would do, and it was certainly the color of the day. All around sat stands and baskets of flowers, mostly white. An abundance of white roses had been brought in from the city for the occasion.

Matthew and his father stood in front of the small gathering with the minister of the church, whose friendship both had cultivated since first relocating to Bavaria. To the minister's right stood a tall, somewhat slender woman whose life had not contained many smiles, but who now beamed from being accorded the honor of sharing this moment with her new friend. Indeed, the smiles on Lola Reinhardt's countenance were coming with greater frequency these days, and the latent beauty that exists in all the women of God's making was beginning to make itself known.

In the front row sat two honored guests—Sabina's aunt from Switzerland, beside whom sat cousin Brigitte. Sabina's heart was delighted that she had come all the way from Berlin and was hopeful that perhaps a true relationship might hereafter be able to form as a result of this visit.

A small portable pump organ had been brought out of the

church and stood to one side, and now began to play a most magnificent rendition of the largo from Dvorak's "New World" Symphony. Its sound seemed soft, almost swallowed up in the vastness of the sky and the mountains and the steeple of the church inside of which it normally gave its services, yet the majestic sounds added to the solemn celebratory mood of the day.

From somewhere behind the corner of the church now slowly walked Sabina and her father, Baron Heinrich von Dortmann. Sabina was attired simply in a reasonably plain white ankle-length dress with a pale blue ribbon for a belt, which blue accented the depths of her eyes to perfection. All the years of counting pennies had made Sabina almost too practical. Though Matthew would have spared no expense on a dress, and though her aunt would have enjoyed nothing better than to have had one made for her, Sabina's final choice was simple, though nonetheless gorgeous, in its design. A matching ribbon wound about small white flowers and leaves, forming a dainty wreath set into the lovely strands of her yellowish blonde hair. She carried a bouquet of white and green, with a white rose in the center, surrounded with white baby's breath and green ferns.

As Matthew watched them advance steadily but ever so slowly closer, his heart swelled.

How could he have ever dreamed that such a day would come to him! In the short month and a half, East Germany and the months he had spent there and all the events leading up to their daring escape had begun to seem like a distant dream that had happened to someone else.

It seemed, he thought to himself as he gazed upon his bride now approaching him on her father's arm, that he had lived three or four lifetimes already . . . and yet the best was yet to come!

～⁓～

In an ancient and distant land, far away and south beyond the Mediterranean, another ceremony was taking place on the same day, at that same hour—not by accident but by joint human and divine appointment, the hour as a result of the former, the occasion as a result of the latter.

A more different setting from the other one could not imagine.

The land, though hilly, was flat when compared with the Alps. The terrain of the country beyond the walls of the ancient city shone brown and arid under the merciless sun, and the temperature of the air everywhere was hot. About the only similarity between the two settings existed in the spacious blue vault overhead, for indeed the same clear sky overarched them both.

One thing was unmistakably the same, however. That was the sense that God's presence had settled over the gathering of those come to celebrate his faithfulness in the lives of a man and a woman who could certainly not be called youths, but who, in the economy of eternity, had yet many years to enjoy together.

The people known as the Jews had always possessed a gift for ceremony. But the celebration in which they were about to participate would register a permanent mark in the minds of many of those in attendance.

For outward appearance, a passerby might have taken the outdoor setting for a traditional Wednesday-afternoon Jerusalem wedding. Though most had been apprised of the uniqueness of this day, a few of the guests might yet remain under the illusion that this would be no different from many such weddings they had attended. They would not, however, remain under it for long. This wedding fit neither Jewish synagogue nor Christian church, and therefore a neutral site had been selected that the ceremony might incorporate both past heritage and present faith into a unity of celebration.

The wedding canopy signifying the bridal chamber, or *huppah*, had been set up early in the day and now stood in front of those who were slowly beginning to gather. The bride was perhaps older than most Jewish young women on their special day. But she who was the center of today's attention had waited twenty-three years to consummate the vows of her betrothal and was all the lovelier and more beautiful as a result of her lengthy period of steadfast waiting.

Neither did the groom have friends to accompany him, nor a father's house in the city from which to make the traditional procession. But he had waited the same length of time to honor the covenant of the betrothal and was not now as concerned with ancient ritual as with present reality.

The enchanting fragrance of hyacinth was everywhere. Containers of force-grown bulbs had been brought in from nearly every florist and nursery in the city, and the mystery of their perfume hung like a mist in the warm atmosphere of the place.

~∽∾∾~

Even as friends, loved ones, and especially her mother and sister Gisela beheld Ursula's quiet beauty under the Jerusalem sun, far to the north Ursula's best friend was about to become a wife.

"Dearly beloved," began the minister of Uelstenberg in German, "you have come today to witness and celebrate . . ."

As he spoke, Sabina and Matthew gazed into one another's eyes with sparkling smiles of such depth that their lips did not even move in consequence. When the minister had concluded his brief opening remarks, the baron spoke his patriarchal blessing and gave his daughter's hand symbolically to the young man he had loved as a son many years before this day.

The minister now turned to Matthew.

"Do you, Matthew, take this woman . . ."

Matthew's mind returned to the day he had first seen sixteen-year-old Sabina von Dortmann bounding up gaily to her father's side. Then had come the introduction that had changed his life forever . . . the look into her eyes . . . the conversation that followed. Then the visit to *Lebenshaus*, exploring the house, the ride, the broken leg, dancing with her at the Schmundt estate, the thunderstorm, the yellow roses, the china box, the underground room.

In but the fleeting split seconds of an instant, not his whole life passed through his brain, but his whole life with Sabina.

It truly had been four lifetimes. The first years at *Lebenshaus* when they were young. The joyous interlude of happy times last summer. The months in East Germany. And now this!

But already the minister had turned toward Sabina.

"Do you, Sabina, take this man . . ."

Sabina's thoughts were full of *das Märchen*. What a romantic her Matthew had been—the horses hidden in the wood, the mysterious picnic basket, the poem lying in the bottom of it!

Yet he had continued to shower her with still more surprises—the horse-drawn carriage, the ball, the message delivered by the little boy, and the red rose.

The poem now carried even more meaning than it had then, and even as the minister was speaking, the verses flitted through Sabina's brain:

> *It is said that love is like a rose*
> > *that grows so sweet, so pure within the heart.*
> *But love is also like a thorn*
> > *that savagely tears my heart apart.*
>
> *Happy time once spent with you gave joy*
> > *and brought the rose in me to bloom.*
> *But then the years apart bore pain—*
> > *like thorns, my memory they pierced too soon.*
>
> *Why then does love, first known,*
> > *within itself such tears and sorrow conceal?*
> *Perhaps because for every rose, the thorns increase*
> > *the deeper splendor the lovely scent reveals.*

She had said the words to him many times last summer, and now her eyes, swimming in liquid love, said it to him in her mind once again. *Oh, Matthew . . . how can you have made me so happy!*

It had all been a lovely fairy tale . . . today most of all!

She was through speaking, and now the minister began to lead Matthew through the words of his promise.

"I, Matthew, take you, Sabina, to be my wedded wife, to have and to hold, from this day forward, for better for worse, for richer for poorer, in sickness and in health, to love and to cherish, until we are parted by death. With God as my witness, I give you this promise."

As his son pledged his love to the lady who would be his wife, Thaddeus McCallum thought back to the night in the middle of the Atlantic when he and Matthew had reflected on their reactions to Baron von Dortmann and the many issues of spirituality they suddenly found themselves thinking of for the first time.

It was, in many ways, the beginning of their adult relationship and their joint quest for truth. In the years since, he and Matthew had enjoyed a father-son friendship accorded to but few men. It had made his life rich beyond words.

Who could have told, thought Thaddeus, where that quest would ultimately lead them? It had led them here, to this very day, to the point of joining, not only the faith the baron had shared with them, but the very ties and roots of family itself with the baron and his daughter.

"I, Sabina, take you, Matthew, to be my wedded husband, to have and to hold, from this day forward, for better for worse, for richer for poorer, in sickness and in health, to love and to cherish, until we are parted by death. With God as my witness, I give you this promise."

Listening to his daughter recite her vows to her future husband, Heinrich von Dortmann's memories were filled with his wife, Sabina's mother. Surely he could be forgiven if his memories strayed from the present to the day when he and Marion had stood beside one another and pledged their own youthful love.

Sabina looked more like Marion with every passing year, the baron thought with a smile, and the resemblance brought no sadness to his heart, only a great and quiet joy.

He missed Marion, but he did not mourn her. His heart was too large to grieve over something their Father had given them the privilege of sharing as a portion of their love—separation.

Their years together had been fewer than he might have enjoyed, but full and rich . . . and complete. Heinrich von Dortmann was not a man who allowed regrets to take root in the soil of his heart. They had bid one another their farewells on the road outside Fürstendorf many years ago. The thought of the agony in poor Marion's eyes as he had whispered his final words of love to her could not help but smite the baron's memory now and then with a stab of pain. But he knew she understood better now what he had been compelled to do, and the thought comforted him.

He was happy now to love Marion by loving the daughter of their union for both of them. And now he had a son to love on Marion's behalf as well!

The baron's focus returned to the present. The recitations had come to an end.

When the vows of bride and groom were completed, the minister passed the communion cup and bread to Matthew. In a departure from the normal marriage tradition, Matthew took it from his hand and served it first to Thaddeus, standing beside him, then took a few steps toward the front row where sat Baron von Dortmann, where he served him the elements in like fashion. He returned to serve Sabina, then partook himself.

Not only did the cup and loaf carry deep spiritual significance to each of the four, but the act of honoring the two fathers who meant so much to the young couple was not lost on any of those who observed it and saw the love and respect in Matthew's eyes as he stood before his two elders.

∽◦∾

Meanwhile, the rabbi spoke the traditional Jewish blessing over the wine. Then followed the reading of the *ketubbah,* the document recording the groom's promise to respect and maintain his bride, as well as itemizing the dowry agreed upon by Rabbi Wissen.

Now the minister, who was conducting the joint ceremony alongside the rabbi, moved to the center, where he faced the beaming bride and groom.

"Do you, Ursula, take this man . . ."

Ursula remembered how lonely she had felt, how she had been almost to the point of removing her ring of betrothal. Oh, how thankful she was that God had been watching over them more perfectly than she had any idea. The long years alone had now vanished into the past and seemed, if anything, a small price to pay for her present happiness.

"Do you, Joseph, take this woman . . ."

For many years Joseph had felt like giving up all thought of ever seeing Ursula again.

Incredible as it now seemed to the eyes of his new faith, God had been with him all the time, even though he himself—he now realized, thanks to the brothers at Bialystok—never really knew him at all.

What a faithful, loving, patient, and altogether generous Father Yahweh indeed was!

The moment their Christian vows were completed, Joseph placed the marriage ring carefully on Ursula's right forefinger.

The rabbi now came forward again and served Joseph from the glass, who then gave it to Ursula to drink. He handed it back to the rabbi, who now took a few steps back.

The assembly grew strangely quiet when the couple turned to the minister again, took a small bite of bread followed by wine from a silver wine goblet, from which bride and groom both partook. This act, symbolizing the completion of their Jewish faith with the personal acceptance of their Messiah's sacrifice, came after the traditional Jewish cup for good reason, and both Ursula and Joseph had prayed together that the significance of the order would not be lost on those witnessing it.

"Now that Joseph and Ursula have given themselves to each other by these solemn vows before God, in fulfillment of their betrothal of so long ago, and have shown their affection and trust by the exchanging of rings and by joining hands, I now pronounce that they are husband and wife, in the name of almighty God, Creator of heaven and earth. Therefore, what God has joined together, let no man nor woman separate."

Though all had been prepared ahead of time for this most unusual mingling of Jewish and Christian marriage ceremonies, there were numbered those staunch Jewish traditionalists, a few of Rabbi Wissen's closest friends, in whose hearts rose a few flutters of offense. But the rabbi had said, when he had made public the news of his daughter's decision, that if he as her father could be open enough to welcome both son-in-law and Christianity into his home with open arms, he hoped his friends could find it within their hearts to do likewise. Most of them, therefore, did their best to honor his wishes, if only for his sake, not because they agreed with him. The years in Russia, many observed, had perhaps made him a little more open than was healthy. In truth, it was not the years in Russia that had exercised this effect on him, but a year in Germany during the war with the very man who, like himself, was giving away a daughter on this same day.

Had the ceremony come several months earlier, the gathered crowd would surely have contained two men who, upon close examination, seemed utterly out of place. Their presence would not have been for the purpose of sharing the couple's joy, but rather for keeping their eyes on the bride's father, as they had been doing for some time. But word had managed to come to them from the north that their superior had been killed in a bizarre incident in Berlin. Never knowing for certain what they were even looking for, they, therefore, had packed their bags, broken off surveillance on the rabbi, bid good riddance to this arid land, and returned empty-handed to Moscow.

The silence lasted but a few seconds more.

The couple now turned from the minister back to the rabbi. Carefully he placed the glass of Jewish tradition onto the ground. With great energy, Ursula and Joseph stomped it to bits.

"Mazel tov!" shouted the congregation of witnesses, and within what seemed like seconds the music and dancing began.

How must the angels have been rejoicing with them to see, at the center of a hundred celebrating Jews in the holy city of Jerusalem, a bride and groom in whose hearts the Spirit of God's Son dwelt.

Truly had salvation come to the house of Wissen and its friends!

∽◦◦◦∽

Far away, the words had just sounded in the happy ears of those seated beneath the Alps:

"I now pronounce you man and wife!"

Matthew bent down and kissed Sabina gently on the lips. Their eyes were closed but for a moment. When they opened them, they held each other's gaze for a second, then smiled.

If the previous summer now seemed but a dream to Sabina, today was certainly no fairy tale!

"Ladies and gentlemen," concluded the minister, "may I have the joy and honor of presenting to you Mr. and Mrs. Matthew McCallum!"

The bride and groom walked beaming through the small assembly, music sounding triumphantly from the organ behind and the church bells above them.

There were the expectant children gathered behind the seats. From his pocket Matthew now produced the handful of coins that in the next instant, by German tradition, were flying through the air to the delightful screams of the youngsters scampering in all directions to retrieve them.

Matthew and Sabina's eyes had only an instant to meet again. But that look said all there was to say.

The next moment they were swarmed about by fathers, friends, and well wishers.

The ancient bells of the church pealed out a resonant blessing of completion, the echoes lifting up and away toward the snowy mountains overlooking the scene.

As the ringing gradually died away in the lofty and expansive distance, those with ears of the heart to discern it might have detected hints of melody carrying on a little longer, and from a higher origin, than could be accounted for by the dying, metallic resonance of the church tower.

In truth, the faint melody came from no bells at all.

It was the sound of angels singing.

❧ 121 ❧

The Busy Kitchen

Winter came round again to the Bavarian alpine village of Obenammersfeld. Its cold this year, however, only added to the warmth in the hearts of those residing at the Chalet of Life just up the slope from the village.

Snow had fallen two days before, and though the sun had returned and the sky promised to remain clear well past the holiday, it would certainly be a white Christmas throughout Bavaria.

Baron von Dortmann had walked down into the village as was generally his custom on most mornings. Usually he and Thaddeus came together, but Thaddeus was too busy today and asked the baron to pick up the delivery that would be waiting for them.

He entered the shop, setting the little bell above the door a-tinkling as always.

"Good morning, Frau Rendt!" he said cheerfully, greeting the baker's wife.

"You are alone this morning, Heinrich."

"Ah yes—Thaddeus and Matthew are busy with their Christmas Eve preparations. They gave Sabina and me strict orders to stay out of the kitchen."

"A pastry just for yourself then?" said the plump woman, opening the case in which stood her fresh-baked delicacies of the day.

"Oh no! You do not think Thaddeus would miss out on your specialty simply because he is unable to join me? No, no, Frau Rendt, he gave me even *more* strict orders to bring his back with me!"

The woman beamed with pleasure. In actual fact, there were so many homemade Christmas goodies already around the house that they hardly needed her pastries today, but neither man would have dreamed of disappointing the good lady now, on the day before Christmas. She had come to nearly set her clock by the daily visits of the two men and received no little satisfaction from their raves.

Wishing her a Merry Christmas and conveying his best to her husband also, the baron left the shop, stopped by the post office for the mail, then began the walk back up the hill to the chalet that was now his home.

Most of the villagers had learned through one means or another that he was, in fact, a baron and that he had spent some seventeen years in prison for no more serious crime than living his faith. None called him *Baron*, however. From his first days here he had let it be known that he would be known only by his name. He possessed no honor above all God's children, and he would not be called by a title that seemed to indicate such. This was hardest to get used to on the part of those who knew him best. Thaddeus was comfortable using his given name. Sabina, of course, would always call him *Papa*. And Matthew he allowed—but only him—to continue calling him *Baron*.

He was on the best terms with the simplest men and women of the village, and even those down into the valley and up the mountains behind them, and spent at least half his days visiting with some one or another of them. He loved nothing more than poking his head into the carpenter's shop in the next village, or traipsing all the way up the mountain with one of the farmers, helping him look for a cow that had strayed off. Even though he put on no airs and rarely spoke of spiritual things to them unless asked, nearly all recognized him for who he was. When he was not present, there were those who called him a saint.

With the mail and bakery bag in one hand, the baron now made for home, munching happily on the pastry of Herr Rendt's that had become his favorite, chuckling to himself as he thought of the smile on the good woman's face when he told her that Thaddeus had insisted on his pastry as always. It was so easy to make others happy, he thought to himself. It was remarkable people did not expend more energy upon it.

He entered the house, calling out to Thaddeus concerning the delivery of his parcel from the village, then went into the living room, where Sabina was placing some last-minute ornaments on the tree.

"Are we still banned from the kitchen, Daughter?" he asked.

"For another hour is all, or so Matthew promised."

"It must be a sore trial for you to be deprived of it on such a festive day as this."

"Don't worry, Papa," laughed Sabina. "I intend to make full use of it this afternoon, and tomorrow!"

Just then Matthew appeared, apron gathered about his waist, flour smeared on his face.

"Whatever are the two of you up to in there!" exclaimed the baron.

"Fulfilling a dream," replied Matthew, continuing on past them and down the hall. He reappeared two minutes later, bearing a cookbook in his hand, then disappeared again behind the closed door of the kitchen.

True to their word, after an hour or so the two men opened the door and emerged, a multitude of smells following them out into the rest of the house.

"We're done!" they announced.

"The kitchen is all yours, Sabina," added Matthew, "although if you don't mind my company, I'll clean up the mess we made and wash our bowls and pans while you are about your business."

"I'd love the company," replied Sabina, jumping up.

The two returned to the kitchen, while Thaddeus took a seat opposite the baron.

"Whew!" he sighed.

"I have a delivery for you from Frau Rendt, Thaddeus," said the baron.

"I thought you just might! And one for yourself?"

The baron chuckled.

"It was a rather short-lived parcel. Unfortunately, it did not survive the strenuous walk home . . . sustenance for the rigors of the climb, you know!"

"I think I understand," rejoined Thaddeus, peeking into the bag the baron handed him.

"My nose tells me that our good friend Rendt is up to his usual quality," he said, removing the pastry.

"Indeed, I think you shall find it so!"

The two men laughed like boys as Thaddeus dug his teeth into the soft sweet roll, the baron relishing his friend's enjoyment of it as much as he had his own.

"Come up to the office with me while you're eating," said the baron. "I want to show you something I wrote this morning."

"This morning—when?" asked Thaddeus, following him down the hall.

"I was up early—about five."

"No sleeping in even on Christmas Eve?"

"I couldn't sleep."

"Doesn't that brain of yours ever rest?"

"No. Besides, I've heard *you* in the office many nights long after *I'm* in bed. You know as well as I do that your brain is just as active as mine."

The two men laughed again, then sat down while the baron handed Thaddeus the page upon which he'd been writing.

For the next two hours they found themselves discussing the relative merits of grace versus accountability with regard to the impact each exercised upon character development. It was well after noon before the two young people heard from them again.

∽ 122 ∽
Chalet Christmas Revisited

As the day progressed, a steady supply of food began to appear from out of the kitchen.

First there had come several new batches of Christmas cookies to add to those Sabina had already baked earlier in the week. The apple strudel that had been a product of the morning's effort of the McCallum duo sat beside their cream-and-chocolate cake, which showed finger marks—obviously men's—around the edges. More cookies continued to appear, batch after batch, until there was easily a three-week supply.

By midafternoon Sabina's own labors began to show, and as day gradually gave way to evening, many last-minute wrappings and mysterious disappearings and goings-on added yet another element of excitement to the day.

At some point during the afternoon, two new enigmatic—but not altogether secretive—long, slender packages appeared, no one knew how, under the tree.

Matthew and Thaddeus had asked to be allowed to prepare the Christmas Eve supper, and now, after 6:00—with the sounds of Bing Crosby's Christmas album sounding softly in the background, and a half dozen candles adding to the Christmassy atmosphere—the four were at last seated around the table to enjoy the traditional McCallum Christmas Eve supper of blintz pancakes. One tall glass pitcher held frothy homemade eggnog, while another stood ready for consumption later in the evening, in front of the fireplace, while they each opened one special gift.

All four looked at each other with radiant smiles.

"When we were alone together last year," said Matthew, "Dad and I spent nearly the whole day of Christmas Eve in the kitchen. We made many of the same things as we have today. We knew we could not possibly eat everything, but it was a way to remember our women without becoming despondent that they were not here to share the season with us. In the kitchen we were able to laugh and enjoy thoughts of how my mother might have done it, or what she would think of the mess we were making, or how you, Sabina, or *your* mother would prepare the old German-style strudel we were attempting to fabricate from an old German cookbook."

"We spent the day making all kinds of goodies," added Thaddeus, "and then we got started on a great turkey dressing whose recipe my wife shared with me on our first Christmas together. Sometime during the day Matthew made the comment that the only thing that could make it all better was if the two of you could have been there to share it with us."

It was silent a moment. All realized the profound significance of the statement, and how wonderful it was that they *had* been brought together again.

"About a month ago, we started talking," Matthew went on, "about trying to recreate our efforts of last year so that we *could* share them with you. So that is what we have been doing today."

"As much as possible," said Thaddeus, "this is a McCallum Christmas, the way Rebecca and I used to celebrate it when Matthew was young, the pancakes, the eggnog, the turkey, the dressing, the cake, the cookies—"

He stopped and took in a deep breath, fighting the emotions that came with memories of his wife.

Thaddeus smiled sadly.

"Of course, all this only makes me miss her the more," he went on. "But there is a healing in it that perhaps is necessary for me. This is my way of bringing you, my new family, all the way into the deepest places of my life, a way of saying that yes, we remember the past, but we are able to rejoice in the present as well, and look to the future with joyful hearts."

"Amen!" put in the baron softly.

"So, with all that said," Thaddeus concluded, "we are now prepared to offer our Christmas toast, aren't we, Matt?"

Matthew nodded.

The two men raised their glasses of eggnog. The baron and Sabina picked theirs up too, and now the four glasses gently sounded together as they met across the middle of the table.

"To the new family of our present . . . and our future!" said Thaddeus, looking first to his daughter-in-law with a smile, and then to the baron. "Words cannot begin to tell the two of you how much Matthew and I love you, and how grateful to God we are that he brought us into your lives so many years ago, and preserved this friendship . . . this *love* between us, all this time."

He took a satisfying drink from his glass, as did each of the others.

"Delicious!" said Sabina.

"Just like mom's, huh, Dad?" added Matthew with a smile, after he had downed a third of the glass.

"I think we did all right, Matt," agreed Thaddeus. "We have, in addition to the other things that were traditional in our family, added a German strudel in honor of *Lebenshaus* for tonight's consumption. It will no doubt not be the equal of your Marion's. But we made one last year, thinking of you in your absence from us, and therefore we wanted to bake another this year, to honor your *presence*."

"It is *we* who are honored, Thaddeus," said the baron.

"Next year I hope you will allow us to treat you to a *Lebenshaus* Christmas," said Sabina, already with anticipation in her voice.

"I was about to suggest that very thing," rejoined Thaddeus. "However, if what I smelled when you were in the kitchen this afternoon is any indication, as well as what I have seen over there on the dessert table . . . we will not have to wait until next year for all of it!"

Sabina laughed. "Well, that is true!"

"May I too make a toast?" asked the baron.

"By all means."

"Then let me reciprocate by expressing how much we too love you." He paused just briefly and a look of melancholy came over his face. "We all have heartaches," he went on, "that the Lord uses to help us mature. Christmas was always special at *Lebenshaus*, was it not, Sabina?"

The baron glanced over at his daughter, and she returned his smile.

"My dear Marion has been on my mind today too. The holiday season is always a time for looking back. But, as you said, this particular day is a time for looking ahead with gladness as well."

He took a great breath, as if consciously exhaling any melancholy that might remain, so as to make all the rest of the season filled with happy *new* memories.

"Ever since our first meeting with the two of you," the baron went on, "my heart suspected there was something special our Father intended to accomplish between us, which, though it has taken many years, he certainly has done. Obviously the radiance on my daughter's face at now being known as Sabina McCallum is evidence of her happiness. For my part, let me simply say that I cannot imagine a lovelier or more peaceful setting than this in which for the Lord to allow me to live these final years of my life. In all honesty I can say that I do not even miss *Lebenshaus* more than occasionally, and then only for fleeting moments. Nor could there be any other individuals on the face of the earth, except of course for Marion, that I could be happier spending those years with than the three of you—daughter, son, and dear friend."

"Thank you, Heinrich!" said Thaddeus. All four raised their glasses again.

"And now," he said buoyantly, rising from the table to begin his role as waiter for the supper, "we invite you to enjoy pancakes à la McCallum!"

∾⌒∾

When supper was over, they retired into the living room to enjoy the tree, the fire, and one another most of all.

"I find myself curiously reminded of an interesting parcel that lay under last year's tree," remarked Thaddeus as he took his seat. "It would seem there has been a revisitation of last Christmas in more ways than one!"

Pretending to ignore his comment, Sabina turned to Matthew.

"When did you receive the rose?" she asked.

"What was it, Dad—two or three days before Christmas?"

"Something like that."

"Why didn't you open it?"

"It was wrapped, like a Christmas package. So I just put it under the tree."

"And there the strange mystery parcel lay," added Thaddeus, "until its perfume began to add to the mystery and make us all the more curious."

"I finally opened it on Christmas Eve," said Matthew.

"You knew it was from me?"

"Of course. Who else knows I love roses . . . who else would have known the promise of the *pink* rose?"

Sabina smiled.

"I really had no idea you would do what you did," she said.

"No regrets, though?"

"Of course not! How many women find themselves actually rescued by a man who has come to sweep her away . . . and then marry her! I'm the luckiest woman alive."

They all laughed at the chivalrous account, then fell silent, staring into the fire.

Thaddeus had just added fresh logs after rising from the table, so the flames coming from the hearth were lively, bright, and crackling. The room was warm and cheery.

Matthew was the first to rise.

"Well, now it is my turn to offer the first Christmas gift of the evening, and perhaps reciprocate from last year."

He walked to the tree, stooped down, and picked up one of the long, slender packages that had appeared just that afternoon, turned and handed it to Sabina, then knelt by her side.

She gazed into his eyes. They smiled. Both knew the mystery was not contained in the content, only the color.

Matthew pointed so she would know which end to open.

Slowly Sabina unwrapped the paper, then pulled out the stem of the rose they all knew was inside, until a small white bud, just beginning to open, was revealed.

"Matthew . . . it's beautiful."

"Every rose we exchange has a story, you know," he said.

"Of course. They all tell the one secret, but in different ways. What is *this* rose's story?"

"The same as every rose's—that I love you, and will *always* love you."

"Why white?"

"Because when Paul talks about how a husband is to love his wife as Christ loved the church, it is always with terms of purity—washing and cleansing and loving her so much that he is able to present her to the Lord holy and without spot or blemish. Paul calls it a mystery . . . a profound mystery, and I can think of no better symbol for it than a rose, full of the secrets of love. Even though in my eyes you are pure and radiant already—the most wonderfully radiant woman in the world!—as your husband I am committed to loving you in that way, giving myself to you as Jesus gave himself for us."

He leaned forward and kissed her gently.

"That is the secret of this white rose—that I will love you, my radiant and spotless bride—for the rest of my life, and that I will *try* to love you in all ways as the Lord would have me."

"Oh, Matthew, you are going to make me cry!" Sabina laughed. "But then you make me cry nearly *every* time you give me a rose. You are such a romantic!"

It was silent a moment, though the fire continued to add its mood to the background of the occasion.

"I believe it is my turn now," said Sabina, rising and approaching the tree. She retrieved the slender parcel she had placed there and handed it to Matthew, also now kneeling beside him. He had given her one of this hue earlier, but she had not yet, until this day, found the perfect opportunity to reciprocate the deepest and most profound message the rose has to tell.

He opened it and pulled out the long stem, at the end of which stood a perfectly formed rose of such deep red as Matthew had rarely seen.

He glanced over to Sabina with a smile. Their eyes met.

There was no need for explanation. They both knew the secret of *this* rose . . . and shared it in their hearts.

∽ 123 ∽
Knotted Strands

Christmas day was as memorable and peaceful as Christmas Eve—festive and happy and full of the good cheer of food, conversation, and song.

An unexpected snow fell the following day. It was not sufficient to make them snowbound, but the holiday spirit had lingered, and no one felt inclined to go out.

The baron began to worry about Frau Rendt by the day after that and therefore made it the business of the morning to pay another visit and to inquire about the Christmas she and her husband had had, as well as to conduct his usual business with her. Thaddeus had been working in the office all morning, however, under some "inspiration," as he said, and begged the baron to secure the goods once again on his behalf.

As the baron set out, he glanced around at the large house with a distinct feeling of pleasure. The chalet that was now Baron von Dortmann's home, which Thaddeus had managed to purchase from Frau Braun in München, was in no way a step down in his estimation from the expansiveness of his own *Lebenshaus.*

Indeed, he had spent so long in a tiny prison cell that this now seemed more spacious and luxurious than he had ever dreamed of enjoying again. There was even space for gardens and enough cultivatable land around the house for a multitude of growing things. The two McCallums' previous efforts of a year ago quickly began to be added to, and the baron's influence was apparent within a month.

The other three were eagerly looking forward to the following spring with huge anticipation, wondering what would be in the baron's mind by then to do with the place!

There had really never been any question that they would all remain at the chalet together.

Too many separations had existed for too many years to rely on mere *visits* with fathers now that Sabina and Matthew were married. Even had one of the older men been inclined to worry overmuch about the privacy of the newlyweds, neither had the desire to be any place in the world other than with their shared son and daughter.

Owing to the unusual fact that both men had outlived their wives, the living arrangement took on a decided and unique patriarchal flavor rather than the more typical matriarchal tone of many homes. None of the three men of the place, however, would have consented to a thing not absolutely to Sabina's liking. In all ways she was the mistress of the house, and they were husband, father, and father-in-law—devoted as puppy dogs to her service.

All three positively adored her.

Sabina and Matthew took up residence together in the lower portions of the large house, where, in addition to their own bedroom, they converted one of the larger bedrooms into a sitting room of their own.

Thaddeus and Baron von Dortmann each had a bedroom of his own on the upper level. That left the last two bedrooms as offices—one to be shared by the two men, the other by Matthew and Sabina.

Following the October 24 wedding, Matthew had taken his bride to the United States for a lengthy honeymoon, one of whose highlights included a visit to the Oval Office of the White House. Their interview with the president was not lengthy but was sufficient for JFK to persuade Matthew to rejoin the diplomatic corps in Germany.

Matthew had agreed, as long as most of his duties could be carried out from Bavaria, with only a trip now and then to Bonn or Berlin. He had years to make up for, that, he said, no job was worth sacrificing for.

Kennedy understood. That would be no problem. Matthew could work out the details with State. Would his father want to continue with his duties as well?

Matthew would discuss the matter with him, he said.

They returned to Germany in the second week of November, and the four had spent the most happy six weeks imaginable together since, getting completely accustomed to the place, setting up their offices, making plans for Christmas, planting what could be gotten in before the onset of winter, and enjoying chats around the fireplace in the evening most of all.

As soon as the Christmas holidays were over, Matthew was scheduled to commence his new post as a liaison between the Bonn government and the U.S. State Department on January 15, 1963.

After reflection, Thaddeus decided to resign from his obligations to Washington. It was time, he said, to think about other things. Both he and Baron von Dortmann had much to write about, and it could not be denied neither was getting any younger. The two had spent the weeks while the young people were gone talking about so many things, and they had already hatched a collaborative book idea. There were also Thaddeus's memoirs and the baron's journals to be gone through. There was far too much to be done, Thaddeus had concluded, to imagine continuing his diplomatic career a day longer.

Lebenshaus of the south, in fact, came in time to occupy quite a different function than had its predecessor in the north. Far from a house of solitude and retreat, indeed the McCallum/Dortmann chalet became such a beehive of activity—with writing and study projects, and constant brainstorming about new endeavors— that a visitor assuming it to be a think tank for some publishing company would not have been far off the mark.

Thaddeus did eventually complete his memoirs, though they were certainly much different from what he had imagined when he had undertaken the project. Using twentieth-century politics as a skeleton, they contained more spiritual observations than diplomatic or political. It was not a best-seller, though it received modest acclaim in the circles where such books are recognized and appreciated.

Baron von Dortmann never did as much with his journals as he had always anticipated. Once out of prison, his own past began to lose the interest it had once had in his eyes. He took more and more to devotional writing, chiefly on topics relating to the nature and character of God.

Notwithstanding the toll his years in prison had exacted upon him, his rugged constitution and unstained conscience served him well. He lived many more years, long enough to take his grandchildren in his lap and tell them of Germany before the wars, even long enough to see them nearly grown.

His writings were eventually published in a series of small

volumes that, in the eyes of those who read and reread and reread them, became classics in the full sense of the word.

Matthew and Sabina, however, did treasure the journals of Sabina's father, and it became one of Matthew's lifetime dreams to find some means whereby to publish them. His work, however, continued to be demanding, and the dream remains yet unfulfilled.

Matthew and Sabina had a son and daughter.

The son they named Thaddeus Heinrich after the grandfathers; the daughter, Marion Rebecca, after the grandmothers.

Their two grandfathers, whom no youngsters could have ever loved more, called them Tad and Mary.

The marriage, perhaps from having incubated so long and begun so late, was strong and happily free of so many of the difficulties that plague younger couples.

Never did either Sabina or Matthew forget how much they loved one another and how grateful to God they were for preserving that love during all the years of their separation.

Hardly a day went by when they didn't remind one another of the secret of the rose.

❦

Author's Note

All the escapes from East to West Berlin documented in *Escape to Freedom* are based on factual incidents, including that in Part VI. An actual tunnel was dug under the wall into the Fischerstrasse cemetery by two husbands who had been separated from their wives when the wall went up. After getting their wives safely out, over a hundred more refugees made it safely through their tunnel in coming weeks, including some very young and very old East Germans. Eventually, however, after a mother and her young child had escaped, the youngster's tricycle was left behind at the gravesite. After some time, it began to arouse the suspicion of the *Vopos*. Coming closer to investigate, they discovered the tunnel. It was filled in and sealed off the following day.

~~~

About the Author

Californian Michael Phillips began his distinguished writing career in the 1970s. He came to widespread public attention in the early 1980s for his efforts to reacquaint the public with Victorian novelist George MacDonald. Phillips is recognized as the man most responsible for the current worldwide renaissance of interest in the once-forgotten Scotsman and one of the world's foremost experts of MacDonald. After beginning his work redacting and republishing the works of MacDonald, Phillips embarked on his own career writing fiction. Since that time he has written and cowritten 48 novels and it is primarily as a novelist that he is now known. His critically acclaimed books have been translated into eight foreign languages, have appeared on numerous best-seller lists, and have sold more than six million copies. Phillips is today considered by many as the heir apparent to the very MacDonald legacy he has worked so hard to promote in our time. Phillips is also the publisher of the magazine *Leben*, a periodical dedicated to bold thinking Christianity and the legacy of George MacDonald. Combining all categories that have made up his extremely diverse writing career, *Dream of Freedom* was Phillips' 100th published work. Phillips and his wife, Judy, make their home in Eureka, California. They also spend a great deal of time in Scotland where they are attempting to increase awareness of MacDonald's work.

*Be sure to look for the final book in the
Secret of the Rose series,
Dawn of Liberty.
Here is a sample from the first few pages of that book.*

∝∾∽

Prologue

In all his purposes for the world, the Creator allows time to help accomplish them.

Whether it be in an individual heart, in the relationships of a family, or in the history of a nation, time teaches, time heals, time strengthens, time deepens roots and gives perspective. For time is an essential element of growth, and a necessary catalyst for the development of maturity and wisdom.

The best things are never arrived at in haste. God is in no hurry; his plans are never rushed.

When he fashioned time, the Creator divided it into segments. Night and day became its measured portions. Months were marked by the sequences of the moon, and the years by repeating quarterly spans of changing climate. He made all things to grow according to these patterns, passing ever and again out of dormancy into fruitfulness and back again, repeating over and over the growth cycle of life's miracle.

Just as he created such natural phases to prescribe duration for growing things, he likewise defined by parallel intervals the progression of the earthly sojourn of his people.

The pilgrimage of one Baron Heinrich von Dortmann had now graduated through the fullness of its natural seasons. His days on this earth had been ones of learning, teaching, loving, and serving, that the bonds of his temporal life might in the end break into the freedom of eternal childness for which he had humbly prepared himself.

His God was not only his Creator but even more was his friend. His was a life whose single prayer was that he might know his God-friend more intimately, and that his life, his words, and his deeds might cause others to know him likewise. His was a life that must spread out, that must plant and nurture and reproduce, and which constantly poured itself into his wife and daughter first, and then all those around him.

He was a man who visibly evidenced the life-spreading, the life-giving, the life-creating character of the primary and foundational essence of the Trinity. For the purposes of the Creator are everywhere bound up in that highest aspect of his triune nature—Fatherhood.

The Fatherhood of God is one that must not merely create, it must continually imbue with *life,* it must generate his *Own* life.

In each tiniest corner of creation does the begetting of the Father's substance and being continue every instant, impregnating new generations of seeds and trees, flowers and grasses, animals and men, with that mysterious yet delicate potency . . . to *live!*

The flourishing fruitfulness of creating Fatherhood invisibly fills every molecule, forever passing itself on and on—every apple containing the seeds to produce ten new trees, each of which is capable of growing ten thousand new apples, which can each produce ten million more in their turn.

In all growing things does this miracle of reproduction and proliferation show us the Father's smiling face. "Look," he says, "look around you. Life is springing up everywhere—because I put *Myself* into all I touch, into every atom of the universe."

Men and women are drawn to the earth; many do not even know why. They cultivate gardens and tenderly care for its trees and flowers and shrubs. The wise among them, however, acknowledge what gives the garden its glory. Kneeling down to plunge their fingers into the moist earth, they recognize that the miracle of God's very creation is before them. When they pluck a blossom from a cherished rose, to offer in affection to a loved one, they perceive their participation in the greatest truth in all the universe—that the goodness of the Creator has been lavished abroad upon the earth for his children to behold, discover truth from, and then enjoy . . . if they will but look up, behold his face of love, and learn to call him Father.

Such a man was Baron Heinrich von Dortmann, late of the kingdoms of Prussia and Pomerania, now child in the heavenly kingdom of his Father, a man for whom the earthly ground he cultivated served as but a foreshadowy likeness of that heavenly garden to which he was now giving his efforts, and the roses he so lovingly tended while here were but faint images of flowerage of a more enduring kind.

In truth, the baron's life itself was a seed, placed in good soil and nurtured by heavenly purposed rains and sunshine, germinating, sending its roots deep and its trunk high, that in time it might bear its appointed fruit: those living blossoms, whose blooms were the radiant faces of others who had become the Father's children by the death-energized sprouting of his life-seed.

Existence continually regenerates itself. Such is the *life* placed into the very universe by its Creator that it can do no other than propagate and rejuvenate. As growing things do not reproduce only once, but pass along not merely the capacity to exist and breathe and grow but the power likewise to *renew* that life, so too did the spiritual life-legacy of Heinrich von Dortmann now spread out and flow into those whom his life had touched, extending in ever- widening concentric circles to future generations, in outflowing ripples of purposefulness in God's kingdom.

The autumn and winter seasons of his life, spent in prison and then in the mountains of Bavaria—though perhaps dormant to the onlooker—were years destined for eternal purpose, during which a multitude of prayer-seeds for family and nation were expectantly planted in the soils of heaven.

The story of the baron's life is necessarily, therefore, one in which the roots from his plant passed on life to an ever-increasing number of human-plants after him, nourishing and enabling them to flourish and bear fruit—thirty, sixty, and a hundredfold. Some of the spiritual seeds planted as a result fell in unexpected places, and the life that would burst forth from them would astonish many. Such, however, is the Father's way. He sends his sunshine and rain to fall on the just and the unjust. Nothing comes back empty. No word from his mouth returns void, but accomplishes the purpose for which he ordained it.

And so, as all life ultimately flows in that great eternal round back into the heart of its Creator, the characters of our saga advanced through the cycles of life. The baron, reunited at last with his beloved Marion, had ascended into the springtime of a happy new time that will know no winter.

Matthew and Sabina had now passed through that wonderful autumn when the bounty of harvest yields fruit from years of labor, and found themselves entering the restful, memory-filled winter years. Now had come the season to observe with glad expectancy the flowering spring and summer for a new generation, even as the country they loved prepared to emerge from its dormancy of separateness and embark upon a new national epoch of unity.

Generations pass that others may be born. The cycles of human life give no occasion to sadness, but rather rejoicing. Should winter's death not come, no eternal springtime could follow. Heinrich and Thaddeus had faded from earthly view, and soon likewise must Sabina and Matthew accompany them beyond the mists of earth's horizon.

Such passings are no end but rather signify completion, fruition, and fulfillment, necessary that new beginnings might begin. What appears to earthly eyes as life's sunset is only the back side of the dawn opening into the greater life toward which we are bound.

God our Father, do we doubt that all things ultimately work for our good and to the growth of your kingdom, both here and in the life to come? Open our eyes to apprehend your designs, that we might fall ever more harmoniously in step with them. Accomplish your eternal purposes in the men and women around us, even those in whom we see no possible light of your presence. Strengthen our faith, Lord, to believe that you indeed love all men and women and are constantly sending rain and sun into the cold chambers where they live so alone with themselves, to soften the seeds planted there by a thousand circumstances of life and by the words and deeds of your people. Awaken the long-dormant hearts of those who have resisted you. Enliven the seeds planted in the human soils throughout the earth, and cause a hundredfold fruit to grow from the plants that spring forth from them. Cause fruit to grow and seeds to be planted from our lives, as we have witnessed in that of the baron and from his legacy. Make us fruitful progenitors of your life, our Father, we pray from the depths of our hearts.

And what is the season at *Der Frühlingsgarten?* What will the breaking of winter's spell in this new German year hold in store for the posterity of the lineage of that ancient family Dortmann and its former estate?

The grounds south of the baron's beloved *Lebenshaus* were not only an earthly garden. The flowers tended by his hand contained no mere temporal tidings. Verily the secret of the rose contains as many depths as does the Father's life itself, for within its blossoms he has hidden his own messages of love for his children to discover.

The baron's Garden of Spring now encompassed his whole nation, and a dawn of many awakenings was at hand.

Take a Second Look!

Find out what thousands of readers have already discovered!

The American Dreams Series

Best-selling author Michael Phillips brings
readers an epic series of love and sacrifice leading
up to the turbulent Civil War.

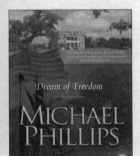

Dream of Freedom

In the midst of a nation's turmoil,
a few will stand. A few will fight.
And one man will make a decision
that has the power to change his
family and the South forever.

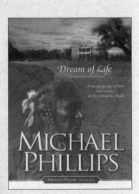

Dream of Life

Secession has begun. Loyalties and
families are divided. And every man
must decide for himself the true cost
of freedom.

BOOK 3 COMING FALL 2007!